# WESLEY MOOR

# Pleasant Surprises

D1608015

This book was professionally typeset on Reedsy.
Find out more at reedsy.com

*For Lisa*

# Contents

# Acknowledgement

A special thanks to all those who helped me along the way:
Lisa – My favorite person
Kris/Matt/BeardSound LLC – Wizards of sound
Lesley – Easy to maim, hard to kill
Allister – Editor extraordinaire
Nicole - Cover design ace
Vince – A classic Philly degenerate
Bryan – Classical musician and murder house resident
Will – Too handsome for his own good
Tim – The most interesting man alive
Matt – Scholar, Kentucky boy, crypto whiz
Elaine – A West Kentucky treasure
Brittany – A pink Starburst if there ever was one
Rob – Ugly runner, great reader
Paul – Mr. Double-Noodle
Julien – Lover of cats and reasonable bedtimes
Tom – Golf god
Dan – Who lent me his sweet hillbilly accent
Erin – Who powered through the gross parts
Scott – Beekeeper and master baker
Stacey – Zuneskies! Double zunes!
Greg – Who gets a lot of credit for reading only 30 pages

# Chapter 1

The devil will have his due, the implacable fellow, and it was Charles Bascom's turn to settle his account. Mexico, blood-drenched and hellishly hostile, certainly had not been the salvation he hoped for when he set out from New Orleans so many months ago. Charles had been an outspoken critic of the war, or at least of its purpose and scope, but, like Jonah, he found himself compelled through divine circumstances to journey across the sea to heathen lands. Instead of Nineveh, however, Charles and his fellow soldiers were purged upon the shores of Veracruz, their directive being to lay siege and conquer, then push inland. Unlike God, the men in Washington weren't looking for repentance from the city's recalcitrant inhabitants; there was no real value in that. What they coveted was beneath the feet of those dirty, distant people: land. Half a continent was ripe for the picking, and the American people were being led to believe that harvest had arrived. It wasn't just land; it was the best kind of land. It was southern land.

Alone, lost, and hotly pursued in a foreign place, Charles could sense that his death was imminent. When young men think about dying at war, if they take the time to consider such an unlikely prospect at all, they imagine themselves falling gloriously in battle amidst great personal heroism. Charles knew and expected differently. He was no longer a young man, and he understood that death would not be glorious and was much more likely to come at the merciless and invisible hand of one of the many

1

exotic diseases that seemed to permeate the condemned and humid air of the Mexican countryside. Consistent with his abysmal luck, Charles had contracted yellow fever almost immediately upon his arrival in Mexico. If he wasn't close to death then, it certainly was a convincing ruse. For most of the bombardment of Veracruz, he lay helplessly on a sweat-drenched and flea-infested cot, fearful that he would choke on his own bloody vomit. The regimental doctor, whose course of treatment consisted of placing a moistened cloth on his forehead, had cheerfully informed Charles that if he pulled through, he could never contract the disease again. "How wonderful," he had muttered to the man while futilely attempting not to fill his breeches.

Surviving yellow fever, it now appeared, was only a brief reprieve. Less than two months after his recovery, he faced death yet again, this time by a statistically less likely source: the Mexicans. At least, he presumed it was the Mexicans. He hadn't actually caught a glimpse of the scoundrels. *What a disgrace*, he thought, *to be cut down by one of the stray slugs from some antique flintlock, which was being fired carelessly from some dirt farmer's hip, no doubt.* In the prewar propaganda, it was commonly suggested that the Mexicans were a fear-filled, ragged group that would rather get drunk and take long siestas than engage on the field of battle. That depiction had been somewhat altered when Charles's regiment took heavy casualties during the Battle of Cerro Gordo, an American victory but also an awakening for some of the untested American troops. Mexican bullets and mortar rounds were as deadly as all others. Still, the perception at home, in the real world, was what mattered.

The men pursuing him through the dense tropical underbrush, if they were in fact men and not ghosts, were definitely not Mexican regulars, generally a clodding lot of marauders. More likely, it was Soñador's outfit, the terrain-savvy guerrillas that Charles and his company had been viciously decimating for the past few weeks. After Cerro Gordo and Santa Anna's flight from Xalapa in the battle's aftermath, the locals were left to fend for themselves against the invading gringos. As a result of its rapid conquests, the US army had spread itself dangerously thin in central Mexico, and its supply lines were vulnerable. Soñador, a poor farmer whose land was raided for the American cause, recognized this vulnerability and abandoned his ravaged home to raise a gang of bandits that could cause problems for the Americans, which they did with great enthusiasm.

Soñador's tactics were small in scale in the beginning and included clandestine nighttime raids on medical conveys and picking off drunken US stragglers (of which there were many) who wandered too far from the rest of the herd. With each success, his ranks began to swell and he became emboldened. Advisors from the Mexican army aided Soñador in refining his tactics and planning his attacks, encouraging him to engage in a war without pity. In the early days of his insurgency, Soñador was just one of a dozen other guerrilla outfits harassing the American lines. All were pesky, but none stood out as a greater threat than any other. It was only after the incident at the Rio Actopan Bridge that Soñador became a priority target of the US command.

During that engagement, Soñador's men managed to bottleneck and massacre more than thirty American soldiers, mostly sick and wounded, as they attempted to cross the river. The loss of life and stolen munitions were enough to rile up the American leadership, but Soñador went a step further. During the attack, his mounted vanguard lassoed three Americans by the neck and dragged them a quarter of a mile down the path, ripping the men to shreds on stones and roots. The eyes of the mutilated soldiers were cut from their sockets and placed carefully in each fellow's mouth. Then the bodies were hung from the thick lower branch of a nearby tree.

A newspaperman traveling with the next American unit to happen upon the carnage wrote a graphic account of the scene that quickly made its way into the major American newspapers, igniting a call for vengeance from the war hawks on the home front. Shortly thereafter, Charles's company of volunteers from Tennessee was given its special assignment: capture the guerrilla Soñador and disband his company of thieves, murderers, and miscreants by any means necessary. The Tennessee men, who had been criticized for their performance at Cerro Gordo but who were considered superior mountain trackers and fighters, enthusiastically accepted their new charge and diligently set about their work.

Successfully pursuing unknown targets that can blend seamlessly with a civilian population is a matter either of finesse or barbarity. With little time to achieve results, and with no means withheld, the volunteers resorted to the latter, "information gathering," it had been called — an excuse for unspeakable savagery.

The company began their pursuit of Soñador with precious little reliable information. After the bandit's last raid, some of the American supplies had appeared in a town southwest of Veracruz called Las Bajadas. That was where they started. Two of the company's hell raisers, Thad and Finney, brothers from Murfreesboro, were called upon to engage in a night of feigned drunken revelry within the town and to leak information to the locals about an upcoming convoy of supplies that would be coming through. The brothers executed their role in the plot superbly, even if they did forget to feign the drunken revelry.

Thad boasted to the bartender in the cantina about his fearlessness in spite of how dangerous the roads could be and how some points were virtually indefensible to a convoy, especially near the Spanish mission outside of town where the road narrowed and the forest was dense. He told the little old man that in two days time he would be passing that very spot with fifteen wagons of supplies, and the brass was just asking for trouble by not giving him enough protective support. Meanwhile, Finney relayed a similar message to a whore named Adelina, who could have coaxed the actual truth of the matter from the young American had she known to keep pressing.

Soñador and his men took the bait and were lured into the trap. As the Mexicans began their assault on the seemingly defenseless convoy, the volunteers opened a hailstorm of fire upon them from hidden positions in the forest. Soñador's bandits took heavy casualties. Those who were captured were viciously tortured for more information about Soñador and his activities. The volunteers learned the names of many of the bandits and tracked them down to their homes, where they were unceremoniously shot in front of their pleading families. Adelina and the bartender from the cantina in Las Bajadas were also gunned down to send a message to the locals about harboring and aiding guerrilla partisans. Charles disagreed with strong-arm tactics against civilians because they were counterproductive and only helped to recruit more enemies. His protestations drew the contempt of his command and were wholly ignored.

Considering how many men the volunteers had killed, it was difficult for Charles to imagine how Soñador had managed to raise enough replacement men to accomplish the annihilation of his company. The more he thought about it, the less likely it seemed. Whoever was chasing him moved soundlessly and rapidly through the jungle, like they could transfer their essence through the intertwined leaves of the canopy. Patiently, curiously, they watched their prey clambering wildly below in a vain attempt at survival. The bandits attacked much differently. They were more like a midsummer tornado: sudden, loud, devastating, and then gone.

A rustling on his left steered Charles to the right. A moving branch on his right pushed him back to his left. So it went for more than a mile, his sins weighing him down and slowing his progress. He knew he deserved death, even a horrific one, but his legs and his heart kept pumping selfishly, desperately attempting to buy himself a few more heartbeats, a few more moments of life. Night was coming, and the jungle was on fire with the brilliant orange of sunset. If he could elude his pursuers for half an hour more, he thought, darkness would descend and the odds would start turning in his favor.

He had scrambled far enough away from the point of attack that he no longer could hear the lamentations of his fallen comrades. At daybreak, his company had been twenty-two men strong. Could he be the only survivor? From where did the enemy come, he wondered, and how did they get so close? They were like apparitions in the bush, leaping out and slitting throats, then disappearing back into the overgrown vegetation. Had these assassins even fired a shot? He could swear that only the volunteers were firing when he decided to quit the maelstrom.

In the distance, he could hear the rush of the Rio Actopan. He panted and swallowed hard. His mouth was dry, but he expected the evening showers to begin soon, and he could refill his empty canteen from the dripping leaves. Thankfully, he had managed to grab his weapons and his gunnysack before taking flight. He counted seven remaining lead minie balls. Quickly, he reloaded and fixed his bayonet. The sounds of the jungle had subsided so that his own sonorous gasping seemed to resonate. Overhead, a snake hawk eyed him curiously.

He had to find a place to hide. Even in the dense forest, he felt totally exposed. Hadn't his company passed a small cave earlier in the day? During his retreat, he tried to backtrack toward their camp from that morning. With all the confusion, he couldn't be sure he was going in the right direction. The area looked familiar, but then again, the forest had looked the same for the past three days.

The forest opened up to a small clearing, where Charles knelt for a moment to collect his breath and consider again the best direction for escape. He listened intently for any sign his pursuers were closing in on him. Silence. Sweat dripped steadily from the tip of his nose. Feeling suddenly stifled by his wool jacket, he shed it and placed it under his knee. Minutes passed, and Charles remained unmolested. Just as he began to hope that he'd eluded death again, he noticed a movement in the high grass near the forest's edge. At first, he could not comprehend what he was seeing. There were a dozen moving shapes in the late afternoon shadows. The dark masses that were closing in on him were black as midnight and had yellow eyes and large, erect ears.

*Jesus*, Charles said as the realization hit him. He was surrounded by jaguars. *Not since Job has a man endured such ill fortune*, he thought helplessly. But there was something peculiar about the movement of the jaguars. Amazingly, they began to rise up on their hind legs. They were men, after all, wearing the hides of the great murderous cats as hoods. Charles had been correct: Soñador was not to blame for the attack. The deadly stalkers appeared to be some peculiar collection of white men and native Mexicans, dressed under their jaguar pelts in tribal garb but also donning the decrepit remnants of rusting pieces of metal armor distributed randomly among them. Charles bitterly noted that the sinewy men were smeared in the blood of his countrymen.

When the weighty realization that he had no means of escape sank in, he bemusedly recalled that natives, Shawnees, had killed his grandfather during a raid near Fort Boone. That was a time when the Appalachian foothills were still dangerous and remote. His grandfather had sacrificed himself so that his wife and their young children could escape on horseback down a backwoods path — or so the legend went. Charles was about to make a sacrifice equal to his grandfather's, but to no heroic end. These men weren't even the enemies his government had commissioned him to kill. His death would be meaningless, and from the looks of his attackers' weapons — brutal.

Burning with frustration and doom, he growled at his attackers. "If you wish to take me," he sputtered, spittle dribbling down his chin, "there is a toll to be paid." The warriors stared blankly at him and continued to inch closer.

With a calm fluidity, Charles swung his rifle to his shoulder and fired into the chest of the warrior directly in front of him, the momentum of the blast knocking the unsuspecting man to his back. Immediately, he dropped the rifle and pulled the pistol from his belt, firing twice and hitting two advancing targets. He ducked, correctly anticipating an attack from behind, a spear, which sailed high and landed harmlessly among the underbrush. With his pistol rounds spent, he resorted to his saber, which he unsheathed with a swift jerk of his elbow. He thrashed wildly at the contracting circle of warriors around him. From the front, they prodded Charles with their spears, distracting him while an attacker approached from his periphery and severed his hand at the wrist with a decisive stroke from a wooden club that resembled a paddle, but lined with razor-sharp volcanic glass stone. Charles screamed in agony and fell to his knees.

The warriors tightened their circle further and began to howl savagely at him in staccato bursts. A shriek from behind the warriors caused them to go silent. The circle opened, and another warrior appeared. He was different from the others. A necklace of tooth and bone fragments lay rigidly on his chest, which was painted blood-red, with two diagonal streaks of black. His head was adorned with a perfect halo of green and yellow feathers, and his face was hidden behind a gruesome mask that was comprised of the front half of a human skull, a spear tip protruding from the ever-grinning mouth. The warrior's eyes burned furiously from behind the sockets of the mask. Judging from the deference of the other men and his ostentatious apparel, Charles understood him to be a chieftain of some sort.

As he approached Charles, the circle of men closed behind him. The leader took stock of the bedlam Charles had caused, then turned his vicious gaze back to Charles, who was kneeling helplessly before him, clutching his blood-spouting nub of a wrist. The chieftain stretched out his open hand to no one in particular, maintaining his baleful focus on Charles. One of the subordinate warriors stepped forward and dutifully placed a dagger in his hand, then returned to his spot in the circle.

Being a melancholy man by nature, Charles had often pondered what it would be like to know death was upon him. Rage filled his heart, and his agony and fear melted away. He released his wounded wrist and deliberately bowed before his executioner. On the ground, his departed hand still clutched his fallen saber. The chieftain stepped forward and lifted the dagger with both hands toward the darkening sky. With a last, quick burst, Charles snatched his saber by the hilt, his left hand gripping his detached right hand, and swiped upward across the leader's torso with all his remaining strength.

The last thing Charles saw before the mob fell upon him was the surprise and fury in the chieftain's eyes. Darkness and bitter satisfaction enveloped Charles as his consciousness faded.

# Chapter 2

**1962**

Violet, beautiful and heart heavy, stood rigidly among the mourners in the foyer. She hardly recognized her own life. Like waking up in an unfamiliar place after a confusing dream, everything around her looked foreign. The room was big and hot. She was surrounded by somber, whispering strangers who nodded and patted each other's starched elbows with consoling hands. She checked her own hands. They seemed distant and common. They could have belonged to anyone. She turned them over, relieved that they responded to her mental impulse. An amethyst ring on her finger caught the light and sparkled; so did her memory. The ring was her dead mother's — *descanse en paz*. She took a shallow breath and prepared for the dull pain she knew would rise from her belly after making that realization for the ten thousandth time. If nothing else, the hurt was familiar and somewhat comforting.

Things began to make sense again. She was at a funeral — not her mother's funeral, but a stranger's. Her mother's had been a long time ago. Violet still felt sick thinking about it. That day had been a complete blur except for the moment just before the casket was closed, when time seemed to stop and Violet looked at her mother's cold, dead face for the last time.

A child running recklessly through a forest of legs brushed Violet's arm, snapping her out of her own head and back to the present. She suddenly remembered what she was doing. She was working. By some weird twist of fate, she had left California and all of its ghosts only to end up living and working in an antebellum mansion-turned-funeral home in Lexington, Kentucky. Her apartment was a large guest bedroom on the second floor. It was in that bedroom, just a few hours earlier, that Violet had made a very important decision while watching the sunrise from her window. After work, when all the mourners were gone, when everything had been tidied up and her work was done, she was going to have some hot tea and a bath, then she was going to go into her room and pack all of her belongings into the same boxes that were never fully unpacked when she first arrived back in April. After that, she was going to jot down a note, lie down on her bed, say her prayers, and then swallow twenty sleeping pills from the bottle she had picked up at the pharmacy the week before. Well, nineteen sleeping pills, she remembered. She'd taken one a few nights earlier. Still, nineteen seemed like enough. Death would be as simple as closing her eyes and falling asleep.

Violet's appearance was elegant and simple. She wore a black cotton dress with a glossy black belt that rested high on her waist. The flipped tips of her dark hair lay lightly upon her shoulders, and her pronounced collarbone showed just above her conservative collar. She had adorned the dress with a small ivory mourning brooch. Her dark complexion starkly contrasted with the brooch and with the light-skinned people all around her.

A sudden burst from the organ sullenly beckoned the mourners to the main sanctuary so the service could begin. As the crowd shuffled to the pews, Violet hung back to help shepherd the stragglers away from their half-smoked cigarettes. Like just about everything else in the old house, there was a beautiful symmetry to the sanctuary. Up front, the casket, encircled by floral arrangements, sat majestically upon the catafalque. A center aisle split the room into two perfectly parallel sets of fifteen pews. The mourners, reverent and hushed, gazed curiously ahead. Violet quietly sealed the room by drawing together the accordion doors between the sanctuary and the foyer. She then crept to her post in the back, an uncomfortable chair with a wicker seat. Paper fans began appearing from purses and from under pews to combat the stagnancy of the air.

Brother Sam, the fat minister who had been sitting in contemplative anticipation during the organ prelude, rose from his ornate velvet seat and approached the wooden lectern. He tugged a white handkerchief from the inside pocket of his sweat-stained suit jacket and gently patted the beads of perspiration forming on his face and neck. After a short pause, his powerful voice cut through the humid air.

"We are here to honor Bill Calloway," he began. "A man who loved his family, who loved his friends, and who loved the Lord. A man who was rewarded for his faithfulness with a multitude of blessings while he tarried on this Earth. Bill and his wife, Loretta, shared forty-seven happy years of marriage. They were blessed with two sons, Jonathon and Timothy, who Bill guided into manhood like a father should, making them the good Christian men they are today."

Violet fought boredom. Having made the decision to end her own life, everything else seemed small and disappointing, much like the coffee she had with breakfast. She had recognized, while sipping from her mug, that it would be the last cup of coffee of her life. The thought was strangely annoying. Orange juice would have been better. She had thought about dumping it out, but she hated to waste anything.

Brother Sam droned on. He spoke kind words about Bill Calloway, but he often spoke very similar kind words about other members of his apparently aging congregation. Violet had seen him eulogize at least four other people. He needed new material. She glanced at the oversized clock above the organ, a special purchase made for the severely near-sighted organist, Ms. Carlene, an eighty-year-old widow who was a wonderful musician but a terrible gossip. Nothing got said that she didn't hear. Her eyesight was gone, but her overcompensating ears were superhuman. She was usually paid some small sum by the family of the deceased, but that was really unnecessary. Ms. Carlene just wanted a chance to catch up on all the latest scuttlebutt.

It was five past the hour. That meant Brother Sam would finish just after the quarter hour. After that, there would be eight minutes of special music and then the final viewing procession. From the size of the crowd, Violet estimated that would take about fifteen more minutes. According to her rough math (considering the distance of the funeral home to the cemetery, the number of cars she'd seen parked in the parking lot, and the time of day), in approximately fifty-five minutes Bill Calloway would be lowered into the ground and the process of forgetting him would begin.

Violet glanced at Mr. Calloway's wife. She too would be dead soon. That's just how it goes. Over the next few years, all of his remaining close friends would drop off as well. Sixty more years down the road and his grandchildren would be equally dead. Then there would be nothing. No one who knew Bill Calloway would remain. Not a single person on Earth would remember the sound of his voice or any of his deeds — all those things that seemed so important today. The only thing left would be a tiny stone marker stating when he was born and when he died, some affirmative proof that he existed at all.

Violet looked at the attendees and tried to imagine their thoughts. For some, she knew, the departure of dear Bill Calloway evoked all of the appropriate feelings of loss and emptiness and sadness. For others, those not as close, like the business associates and the acquaintances, she knew there was probably very little thought being given to Bill. Those folks, hypnotized by the natural and practiced rhythm of Brother Sam's sanctimonious voice, were probably letting their minds toy with the not altogether unpleasant thoughts of their own funerals (down the road, of course). No doubt they would be triumphant affairs. Violet's own funeral would be in two days, she estimated, and would be attended by only one person: her boss, Henry Pendleton. That was a bitter thought, but then again, she reveled in the self-abuse.

Brother Sam paused to take a sip of water. "When I got a call from Loretta last week," he continued, "saying that Bill was over at St. Joseph's, I paid my old friend a visit. I walked into his hospital room and was met by that familiar smile. I said, *Bill can I get anything for ya.* He said, *Yeah, how bout a dozen donuts from Spalding's.*"

The congregation enjoyed a muted laugh.

"But that was Bill, confident and cheerful all the way to the end. I said,

*Bill, you sure are in a good mood.* He just laughed and said, *Brother Sam, I wanna see Jesus with eyes that aren't clouded by tears."*

A chorus of amens erupted from the mourners.

"And that's why we can all smile today, knowing that Bill was born again and washed by the blood of the lamb. He was forgiven. Bill knew that when his heart stopped beating there would be a whole new life waiting for him on the other side. And in that life, he doesn't have cancer and he doesn't feel pain, he just basks in the glory of our Lord."

As Brother Sam reached his crescendo, he extended one of his arms dramatically toward Heaven.

"Yes, friends, he is walking with Jesus today. And if you know Jesus the way Bill did, then you will see his smiling face when we are all reunited on the other side. When we all get to Heaven, what a day of rejoicing that will be. When we all see Jesus, we'll sing and shout the victory. Let us pray."

After the service was over and the casket was closed, Violet helped Loretta Calloway into the waiting Cadillac that would take her to the cemetery. The elderly woman clutched Violet's forearm in that firm but shaky way that old people do.

"Bill looked so handsome today. I almost expected him to climb out of the casket and come home with me."

Violet smiled compassionately. "Mr. Pendleton cares very much for his guests and does good work."

At that moment, both women caught a glimpse of Henry Pendleton as he leaned into the passenger side window of the hearse ahead of them. He was saying something to the driver. While he almost never observed the actual funeral services anymore, he still made a point of watching the funeral processions embark on their macabre parades to the cemetery.

His countenance was enigmatic. The severe paleness of his blue eyes and heavy eyelids projected a perpetual weariness, and his lips were set in a natural and incurable smirk. His hair was dark and thick with subtle curls. He combed it carefully in a way that suggested wealth. His cheekbones were high and his skin was taut and flawless, all of which made him appear much younger than his stated age of forty-four. Violet attributed his youthful appearance to the fact that he had no vices.

She had no complaints about her employer. He was frank and courteous, perhaps even genteel, but never condescending. Henry kept to himself and zealously attended to his work and his greenhouse hobbies. He expressed no interest whatsoever in Violet's private affairs, much to her relief. She felt sorry for him, knowing that he would certainly be the one to find her body tomorrow morning, or maybe tomorrow afternoon.

"It is a special gift, you know," Mrs. Calloway continued, "to make the dead look like they are at peace. It takes a certain peculiarity — a closeness and acceptance of death. Mr. Pendleton has the gift."

Violet could not disagree.

Violet rode shotgun in the hearse on the way to Lexington Cemetery, which was more of an arboretum and botanical garden than a graveyard. When she was first hired, Henry brought her there so that she could familiarize herself with its labyrinth of pathways. It had the beautifully nostalgic and remote feel of a Robert Frost poem, despite being located just a quarter mile north of the bustling city center. During their visit, Henry, whose interest in the botanical sciences bordered on obsession, seemingly pointed out nearly thirty species of trees growing among the tombstones.

"That, my dear, is a hackberry," he said triumphantly, "very good for making tobacco sticks. And that is a tulip poplar. Many of the first homes in this area were built out of those."

It was spring then, and the multitude of weeping cherry trees flanking the southern entrance of the cemetery's main avenue were in the height of their magnificence. In addition to the dogwoods, southern magnolias, sugar maples, and fern-leaf beeches, Henry also pointed out the flora growing in the underbrush, using each plant's scientific name. His effort was lost on Violet. To her, they all just looked like weeds.

Bill Calloway's funeral procession passed through the cemetery's stately wrought iron gateway near the Romanesque visitor's chapel, then cut through the oldest sections of the cemetery, in full view of the monuments of its most honored residents, including the legendary statesmen, Henry Clay. His stone figure presided solemnly, fatherly, over the rest of the grounds atop a 120-foot, Corinthian-style limestone column that stood higher than the treetops. The statue's right hand was outstretched toward downtown Lexington. Violet thought it looked like he was checking his watch, waiting patiently for something, perhaps for the city to join him in death — one of her typical dark thoughts. According to Henry, the giant basswood tree beside Clay's tomb was nearly two hundred years old and therefore had been growing since before the signing of the US Constitution. "How about that," she'd replied.

The tombstone placements in the older sections were dense and sporadic, but Violet considered many of the tombs to be beautifully artistic. She particularly liked the tomb exhibiting the statue of a robed woman stepping on a fat, woebegone serpent, her stone face placid and angelic, sheltered for all time beneath a dome of gothic design. The newer sections featured straighter rows, flatter surfaces, and less distinct tombstones, the sterile efficiency of the modern age — a pity.

Any time Violet and Henry would come to the cemetery to make preburial preparations near the gravesites, Violet would set up the canopy and folding chairs and place floral arrangements while Henry wandered aimlessly around the property. He tended to stay in the oldest sections, where he examined the headstones, smirking to himself and sketching some of the trees in a small notepad he kept in the pocket of his slacks.

Directly adjacent to Lexington Cemetery, on the other side of a protective row of eastern hemlocks and a wire fence, was Cove Haven Cemetery. It was unkempt and overrun with high grass and weeds. The volunteers who maintained the grounds could only afford to have it mowed a few times a year. It stood in stark contrast to the immaculately maintained grounds of the Lexington Cemetery. Violet learned from Henry that Cove Haven was created to solve a very troubling problem for the city founders. They needed a place to bury the Black residents. Even in death, the old racists had to be exclusive. Violet's father had once told her that everyone was brown once they were covered in dirt. If nothing else, he had a sense of social justice, one of his few positive attributes.

Bill Calloway's procession passed the Gardens of Remembrance, Tranquility, and Serenity, as well as a section known to the groundskeepers as "Baby Land," a ghastly name that Violet hated. Finally, the hearse arrived at its destination and the pallbearers were called upon to perform their duties. The sun was near its midday height, and it shone brightly down on the gathering through perfectly clear skies.

Violet had been to the cemetery earlier that morning to oversee the arrangement of the folding chairs, the burial canopy, and the easel that would hold Mr. Calloway's photograph. Afterward, she thought about scouting for a suitable plot for her own final resting place but realized that she didn't have nearly enough money saved up to pay for one. She would have to be cremated, which was probably for the best. She felt no need to be remembered. She only wanted to forget and be forgotten.

The mourners parked on the edges of the paved pathway near the burial site and then solemnly trudged toward the last act of the show. When all had gathered, a merciful breeze fluttered through the crowd, a temporary reprieve from the sadistic humidity. Brother Sam, who never liked to be too far from a pitcher of lemonade, was succinct in his final remarks, "dust to dust" and so on. No one, except perhaps Loretta, really seemed to mind. Everyone was growing weary of remembering Bill Calloway. They had their own concerns to worry about, after all, and they were still alive to worry about them.

In the distance, Violet noticed a short man wandering alone through the headstones. Periodically, he would stop and carefully observe a grave, then glance over at the burial ceremony. He appeared to be well dressed, wearing a light-colored suit with a white shirt, dark suspenders, and an open collar where Violet suspected a bow tie had recently been removed.

When the ceremony was over, the man casually made his way over to Violet, nearly startling her from behind.

"Excuse me, are you with the funeral home?" the man squeaked, politely removing his hat from his head and holding it close to his chest with the nubby little fingers of his right hand. He had thinning, dirty blonde hair, which exacerbated a bulbous forehead.

"Yes," she replied warily, "can I help you?"

Upon closer review, the man appeared even shorter than before. Violet stood nearly an entire head above him. His suit also suffered in Violet's regard upon close inspection. It was wrinkled and stained to the point of absurdity. That, plus the fact that his right eye was not perfectly in sync with his left, made the unfortunate man look like a broken puppet.

"I'm from Atlanta," the man said in his thick Georgia accent. "I've been visiting my aunt in the hospital here. Unfortunately, it's not looking good."

"I'm sorry to hear that," said Violet as she took half a step backward to create a bit more distance between herself and the stranger.

"I need to start making some preparations for her. That's why I'm here today. I'm supposed to be viewing a plot with someone from the cemetery office in a few moments."

Violet smiled and nodded.

"It's the curse of responsibility," he continued, pursing his thin lips. "My parents are too old and feeble, God bless them, to help her, and my brothers are all good-for-nothings." He sighed deeply as he looked toward the fresh pile of nearby soil. "That's why she sent me, my mother that is, to help poor Aunt Dilsey. But that's neither here nor there. Say, who's the director of the funeral home you work for?

"That would be Henry Pendleton. I'll get you a card from the hearse. You should call Mr. Pendleton and set up a meeting."

The man scratched his unshaven jaw. "Pendleton, you said? Yes, I'll have to do that. After all, my aunt is very sick."

Violet smiled and started to turn toward the hearse, but the man reached out his hand, just inches from her elbow.

"How long have you worked with Mr. Pendleton?"

Violet looked down at his outstretched hand, then took another half step backward. "Only since last spring. I just moved here from California."

The man nodded toward Violet's left hand. "I see you're not married. What brings you all the way to Kentucky?"

"I'm sorry, Mr. … what was your name again?" Violet's uneasiness was becoming more transparent.

"Rhodes," he said, smiling.

17

"I'm sorry, Mr. Rhodes, but I've really got to finish up here and get back. I've got a lot of work to do at the funeral home."

"Of course," he replied. "I'll let you get to it."

"Let me get you that card."

"Don't trouble yourself," he said, tipping his hat, "Lexington's not too big — at least not as big as Atlanta. I'm sure I can find y'all."

He bowed slightly before placing his hat back on his head. As he walked away, Violet noticed for the first time that he was leaning heavily on a thin wooden cane.

"See you soon," he called over his shoulder.

"No," Violet said under her breath, "you won't."

# Chapter 3

**1962**

Violet was finishing some dusting in the funeral parlor when she heard yelling from the backyard. She ran out the rear exit and was shocked to see that the source of the bellowing was the funeral home's next-door neighbor, Paul Trimble. The apparent object of his anger was Henry, who stood before him, arms crossed and resolute during the verbal barrage.

"You're a son of a bitch, Pendleton," Mr. Trimble screamed. "You'll regret this. I promise you that."

The present moment excluded, Mr. Trimble had been a pleasant enough neighbor, always waving when he saw Violet or Henry out and about. He was a good-looking older man, probably around fifty years old, with a full head of salt-and-pepper hair.

Violet stepped off the back porch and approached the two men as the confrontation came to an end. She couldn't help but stare in wide-eyed surprise as Mr. Trimble stormed past her and back toward his own house.

"What?" he snarled at her.

She shook her head innocently. His normally tan complexion was nearly crimson as he shredded some papers he'd been clutching and violently threw the debris toward the funeral home.

When he was gone, Violet made her way over to Henry, who watched the other man's departure with serene composure.

"Whoa," Violet said, "what was that about?"

Henry gave a roguish smile. "Mr. Trimble is very cross with me."

He pulled a small bottle of stomach ulcer medication from the pocket of his trousers, shook one of the pills onto his palm, and popped it into his mouth.

"I'll say. Is there a reason?" Violet asked.

"Oh yes," he replied, before throwing his head back and forcing the pill down his throat.

Violet waited, but no explanation was forthcoming. "Okay, well, I guess I am going to turn in for the night."

"Have you tidied up the sanctuary?" Henry asked, glancing at his watch.

"Yes, it's all finished," Violet replied.

"Very good. I think you did an excellent job today. You are making things much easier for me."

Violet forced a smile. "Thank you. Well, if that's all…"

"Actually, Mr. Trimble's hysterics have set me behind schedule a bit. Would you mind helping in the greenhouse?"

"Sure," Violet replied dutifully.

Henry's greenhouse, his pride and joy, was large for a noncommercial structure. It was positioned in the backyard in such a way as to maximize the amount of sunlight it received, taking into consideration the curvature of the Earth and myriad other factors Violet found tedious and uninteresting. Despite being named after a flower, Violet had little interest in plants. She confessed to Henry that she could not name a single plant in his entire greenhouse. To that end, Henry explained that the collection he maintained was highly exotic and extremely rare for this part of the world and that few people outside of those trained in the field were able to identify each species accurately. When she asked why he didn't have more flowers, he told her that he preferred plants that contained "intricate or unique internal qualities" over the ones that "merely exhibited flashy exteriors." If his goal was to throw an even wetter blanket on the already desperately boring field of botany, he had succeeded.

The greenhouse was even more humid than the early evening air outside, and Violet immediately felt perspiration on her temples upon entering. Although she lacked a finer appreciation for what Henry was doing, she recognized the beauty of the room's color and symmetry. She felt there was a certain balance and comfort to everything being exactly in its place and a master gardener nearby to tend to each plant's needs, utilizing his expert knowledge.

Henry checked several thermometers placed throughout the structure and, satisfied with the results, looked back to Violet.

"Starting by the door and working your way around the right wall, inspect the plants on that side for bugs, discoloration, or anything else that looks odd," he instructed.

Violet nodded and quickly began her check. She flipped up leaves and prodded carefully near the stems of each plant. She was not totally convinced she would recognize something out of the ordinary if she saw it.

"Oh, wait a second," she said suddenly, "this one doesn't look so good."

Henry made his way over to where she stood. They both leaned in for a closer examination of a drooping plant that was beginning to show brown discolorations on its leaves.

"Yes," he said with irritation, "this particular plant has been giving me a lot of grief lately."

"What is it?" she asked.

"This," he responded joyously (as he always did when talking about his plants), "is a guarana plant, Paullinia cupana. It is native to tropical regions of South America."

"Oh," Violet said.

"When healthy, a guarana plant will produce some very peculiar seeds. You see, they come in thick clusters of red buds. When split open, the seeds inside look like eyeballs. There are some very interesting legends among the native South Americans about this plant. You will have to remind me to tell you sometime. The guarana seed is used for a variety of medicinal purposes among the natives, but essentially it is a stimulant. It has more caffeine than a coffee bean."

"That's very interesting," Violet said, only partially lying. "I actually just meant, what's wrong with it."

"Oh, sorry," he chuckled, "you know how I enjoy talking about my little friends here."

"That's all right." Violet smiled.

"To answer your question, everything you see in here, indeed, almost every plant you see anywhere, is fighting to live. In the harshest climates and the most remote unforgiving terrains, you will find plants that have somehow managed to overcome tremendous odds to survive. But this one is different. I'd say this one is just looking for any excuse to die."

Violet shrugged. "It's not like plants make decisions to live or die. They can't make decisions at all; they have no central nervous system. They're just plants."

Henry appeared to think carefully about Violet's assertion. "That's true," he finally responded. "They cannot think, at least not like you and I think. That may not be so bad, though; humans are dreadful thinkers sometimes. But you presume that is the end of the story. Either something is human or it isn't. Human or nothing."

"I know it's not nothing. It's just a plant."

"You know, I've read about some pretty radical theories concerning plant and human interactions. It has been suggested that there is a bond between humans and plants that goes beyond what we are capable of explaining."

He glanced at his watch again with consternation.

"Is something wrong?" Violet asked.

"No, I'm just pressed for time is all. I am supposed to meet a friend in about half an hour, and I'm afraid I'm going to be late."

Violet was surprised. In the four months she'd been working for Henry, she'd neither seen nor heard him speak of anyone other than his clients. "I can take over here if you'd like, and you can go ahead," she offered.

Henry shook his head doubtfully. "No. It would take me at least half an hour to explain all that needs doing." He ran his fingers through his hair then rubbed his chin, brooding.

"Actually," he continued, "if you really don't mind helping, then maybe you could go and meet my friend. Do you have any other plans this evening?"

Violet hesitated. Yes, she had plans, very important plans.

Before she could respond, Henry continued, "I believe you've met this gentleman before. He's my attorney, Brian Todd."

Indeed, Brian had been meeting with Henry the very day Violet first showed up on the funeral home's doorstep looking for work.

Violet stiffened up. "I vaguely recall him," she muttered, "but I don't think I can be a substitute if he's expecting you."

"Well," Henry said, "to be honest, he's not exactly expecting me either."

Violet tilted her head in confusion. "I don't understand."

"Today is his wedding anniversary. Tragically, his wife was killed shortly after they married."

"Oh," Violet said quietly, "that's terrible."

"It has been a few years, but Brian still thinks about her a lot. It makes him a bit...melancholy. I planned to meet up with him this evening to make sure he doesn't go overboard, if you know what I mean, but I just can't be in both places at once."

Violet did not want to go. "Do you even know where he'll be?"

"Without a doubt he'll be at a bar called Cuppy's at 5th and Broadway," Henry assured her.

Violet stewed on the request.

"If this makes you uncomfortable, please don't worry about it," Henry said. "I'm really sorry to have to ask such an odd favor. I wouldn't do it if I weren't worried about his safety."

Violet felt the all too familiar yoke of responsibility being mounted on her shoulders. "No, it's fine," she said. "I'm glad to help. I'll call myself a taxi."

"Actually, you have a driver's license, right?" he asked.

"Yes."

"Then just take my car."

** ** ** **

All day, Violet had been planning her disappearance. She wanted nothing more than to slip unnoticed from life's shores into death's dark abyss. Having no friends and no personal or family connections outside of

California, she felt she was already neck-deep in those lonely waters. However, as she carefully made her way downtown in Mr. Pendleton's car, a black Cadillac Superior Crown Royale hearse, she felt like the most conspicuous person in Lexington.

She had not been behind the wheel of a car for many months and, being otherwise out of practice, she established a very deliberate pace. Almost immediately after pulling onto Leestown Road from the funeral home's driveway, a line of cars began to accumulate behind her. It was nearly evening, and most of the motorists had their headlights on, even though the lingering summer sun had not quite set. Much to Violet's chagrin, her slow progress and the line of cars behind her looked like a late evening funeral procession. Out of courtesy and respect, oncoming vehicles pulled to the side of the road and stopped until the long line of traffic had passed. Violet was mortified, but having already come nearly halfway, she was forced to continue the inadvertent motorcade toward her destination.

Violet's embarrassment and stress merged into general agitation, which was further exacerbated when all the downtown parking spaces were filled and she was forced to engage in a horrendous parallel parking attempt. After several starts and stops and some minor contact with the front bumper of the car parked behind her, she decided the space would not accommodate the long hearse. In frustration, she peeled out and parked next to a fire hydrant two blocks from Cuppy's. Considering her plans for later that evening, parking tickets no longer served as an effective deterrent.

Cuppy's was a middle-of-the-road tavern tucked between a men's clothier and a tobacco and newspaper shop. The brick edifice, which was starting to show its age, had been painted blue in lieu of much-needed renovations. The door was propped open, and Violet, having experience going into bars looking for her father (many much seedier than Cuppy's) strode confidently inside. It was about what she expected. The place had two sections. Up front was the bar, complete with a panoply of colored bottles displayed prominently on glass shelves in front of an oversized mirror. In the back, beyond a simple wooden banister, was a handful of desolate tables where lunch and dinner were served. Overhead, a solitary ceiling fan churned the stagnant air with no perceived effect.

After surveying the room, Violet recognized Brian sitting alone at one end of the bar. He was hunched over his freshly poured drink, staring dolefully into the amber liquid like he was seeking answers from a Magic 8-Ball. Violet casually approached the bar and took a seat two stools down from him. Other than a couple of workmen sipping on beers and listening to a Reds game on the radio at the other end of the bar, the place was empty.

"What can I get you?" asked the bartender, a balding middle-aged man with a handlebar mustache who seemed to materialize out of thin air.

"Just a Coke, please."

The man gave Violet a quick second glance and then filled a small glass with Coke and plopped two maraschino cherries on top. He winked at her as he placed it on a cocktail napkin.

Still trying to shake off her miserable driving experience, Violet flipped the hearse keys onto the bar and rubbed her right temple with her fingertips. She sat in silence, trying to determine how she was going to approach Brian.

"You look familiar," he slurred before she could put a plan into motion.

"I'm sorry?" she responded, clueless as to what he'd said but grateful that he had started the conversation.

"I said you look familiar," he repeated with a little more clarity.

"Do I?"

"Yes, you do. I've seen you before."

He closed his eyes and tapped the fingers of his right hand on his forehead like he was punching figures into a calculator. After a few seconds, he stopped and pointed triumphantly at Violet, then groggily opened his eyes.

"You work for Henry Pendleton at the funeral home, don't you?"

Violet gave an unenthusiastic nod.

Brian looked in awe at the glass in his hand. "By God, I think I'm even sharper when I'm drunk." He gulped the rest of his drink and tapped the bar with his empty glass. "Gimme another one, Freddy."

The bartender, who was trying to catch the game, sluggishly pushed himself away from the radio and back toward Brian.

"Same stuff?" he asked.

Brian nodded, then turned to look at Violet. "So, Henry sent you down here to keep an eye on me tonight, did he?"

Violet gave a little shrug. "He was worried about you, I guess."

Brian laughed. "The mortician is worried about the lawyer, Freddy. What's that tell you?"

"Nothing good," the man replied over his shoulder as he reached for a bottle of top-shelf bourbon.

"So worried, in fact, he sent his little Mexican housekeeper to make sure I went to bed on time," Brian added caustically.

Realizing just how drunk and unpleasant Brian had become, Violet snatched the keys from off the bar and quickly spun on her barstool toward the exit. She felt horrible for Brian, but she was hardly in the mood for such nonsense.

"Ahh, lighten up, I didn't mean anything by it," Brian said half-heartedly. "Here, what are you drinking? I'll buy you another. Tequila? Margarita? Cerveza?" he asked in an over-the-top Mexican accent.

What little patience Violet had when she entered the bar was fully exhausted. All she wanted to do was go back to the funeral home, take her pills, tuck herself in bed, and leave all of life's irritations behind. Actually, that was the thing she wanted second most. What she really wanted to do was splash Brian in the face with her full glass of Coke. So vividly, could she imagine the maraschino cherries bouncing off his stupid forehead, she actually reached for the glass, but before she gave in to the impulse, she paused and reconsidered. Despite his insults, she still pitied him.

"Did I offend you in some way?" she asked directly.

Brian gave her a sideways glance and smirked. "No, you didn't offend me. C'mon, sit down. I'm sorry, I'm a little intoxicated." He patted the stool next to him. "I'm harmless. Just full of piss and vinegar."

Violet glanced uncertainly toward the bartender, who nodded his grudging endorsement of Brian's assertion.

Brian patted the stool again. "C'mon, I'm sorry."

Violet eyed him warily. Brian, who had come directly to Cuppy's after work, was still wearing his gray business suit, his tie loosened to an almost

26

comical degree. He seemed tall to Violet, despite stooping over his drink, and he had a nice, albeit bleary-eyed face. He was a younger man, but anguish, which clearly wore heavily on him, was setting the groundwork for premature creases on his brow.

"What's your name?" he asked.

"Violet," she replied as she returned to her stool.

Brian chuckled. "You know, last year your boss came down here himself."

"He would have been here tonight too," Violet explained, "but he got held up by his neighbor. They were arguing in the backyard this afternoon."

Brian's eyes suddenly lit up with interest. "Was the guy's name Paul something?" He tapped his forehead like a calculator again, but this time the computation was not forthcoming.

"Trimble," Violet offered.

"Yeah, Trimble. So, no kidding, they were arguing this afternoon? Could you hear what they were saying?"

"Not really, I was inside for most of it. I did hear Mr. Trimble tell Henry that he was going to regret something. Then he stomped away."

Brian laughed.

"What? Why is that funny?" Violet asked.

"Nothing. Just this afternoon I was wondering if ol' Trimble had been served yet. I guess that answers that question."

"Served what?"

"The summons we issued. Henry is suing that piece of shit, and I'm helping him do it."

Violet looked surprised. "Why is he suing him?"

"That's privileged information," Brian said, suddenly taking a more serious tone.

"No it isn't," Violet scoffed. "I could go get the complaint from the clerk's office tomorrow morning if I wanted to."

Brian smiled coyly and took a sip of his drink. "What do you care? You've got no stake in it."

"I thought lawyers loved talking about their cases."

"No," Brian corrected, "only lawyers who have no personal lives love to talk about their cases. They do it because they have nothing else to talk about."

Violet rolled her eyes and turned back toward her Coke. The next few moments passed in an uncomfortable silence, neither could think of what to say next.

"He's suing for trespass," Brian relented.

"Trespass to land or chattels?" Violet inquired.

Brian's eyes opened wide in exaggerated surprise. "Well, look at you and your big legal brain. Trespass to land, Miss Lawbooks. He's been trespassing on Henry's land continuously for over a year."

"Don't be so condescending, Mr. Todd. I was prelaw in college."

"But you didn't take the plunge with law school, huh? Well, good for you and your good fucking choices. Practicing law is for the birds."

Violet rolled her eyes. "So, you were saying — Trimble's somehow been trespassing on Henry's property?"

"He hasn't, but his pool house has. Last year, Trimble began construction on a big swimming pool and a pool house near the property line. As it turns out, he was a little too near the line, three feet over according to Henry."

Violet nodded with interest.

Brian continued, "Henry apparently told Trimble that he thought he had gone over his property's boundaries, but Trimble just laughed it off. He said the legal descriptions on the deeds weren't clear, and what was a few inches between neighbors anyway? Henry dropped the issue, and nothing happened, except that ol' Trimble has made some very expensive additions to the pool house. I hear it is quite a magnificent structure at this point."

"So what is Mr. Trimble's legal position?"

"Well, the only real argument he can make is that he didn't cross the property line. The properties at issue were surveyed a very, very long time ago, and it is possible none of the markers listed in the legal descriptions on the deeds are still there. In the old days surveyors would use trees or big rocks or other little landmarks like that as points of reference. It's been over a hundred years since the properties were surveyed, and a lot could have changed since then. The only other defense would be for adverse possession, but he's not even close to that one."

"I don't know what adverse possession is," Violet admitted.

"You're gonna have to hit the library more, Miss Lawbooks," Brian teased. "It means that if one person openly and notoriously makes a claim on a piece of land owned by someone else, and nothing is done about it for fifteen years, then the property legally goes to the squatter."

"Really?"

"Well, there's a little more to it, but that's it in a nutshell."

"That doesn't seem right."

Brian shrugged. "It is what it is. Regardless, the pool house doesn't qualify. What's hilarious is that if Henry wins, Trimble will have to either tear down the building or compensate Henry for the land that's been taken."

"If Henry knew that Mr. Trimble was on his property, why did he let him finish building the pool house before suing him? Why did he let Mr. Trimble spend so much money?"

"What do you mean *why*? I think it's perfectly clear."

Violet raised a perplexed eyebrow.

"He hates the guy."

Violet scoffed. "Henry doesn't hate anyone."

"So you know everything about him now that you've known him for four months? Trust me, he hates him. It's okay, he's allowed to hate someone if he wants."

"But isn't Henry like some sort of holy roller? He's always reading the Bible. Doesn't it specifically say to *love thy neighbor*?"

"I think it says to love thy neighbor as you love thyself."

"Yeah?"

"So, maybe he's doing exactly that. Maybe he hates himself too."

Violet grinned. "Sounds like you spend a fair amount of time in the Good Book yourself."

Brian nodded vigorously as he simultaneously finished his bourbon. "Oh yeah, I love it. I read it all the time."

"Any book in particular?"

"Oh, you know, Genesis, Revelations, 2 Corinthians — all the hits, really."

Violet smiled.

"Henry's a very strange bird, you know that, right?" Brian tapped the bar with his empty glass and motioned to Freddy, who was preoccupied with the Reds game, which had entered the ninth inning.

"He seems all right to me, just keeps to himself mostly," Violet said indignantly.

"You don't think it's weird that he spends so much time in that god-forsaken greenhouse? What else have you seen him do other than work?"

"He reads a lot and goes for walks."

"Yeah, in the cemetery. I really don't know how someone can care so much about the dead when he doesn't give a shit about anyone who's alive."

Violet shrugged. "He seems to care about you."

"And you're saying that's not weird?" Brian countered.

"How did you first meet up with him?" Violet asked.

"That's another thing. He comes to the firm where I work out of the blue a few years ago and asks specifically for me. The secretary tries to get him to speak with one of the senior partners, but he would have none of it. When he introduces himself to me, he tells me that he's been a close friend of my family for a long time. He says he knew my granddad. I was like, *okay*. It was all the same to me. I was just glad to have a new client. One that had some money to boot."

"Will he win his case?"

"I don't know. He certainly thinks he will."

"Don't you?"

"I don't know, maybe."

"Don't you care?"

"Look, I'll do the best I can for him, that I promise. But I'm not going to bear someone else's cross. When I was fresh out of law school, I didn't take the time to separate my clients' problems from my own personal problems — as far as I was concerned, they were one and the same. I quickly learned that the weight of other people's troubles can crush you if you're not careful. Now I just do my best and let my clients do the worrying. Besides, if rich guys didn't have pissing contests like this property dispute, I'd be out on the street."

A heavy silence fell between the two.

"You seem sad," Brian blurted.

Violet was caught off guard. "Do I?"

Brian narrowed his bleary gaze at her and softened his tone. "Yep."

Violet just shrugged.

"Did Henry tell you today was my anniversary?"

Violet nodded somberly and fixated on her untouched Coke.

"She's dead."

"I'm sorry," Violet whispered. The words sounded hollow, meaningless.

"Don't worry," Brian replied, placing his hand on Violet's and patting it with feigned sympathy. "I've been told by several people, very smart, very well-to-do people, mind you, that it must have been her time." He withdrew his hand and scratched the back of his head. "So, if you're concerned about the timing issue, like I was, don't be."

Suddenly, Brian pounded his open hand on the bar with such force, it caused Violet to jump. When Freddy looked up, Brian pointed vehemently toward his empty glass. "You know how to order nicely, Brian," Freddy said and then turned up the radio. Brian, in response, leaned over the bar and smashed his empty glass violently on the tiles below, scattering a hundred shimmering pieces across the floor, some landing in crevices where they'd never be seen again.

"May I please have another," Brian said in a British accent.

"Goddamn it, Brian!" Freddy snarled as he stomped across the glass shards. "Pay your tab, you've had enough."

"You don't know one single fuckin' thing about when I've had enough," Brian huffed. "Now do your job and pour me another glass."

Freddy just glared back at Brian.

"I'm trying to celebrate my anniversary. Is that such a crime?" Brian asked.

The bartender continued his steely glare.

"That wasn't a rhetorical question," Brian growled.

"You've done your damage, Brian. Now, I'm warning you, go sleep it off.

I won't ask you to leave again."

Violet looked down at her hands, which she nervously rubbed together.

"You know how this is going end," Freddy stated as he surreptitiously slipped the big gold ring off his right middle finger.

"Psshht, I don't know shit," Brian lamely retorted.

"You got that right," Freddy said as he swiftly delivered a straight right from across the bar that instantly sent Brian to the dirty floor.

Freddy winced and gave his hand a couple of shakes before putting his ring back on. "Sweetheart, could you hand me his wallet? It's in his front left jacket pocket." Stunned, Violet obeyed.

"Don't worry," Freddy said, "we've got a little arrangement, Brian and I."

He opened the wallet and pulled out enough bills to cover Brian's tab and the damage he caused. He then handed the wallet back to Violet, who stood dumbfounded over Brian's motionless body. She wasn't sure what to do next. Certainly, no one could blame her if she just left him there on the floor. He had been a proper asshole that evening. But she couldn't help but feel an obligation to Henry, who had tasked her with keeping an eye on him. Plus, there was the omnipresent guilt.

"What are you going to do with him?"

Freddy thoughtfully leaned on the broom he'd gotten out to sweep up the glass shards. "If he doesn't wake up before closing time, which he won't, I'll just prop him up beside the building when I lock up. Don't worry, nobody will mess with him. They'll think he's just a bum."

With his clothes all disheveled and dirty from the floor, Violet agreed that he looked the part. She sighed, then opened Brian's wallet and flipped through the remaining bills.

"How much to carry him to my car?"

The bartender gave her a cheeky look. Violet rolled her eyes. "It's not like that."

"Of course not," he said before turning to the two workmen at the other end of the bar, who were polishing off the last of their beers. "Hey, yous want Brian to pay your tabs?"

# Chapter 4

**1962**

Violet had no idea where Brian lived, and although she could have checked his driver's license, she knew she couldn't lift him out of the back of the hearse anyway. The two brawny men from Cuppy's had a difficult, albeit raucously merry time of getting him placed there to be begin with. Besides, he looked pretty comfortable sprawled out in the same spot where Bill Calloway lay just a few short hours before.

It was past midnight when Violet got back to the funeral home. She parked in the side lot, leaving Brian to his carefree slumber. Although she expected Henry to be waiting up for her to hear about the details of her evening, she found the place dark and quiet. In a way, Violet felt let down. When Henry had asked for her help, she assumed her duties with an earnestness that was equal to an important task. What initially seemed like Henry's sincere concern for a troubled friend now appeared superficial. Moreover, Henry's concern for Violet's well-being and safety also seemed suspect. He'd sent her to a bar in the middle of the night to pick up a drunk man she barely knew, and he couldn't even stay awake long enough to see if she returned intact.

Violet got on with her normal nighttime routine. She brushed her teeth, washed her face, and filled a glass from the kitchen with water. By the time she reached her bedroom, her anxiety was building. She paused at the threshold and took a slow breath before flipping on the light switch. Henry had spared very little expense in refurnishing the funeral home when he bought the old mansion and undertook the badly needed renovations; the guest rooms were no exceptions. Unlike some would-be restorers, he had a very good eye for tasteful décor and the subtle luxury needed to match the grand design of the structure's architecture. Many of the pieces of furniture in her room were expertly restored antiques, the centerpiece being the four-post bed sculpted out of walnut. Despite its comfortable amenities and aesthetic features, the room seemed just as foreign to her as it did when she first moved in. Everything was tidy and neat, giving it the appearance of a well-curated room in an historical home. She imagined a waist-high velvet rope stationed across the doorway keeping a slow-moving line of museumgoers safely out of reach of the artifacts within.

To keep her frenzied mind from racing, she tried focusing her attention on the things she still needed to get done: her death chores. The room was stifling, so she opened the window before getting to work. Next, she took two cardboard boxes from the closet and set them next to her vanity, also an exquisitely refinished antique. She labeled the first box "trash" and the second one "charity." Her makeup, perfume, a handful of cheap earrings, hair clips, undergarments, and personal hygiene items she tossed into the first box. All her other clothes and an envelope full of cash (her unspent salary) she placed neatly in the second box. The only item that gave her pause was a cheap jewelry box her father had given her as a child. When opened, a small ballerina was supposed to pirouette continuously to the song "You Are My Sunshine," but that feature had been defective for more than a decade. She tossed it into the trash box as well.

When almost everything had been sorted, she sat at the vanity and stared dolefully into the mirror until her vision blurred and the reflection became unrecognizable. A soft breeze penetrated the room and lifted the curtains wistfully, stretching out far enough to graze lightly against her leg. Violet brushed her hair methodically until it was perfectly straight, then tossed the brush gently into the trash box. She thought about digging out her makeup so she could freshen it up one last time, but it occurred to her that it likely would just get smeared on her pillow in the end. Her priority was to leave as little mess as possible.

She glanced around the room once more and ran through a mental checklist of things left to do. When she was satisfied that everything else had been accomplished, she got out a pen and a single piece of paper. For the next half hour, Violet numbly set down a concise recitation of the events that led her to her decision. She stuck mostly with the facts but allowed some emotion to seep through as well. She ended with two apologies and signed only her first initial. With great deliberateness, she folded the note into horizontal thirds and sealed it in an envelope on which she wrote *Henry - Please Open.* She leaned the envelope conspicuously against the mirror, then reconsidered and slid it under the door into the hallway. With that, all of the housekeeping was done.

Still wearing her black dress from the funeral, she got up from her seat at the vanity and approached the nightstand upon which she'd placed the glass of water. The sleeping pills were in the nightstand's solitary drawer. She had purchased them a few weeks before while dealing with a bout of insomnia but had only taken one of twenty. The remaining nineteen should easily do the trick.

At last, the moment of truth had arrived. Cognizant of the absolute finality of her actions, she considered one last time whether she was doing the right thing. Calmly, peacefully, she asked herself two simple questions: *Do I have anything to live for? Can I ever be happy again?* She contemplated the questions deeply. The answers to both, she decided without emotion, still was no. It was settled.

Practicing her final resting position, she lay down on the bed and painstakingly smoothed out every crease in her dress. When she was satisfied that everything was in order, she took one last glance at her mother's ring, folded her hands, and rested them softly on her stomach. Finally, she let her head fall gently on the soft pillow.

*Once I take these pills, I will never rise from this spot*, she thought.

A tear streamed down her cheek as weariness overcame her. She was glad she elected not to put on more makeup; it would have streaked.

*Enough dawdling*, she thought. *It's time.*

In one last act of contrition, she closed her eyes and started a meandering prayer.

# Chapter 5

**1845**

Sheriff Carr dozed in his chair, puffing his pipe just frequently enough to keep it lit. He was exhausted, as was the oil in his tableside lamp. The dying flame flickered wildly as it approached oblivion, projecting excited shadows on the wall and ceiling of his little cottage. Mrs. Carr was already in bed, asleep. As was their nightly routine, she turned in first and then made several unheeded calls for Sheriff Carr to join her. He loved his wife but also enjoyed spending a few quiet moments to himself at the end of the day, reading one of the local newspapers and thinking.

During the waking hours, the city bustled, and his ever-increasing duties as the primary guardian of the peace necessarily placed a high premium on solitude. The citizens needed his protection, the politicians needed his advice, the newspapermen needed a statement, and the deputies needed his guidance. For a man well past his prime, the work was taxing, and every day it lost some of the luster it once held. At night, he enjoyed sitting contemplatively in his favorite chair for as long as his drooping eyelids would allow, eventually slipping quietly into the bedroom and under the covers. Mrs. Carr always greeted him with a sigh of deep, unconscious satisfaction when she felt his warmth next to her. She didn't particularly like the routine but knew what it meant to her husband and allowed the practice to continue.

Able to forestall sleep no longer, the sheriff raised himself from his chair with a low grunt. He took one last draw from his pipe, then snuffed it out and placed it carefully on the nearby mantel. Relentlessly aching muscles and bones had become so common to him, he could no longer remember what it felt like to be comfortable. But there was nothing to be done about it. If he wished to remain among the ranks of the living, aches and pains were part of the bargain. Being a generally well-contented man, the sheriff harbored no bitterness toward aging and its debilitating effects. During the course of his life, he'd enjoyed remarkably good health and had escaped the clutches of death both on the battlefield and in the barroom. Unlike many, he'd been given a fair enough shake.

Just as he began puttering toward the bedroom, the glint of a lantern caught his eye from outside his front porch window. Someone was approaching the front door. The sinews of his aching frame instinctively tightened as he reached for his pistol, which he always kept nearby. A few moments later, a gentle knocking came at the door. Carefully, the sheriff unhitched the bolt and cracked the door open just far enough to see the face of Jacob Bell, one of the night watchmen from the Sandersville Precinct, located just north of Lexington.

"Jacob?" Sheriff Carr said when he recognized the young man.

"I'm sorry to disturb you so late, but you're needed at Berwick House," Jacob replied, breathing heavily.

The sheriff's chest tightened at the mention of Berwick House. He knew immediately, considering the late hour and the solemnity of Jacob's expression, that a terrible tragedy had occurred. "What's happened?" he whispered, almost inaudibly.

"It's Anna Driscoll, Sheriff. She's dead."

Sheriff Carr lost feeling in his legs. The words penetrated him like the stinger of a monstrous wasp, and for a moment he thought he would tumble to the floor. Luckily, his ferociously strong grip on the doorknob prevented his fall.

"Are you certain?" he finally managed.

Jacob nodded grimly. "I've seen it myself. It looks like it may have been Pleasant's doing."

"My God, it can't be." The numbness of his legs contrasted perfectly with the sudden pain in his chest and shoulder.

Jacob shrugged. "That's why we need you right now, Sheriff."

"All right. Go to the livery and get a horse ready for me," the sheriff ordered. "I'll be out in a minute."

Jacob obediently scampered off, and Sheriff Carr quietly closed the door and sighed a deep pensive breath as he considered the insidious news. Never had he been so weary. He felt like a traveler who, after a long and arduous journey, believed his destination to be just over the crest of the next hill, only to discover upon reaching the summit that a vast chasm lay on the other side. He needed time to further compose himself, but he could not linger. Quickly, he went to the bedroom and delicately touched the shoulder of his sleeping wife.

"What is it, dear?" she asked without opening her eyes.

"Jacob Bell was just at the door. Something's happened, and I'm needed straight away," he whispered.

Mrs. Carr squinted into the darkness. "Is there any danger?"

"No, it's nothing to worry about. Now, go back to sleep. I should be back in time for breakfast."

He dared not mention the news of Anna Driscoll's death. In truth, he did not know if his wife would be able to bear it, so close was her relationship to the poor girl. He knew that she would harangue him later for withholding the information, but under the circumstances ignorance was an exquisitely blissful condition, and the sheriff dared not rob his wife of one last unburdened night of sleep.

"Be careful, Joe," she murmured before shifting under the blankets and nuzzling back into her pillow. She'd become accustomed to her husband's professional comings and goings and had learned when it was appropriate to worry. If he told her there was no danger, she trusted him.

The sheriff put on his riding jacket and boots and then carefully secured his pistol in its holster. Jacob was already mounted and waiting for him just outside the front gate. He held the reins of the sheriff's freshly roused horse, which champed uncomfortably at its bit. The sheriff mounted and the two men commenced a brisk trot toward the edge of the city, where the northerly road leading to Berwick began.

The summer's heat and humidity finally had given way to cool autumn evenings, making the ride through the country darkness quite temperate. A light fog had fallen in certain dips and valleys along the way, and fireflies appeared sporadically throughout the woods and across the tobacco fields, giving the night a mystical aura. Sweet-smelling corn mash permeated the air from the north-county bourbon distilleries, creating in Sheriff Carr a great urge for a few sips of the spirit. Unfortunately, he'd long ago abandoned his flask for more righteous pursuits. In times like these, he missed it.

The sense of tragedy and scandal was palpable. Anna Driscoll was very popular in the community and greatly respected for her kindness and generosity. Sheriff Carr regarded her with more tenderness than his own stepdaughters, his wife's girls from a previous marriage. They were good women but a little distant with him. He could never replace their dead father, and he never tried. He just made sure they were taken care of, them and their mother. Both had married and moved east to more comfortable lives. For her part, Anna returned the Carrs' affections and graciously played the part of doting daughter.

The sheriff's initial shock gave way to anger, and although he tried to control it, rage was burrowing down deep inside him, like it did in his younger days when he was a wild and reckless man — a dangerous man. With great bitterness, he wondered if, at long last, the sins of his past were finally catching up to him. He realized it was foolish to have believed that his late conversion from wicked ways would spare him the wrath of Providence. The thought that his past ruthlessness was somehow being visited on his innocent loved ones as proxies made his journey to Berwick all the more difficult.

He arrived just before midnight, and every candle and lantern on the estate appeared to be aflame, making the recently completed mansion shine like a great beacon in the darkness. It was the most magnificent estate in Fayette County, notwithstanding Mr. Clay's mansion, Ashland, and it represented all of the splendor of the bountiful region. But knowing what awaited him inside, passing through the great Ionic columns on the portico of the mansion's façade made him feel like he was entering the sepulcher of an ancient deity. The gathered staff sat silently and bewildered in the south drawing room, their heads and hearts bent under the tomb-like gravity of the house.

"Where is Mrs. Cullen?" Sheriff Carr asked gruffly.

No one answered.

"Now, I'll have an answer, damn it!" he bellowed, stirring great fear in his audience.

Miss Martha, an ancient woman who had long been in the employment of the Driscolls, reluctantly answered. "She's upstairs with Mrs. Anna."

"What's she doing up there?" Jacob asked angrily, "I thought I told all y'all to stay down here till I got back with the sheriff."

Miss Martha nodded and averted her eyes back to the ground. "We know. That's why we're sittin' here. But Mrs. Cullen said she wanted to sit with her until the law arrived. She said she couldn't stand to think of Mrs. Anna all alone up in that room."

"The whole reason I wanted to keep y'all outta that room was so nothing would get moved around before the sheriff got here. That ain't too hard to understand, is it?"

Although Jacob was attempting to emulate the sheriff's severe tone, in comparison he seemed as meek as a child.

"We told her to leave it be, but she said she couldn't stand to think of Mrs. Anna up there by herself. She told us to hush up and sit still, and that's what we've done."

"Enough," Sheriff Carr said. "Put on some coffee for me and Jacob. The rest of y'all stay put. Nobody is to leave this house, you hear?"

The sheriff turned to Jacob. "Well…"

Jacob stared blankly back at him.

"Are you gonna show me, or do I have to buy a ticket first?"

Jacob apologized and hastily led him up the main staircase and down the second-floor hallway to the door of the master suite, which appeared to have been kicked open.

When the sheriff and Jacob entered the room, Mrs. Cullen was sitting in a small wooden chair next to the bed where Anna lay. Mrs. Cullen was a stout, middle-aged, Irish, housemaid with red hair and a colossal bosom. She gazed sullenly at Anna's motionless body and sobbed lightly. Her obvious distress was no surprise to the sheriff. She'd been hired as Anna's wet nurse over two decades earlier. Loyalty and love had kept her with Anna from the very start. Her dedication was further bolstered by Anna's reciprocal affection. Anna harbored such fondness for the woman, the only immutable condition she'd made to Pleasant Driscoll's proposal of marriage was that Mrs. Cullen be taken on as the head maid in their new household.

"I haven't messed with nothin'," she said upon the sheriff's entrance.

"Come stand with Mr. Bell over here for a moment while I inspect the room," Sheriff Carr demanded, not unkindly.

Mrs. Cullen obeyed, reluctantly breaking her vigil over Anna's body. The sheriff moved the chair in which she'd been sitting out of the way and surveyed Anna Driscoll carefully. A dull pain again permeated his shoulder as he leaned over her body, which lay perfectly arranged on the bed. She was still very beautiful, even though all the color had abandoned her placid face, replaced by the pallor of death. Her eyes were closed and her hands were neatly stacked on her chest. He drew closer and closer to Anna until his ear was just inches from her mouth.

"We think that…" Jacob began.

"Shush!" Sheriff Carr hissed.

The room became very still, the only sound the implacable grandfather clock in the hallway. After a dozen sonorous ticks and tocks, Sheriff Carr once again stood upright. He sighed with disappointment. Jacob and Mrs. Cullen watched him with curiosity.

"When I was a young boy, my father took me to the funeral of my Uncle Gabe, who'd been kicked in the head by a mule," he said. "It was one of those makeshift frontier affairs, nothing but a crudely fashioned pine box and a hole in the ground. Imagine everyone's surprise when Uncle Gabe sat straight up in his coffin midway through the eulogy. He saw me and

42

yelled *Freddie, get my whisky! They think I'm dead!"*

A humorless grin crept across the sheriff's face. "Can you believe no one had checked that he actually stopped breathing? As you may expect, that made quite an impression on me."

"Why did he call you Freddie, Sheriff?"

The sheriff grumbled, "He'd been kicked in the head, Jacob. He didn't know what he was sayin'."

The sheriff strolled about the room, scrutinizing every detail. A length of rope lay on the floor near the bed.

"Where'd this come from?" he asked.

Mrs. Cullen shrugged.

"Sheriff, I believe that's the murder weapon," Jacob volunteered. "Look at her throat."

The sheriff gently tilted Anna's chin upward. Her skin was cold. Her neck was discolored and severely bruised. It appeared Jacob was correct. While he certainly was no stranger to death, Anna's battered neck distracted him in a way he'd never felt before. The more he considered her, the more his head began to swim. His legs were on the verge of betraying him yet again, so he plopped down on the chair Mrs. Cullen had relinquished a few moments before and leaned his elbows forward on his knees. From his jacket pocket he produced a worn handkerchief and dabbed away the perspiration forming on his brow.

"Why is she wearing a formal dress, Mrs. Cullen?" he finally managed to ask.

"Mrs. Anna and Mr. Driscoll went to a dinner party tonight in town at Philip and Ivy Carter's house," the maid replied miserably. "Oh, that I could change what happened!"

"Take a breath, Mrs. Cullen," the sheriff said, his composure regained, "and tell me exactly what you saw from the time the Driscolls got home from the party tonight until right now."

"The whole time?"

"The whole time."

Mrs. Cullen nodded reluctantly and searched her memory. "Actually, I think I'd better start the story a little earlier than that."

Sheriff Carr extended his hand somewhat sarcastically, inviting her to continue.

"Before they left this afternoon, I heard them arguing about something here in the bedroom. Heaven knows I'm not the type who would listen in on a private conversation, especially between the Driscolls, but I'd never heard them raise their voices at each other before and it scared me."

"What were they arguing about?"

"I'm not sure. Like I said, they were in this bedroom, and I was down the hall yonder, so everything was muffled. I came up the hall a little closer and started polishing the old clock so I could hear better."

"Not the type who would listen in on a private conversation, you say?" Jacob chided.

"I told you this was different," she retorted. "It was still hard to hear what they was saying because they stopped their hollerin', but Mr. Driscoll was talking fiercely, you know, viciously. He told Mrs. Anna he was ruined and that it was all her fault."

Sheriff Carr stiffened. "What did he mean?"

The maid shook her head. "I couldn't tell you. Mrs. Anna was crying, though, God bless her."

"Did you hear anything else?"

Mrs. Cullen lowered her head. "I did, but I wish I didn't. I wish to God I didn't."

"Mrs. Cullen, I know you loved that lady over yonder, but I don't have time for beating around the bush. I'm trying to understand what happened to Anna. I wasn't here when all this hollerin' and carryin' on happened, but you were. I have to know what you know if I'm gonna do my job."

Mrs. Cullen swallowed hard and composed herself. "Mr. Driscoll said something real mean to Mrs. Anna, and it don't make no sense to me. I mean, those two had been so happy. I don't think I've ever seen two people better suited for one another in me whole life."

"I know how they were together," Sheriff Carr said sullenly.

Mrs. Cullen shook her head. "He was always bringing in these beautiful

44

bouquets of wildflowers for Mrs. Anna, and she'd sit and stare at him like he hung the stars while he talked about where he'd found 'em. Other times, they'd go out riding on the property and I wouldn't see 'em for the whole day, but they'd come back to the house glowing bright as you please, just from being together. There was never a cross word between them. That's why the staff admired 'em so much. It was like we all got to feed on that brightness they had together. We'd watch 'em and we'd feel like we was loved too."

Mrs. Cullen's face fell. "I don't know what we'll do now. Everything's busted."

Sheriff Carr's tone began to change. "You still haven't told me what Pleasant said to Anna. I'll have the truth, by God, and I'll have it this minute."

Tears sprang afresh from Mrs. Cullen's eyes. Between sobs, she answered, "He told her that she had finally failed him completely. He said he wished they'd never even got married."

"Hogwash, he'd never say such a thing," the sheriff scoffed.

"It's the truth, I swear it. I think part of it has to do with the secret they had. I swore I'd never say nothin' about it, but I reckon it don't matter no more. Fact is, Mrs. Anna was never gonna have any babies. They'd got a doctor from Philadelphia to come down here and check her out, and he told 'em that she was barren. Nobody else knew. Mrs. Anna only told me when I found her crying in the garden one day. Poor creature."

"I didn't know that," Sheriff Carr admitted.

"After he said those terrible things, Mr. Driscoll left Mrs. Anna in the bedroom and went down to the carriage. He looked so cruel. I don't think he even saw me standing outside their room. I went in after and asked Mrs. Anna if she was all right, but she just wiped her tears up and smiled at me. I could see it plain as day, though."

"What?"

"She was broken. Broken in a way only something real special can be broke. Her spirit was dead, even if her body wasn't yet."

Miss Martha poked her head into the room. "Coffee's done," she said.

"Just set it down on the dresser there," the sheriff instructed.

After seeing Anna's lifeless body and hearing Mrs. Cullen's gossip, the thought of drinking coffee made the sheriff feel like retching. Jacob apparently did not feel the same trepidation as he immediately took a large sip from his mug.

Mrs. Cullen twisted her hands nervously as she continued her story. "I was in the warming kitchen, sitting in the rocking chair, when they got back tonight. It's my custom to stay up when they go to parties so I can fetch what they need when they come back home. Sometimes its just a glass of water, sometimes it's nothing at all. Either way, I like to be there for 'em just in case."

"Did you hear them come in?"

"I'm ashamed to say, I didn't. I must have been asleep. I suppose it was the commotion upstairs that woke me up."

"The door breaking in?" the sheriff asked, nodding past Mrs. Cullen to the splintered doorframe behind her.

"That's right," she said, glancing over her shoulder at the damage, "then there was heavy footsteps across these here floors. It was definitely a tussle of some sort. When I heard that I was scared and didn't know what to do. I thought it might be some kinda intruder or something like that. When the tusslin' noise stopped, I crept real slowly up the stairs. The only light was coming from this here room."

Mrs. Cullen again swallowed hard and furrowed her brow. "I was real scared to look, but I did anyway. That's when I seen Mr. Driscoll putting Mrs. Anna on the bed all gentle-like. He closed her eyes with his hand and straightened her up real perfect. I didn't know what I was seein', and before I knowed it, I blurted out, *What's wrong with her? Is she sick?* Mr. Driscoll didn't even look at me; he just stroked her cheek with the back of his hand and said, *She's dead.* He said it like he was tellin' me it was raining outside, or like he was tellin' me what time it was — no emotion at all. Well, after hearin' that, and how he said it, I got this chill that ran straight to me bones, my head felt like it had been slugged. That's when I noticed the rope laying there on the floor, in that very spot. *You killed her!* I said to Mr. Driscoll. *You done choked her to death.* He still didn't look up at me. It was like he was entranced or something — could be he was possessed by Lucifer himself."

"Did he tell you what happened or say anything else?"

"No, he just kept staring at her and pettin' her face. Then he kissed her hand and got up real sudden. I thought he was coming to strangle me too, so I squealed like a stuck pig. But he just walked right passed me, down them stairs, and out that front door. I don't know where he's gone. The stable boy, William, came in a few minutes after Mr. Driscoll left and told me that he got on his horse and rode off in a hurry. I was near hysterical at that point and didn't know what to do, so I sent William over to the neighboring estate to get Mr. Clinton. He done it, and Mr. Clinton come real quick. He checked on Mrs. Anna, and seein' as how she was dead, he took a look around the house carryin' his pistol to make sure no one was still here. He told me to go fetch William 'cause he wanted William to go get the precinct watchman, but I told him I couldn't leave Mrs. Anna. I could tell it made him cross, but I wasn't budgin', so he went and got William hisself. Folks has been coming and goin' since it happened, but I've not left her side."

"Jacob, was Mr. Clinton still here when you arrived?"

"No, he'd already gone. His house isn't far, though, you want me to go get him?"

Sheriff Carr nodded, then turned his attention back toward Mrs. Cullen. "I'm gonna take some notes about what you've said and what I've seen while he gets Malcolm. I don't suppose I can convince you to go back to your quarters and get some rest while I work, can I?"

To the sheriff's surprise, Mrs. Cullen immediately stepped out into the hallway. However, a few moments later she stubbornly returned with another small wooden chair and stationed herself near the bed. The sheriff was irritated, but he couldn't fault her undying loyalty. He scooted his chair to a nearby writing desk and produced a small pocket journal from his jacket. Using the ink and pen on the desk, he transcribed his initial inspection. Every so often, he paused to stretch out his arm and shoulder, which continued to bother him with a nagging pain.

A half hour later, Jacob knocked on the open door. "Sheriff, Mr. Clinton is outside."

"All right," the sheriff said. "Tell him I'll be right out. After that, I want you posted at the front entrance. No one without a badge is allowed in this house without my permission."

The sheriff concluded a thought in his notebook, then shut it up and tucked it back into his jacket. He patted Mrs. Cullen's shoulder as he exited the room.

Malcolm Clinton was standing alone under the immense front portico when Sheriff Carr emerged from the house. Mr. Clinton was a handsome, albeit somewhat foppish gentleman who worked in the city as a banker but also ran a sizeable tobacco plantation near Berwick. He and Sheriff Carr had crossed paths at many social events over the years, all of which the sheriff attended out of political obligation and Mr. Clinton attended out of personal delight.

"I apologize about the late hour," the sheriff said as he shook Mr. Clinton's gloved hand.

"Please, Sheriff, think nothing of it. These are grim circumstances. What can I do to help you?"

"I was speaking with Mrs. Cullen about what happened, and she told me that William came and got you shortly after Mr. Driscoll left Berwick tonight. Did you happen to see him on the road when you came here earlier?"

"No, Sheriff, I'm sorry to say I didn't. I was quite confused at the time as to what was going on. At first, I mistook poor William for a villain of some sort and nearly put a slug through his head. Fortunately, he was able to explain that something had happened at Berwick and that my help was needed."

Mr. Clinton then cocked his head. "From your question, I take it you are of the opinion Mr. Driscoll is to blame for what happened?"

The sheriff grunted in the affirmative.

"How heartbreaking. Could it have been a transient or some sort of rogue?"

"No. According to Mrs. Cullen, she was the only one in the house with the Driscolls when it happened. She heard a skirmish and saw Pleasant hovering over Anna's body on the bed."

"Do you think Mrs. Cullen is telling the truth?"

"I believe so. She'd have no reason to lie."

"I suppose not," Mr. Clinton admitted. "The strand of rope up there is the instrument of murder then?"

"I think so. Anna's neck is bruised all to hell. I think her windpipe is crushed. Did anything else grab your attention when you first saw the room? I guess you were the second person on the scene behind Mrs. Cullen."

Mr. Clinton sighed thoughtfully. "Only that Mrs. Driscoll had been meticulously laid upon the bed, but honestly I didn't linger long enough to truly examine the scene. It was quite ghastly. I quickly checked the house to make sure no one was hiding therein, then I sent William to get Mr. Bell."

"That's what Mrs. Cullen said."

Mr. Clinton slapped the back of his right hand into the palm of his left. "I knew something was wrong with them tonight. They acted so peculiar. But how could I have predicted this?"

"What are you talking about? When did you see them?"

"Well, Rachel and I saw them at the Carters' dinner party. Frankly, I'm surprised they had the courage to show up at all, considering Pleasant's recent misfortunes."

"Misfortunes?"

Mr. Clinton looked somewhat surprised. "Being Mr. Driscoll's banker, I was the first to know about his wretched turn in circumstances, but I kept it buttoned up as a professional courtesy. Nevertheless, somehow it leaked out and became gossip fodder for the socialites. So, you've not heard?"

Sheriff Carr glared impatiently at him.

Mr. Clinton cleared his throat awkwardly. "Right, well, it seems that Berwick's vineyards have been blighted by some unknown disease of the vines — poor fellow. This year's crop is totally lost, and it is not known if the land will ever produce a grape yield again."

Sheriff Carr could appreciate the unpleasant nature of the news but could not comprehend its true impact. "I know the vineyards are very important to Berwick," he said, "but it isn't the only source of income. They've still got tobacco, the orchards, and the livestock, not to mention last year's vintage."

"All true," Mr. Clinton allowed, "but I'm afraid it is a matter of debt and available collateral. You see, Mr. Driscoll mortgaged his entire estate for a loan to build Berwick House and for the startup capital for the vineyard. It is always risky to make a loan based on an agricultural endeavor, but we all had such confidence in Mr. Driscoll's genius and his unflappable optimism that we gave him the loan. He'd produced a very small trial vintage out of his hybrid grapes, and everyone agreed it was the most exquisite wine produced outside of Europe. We thought he was going to make a lot of money. But there was no way to anticipate this blight."

"I acknowledge it is a regrettable setback, but it hardly seems ruinous, with the estate's available resources," the sheriff argued.

"Unfortunately, time was the real enemy. The loan was constructed to be of a very short duration, per Mr. Driscoll's express wishes. A bulk payment is due before the end of the year, and he simply has no liquid finances with which to fulfill his obligation. His equity in the house and the rest of the estate is surprisingly little. He was just getting started, after all. Even before tonight's tragedy, there was little doubt he would default and the bank would be forced to possess the collateral."

Sheriff Carr placed his hands on his hips. "Surely your bank could have restructured the loan to manageable payments spread out over the coming years so he could attempt to diversify his holdings and make good on the note."

"'Twas my thought exactly," Mr. Clinton awkwardly agreed, "but Mr. Driscoll was deemed too volatile by the bank's board of directors. As with any responsible financial institution, the best interests of the bank, and of its clients, are placed in the forefront. Immediate foreclosure on the property upon the impending default was deemed most prudent by the board, despite my personal misgivings."

"I'm sure Mr. Driscoll did not take the board's decision lying down. I know him well. He's capable of confounding the devil himself with his cleverness. It's hard to imagine that he had no ingenious solution to the problem."

Mr. Clinton's mouth seemed to twist with irritation. "Oh yes, Mr. Driscoll made several bombastic overtures to the board, which frankly secured their collective opinion regarding his instability. The amount of money at stake was simply too great to wager on his novelties. Most of his ideas would have required a further investment from the bank. It was out of the question. I fear that, for the bank's sake, I will need to step into a receivership role so that I can undo Mr. Driscoll's mismanagement."

"Fine," Sheriff Carr said crossly, "the Driscolls were on the brink of financial collapse and the bank could do nothing to help. You still haven't told me how they attracted attention to themselves tonight at the Carters' party."

"You mistake my previous statement, Sheriff. To everyone else I'm sure the Driscolls seemed perfectly normal, albeit somewhat sedate. Certainly, they made no grand scene or anything of that nature."

"But somehow you knew that things were off-kilter?"

"Precisely."

"Well, please do go on, Mr. Clinton, time is wasting."

"Of course. Like I was saying, I knew that something was wrong between the Driscolls, not because of their countenances toward the other guests, but because of subtle changes in their behavior toward one another. As you know, they have been a very popular and well received young couple in Lexington since their marriage several years ago. Indeed, they possess, rather I should say *did possess*, a certain liveliness that energized those fortunate souls caught in their orbit. I must confess that on more than a few occasions I myself had been hypnotized by their presence. I suppose there is solace in knowing that I was not the only one to feel so. Nevertheless, my surveillances of them, even if uncomely, imparted upon me a baseline on which to judge their customary behavior. It is only in the light of my previous observations that I discerned their departure from the norm tonight."

"Get to it, man, what happened?"

"Bear with me, Sheriff, I'm coming to that. As was their custom, when the call to dinner was made, the Driscolls fell to the back of the throng making its way into the dining room. I'd witnessed them do this on several prior occasions. Essentially, Mrs. Driscoll would take advantage of the group's inattention and gently clasp Mr. Driscoll's arm and elegantly tiptoe closer to him so as to whisper something in his ear. I durst not speculate as to the content of the messages conveyed, as I do not wish to tread impolitely upon the conjugal affairs of others, but without fail, it would elicit from Mr. Driscoll a rascally grin and wink or some other reception of obvious delight."

Sheriff Carr raised his eyebrows.

"Please don't mistake me," Mr. Clinton interjected, "there was nothing uncouth about it. To the contrary, it was quite beautiful to see a husband and wife still in love with each other and not someone else's wife or husband, as seems to be fashionable in Lexington society these days. So moving was this habit of theirs, I found myself watching for it every time they were in our company."

"Sounds as though the grass appeared greener," the sheriff said.

"Certainly not, Sheriff." Mr. Clinton snorted indignantly. "I viewed the Driscolls' display as I would a great work of art which can inspire wondrous feelings in the observer without any desire to physically interact with it. You insult me, sir."

"All right, begging your pardon. Please continue," Sheriff Carr said with half-hearted contrition.

Mr. Clinton resumed. "Tonight, something different happened. Sure enough, Mrs. Driscoll whispered into Mr. Driscoll's ear when the attention of those gathered was diverted to Mr. Clay, who was leading a rather impassioned colloquy regarding the current vicissitudes with Mexico, but her message did not meet with its usual reception. It was as though she'd whispered into the ear of a graveyard statue. Mr. Driscoll finished his brandy and stared vacantly ahead. There was no grin, or wink, or bow. For the briefest of moments, I detected a worrisome look of dismay on Mrs. Driscoll's face, then nothing. She recovered, and it was like nothing had been said at all. The rest of the evening was quite typical in every regard."

"This is your grand evidence of marital woe?" Sheriff Carr cried. "My

God, if you were to see some of the looks my wife gives me, you'd probably think she were prepared to set me on fire in my sleep. This harsh look you speak of…"

"I did not say it was a harsh look, Sheriff," Mr. Clinton corrected. "It was a worried, almost desperate look."

"Whatever the case may be, a single look between spouses does not amount to the weight of a single bean on the scale of justice."

"Regarding anyone else, I'd agree with you wholeheartedly. But if you truly believe the scene I just described between the Driscolls meant nothing, then you don't know them as well as you suppose," Mr. Clinton said resolutely.

Jacob approached and patted the sheriff's elbow. "Sheriff, Deputies Casey and Powell are here. They're waiting for you in the library."

The sheriff gave Mr. Clinton a pensive glance. "Sir, I thank you for your help. You've given me a lot to think about."

"Just let me know if you need anything else, Sheriff. Good luck."

The men shook hands again, and Sheriff Carr trudged back into the house. Tom Casey, a nine-year deputy, and Trevor Powell, a late teen still in his first month on the job, stood impatiently near one of the bookshelves in the handsomely outfitted library.

"What's the story, Sheriff?" Tom asked when the sheriff entered the room. He quickly returned a book he'd been glancing at to the shelf. Trevor crossed his arms over his skinny chest and focused intently on the sheriff.

"This is what I've got so far," Sheriff Carr began. "It looks like the Driscolls argued this afternoon before going to a dinner party in town. At the party, one of the guests noticed them acting a bit out of character. We don't know what happened when they first got home, but shortly thereafter there was a ruckus upstairs. Mrs. Cullen heard the bedroom door kicked open and scrambling footsteps. When she got upstairs, she saw Pleasant putting Anna on the bed and acting quite bizarre. She screamed, and he left. There's a length of rope on the floor up there, and death appears to have been caused by strangulation."

"Any idea where Mr. Driscoll is?" Trevor asked.

"All we know is that he's headed north on horseback."

"We got another Patrick Boyle situation on our hands?" Casey inquired with ill-disguised glee.

"Who is Patrick Boyle?" Trevor asked.

Tom rolled his eyes with feigned exasperation. "Don't you read the papers at all? He was a blacksmith from the Meadowthorpe precinct. Few years back, he fell under some mental disease and murdered his family — two young boys, a teenage daughter, and a pretty little wife."

"Christ," Trevor replied. "What happened to him?"

"After he done his deed, he turned coward and couldn't take his own life, so he hit the road. Sheriff Carr and I had a good idea where he was headin', and we beat him to it."

Sheriff Carr clucked his tongue in disgust.

"Did you get him?" Trevor asked.

"Oh yes," Tom smirked and cut a knowing glance at the sheriff. "We got him real good."

"Did he come at y'all or something, like an attack?" Trevor prodded excitedly.

"Hell, no." Casey laughed. "Boyle was beshit with fear at the sight of us. It was a stench that followed him to Satan's doorstep."

The story's somewhat ambiguous ending caused a frown to creep across Trevor's face. "What are you tellin' me?"

"I'm tellin' you that some sons of bitches get justice a little quicker than others when it's clearly what they deserve. You gotta get the rocks out of your skull, Deputy."

Trevor frowned at the insult.

"What say you, Sheriff? We got another Boyle situation?" Tom asked again.

Sheriff Carr bristled at the deputy's swaggering attitude. "I think you know what kind of situation it is," he replied brusquely.

Tom smiled. "C'mon, Trevor, let's round up the boys. We gotta get goin.'"

After the deputies stalked out, Sheriff Carr once again made some notes in his pocket journal. He felt awful, both physically and emotionally. The options that lay before him were sadistic. Before he could straighten out his thoughts, a commotion arose at the front entrance. Mr. Clinton's shrill voice cut clearly through the house so that the sheriff recognized it even from the library.

Greatly perturbed by the interruption, he ambled toward the hubbub.

"What's the trouble here?" he growled.

"Sheriff, I was just doin' what you asked," Jacob said apologetically. "Mr. Clinton wanted to come into the house, and I told him no one could come in without your say so."

Mr. Clinton shifted uncomfortably. "I didn't want to bother you with such a trifling concern, Sheriff, and I'm truly embarrassed to bring it up, but it is meaningful to my wife, and now that your attention has been called to the matter, I feel I must explain. Recently, Rachel loaned Mrs. Driscoll a literary magazine that she is quite fond of called *The Pioneer*, I believe. When I was in the Driscoll's bedroom earlier, I noticed it was lying on Mrs. Driscoll's bedside table. I meant to grab it before I left, but with Mrs. Cullen's hysterics and whatnot, I forgot. I know this is quite trivial, but there will be a lot of change and commotion at Berwick in the coming days and weeks, and I fear it will be lost in the tumult."

"Malcolm, my God, are you so callous? Anna is not three hours dead!"

Mr. Clinton's face turned crimson with embarrassment as he stammered, "M—my deepest apologies, Sheriff, if I'd known that I'd be detained by Mr. Bell here and that your attention would be required, I'd never would have attempted to retrieve it."

"Rest easy," Sheriff Carr said derisively. "I'll see that you get Rachel's precious storybook."

"Please, Sheriff, do not trouble yourself. Just let me upstairs for a moment, and I will retrieve it myself."

"You have been most helpful tonight, Mr. Clinton, but I feel it is time for you to go. I will personally ensure that Rachel's belongings are returned to her."

"Of course. Thank you, Sheriff," Mr. Clinton said with thinly veiled disappointment. "The things we do to keep our wives happy, right?"

Sheriff Carr scowled. "That's a helluva thing to say in this house."

# Chapter 6

**1962**

A succession of mighty screams resonated through the funeral home just after seven in the morning. Violet, roused by the bellowing, opened her eyes and groggily studied the ceiling. She lay in a clouded stupor as the events of the previous evening came rushing back to her. Panic seized her, and with a jolt of adrenaline, she rolled off of the bed, somewhat expecting her disembodied soul to look down on its former shell. Instead, she found only her slightly rumpled blanket and pillow.

Sunlight gushed into the room and cast everything in the warm glow of dawn. With great difficulty, Violet fought to regain her composure. The pill bottle sat harmlessly on her nightstand, exactly where she'd left it a few hours before. She couldn't believe it. In her exhaustion, while balancing on the cusp of her own mortality, she'd fallen asleep before committing the fatal act. Through her open window, she heard the heavy-handed pounding of fists on glass and muffled calls for help. She peered outside, shielding her face from the bright sun, and squinted down to the rear parking lot. To her chagrin, she recalled that Brian was locked in the back of the hearse. Indeed, it was him who had been howling so miserably. It was a scene she was never supposed to have witnessed and one she felt unprepared to handle.

To Violet's relief, Henry meandered into view from the direction of the greenhouse. He strode toward the commotion with a look of curiosity and amusement. Violet watched as he unlocked the back hatch of the hearse with the spare keys hidden in a magnetic container under the back fender.

When the door swung open, Brian toppled out onto the pavement. He scrambled to his feet but then immediately doubled over in a fit of vomiting. Henry watched stoically as the disheveled lawyer clumsily attempted to remove a dangling strand of viscous saliva from his mouth with a curled finger. When the strand stuck to his finger, Brian shook his hand wildly until he accidentally slung it onto the hem of his suit pants.

From her perch, Violet could not hear the ensuing discussion between the two men, but Brian's contrition was evident enough. He hung his head and pointed at the hearse then rubbed his temple and shrugged as though explanation were impossible. Henry said something then turned and pointed toward the funeral home. Both men suddenly realized that Violet had watched the entire scene unfold and all gazed awkwardly at one another until Violet abruptly shut her window and pulled the curtains closed.

Her face burned with humiliation, both for herself and for Brian. She debated whether to hide in her room until Brian had gone or go downstairs and confront the situation head-on. As attractive as the first option seemed, she knew that if she didn't air things out with Brian and offer him an explanation, it could possibly damage his relationship with Henry. That was the last thing she wanted.

Violet freshened up in the bathroom then made her way downstairs toward the sound of voices in the kitchen. As beautifully designed and remodeled as the rest of the mansion was, the kitchen was rather mundane. Henry had opted for unobtrusive functionality in lieu of flashier and more modern alternatives. When she entered the room, Brian was sitting with his elbow propped on the green-swirl Formica tabletop, his head resting in his hand. Henry was busying himself at the stove, cracking eggs, buttering toast, and laying bacon in a frying pan. Violet was surprised to see Henry cooking, since she was the one who always prepared their meals, if any meals were to be prepared at all. More often than not, she and Henry would fend for themselves, often just scavenging off of the leftover cold cut and cracker trays from the hospitality room.

Quietly, Violet took a seat opposite Brian on one of the matching green upholstered chairs that came with the table. He didn't acknowledge her.

"Good morning, Violet," Henry said when he noticed her.

"Good morning," she replied somewhat hoarsely. "Need some help?"

"No, please relax. I'm taking care of breakfast today."

He poured two cups of coffee and placed them before Brian and Violet. Brian immediately reached for his mug and blew impatiently across the steaming black liquid before taking a couple of scalding sips. Violet was content to cradle her mug in her ever-cold hands. Henry cheerily returned to his endeavor, leaving Brian and Violet alone at the table.

"How do you feel?" Violet asked.

Brian just scowled at her.

His disdain irked her. After all, she had been thrust into a very difficult situation, one she felt she handled pretty well. "Your fault, not mine," she said matter-of-factly.

Brian's eyes widened in disbelief. "Are you serious?" he hissed. "You think I chose to be kidnapped and locked in the back of a fucking hearse?" He lowered his voice further. "I literally almost shit myself when I woke up."

Violet scrunched her face in disgust. "You were the one playing 'drink all the bourbon' last night. Besides, you'd be thanking me if you knew what the alternative was."

"Thanking you? Are you high?"

Before Violet could respond, Henry scurried back over and placed two plates on the table. "*Buen provecho*," he said, smiling.

Violet noticed that everything on her plate was burned, except for the eggs, which were somewhere between runny and raw. She forced a smile and nodded her appreciation to Henry. The smell and appearance of the food seemed to make Brian queasy. He clenched his jaw and breathed a few shallow breaths before returning to a hard-fought equilibrium.

"Eat up," Henry said. "I promise you'll feel better."

Brian apprehensively picked up a fork and evaluated the plate before him, but the prospect of actually putting any of the blackened morsels in his mouth proved unfeasible. He pushed the plate away and leaned back in his chair.

"Can we just get this over with?" he asked dejectedly. "Are you firing me or not?"

Henry looked surprised. "Why would I do that?"

Brian scoffed and looked incredulously across the table. He then looked down at his unkempt state and motioned at himself like a game show model displaying a prize.

"Look, I'm really sorry about all this. I know it's unprofessional, with all the screaming and the vomiting and what have you. I honestly have no clue what happened last night."

"Maybe Violet can fill in some of the details there," Henry suggested.

With the aid of her coffee, Violet forced herself to swallow down the bite of toast with which she had been laboring.

"Well," she said, shifting in her chair, "I found Mr. Todd at Cuppy's, like you said I would."

Both men looked intently at her as she spoke, one with thinly veiled amusement, the other with thinly veiled contempt.

"Mr. Todd was having a few drinks and telling me a bit about his...uh..."

Violet feared that mentioning Brian's dead wife would cause him to spontaneously combust, so she switched gears.

"That is, he was telling me a little bit about your lawsuit against Mr. Trimble."

"Is that right?" Henry said, cutting Brian a surprised glance.

Brian looked alarmed. "Well, I wasn't really talking about the details of the case; I was just kind of speaking about the law in general. Just describing a few basic legal principles for her, in layman's terms."

Violet took offense at being called a layman. All she'd done was try to help the man, and in return he insulted her. She turned sharply toward Henry. "It seems Brian isn't very confident that you will prevail." She glanced back at Brian and feigned confusion. "Or was it that you didn't really care if he prevailed? I forget how you worded it."

Brian laughed nervously. "That's not what I said," he reassured Henry. "I merely said there was no way to be one hundred percent certain about the outcome of a case when it's left in the hands of a jury. Like we've already discussed, I think you have a very strong case, and I think we have a good chance of getting the result you want."

Henry smiled graciously. "Don't worry Brian, I'm not upset with you. Violet is like my right hand around here. You can discuss the case with her freely. Besides, I like our chances too."

Brian looked relieved.

"Why is that?" Violet asked.

"Well, besides having a very skilled attorney on my side, I am confident the surveyor will find all of the historic property markers, even the buried ones, and they will justify my claim."

Violet couldn't tell if he was being totally sincere in his praise of Brian. From the uncertain look on Brian's face, he couldn't either.

"Anyway," Henry said, "you were telling us about what happened last night."

"Right," Violet continued. "Well, Mr. Todd became a bit…belligerent… with the bartender, and they got into a fight."

Brian rubbed his tender jaw. "Well, at least that explains why my face feels like it went three rounds with Cassius Clay. Freddy and I have a bit of a love/hate relationship," he explained. "I probably got some good licks in too."

"Well, you hit the floor pretty hard, does that count?" Violet goaded. "Anyway, you were out cold, so I asked Freddy what he was going to do with you, and he said he'd set you outside on the street if you didn't wake up before the end of his shift."

"That bastard!" Brian growled.

"I got a couple of guys from the bar to pack you out to the hearse, which Henry let me drive last night, and I brought you back here. It was the best thing that could have been done under the circumstances."

Brian grimaced and rubbed his temple with his fingers. "I can't believe that asshole let you drag me out of there and put me in a hearse!"

Violet was in disbelief. Brian still couldn't admit that she'd helped him. "Didn't you hear what I said? He was going to put you out on the street."

"No, he wasn't," Brian replied.

"He seemed pretty serious to me."

"He was playing a joke on me, on both of us, really. He wouldn't have put me out on the street. He would have helped me back to my apartment."

"You think that the man that knocked your lights out was just going to tote you around Lexington, out of the goodness of his heart, and tuck you into bed at your apartment?"

"Of course he was. He's my landlord. I live above the bar."

Henry, who had put all the pieces together when he first saw Brian in the back of the hearse, burst out laughing when the revelation was finally made to Violet. She was dumbstruck.

"Obviously, I didn't realize…" she stuttered.

Brian just scowled as Henry fought to compose himself. "Lighten up, you two," he snorted.

A car horn sounded from the parking lot.

"Thank God," Brian said. "That's my cab." He thanked Henry for his untouched breakfast and apologized again for his scene in the parking lot. He said he'd call later in the week to talk about the case and then hurried out the door. When he was gone, the kitchen fell silent, and Violet felt like crying. She was ashamed, and angry, and bitter, all on top of the tornado of emotions associated with her botched suicide. She even felt annoyed with Henry, who not only created the whole embarrassing situation with Brian, but also had the gall to laugh about it in her face.

He seemed to pick up on Violet's mood.

"I'm sorry I laughed about what happened," he said. "I know you were doing the best you could last night."

Tears started welling up, which made her even angrier.

"I don't think you should have sent me there."

"No, I suppose not," Henry agreed. "That was unfair to you. But, as you can tell by my cooking, I'm not perfect."

Violet forced a smile and patted her eyes with her napkin.

Henry looked thoughtfully at her. "May I share a story with you, Violet?"

"I'm not sure now is a good time, Henry. I don't feel very well this morning." She pushed her chair back from the table and started to get up. "I'd like to go rest in my room, if you don't mind."

"Please, indulge me," he persisted. "It will only take a few minutes."

Violet sat back down.

"When I was still training to be a mortician," he began, "my class spent several weeks in the morgue of a hospital in Louisville working with cadavers. One night, while I was leaving, I noticed a man dressed in maintenance overalls sitting in one of the waiting areas. He was chewing on his nails, clearly fretting about something. That was pretty typical for a hospital waiting area, so I didn't pay it much mind. The man was still there the next day, though, and the day after that. Each time I saw him, he looked more worried and more exhausted. On the fourth day, he was still in the waiting room when I arrived at the hospital, but he was gone when I was on my way back out. It made me wonder if something had happened. But again, I didn't give it too much thought.

"Incidentally, I happened to come across the man outside in the parking lot, weeping. I don't typically like to intrude in the affairs of others, but compassion overcame me in that moment, and I asked if he was all right. He thanked me for my concern and said that he was fine, but I could tell that there was something else he wanted to say. *Want to get a cup of coffee?* I asked him. He did.

"As we sat in that midnight diner, he proceeded to tell me the most heartbreaking story I'd ever heard. Every now and then, I find myself thinking about his tale, and each time I do, I feel the same miserable ache I did when I first heard it."

"I'm really not in the mood for this," Violet interrupted.

"Please, Violet, it's quite brief," Henry said before continuing. "The man had married young. His wife was a serious woman, plain and dutiful. Together, they started a little country store that did a modest business in a modest community. But they persevered and grew the store over the years and fell into a comfortable but hardworking lifestyle. Along the way, they had a son, who was a precocious lad. Although well-meaning, the boy often caused mischief and created many headaches for his parents.

"One day, while the man was working alone, a very beautiful woman walked in, whom he had admired from behind his counter on several previous occasions. The woman typically went about her business with tired disinterest, quietly purchasing some milk or dish detergent, but on this particular day, something was different about her. She looked especially alluring as she browsed his shop, seductively caressing various items on the shelves. The shop being otherwise empty, he approached and asked if there was anything he could help her find. *Looks like you do a pretty good business here*, she said to him. He told her, *I do pretty well for myself.* The woman sauntered over to the clothing section. *This is a little embarrassing,* she said, *but I'm looking for a particular kind of undergarment, and you don't appear to have it in stock.*

"The man was shocked. His wife always fielded questions about women's apparel. When she wasn't around, which wasn't often, those types of questions were left unasked. The woman came close and whispered in his ear, *I want something silky like I've seen in the fashion magazines.* Her warm breath on his neck and the irreverence of the request made him tremble with a sudden desire he'd never felt before. *I could probably order something like that*, he told her. *Come back in exactly two weeks, and I'll have it for you.* She thanked him and left the store, hips swinging dangerously from side to side as she exited.

"The man filled out the order form and sent it off in the mail. For the next two weeks, he eagerly awaited its arrival and made sure he was the first to intercept all shipments of new inventory. In the meantime, he allowed his mind to run wild with fantasies about the woman. He was excited in a way he hadn't felt in years, but the more he thought about the woman, the more his tedious wife and mischievous son drew his disdain.

"The package finally arrived, and the man ensured that his wife would be out of the shop the day the woman was scheduled to return. Again, the woman arrived when the store was empty. She looked even more tempting than before. To the man's delight, when she came in, she locked the door behind her and flipped his 'open' sign to 'closed.' *Do you have something for me?* she asked. The man nearly fell over himself retrieving her package, which he'd hidden among his other stock. The woman followed him into the stockroom and marveled at the lascivious garment he produced.

"*I suppose I'd better try it on*, she told him. The man started to leave the storeroom to give her privacy, but she caught him by the arm. *You know, I haven't got a thing on underneath this dress,* she told him."

"Please stop!" Violet exclaimed. "This is making me very uncomfortable, and I don't think this is an appropriate story for you to be telling me."

"Please bear with me," Henry entreated. "You have to know what was motivating the man in order to fully understand what happened next. You see, that was the beginning of a month-long affair between the storeowner and the woman. She would come to the store and slip notes to him, giving him instructions on where to meet her for their next tryst. With each meeting he wanted her more and more. When he finally suggested that they run away together, the woman flung her arms around him and agreed.

"She instructed him to liquidate all of his assets so they'd have some cash for their new life together. When everything was ready, the man went to his wife and confessed the affair, as well as his intentions to leave. Although she was a stoic woman, the news came as a great shock to her. She begged him to think of their son, who needed his father. *Just tell him that I had to go away. Maybe I'll see him again someday*, the man told her. The man then took some of his belongings and an envelope full of cash he'd pulled together from his personal and business accounts. He couldn't help feeling bad about the condition in which he was leaving his wife, but his own selfish desires and needs overcame any compulsion he felt to stay.

"So, the storeowner and the woman set out together. They decided to stay in a hotel the next town over while they made their final decisions on where to go next. On the way, the woman noticed that the man was still wearing his wedding ring. *Aren't you going to take that off?* she asked. When the man slipped the ring off his finger and gave it to her, she promptly tossed it out the window. The man was a little perturbed by that, since the ring was made of gold and could have been sold for some extra cash, but he wanted to make the woman happy.

"A little farther down the road, the woman turned around in her seat and looked at the man's trunk full of clothes, which he'd placed in the bed of his pickup truck. *I don't know why you brought all that stuff,* she said. *I don't like the thought of you wearing your old clothes. That life is over for you, isn't it?* The man explained that they were the only clothes he had, but the woman didn't care. *Please get rid of them. It makes me think you might change your mind and go back.*

"Still eager to prove his loyalty to her, the man stopped the truck on a bridge over a little country creek and dropped the heavy trunk into the water below. He watched as it bobbed a couple of times and then sank below the surface of the shallow water. The woman gave him a kiss, and they continued on their way. Later that evening, as he and the woman lay in bed at the hotel, a frantic banging came at the door. To their dismay, it was the storeowner's wife. Somehow she'd managed to find him. She showed the storeowner a note she'd found in their son's room. It read, *Dear Mommy, Please do not worry about me. I am going with Father. I am going to bring him back home. I will be back soon.*

"The man rushed out to his truck, but the boy was nowhere to be found. The man explained that the boy couldn't have come with him, since there was no place in the truck he wouldn't have seen him, but the storeowner's wife was adamant that the boy was not at home.

"A sick feeling crept over the man. He sped as fast as he could down the road until he arrived at the creek he'd crossed earlier that afternoon. He scrambled down the embankment and splashed into the waist-deep water where he'd dropped his trunk. After a frenzied search, he located the trunk and hauled it over to the muddy embankment. He unlatched the lid and opened it up to find the drowned body of his six-year-old son lying curled up on top of a pile of drenched clothes. The little boy's fingernails were torn from scratching futilely at the inside of the box. All the man could do was take the boy's cold body in his arms and cry bitterly.

"Things unraveled quickly for the man after that. When his mistress heard about what happened, she disappeared into the night, along with his cash. His wife demanded a divorce and then moved west. Everything he once had was gone, his wife, his money, his mistress, his reputation, and, most importantly, his son. He was left only with the unforgettable memory of what he'd done."

"What is the point of such a horrible story?" Violet whimpered.

"I asked the man the same thing that night," Henry replied. "He told me that after everything happened, he was ready to end it all. He even went to the Seelbach Hotel with plans of jumping, but when he got to the roof and looked down onto Walnut Street, he happened to see a billboard advertisement for a local bank. It featured a big piggy bank and the phrase *Don't steal from the future.* The man stood on the ledge for a long time, but ultimately, he took the message as a sign, and he did not jump."

It suddenly occurred to Violet why Henry was telling her the story. "My note!" she gasped. She had completely forgotten about the suicide note she had slid under the door and into the hallway. Henry nodded and took it out of his jacket pocket.

"I saw it last night when I came to talk to you about how things went with Brian. After reading it, I rushed into your room and saw that you were sleeping. I noticed the pill bottle on your nightstand and counted the pills. I stayed with you until I was certain you were fine."

Violet didn't think she could be any more humiliated. She wished she could vaporize into thin air. She pointed at the note. "So now you know everything. Who are you going to tell?"

Henry looked somewhat hurt. "Violet, I understand that circumstances have changed, that your expectations were different when you composed this, but the mere fact that it exists tells me that you feel compelled by truth."

Violet looked away from Henry and fixed her gaze on her plate, which somehow looked even less appetizing than before.

"You think that you can't face the consequences of this truth?"

"I guess it doesn't matter," Violet said morosely. "Tell whoever you like."

"Why, because you don't intend to be around to deal with it?"

Violet shrugged.

Henry grew visibly irritated, but he tried to maintain his composure. "I acknowledge that you are the captain of your own ship, Violet, and that you can choose to steer yourself toward whatever waters you please, even if it's the swirling abyss. But please let me finish my story before you close your mind.

"After the man decided to live, he started over. He got an apartment and a night shift job in an office building downtown. It was humble, to say the least, but it was progress. On a cold November night years later, he was taking a back-alley shortcut home when he heard a noise from inside a dumpster along the way. Lying among the waste and filth was a tiny, naked baby girl — an innocent child whose only crime was being born to a poor and confused young mother. Half-frozen, she had been left to die in a heap of trash. The man carefully picked her up, warmed her inside his jacket, and walked her all the way to the hospital. Which is where I had seen him, waiting anxiously four days straight for the news that she would survive.

*"Don't steal from the future,* he told me again, this time crying with joy. *That sign. It was a message to me, but it wasn't about me. It was about that little girl. If I'd done it. If I'd jumped. I would have stolen the most important moment of that child's life away from her. She would never have been found."*

Henry sat down and passed the note across the table. "Do you know how few people are actually looking for opportunities to do good in this world? You can be that person and find purpose for yourself. Don't steal from the future."

Henry looked at Violet with such earnestness, she couldn't help but feel comforted. It was obvious that he cared about her. She picked up the note and stood to leave.

"Violet, please don't..." Henry started but had to choke back his emotions.

"I won't," Violet said.

# Chapter 7

Charles Bascom had never been in such terrible, unrelenting agony in all his life. After making his heroic stand and cutting down the murderous chieftain with his saber, the jaguar warriors pummeled him lustily with their brutal stone weapons, but for some unknown reason they spared him the death blow. Amazingly, after they got in their licks, they even seared his severed nub of a wrist with a red-hot iron so he wouldn't bleed out. He didn't understand it, but he was glad to be alive. At least he was glad at the time.

In the three days since being captured, he and four other captives from his company had been shackled together at the neck and forced to march almost nonstop over the treacherous jungle terrain. The tight-fitting iron collars, no doubt introduced by the conquistadors of old, were linked together by heavy chains that clinked and clacked with every step. To make the trek even more uncomfortable, each man's hands were bound behind him with tightly knotted hemp ropes, and their ankles were tied so that anything more than a quarter stride was impossible. Because Charles's right hand had been hacked off, his arms were tied excruciatingly tight at the elbows, forcing him to puff out his chest and arch his shoulders back. The awkward posture, in addition to the tight collar, made him feel suffocated. He huffed and puffed as he plodded along, unable to fully catch his breath.

While the slow asphyxiation and the pain radiating from his mangled arm and broken ribs were torture enough, perhaps the most maddening thing of all was the mosquitoes, which he was unable to slap away due to his bondage. At any given time, he felt half a dozen tiny pricks on his skin, the bloodthirsty insects feasting on him until they fell to the forest floor, their bellies too gorged for their tiny wings to lift. There was little consolation in trampling them. It was death by gluttony, and Charles, whose empty stomach felt like it was gnawing on his spine, was envious. Each of the captives tried to help the man ahead of him by blowing or spitting on the pests as they landed, a small relief, but one Charles could not enjoy as he was the last person in line. Still, he was glad he was not alone.

He knew his fellow captives well. His company had been fighting and surviving together for several months, and they shared a bond that can only be forged in combat, where life is uncertain and independence is dangerous. Leading the procession were Thad and Finney, the brothers from Murfreesboro who'd run the reconnaissance mission in Las Bajadas that baited Soñador into an ambush outside of the village. Charles was not surprised that they were still alive. Although they were both young and very stupid, they were muscle-bound, gritty, and resilient.

Next in line was Josiah, a mountain man from Sevierville who'd been added to the special company due to his mountain tracking experience and general comfort in the wilderness. During the ambush, he had taken an arrow just under his collarbone and another through his calf. Neither had been fully removed, just snapped off a few inches above his flesh. Josiah was reticent and proud, too proud to complain, but still it was clear he suffered greatly.

Fourth was Virgil, the antithesis of Josiah, brash and charismatic and the self-proclaimed future governor of Tennessee. He often bragged that his father once stood as a second for Andrew Jackson during one of his famous duels, but the claim was dubious at best. Charles didn't trust him. He suspected Virgil's sense of self-preservation was far greater than his sense of loyalty.

Last of all was Charles. Just a couple of years shy of forty, he was the oldest enlisted man in the company. Some of the men called even him Uncle Chuck, a name he truly despised. When he was reunited with the other survivors of his company, they seemed ill pleased to see him.

"Did anyone get away?" he'd asked.

Josiah spat, his saliva red with blood. "We thought you did," he said sullenly.

Charles was in bad shape, but he knew he was still doing fairly well in relation to some of the others. In addition to his grievous battle wounds, Josiah was also showing the early signs of yellow fever, a horror Charles knew all too well. Even worse than him was Finney, who started the march well enough but made a grave mistake on the second day. Having managed to somehow loosen the rope binding his wrists, he whispered to the others that he could make a run for it if he could somehow get out of his iron collar. Virgil endorsed the idea and told him that all he needed to do was unscrew the linch pin near the nape of his neck and he'd be free.

Charles alone condemned the plan, telling Finney that even with a full day's head start, the jaguar warriors would swiftly track him down and kill him, and maybe the rest of the group as well.

"But if I can get away, then I can go get reinforcements and we can slaughter these sons of bitches for what they done," he replied, blinded by hope.

Charles continued to plead his case, but Finney was resolved. Night fell, and he began to furtively unscrew the pin on his iron collar, one secret turn at a time, careful not to reveal that his hands had come unbound. When the pin finally came loose, Finney darted silently and nimbly into the underbrush, albeit still hampered by the rope on his ankles. There were only four warriors actually guarding the prisoners. Two of them were ten or so yards ahead of the pack, the navigators, and the other two were about twenty yards behind, the motivators. The rest of the war party was in the forest, scouting and hunting, Charles presumed. From time to time, he had spotted one of them moving liquidly through the vegetation, his jaguar pelt shimmering in the rays of sunlight that managed to penetrate to the forest floor. He wondered how many of them were out there. It had to be a lot, considering how easily they'd obliterated his company.

At first, it appeared that the guards hadn't noticed Finney's escape. It was very dark, and he had been surprisingly quick. Fifteen uneventful minutes later, Charles even allowed himself to believe there was a chance he'd actually gotten away. That was when three of the jaguar warriors emerged from the darkness, carrying the breathless runaway by the arms and legs. Without a word, they retied his hands and reconnected his iron collar.

One of the warriors, a white man with an old European-style mustache and goatee bearing a strange resemblance to Don Quixote, produced a thin flint dagger while the other two secured Finney's head in a tight hold. As swift as a striking rattlesnake, the warrior surgically stabbed each of Finney's eye sockets, destroying the tender jelly and causing Finney to produce the most blood-curdling scream Charles had ever heard. Cursing and wailing, he shook his head wildly from side to side, slinging viscous gore onto Josiah and Thad from the carnage of his face. The warriors spoke firmly to Finney in a language Charles did not recognize and nudged him forward with shoves in the back, seemingly instructing him to close his mouth and keep moving, but the mutilated man only spat and cursed back at them. Overcoming his recalcitrance simply took placing the blade of the dagger gently next to his genitals. Suddenly motivated, Finney fell in step with the other captives and soldiered on. There was no more talk of escape after that.

Not far down the trail, it became apparent that Josiah was growing too weak to continue. He stumbled and fell repeatedly, each time violently jerking the chains linking him to the necks of Virgil and Finney, who in turn jerked the necks of Thad and Charles. Frightened by Finney's recent experience with the warriors' motivation tactics, the men encouraged Josiah and aided him as best they could, but the yellow fever was on him in full force, and his strength gave out for good.

"Let me die," he moaned after falling face-down in the dirt.

To the surprise of the Americans, the natives stopped the march and whistled a signal into the forest. Several warriors appeared, and after a short conference, they constructed a crude sled out of fallen limbs and loose foliage. Josiah was unshackled and placed upon it. Thad, the strongest and ablest body left among the captives, was also released from his bonds and harnessed to the makeshift sled using thin hemp ropes and a variety of clever knots. But saying that Thad was the strongest among them was like saying he was the strongest kitten in the litter. In his diminished state, he groaned and cursed mightily as he toiled under his new yoke. Virgil was moved to the first collar so that blind Finney was not leading, and Charles was put in the third collar. The last two collars, which were vacant, were tied around Charles's waist. From there, the procession slowed considerably.

Charles knew his mental faculties were far from sharp. In truth, he was close to delirium. Still, he could not understand why the survival of the captives mattered so much to the warriors. It was very doubtful that they were being taken for ransom or as prisoners of war, since the warriors, who ostensibly lived in remote seclusion, probably cared very little about the war between Mexico and the US. And while it wasn't uncommon for captured sailors to be impounded into the service of a victorious enemy vessel after a battle at sea, the warriors were mountain dwellers, not mariners, and the men were not fit for any type of service or labor. In fact, it was unlikely Charles and the others would survive much longer, even if they received medical attention, which was very unlikely. Healthy men would have found the march extremely strenuous, and the Americans hadn't eaten a scrap of food since the morning of the ambush.

The warriors, on the other hand, were astonishingly tireless. Silently, stoically, they made their way through the jungle, rarely speaking and never resting. Each warrior kept a pouch tied to his waist and would occasionally eat a pinch of something from within. Charles couldn't tell what it was, most likely some berries or grains. He would've given anything for a taste.

The Americans no longer feared death, but the incident with Finney made it clear that misbehavior would not result in execution, just severe discomfort. After a short whispered debate, Charles, Thad, and Finney agreed that if the path led them near another cliff or river, they would all jump together and put an end to their misery. Whatever the natives had planned for them, it was bound to be unpleasant. Better to end things on their own terms. Virgil did not like that idea and argued passionately against it, but his iron collar mandated his participation in all actions of the majority. As it happened, the opportunity for self-destruction never came. Instead, the procession reached its destination.

After being in the jungle for so long, the enormous stone structures of the ancient ruins were shocking and fearsome. Josiah was unconscious and Finney was blind, but the other three marveled at what they saw. As they entered the city, the jaguar warriors who'd been scouting on all sides of the marching group began to reassemble with the main party. Charles counted twenty-two.

"Jesus," Virgil muttered.

"What do you see?" Finney asked, his voice wavering. He had been a brave enough man before his failed escape, but losing his sight reduced his courage greatly.

"Some kinda Aztec city," Virgil replied.

Even poor men from Tennessee had heard about the Aztecs and their bloody practices. In the prewar propaganda, the term "Aztec" had been synonymous with savagery. A sense of dread enveloped the haggard Americans.

"But there ain't no more Aztecs, right?" Thad asked. "I mean, they was killed off by the Spanish."

"Could have fooled me," Virgil replied as he surveyed his surroundings. "Must be some undiscovered tribe."

"There's a difference between undiscovered and undisturbed," Charles interjected dryly.

Were it not for the bleakness of their current circumstances, the scene would have been quite beautiful. The ruins were nearly overrun with vegetation, as though the rainforest were swallowing the looming structures whole and reclaiming them as part of the landscape. Pools of collected rainwater in leaves and puddles glistened and shimmered as the evening sun peeked through the openings in the canopy. But just like nature, where death and beauty are opposite sides of the same coin, the shining city was shrouded with a sense of foreboding.

As they trudged along, grim-looking watchmen stationed high atop the stone edifices greeted prisoner and warrior alike with pitiless and indifferent glares. Fear and death permeated the humid air, making Charles wish they were all back in the jungle. The density of the vegetation and the winding path made it difficult for him to fully appreciate the scope of the city, but he sensed its vastness. The procession followed a dirt path that ultimately snaked into a central plaza, a spacious grass clearing surrounded by lesser temples and palaces and a towering pyramid on the far end that had six massive levels, each one tapering in length but all at least twenty feet high. Each level had numerous and symmetrical recesses, making it appear as though the entire thing were constructed of hollowed-out stone boxes. The top of the pyramid appeared to be truncated, suggesting a more ornate temple had once stood at its peak but had deteriorated over the centuries. On the side facing the courtyard, a massive staircase ran from the ground all the way to the top.

The plaza teemed with activity. Jaguar warriors and lower tribesmen were corralling groups of Mexican villagers, as well as other indigenous-looking people, into a line at the foot of the monstrous pyramid. The Americans were led to a holding area in front of a temple near the western end of the plaza. The small building, which was in an advanced state of deterioration, was covered in carved stone panels depicting the terrible and savage feats of a vengeful pantheon of ancient gods.

In the center of the plaza was a small garden being tended by a number of older tribesmen painted in red and green stripes and carrying crudely fashioned farming tools and earthen water basins. The perimeter of the garden was lined with torches atop long wooden pikes, each one skewering a stack of human heads in varying stages of decay.

"What are they growing over there?" Thad whispered.

"It ain't new potatoes," Virgil answered.

The sun had almost set, and it was getting difficult to see, even with the torchlight. "I think it's some type of sage plant," Charles said, squinting.

The tops of each plant were flowering with purple bell-shaped petals. From a distance, the corollas protruding from the blooms looked like long white feathers.

"I guess they want to make sure we are perfectly seasoned," Virgil muttered.

"Do you really think they're gonna eat us?" Finney asked. "Tell me what you see!"

"It's what I don't see that bothers me at the moment."

"What don't you see?"

"Animals," Virgil answered bitterly. "All these people and not a single chicken or goat."

A group of seven shamans chanting in low voices marched slowly and solemnly around the garden. Each wore a long robe, reminiscent of the sort donned by Franciscan monks. The lead shaman dangled an ornate thurible from his outstretched hand, smoke billowing out the top.

Puzzled, Thad asked, "Are they heathens or Catholics?"

"Is there a difference?" Finney joked, despite himself.

Virgil, the only practicing Catholic in the company, took offense. "We'll see how funny that is in a few minutes when we all stand in judgment. You'll surely wish you'd taken the holy sacraments when you watch me stroll into Heaven while you boys are cast into the pit."

"I don't think none of us need trouble ourselves with thoughts of Heaven," Josiah muttered grimly from his sled. It was the first thing he'd said all day. "Not after what we done."

Thad looked down at the dying man in disbelief. "I'm glad you decided to wake up now that I've finished pulling you through the whole fucking jungle."

Josiah forced a smile. "Now be a good boy and fetch me a glass of lemonade."

As the others squabbled, Charles continued to survey the plaza. "It can't be," he suddenly said in disbelief.

"What?" asked Finney, again distraught at his inability to see what horrors awaited him.

"It's him."

Standing alone, near the base of a temple on the eastern side of the plaza, was the chieftain that Charles had nearly cut in half, his headdress of yellow and green feathers and his horrific skull mask unmistakable in the torchlight.

"The man, in the mask over there," Charles said, unable to point but nodding in the chieftain's general direction. "I killed him in the forest. I sliced him to ribbons."

"I'd say you're mistaken," said Virgil. "That man doesn't have a scratch on him."

"You don't understand," Charles said in bewilderment. "I opened that man up like a bag of grain. I saw it."

"How do you know it's the same man?" Thad asked.

"Same paint, same size, same mask."

Virgil scoffed. "All these monsters look exactly the same. If you killed one that wore a fancy skull mask, don't you think one of his little buddies could have picked it up for himself?"

"Look closer, Virgil. They're not all the same. Some of these fellas look like us." Charles said warily. "Still, I'd swear that was the same man I cut down in the jungle. Something is off here. Something is not right."

"I tend to agree," Virgil said sarcastically. "The skewered heads did a pretty good job of convincing me.

"Me too," Thad agreed, completely oblivious to Virgil's mockery.

When the sun dipped below the horizon, the group of shamans that had been circling the sage garden changed the route of their procession toward the great pyramid. As their chants became louder, the jaguar warriors and their fellow tribesman knelt in a show of respect. Only the warriors guarding and corralling the prisoners were left standing.

"What's happening?" Finney asked, sensing the change in atmosphere.

"I think they are starting some type of ceremony," his brother whispered.

The group of shamans prostrated themselves at the foot of the pyramid and bowed seven times, each time touching their foreheads to the ground then reaching up toward the glowing twilight of the evening sky. When they finished, an enormous, bald-headed warrior painted blue from head to toe emerged from the lowest level of the pyramid. He was wearing only an animal hide loincloth and carrying a large stone mallet. Around his neck hung a prominent crucifix. The blue man bowed reverently at the group of shamans, then slowly ascended the great stairs of the pyramid, each lumbering step falling heavy and methodical, like a fairytale ogre.

Once atop the towering edifice, he extended his mallet and beckoned to the line of assembled prisoners. Two fearsome-looking warriors grabbed the first man in line, a quivering peasant farmer, and escorted him to the top of the pyramid. Upon reaching the summit, the blue man indicated that he wished for the man to kneel. Frightened, the farmer hesitated. One of the escorts slapped the back of his knees with the length of his spear, forcing him to lurch forward. The blue man towered over him and raised his long blue arms toward the sky. Then he appeared to bless the man with the sign of the cross.

"What in the hell?" Thad exclaimed.

"It's like some form of pagan Christianity," said Virgil, suddenly hopeful. "Maybe they are just doing a mass."

The escorts forced the peasant to place his head on a low stone altar in front of the blue man, who raised the stone mallet above his head and brought it crashing down on the crown of the little man's head with a sickening crunch. His legs jerked and his spine went rigid, then he slumped limply to the ground. The two escorts used smaller stone hammers to chip away skull fragments until the peasant's brain lay exposed, allowing the blue man to reach into the open skull with his massive hands and remove the brain like he was plucking a walnut from its shell. Triumphantly, he held it over his head for the crowd to see. The warriors and tribesmen in the plaza crossed themselves and chanted a singsong "Amen" while the blue man pulled the brain apart with his hands, placing one half in a bowl to his left and the other half in a bowl to his right.

"Is this normal for mass?" Thad asked, dumbfounded.

Virgil was too shocked to speak.

"They killed someone, didn't they?" Finney whimpered.

Charles had been so caught up in the gruesome scene, he was startled to notice a presence behind him. To his dismay, he discovered the chieftain from the ambush had quietly sidled up next to him and was inspecting him through the bone sockets of his horrific mask. There was no mistake; Charles had seen the same hateful eyes before. He was shorter than Charles, but lean and muscular. With a fierce jerk, he grabbed Charles by the stub of his right wrist, making him grimace in excruciating pain. The chieftain shook with rage and murmured furious words that Charles did not understand, the sour smell of gore and smoke radiating from him. Charles tried to pull away, but the chieftain swiftly drew a dagger and held it to his throat, his eyes growing wide with bloodlust. Another idea seemed to occur to him, and he deftly removed Charles from his iron shackles. Once freed, he struck Charles viciously in the kidney with the hilt of his dagger. Charles doubled over and his vision narrowed, but he fought to remain conscious. If there had been anything in his stomach, the pain would have forced him to retch it up.

The chieftain pulled him back up to his feet and dragged him violently toward the pyramid as the other Americans looked on in astonishment. The scene went largely unnoticed by the people in the plaza, who were fixated upon the skull-hammering blue man until the chieftain cried out in a fit of rage. He called up to the executioner, yelling a long series of angry words and then motioning for the escorts who heeled to him like dutiful hounds.

Charles was still trying to catch his breath as the warriors dragged him up the pyramid and dropped him at the feet of the blue man. He had no strength left to resist them. From the plaza below, the chieftain barked at the blue man and furiously gestured a hammering motion, but the blue man seemed apprehensive. He looked to the escorts, who only glared back at him.

It was only after the chieftain began ascending the steps himself, dagger in hand, that the blue man finally acquiesced. He hastily blessed Charles with the sign of the cross and waited for the escorts to thrust him into position on the stone altar, still warm and sticky with the blood of the previous sacrifice.

Charles's gaze fell upon the plaza and beyond. He couldn't help but marvel at the situation. *What an outrageous way to die*, he thought, though not bitterly. He was too exhausted to hate.

"Just get on with it already."

# Chapter 8

*A person who's going mad doesn't know he's going mad*, Charles reassured himself for the tenth time. *My name is Charles Bascom. I'm from Lebanon, Tennessee, and I'm serving in the 2nd Regiment of Tennessee Volunteers.* He repeated the information in his mind over and over, but it did not have the ring of truth. He gazed up from his cell, a tiny five-by-five-foot stone pit with a thatchwork of thick reeds crisscrossing overhead, barring his escape. The night sky was clear and placid.

*If I think hard enough, I will remember how I got here. I just need to focus my mind and remember. I need to concentrate, and everything will come back to me. My name is Charles Bascom. I'm from Lebanon, Tennessee, and I'm serving in the 2nd Regiment of Tennessee Volunteers.*

It was no use; the words meant nothing to him. He'd gotten the information from the commission papers in his jacket pocket, but the name did not feel like his own. Once again, his frustration turned to panic, and he screamed as he yanked furiously on the barrier above him.

A hand tugged on the hem of his pants. It was the Mexican, his cellmate. The man put a finger over his lips and indicated that he wanted Charles to be quiet.

"Why?" Charles shouted. "Nobody will come. Nobody remembers that we're here. They left us!"

Again, the Mexican just touched his finger to his lips and motioned for Charles to sit down. Charles obeyed. It was tight enough for the two men

81

without one of them blustering about like an idiot. He hated the suffocating closeness of the pit, but the Mexican did not seem to mind. Silently, the gaunt man sat in the darkness with his head bowed and his legs stretched out in front of him. He wore the clothes of a peasant, torn breeches, a stained and ragged cotton shirt, and brown leather boots with holes in the soles. His black hair was long, well past his ears, and thick with grease. A short, rugged beard covered his cheeks and chin.

Charles, it seemed, had also grown a short beard. How long had he been in this godforsaken place? When he first regained consciousness, his mind was a blank slate. He couldn't even remember how to speak. He just shrieked and clambered about the cell like a wild animal. Slowly, things came back to him, simple words at first, then more. The Mexican had just watched him, curiously, patiently.

Suddenly, more words careened through his mind like they were being dumped from a bucket, foreign words — Spanish! Did he know Spanish?

"*Quien eres?*" he blurted.

The little man seemed surprised. He shifted forward eagerly and spoke rapidly. The words all ran together, and Charles couldn't understand them. He shook his head in frustration.

"*Despacio,*" he said. "Slowly."

The man nodded and started again, carefully saying each word in a steady staccato rhythm. "I'm a poor farmer," he began again in Spanish. "I was taken by the warriors and brought to this place."

Charles nodded his understanding. He did not remember any warriors, but it certainly appeared that they'd been captured by someone.

"Who are you?" the Mexican asked.

Charles shrugged. "I'm not sure."

"Don't worry," the man said with a rueful grin. "It will come back to you soon. How's your hand?"

Charles looked down at his hands, first his left and then his right. He flipped them over and inspected them carefully.

"What do you mean?" he asked. "They are fine."

The Mexican pointed at the right one.

"Was something wrong with it?"

The man smiled. "It will all come back to you soon," he repeated. "First you will remember yesterday, then the day before, and so on and so on."

There were images in his mind, but they were muddled. There was a blue monster chasing him, towering over him, threatening to kill him. He was in pain, red and black and yellow pain, like fire. But then a man appeared — a leader, and somehow he stopped the monster, controlled him. He remembered other men, friends of his, who were hurt and dying. Then they all ate. They were hungry, but whatever it was, they didn't want it. What was it? Something they were forced to chew and shallow. He wanted to spit it out, but he couldn't.

The images retreated, and Charles cursed in frustration.

"It may take another day yet," the other man said as he rested his head back against the stone wall and gazed through the reeds at the night sky. "Don't worry. I do not think they mean to kill us."

"Who?" Charles asked.

"The warriors. Some they killed and some they saved. We have a purpose still, I think."

"If we have a purpose, then why we are rotting in this pit?"

The Mexican shrugged. "They are saving us for something."

Charles growled. "If I could just remember what happened…"

Sadness crept over the Mexican's face. "Sometimes forgetting is better."

Restless, Charles stood up again and examined the barrier above them. "I bet we can cut or break through these reeds. It will take some time, but if we can find a sharp stone or apply some pressure to the right spot, we can get through it."

"Perhaps," the Mexican replied somberly, "but it is no use. If we run, the warriors will find us. We cannot escape, even if we get out of this pit. You will remember soon."

The other man's pessimism was irritating, but Charles would not be deterred. "Suit yourself. I'm getting out of here, though."

Charles scoured the floor with his hands, searching for anything that could be used as a tool. Nothing. He felt inside his trouser pockets. Nothing.

Then he remembered his belt. He unfastened it and yanked it through the belt loops of his trousers, the leather popping as it went. He looped it through the reeds overhead and tugged downward. The barrier shook, but there was no sign of any structural weakness. He wrapped one end of the belt tightly around each hand and hooked his boots through the thatch work near the Mexican's head, letting the full weight of his body test the durability of the reeds. Violently, he bounced up and down while simultaneously jerking the belt with his arms. When it was clear that a particular segment was not going to give, he looped the belt over the next segment and tried again. Hours of furious labor passed, but the barrier would not crack.

Defeated, Charles plopped back down on stone floor.

"Thanks for the help," he said in English, but the Mexican just gave him a disinterested glance.

"I need something sharp," he muttered to himself.

Charles ripped one of the brass buttons off of his uniform and started scraping it against the wall.

"You are digging out?" the Mexican asked, clearly amused.

Charles tried to ignore him, but the man's apathy annoyed him. "I can use the stone wall to…" Charles could not remember the Spanish verb meaning "to sharpen," so he mimed a cutting motion. "I can use this on the barrier or maybe as a weapon." He held the button at his neck and imitated a slicing motion.

The Mexican grinned and leaned his head back against the wall.

*What a useless man*, Charles thought. *If he thinks I'm going to help him when I get out, he is sorely mistaken.* Newly determined, Charles went back to work rubbing the button against the wall, periodically turning it over to even out the sides. He labored continuously until the sun began to rise and fill the little pit with light. The product of his efforts was a brass nub about as sharp as one of his bicuspids.

"Shit," he yelled, then flung the mutilated button against the wall, where it bounced off with a clink.

He was about to try screaming again when intense anxiety suddenly overwhelmed him. Desperately, he scrambled in vain against the walls, thrashing his arms about like a man floundering at sea.

"What's happening?" he cried. "Help! *Socorro!*" he pleaded to the Mexican, but the man just watched sternly as he struggled.

The anxiety and panic kept building until Charles was on the verge of banging his head against the stones to discharge the mounting pressure. Finally, there was a release, and all of his lost memories swallowed him up like an avalanche. Everything came back to him. He remembered the ambush in the forest and his fellow soldiers. He remembered the forced march and the ancient ruins. With horror, he also remembered the chieftain and the pyramid, how his head lay on the blood-covered stone altar and how he waited for the blue man's stone mallet to crush open his skull. If it hadn't been for the appearance of the man in the fine clothing, the leader, his brain would have been plucked from his head like the others. The man had called up to the executioner in a calm, commanding tone, then Charles had been led back down the pyramid, past the seething chieftain, and back into the ranks of his astonished fellow Americans.

A shaman then force-fed each of the soldiers some freshly snipped diviner's sage from the sacred garden. That's when the hallucinations began. Terrible images appeared to him, decaying, maggot-ridden corpses and gruesome scenes of death and suffering. The terrible stone gods engraved on the temples sprang forth and devoured the earth and sky around him in depraved and lusty ecstasy. Everything was tinted in a red hue, dark and thick like blood. Then there was pain, excruciating pain. Every nerve in his body exploded in agony before going numb. Finally, there was stillness — perfect, black, infinite tranquility. That was when he'd awakened in the stony pit, wild and witless.

The Mexican's face showed clearly in the early-morning sunlight. His brown eyes were framed by dark sockets above his flat nose.

"Now do you remember?" he asked serenely.

Charles quivered and stared at his hands. "Yes."

"You have seen some terrible things, no?"

Charles nodded.

"As have I." The Mexican sighed. "Now you understand, forgetting was a blessing. There are things we must talk about. Before, you wouldn't have understood, but now, I think you will. When you were captured, they took your hand, correct? It must be true; I saw it regrow before my eyes."

Charles gazed in awe at the hand in question. He flexed it and turned it over, then flexed it again. It was perfect. "How?"

"It was the same with me. When I was taken, they cut off all of the fingers on my right hand. It was very distressing. I was quite fond of them. And the pain…" He rolled his head in remembered agony. "But now, here they are." He wiggled them as proof.

Charles continued surveying his own hand. "It looks normal. There's no pain."

"True, there is no pain, but do you feel something else?"

"I suppose there is…" Charles did not know the word for numbness. "There is no feeling."

The Mexican's eyes sparkled. "Yes, exactly. The pin on your jacket, take it off."

Charles had forgotten about the pin. Embarrassed, he took it off. The pin would have been a much better tool than his brass button. The Mexican must have thought the same thing; his eyes were laughing.

"May I see it?"

Warily, Charles handed it over, and the Mexican examined it with great interest. He pointed above Charles's head.

"What do you think of that spot?"

Charles looked up and tried to find the place to which he was referring. "Where?"

"Just above you," the Mexican said as he repositioned himself.

"You will have to show me. I don't see what you are talking about."

"Never mind. It was nothing."

The Mexican was once again reclining against the wall. Charles was confused. "Where is my pin?"

"What do you mean? I gave it back to you," the Mexican said innocently.

"What game are you playing? You didn't give it back to me."

The man smiled mischievously and nodded toward Charles's leg. The pin was pushed directly into his calf.

"You did not feel that?" the Mexican asked with feigned surprise. "Strange."

Charles plucked the pin from his calf and rolled up his pant leg. A small red hole appeared where the pin had been, but there was no pain and no blood.

"That is quite shocking," said the Mexican. "I bet your heart is racing right now."

Charles paused. Strangely, he could not feel the familiar rhythmic beating in his chest. He held his breath and waited. Nothing. "I'm still dreaming," he concluded.

The Mexican raised his eyebrows and knocked his right fist on the stone. "Seems like you are awake to me."

"Live men have heartbeats; they feel pain. If this is real, then I'm a dead man."

The Mexican smiled. "Perhaps. Perhaps not. Perhaps death is not available to us."

Charles laughed. "That's quite a leap. You think we cannot die because you stuck a pin in my leg and I don't go howling like a fool?"

"Did they feed you a strange plant from their sacred garden?" the Mexican asked.

"Yes, and it gave me fantastic visions. I'm still having them right now."

"No," he replied somberly. "The visions are over. We are changed. There was magic in those leaves."

For the first time, Charles noticed that the Mexican's left hand was hidden behind his back. It had been hidden the entire time he'd been conscious.

"Why are you hiding your hand?" he suddenly demanded. "What do you have?"

The Mexican smirked. "A little assassin." Slowly, deliberately, he brought his hand to his lap. Writhing around his arm was a large viper, its scales shimmering olive, black, and tan in the sunlight filtering through the reeds. The Mexican's fingers clutched the snake tightly behind its triangular head.

"Good God!" Charles exclaimed as he drew his legs toward his chest and pressed his back tightly against the wall. "Have you been holding that goddamned thing the whole time?"

"This is a *nauyaca*," the Mexican proclaimed. "Some call it a yellow beard viper." He brought the snake's head close to his face and examined it. "I'm not sure why, though."

"Why do you have that?"

"He dropped right in my lap, if you can believe it, just like you. We were very lucky not to get bitten; this species is very ill-tempered and quite venomous. My uncle was bitten on the hand by a nauyaca when I was a boy. I still remember very well. His arm swelled up and his hand began to rot. My uncle was a strong man, but he screamed in pain. The bite killed him. They told me the poison went to his head."

"We've got to kill it right now."

"I will," he promised. "But first I must see something. It has been hard waiting, but I wanted to make sure you had eaten the leaves too."

A wave of understanding washed over Charles. "Are you mad? We are not immortal. The sage has just dulled our senses, and soon enough they will be back to normal. That snake could kill us."

"Perhaps," the Mexican purred. "I am eager to find out. But not on myself, of course."

"You would murder me in cold blood?" Charles asked angrily.

"It is not murder. It is vengeance," he hissed back.

"Vengeance? You are mistaken. I have done you no wrong."

Rage distorted the Mexican's face. "There is no mistake. Your army came to my farm and demanded food. I gave everything I had, my crops, my livestock, my supplies. Everything they asked for, I handed over. It was not worth my life. But then they looked at my wife. They were hungry for her too. I told them to leave, but they would not go. They took her by force, in my own home. I could hear her crying out to me, pleading for me to help her. But I could not. I had no guns, no strength. She was a fearsome woman, though. She stole a knife from a soldier who was raping her, and she stuck it in his belly."

The Mexican's eyes deadened. "They shot us both, then burned my farm. My wife died. I lived."

Charles was aghast.

"Do you know me now, gringo?"

"Soñador," Charles whispered. Though his company had been pursuing the bandit for weeks, no one had a good idea what he looked like. It was surreal to face him. He was small but still fearsome.

"I was weak when they came to my farm. But then I grew strong. You have seen my strength, no? Since then, I've killed many like you, and I will kill many more."

Charles tried to think on his feet. "We have a common enemy. We should put our differences aside for now and work together to get free."

Soñador laughed. "You are the greatest enemy I have, gringo."

Quickly, Charles changed tactics. "But you think we are immortal. What if you are right? What if the snake bites me and I live? You think I'll forgive you for trying to kill me?"

"If I'm right, and you live, then there is nothing you can do to me, we have both eaten the leaves. If I'm wrong, then you will be dead and I will celebrate."

Soñador was resolved, and there was nowhere to go. "God, I hate snakes," Charles said in English. "If I'm getting bitten, then so are you."

With all his strength, he lunged at Soñador.

# Chapter 9

## 1962

Violet sighed deeply as she shuffled around the casket showroom behind Randall T. Lick. Everyone was a little crazy, she was the first to admit, but Mr. Lick was literally certifiable. Twice a month, the garrulous old pervert visited from Eastern State Psychiatric Hospital to apprise himself of the latest caskets and funeral services offered at Pendleton's. It was a morbid obsession, one that Henry indulged with remarkable grace. The same could not be said for Randall T. Lick. Upon first meeting the man, Violet made the mistake of asking him what the T. in his name stood for. "Titty!" the old man cackled gleefully, one hand latched onto his worn suspenders, the other vigorously squeezing an invisible breast in the air. Repulsed, Violet had curled her lip into a grimace that only intensified his delight. Henry claimed that he was harmless, but Violet was wary.

Every visit was the same. Randall would barge in and demand a tour — one he could never hope to finish due to his arthritic knees — but one he felt he was entitled to as a future customer.

"I wanna know what I'm paying for, Bootie-boo," he told Violet once.

"You haven't paid for anything yet," she reminded him.

"That's right," he said smugly, "and don't you forget it."

In reality, he only asked for a tour as an excuse to get into the sanctuary so he could waddle over to the organ and mash his stubby fingers on the low-register keys. The crazy bastard must have sensed that the ominous reverberations set Violet's teeth on edge. He absolutely reveled in provoking her. Knowing this, she reveled in ignoring his antics, even when they involved appallingly creepy and demeaning undertones. During his last visit, he'd winked mischievously at the man who dropped him off and confided, "I'm gonna get another baby on Bootie-boo over there, and she's behind me one hunnert percent!" Violet managed a weak smile, but only because she was fantasizing about driving her palm into his bulbous nose. She'd only recently scraped together enough mettle not to kill herself. Dealing with Randall seemed like an undue and ill-timed test of that resolve.

With all other formalities out of the way, Randall liked to examine the caskets, a comical sight considering his short stature. The way he stood on his tiptoes to peer inside each one reminded Violet of a child reaching for a cookie on a high countertop. The insufferable back-and-forth was the same as always.

"How much for this one?" he asked gruffly.

"Three hundred," Violet replied impatiently.

"Did you raise it? It was only two hundred last month!"

"No, it's the same as last month. Three hundred."

Randall squinted suspiciously at her then moved to the next one, the one he really wanted but always criticized in an attempt to bolster his bargaining power. It was the most premium casket Henry sold, the Marquis.

"I figured this old Bertha would still be here." He laughed. "I doubt you'll ever sell this heap."

Violet shrugged.

"Might as well chop it up for firewood. Folks would sooner get buried in a pine box than this atrocity. Though I reckon it might be fittin' for a Prestonsburg butcher, if you know what I mean."

She didn't.

"What was y'all askin' for this one again?"

"Seven-fifty."

Randall clucked his tongue and laughed. "You have to bring in a helluva lotta railcars for that kinda cheddar."

Anxiously, Violet checked her watch. Only a few more minutes until the bus from the hospital would be back to pick up the little debaucher and get him out of her hair. She could hardly wait, but not just to be rid of Randall T. Lick; she had other things on her mind, exciting things. Maybe it was nothing. She still couldn't be sure that her imagination wasn't running wild. It all started with a simple look, a moment of hesitation. She thought she knew what it meant but couldn't be sure. It had only been a single passing glance, but now it was driving her, obsessing her.

The front door of the funeral home opened and closed with a familiar heavy thud. A plump, middle-aged man in a sterile white uniform plodded merrily into the casket showroom where Violet and Randall were waiting.

"All right, Randy," the man said in a condescending singsong tone that immediately drew Randall's ire. "It's time we headed back to the hospital. Our friends are waiting for us." When he dropped Randall off earlier in the afternoon, the man had confided to Violet that he was trying a different tack with the salty old patient. He was going to start killing him with kindness. So far, it didn't appear to be working.

"None of those crazy fuckers are friends of mine," Randall spat back.

The plump man gave a tsk-tsk. "Sounds like you woke up on the wrong side of the bed this morning."

"It was a better bed than you woke up in," Randall snarled.

The man put his hands on his hips with mock consternation. "What if I told you I woke up next to a beautiful woman this morning?"

Randall looked over to Violet and smirked. "Bet she was a whore."

The man ran his tongue forcefully across his front teeth with a slight sucking sound. "All right, you little shithead, have it your way. Get your ass back on the bus."

Randall cackled merrily and reached a hand out to pat Violet's backside, but she deftly smacked it away with an audible whack.

"Prickly little peach," Randall murmured as he hobbled out with the plump man's assistance.

"Be back in two weeks!" he called over his shoulder. "If I'm here sooner than that, I reckon I'll be stiffer than a pecker, Bootie-boo!"

As soon as the door clicked shut, Violet dashed up to her room. The bus had been a few minutes late, so she was going to have a little less time than she planned. Henry had been preparing the latest body for an hour and half already. He never took much more than an hour and forty-five minutes. When he finished, he would need her assistance carting the casket out of the embalming room in the basement. She had to be finished before then so he wouldn't come looking for her. Hurriedly, she went into her closet and shuffled through her dresses until she found the one with the blue polka dots, a fairly hideous creation that she never wore. It had two small pockets sewn onto the front, some poor designer's misguided concept of fashion. Inside the left pocket was a small, freshly cut metal key. It was made to order, but she didn't know if it would actually work. In a few moments she would have her answer.

With her heart racing, she scurried back into the hallway and paused, listening intently for any sign that Henry was out of the embalming room and lurking about the house. Silence. For a split second she felt a tug of doubt, but it was far too feeble to overcome her determination. She dashed down the hall toward Henry's room, stopping short at the little broom closet that had seemed so innocuous a few short weeks ago, before Henry gave her that look, that fleeting glance that sparked the fire in her belly, that had reignited a dormant pep in herself. She tried to temper her excitement. Finding the strength to step back from the dark place she recently found herself had been tough. She needed to make sure she could stoically accept disappointment if the key didn't work.

Normally, a moment of inspiration happens when the light bulb finally comes on for someone, when there is illumination in the figurative darkness. For Violet, it was the exact opposite. Her journey began just as a light flickered out. A week earlier, she had been reading quietly in the sanctuary, her legs stretched out on the front pew, when a curious-looking bulb near the front lectern died with an almost imperceptible pop. At first, Violet was unsure what she had heard; the bulb had produced so little actual light, she hardly noticed any difference in the brightness of the room. She eventually spotted the dead bulb because it was one of a matching pair and its mate was still burning bright. Unlike modern bulbs, it featured a tangle of spiraling filaments within a hand-crafted glass casing. Ever so briefly, she mourned its demise as she gently unscrewed it from the fixture. She was a sucker for relics from a more elegant time. On the other hand, she was grateful for a chance to abandon the tedious gardening book she had borrowed from Henry to go in search of a replacement bulb that would complete the pair. A task that was easier said than done.

The first-floor supply closet, a converted kitchen pantry, contained a great variety of bulbs, but none like she needed. She checked the root cellar, then the old icehouse (which had been converted to storage), and even the greenhouse. No luck. She would have asked Henry where to find a replacement, but he was strolling around in the woods behind the main part of the estate with his trusty notebook, and she had no desire to traipse through the tick-infested weeds in order to find him. That was when she remembered the broom closet in the hall on the second floor near his bedroom. It was worth a try.

The closet was small and dusty, its main function being to house the hot water heater. Although she did almost all of the cleaning around the house, she never had any occasion to visit the closet before. A solitary light dangled from the ceiling, but even after pulling the chain and shedding light on the issue, there was little to see. A number of paint cans were stacked on shelves along the wall, along with some scraps of crown molding left over from the remodeling. There were a few decrepit cleaning supplies, including a crusty mop sitting in a rusty bucket, and several stacks of old newspapers that were probably being saved as kindling for winter fires. Violet gave a cursory look around and quickly abandoned any hope of the room producing an antique light bulb. When she turned to leave, she was startled to find Henry standing in the doorway.

"Can I help you find something?" he asked, smiling.

And that's when she saw it: the look. It was nearly imperceptible. Perhaps he had raised his eyebrow a millimeter more than normal, or narrowed his gaze in a way that she'd never seen before; in hindsight she couldn't put her finger on what was different about this particular look, but she was certain she didn't imagine it. In the fraction of a second it took her brain to register what her eyes had seen, she knew: Henry was hiding something.

"I'm looking for a replacement bulb." She smiled back as she handed him the dead one. "This one burned out, and I can't find anything like it."

Henry turned the bulb over in his hands and cocked his head to the side as he inspected it. "Unfortunately, I don't have a replacement for this one. We may need to go antiquing to find another. In the meantime, we can just put a couple of the modern decorative bulbs in the fixture.

"Works for me."

As Violet was leaving the closet, Henry pointed toward the floor near her bare feet. A spider was scampering toward a pile of newspapers in the corner. Violet leapt forward and let out an involuntary squeal. Henry grinned as he stepped on the fleeing arachnid and smeared its tender insides across the dusty wooden floor.

"Loxosceles reclusa," Henry said.

Violet's heart was still racing. "Are you casting a spell?"

Henry laughed. "No. That's the scientific name for what I just smashed. It's better known as a brown recluse."

"Are they poisonous?"

"From what I recall, their bites are known to cause necrosis. I don't think they're deadly, but I'm not an arachnologist."

"So, it might rot my skin, but it won't kill me?"

"Don't worry, they're not aggressive," Henry assured her. "I'll spray some insecticide, and hopefully that will take care of them. This closet is an absolute breeding ground. I see one every time I come in here. You'd be best served to just steer clear."

He flashed the look again.

Violet shuddered. She hated spiders. She wanted all spiders in the world to die in a fire. "I think there's one in my hair!" she screeched while flailing her hands near her head, unable to bring herself to make actual contact.

Henry came closer and inspected her head. "No, you're clean. Your mind is just playing tricks on you."

He turned off the closet light and pulled the door closed while Violet recovered. Both went on about their business, but as the day passed Violet couldn't shake the memory of Henry's split-second look. There was something in the closet that he didn't want her to see.

She had to go back and give the spider-riddled closet a good once-over if she ever expected to get over the gnawing feeling in her gut that something was amiss. The problem was that Henry was always floating around the house, and she didn't want to arouse his suspicion by getting caught dallying in the closet a second time. After biding her time for an insufferable few days, her big chance finally came when Henry unexpectedly announced that he was heading into town to run a few errands. He didn't say what the errands were, and Violet didn't ask. As soon as the hearse turned onto the highway, she went into full detective mode.

Armed only with a fly swatter for squashing spiders, she returned to the closet and rummaged through the junk. She was very excited to finally be searching, but she had no idea what she was searching for. Disappointingly, the paint cans were just paint cans and the newspapers were just meaningless newspapers. Feeling frustrated and betrayed by her instincts, she skulked about the closet, her searching gaze darting from point to point. It would have been easy to give up, but she wasn't willing to admit defeat. It wasn't until she got down on her hands and knees that she found a tiny latch and button at the base of the storage shelves holding the paint cans. Depressing the button revealed that the shelves were hinged. They swung soundlessly away from the wall, exposing the outline of a two-by-two-foot panel and a small keyhole. Violet gasped. She'd been right. The closet was more than it seemed. The discovery only stiffened her resolve.

Violet closely inspected the keyhole and recognized its peculiar shape. She'd seen it a dozen times in the past few months. It was a casket lock. Henry must have removed it from one of the caskets and repurposed it in the custom panel. She was impressed by his ingenuity but also a little disturbed. What could Henry possibly consider sensitive enough to warrant such an elaborate hiding place? Two things immediately came to mind: one was money, and the other was something more sinister. She didn't want to rush to judgment.

Finding a potential key for the lock had been surprisingly easy. The funeral home only sold one type of casket with locks, the Imperial, and

Violet believed that Henry had a universal key for all Imperials on his key ring. Figuring out a way to get a hold of that key unnoticed, however, was considerably more difficult. Cleverly, she contrived a reason to borrow the hearse: she told Henry she needed some new reading material from the library, and it was too far to walk in the summer heat. It was a ruse based primarily in truth. The thought of pawing through another one of his gardening books made her want to pull her hair out, and the library was a good five miles away. Henry, who was eager to help her pursue scholastic endeavors, enthusiastically endorsed the trip. More importantly, he put his keys into her hands.

Just as she suspected, one of the keys appeared to be a dead ringer for the secret lock, so she took it to a hardware store on her way to the library and had a duplicate made. The thin-whiskered teenager behind the counter had been reluctant to make a copy, since he'd never seen anything quite like it before and wasn't sure any of the blanks would work right. His ambivalence dissipated when Violet gave him her best doe-eyed pout and let the shoulder of her dress slip, briefly revealing her bra strap. She wasn't proud of herself, but she was in a hurry and the boy needed to be motivated. At the library, a gritty detective novel seemed appropriate, so she checked out *The Big Sleep*.

That was Monday. Four days passed before she finally got her chance to delve back into the closet to try her key. If it hadn't been for the intolerable Randall T. Lick, she would have had all the time she needed. When Henry was preparing a body, he liked complete isolation. He never came out before he was finished, and he had strict standing orders not to be disturbed. He even locked the door to the embalming room behind him. Violet bristled. She hated Randall T. Lick. Which reminded her of something Brian had said to her at Cuppy's a few weeks earlier. According to him, you're allowed to hate whomever you want. She shook her head. She didn't want to think about Randall T. Lick, and she certainly didn't want to think about Brian. She focused on the task at hand, the keyhole.

Breathlessly, she inserted the key. It fit. Sweat was beading on her brow. She twisted her hand to the left, then to the right. Nothing happened. The key didn't budge. She tried again, first applying more pressure both ways, then wriggling it around as firmly as she could. Still nothing.

"Damn it," she muttered as she pressed her head dejectedly against the wall.

She had been so certain the key would work. It looked and felt exactly like the one on Henry's key ring. There was no question the boy at the hardware store had given it his best effort. His heart had definitely been into it, and probably another vital organ, but it appeared he lacked the skills to pull it off. Violet didn't blame him. It was possible she simply had the wrong key duplicated. It just fit so perfectly.

She growled in irritation but told herself it was only a setback. One way or another, she was going to open the panel. As an afterthought, she pulled the key back ever so slightly in the keyhole and flicked her wrist to the right. Amazingly, it turned with a satisfying click, and the tiny door swung inward. Violet's heart leapt.

"Yes!" she whispered.

She checked her watch. There wasn't much time left. If Henry wasn't already done prepping the body, he was damn close. Violet knew she should close the door and wait for another opportunity to investigate further, but she was far too caught up in the thrill of her success to play it safe. Without further hesitation, she clicked the small flashlight she'd brought from her room and turned off the dangling bulb. She plunged head-first through the tiny door, snagging her dress on a loose nail and causing a slight tear, a small casualty. She couldn't care less.

Once inside, she discovered that there was enough room to stand, so she did. The space wasn't much larger than a phone booth, and in the darkness she nearly stumbled over a small stool underfoot. Her stomach tingled with nervous excitement. She felt happy and proud. She'd followed her intuition and overcome some tricky obstacles to get this far. She felt like Philip Marlowe, or at the very least a badass Nancy Drew. Finally, it was time to find out what Henry was hiding.

She shined the small flashlight all around her. Each wall, with the exception of the one with the door, had a waist-high shelf attached to it. The shelf to her left contained stacks of old books and rolled-up parchments.

Desperately, she wanted to open them up and thumb through their contents, but she didn't dare touch anything before coming up with a plan for covering her tracks. The other shelf held a medium-sized wooden box, a small tin box, a movie reel container, and a bizarre wreath displayed in a glass encasement. The shelf directly opposite the door was cleared off except for a couple of small candles — a viewing table, she surmised.

Violet was giddy. She knew it was wrong to snoop into someone else's personal affairs, especially her employer's, especially when he was also acting as her landlord, and especially when he knew her darkest secret, but she felt utterly compelled to press on.

Overhead, Violet noticed a narrow beam of light. She stood and found that there was a small peephole in the wall that peered out into the hallway between the door of the broom closet and the door to Henry's bedroom. Mentally visualizing the wall from the hallway side, she surmised that the peephole must be integrated into a sconce or maybe a portrait. She'd never paid much attention to that particular wall and couldn't remember what was on it. Whatever it was, it must have been pretty inconspicuous. It also made her uncomfortable about what other possible peepholes might be set up throughout the house. The mysteries were starting to multiply.

As she shuffled around the tiny area, she scuffed her shoe against something hard on the floor. Upon closer inspection, she discovered a dirt-covered stone marker, much like the tiny markers in Baby Land at the Lexington Cemetery. Without touching it, or otherwise wiping away the dirt, she could barely make out a single unfamiliar word etched in all capital letters on the stone surface. She said the word out loud, but it felt foreign on her tongue.

The light flickered overhead. Immediately, Violet switched off the flashlight and raised herself back up to the peephole. She blinked hard, but the image of the hallway would not come back into focus. Suddenly, it dawned on her that someone was trying to look in. It was Henry! A wave of panic flooded over her. She'd been a fool. Her lack of patience was going to get her caught. There was no way to escape without being seen. All Henry had to do was open the closet door to see all the mischief she had been getting into.

In the darkness, she squatted down, reached through the panel, and pulled the hinged shelves toward her until she heard them latch back into place against the wall. She then pushed the secret door closed as well, hoping that she would be able to reopen it from the inside when the coast was clear. If not, she would be forced to call out for help and bang on the walls until Henry rescued her. If that happened, she might as well march straight into her room and gather up her belongings. There would be absolutely no way to interpret her snooping as anything other than...well, snooping.

She looked through the peephole again. The hall was empty. Henry was gone. She exhaled slowly and relaxed her tense body, but her relief soon gave way to new anxiety as she heard the bulb from the closet click on. She caught a gasp in her hand and held her breath. If she could hear the light switch being turned on, then Henry would be able to hear the slightest movement from her side of the wall as well. She waited, not daring to move a muscle for fear the floor would creak beneath her feet.

What was she going to say if Henry opened up the secret panel? She thought about stealing a line from Bugs Bunny: "Must've taken a wrong toyn in Alba-coykey." Perhaps adding a little levity to the situation would buy her a chance to beg for forgiveness. She couldn't hear anything from the closet side of the wall, and the tension was mounting with each passing second. The dread of being discovered made her skin crawl. Then she realized her skin wasn't crawling; something was actually crawling on her skin. With horror, she remembered the spiders. It took all her might to suppress the scream that nearly burst out of her lungs. She also had to fight the nearly uncontrollable urge to frantically slap at her left thigh, where she felt the grotesque little monster scampering about, knowing that the slightest movement might alert Henry to her presence. It was a superhuman effort, one that exhibited true determination and force of will, but it came at a cost. The pressure building inside of her, unable to escape through the normal channels, concentrated itself, then found an auxiliary exit. To her mortal embarrassment, Violet broke wind — loud and hard.

Certain that the game was up, she thrashed wildly at her legs until she was satisfied that nothing could have survived the melee. Then, desperate to escape, she groped in the darkness until she found a latch that opened the secret door. Quickly, she reached awkwardly through the bottom of the hinged decoy shelves and pressed the release button before tumbling out into the empty broom closet. She raised her head and looked around. Henry was gone.

With all the dignity she could salvage, Violet once again closed the secret door and secured the hinged shelves into place. She straightened her dress and quietly exited the closet, keeping the light on, since that was how Henry had left it. In the hallway she could hear footsteps going down the staircase, the only way to get to the first floor. She had to act quickly. As soon as Henry reached the first floor, Violet dashed into her room on her tiptoes and stepped out of her window onto the second-story porch. With all the bravery she could muster, she ambled over the guardrail and shimmied to the lattice upon which ivy crept up the side of the house. Like the worst cat burglar in the world, she managed to climb down the lattice, bringing handfuls of ivy with her.

Once on the ground, she ran to the entrance of the basement on the north side of the house, taking care to duck under all of the windows as she went in case Henry was looking out. Thankfully, the large wooden doors to the basement, which looked like the storm cellar at Dorothy's house in *The Wizard of Oz*, were propped open and Violet could slip right in. She plopped down on a chair in the corner, wiped the sweat off of her head with the back of her hand, and fought to control her breathing. A few moments later, Henry came strolling in. Most people look haggard after completing difficult work, but he was the opposite. He always looked refreshed and relaxed after doing his work. When he spotted Violet, he appeared surprised.

"There you are," she said to him with a contrived mixture of boredom and nonchalance.

Henry raised his eyebrows slightly. "Oh, I was just looking for you too. I guess we just missed each other."

"Must've taken a wrong toyn at Alba-coykee," Violet said playfully.

"Pardon?"

"You know, Bugs Bunny."

"I'm sorry, I…" He trailed off.

"Nothing, never mind." Violet was doubly glad Henry hadn't found her in the secret room. Her joke would have been dead on arrival.

"What happened to your dress?" he asked, noticing the small rip.

Violet was a terrible liar, so she decided to stick to the truth as much as possible.

"I snagged it earlier," she replied. "I'll have to mend it later tonight. It's kind of a drag."

"I've got some thread if you need it," Henry said as he held up a spool of the thread he used to sew eyelids shut.

Violet, stunned, wasn't sure what to say.

"Relax. It's just a little mortician humor," Henry said, grinning. "I guess I'm no Buns Bunny."

Violet giggled. "Bugs."

"Of course. Bugs."

Violet felt guilty about her surreptitious activities. Henry was strange, but he was a kind man, and he'd been very good to her. She was betraying his trust by going behind his back and sifting through his things. That being said, the excitement of the past half hour left her more invigorated, happy, and alive than she'd felt in a very long time. Her investigation had to continue. Already a new question was gnawing at her. As she helped Henry cart the newly prepared body over to the lift, the strange word she'd read on the stone marker echoed in her head.

She had to find out what BERWICK meant.

# Chapter 10

**1824**

**(A Midsummer Soirée at Russell Cave)**

"Press on," Pleasant's mother counseled him as he sat glumly on the old white mare, his worn satchel slung over his shoulder. "Press on until you scarce can summon the strength to persist at your task, then collect your remaining might and press harder still. Do not reserve your energies out of fear you will exhaust them. You will not, and neither will you falter. Your efforts will only bolster your endurance. Press on with reckless abandon, and you will lay claim to a magnificent destiny." Her advice was fervent but cold as iron. Pleasant was only thirteen then and still frightened of the unfamiliar. He wanted to beg her to let him stay. The sodden little cabin they shared was all he'd ever known. If staying meant tending pigs and toiling in the tobacco patch for the rest of his life, those were terms he was prepared to accept. Transylvania University seemed like a distant and fearful place, though it was only a day's ride away.

His mother must have seen the reluctance in his face that morning. "You've got every advantage you need, son," she told him. "You're smarter by half than any person I've ever known, and you're a Driscoll. That's a name that means something in this state thanks to your father. You may not have two coins to rub together, but it's no matter. Poverty is a temporary condition for enterprising men in this country."

"What about you?" he had asked as stoically as his shaking voice would allow.

"Your aunt and uncle are just down the holler. I've already told you, that's not something you should worry about. Your task is simple: learn all you can and make something of yourself."

That was three years ago. Since then, he had followed his mother's advice as faithfully as possible and in the process came to embrace a whole wide and beautiful world of knowledge and culture. Greedily, he consumed information. In addition to his regular coursework, he attended as many special lectures as he could afford and participated in every extracurricular activity that would fit into his nearly impossible schedule. Still, his voracious appetite for learning never felt satiated. He was always hungry for more. Math was his first love. That was his ticket to the university in the first place. He first discovered his prowess in that subject while attending a dank little one-room schoolhouse near Fort Boone, where he surpassed the instructor's mathematical knowledge in the span of one semester. After that, he'd sent off for worn out copies of Euclid's *Elements* and other classic mathematical treatises, merrily working his way through them in his leisure time. He also loved science, math's sweet sister, because he knew it was the key to unlocking the secrets of the natural world. What surprised him, however, was how easy he got along in everything else. Not only did he have an aptitude for language, acquiring a fluency in Latin and French and a speaking proficiency in Spanish, but he also had an ear for music and became quite adept at playing the piano and fiddle. Anything that tickled his fancy, he tried, and more often than not he discovered he had a knack for it. Drama, poetry, sketching, even dancing — he flourished in all he did, and each success gratified him to the marrow of his bones.

There were times, though, late at night, as he strained his eyes poring over his studies by candlelight, that exhaustion caught up to him. During those rare episodes, he would go outside and stare up at the night sky and quietly ponder the vastness of what lay beyond. He felt so small, he virtually disappeared. By the time he returned to his desk, he was rejuvenated. There was nothing quite as invigorating as coming back into existence after being swallowed up by the universe.

Unlike many of his classmates who came from wealthy families, it was a constant battle for Pleasant to keep himself fed. He earned money where he could, mostly working as a clerk for the surly merchant with whom he boarded, but also tutoring French, sometimes only staying a lesson or two ahead of his pupils. As he began the last year of his degree, his professors advised him it would be wise to make an appearance in Lexington's high society so that he might bolster his prospects upon the completion of his degree. Pleasant had a willing spirit, but he wore the uniform of destitution. It took months for him to scrimp together enough money to purchase the evening attire of a proper gentleman. If not exactly the height of recent fashion, the clothes were in passably good condition, despite being mostly second-hand.

All he needed was an invitation to an exclusive event. That's where his friend and classmate, Jeff, an aristocratic Mississippian who was lucky enough to claim a whole tangle of connections thanks to his high birth, was able to lend a hand. Jeff boarded with Joseph Ficklin, a family friend who served as the editor of the *Kentucky Gazette* and as Lexington's postmaster. Ficklin was a mighty pillar of the community, having defended it against Indian attacks during its earliest and most vulnerable days, then prospering as the burgeoning city grew out of the wilderness. Through Ficklin, Jeff managed to secure invitations for himself and Pleasant to a lavish midsummer party at Russell Cave. Jointly sponsored by Lexington's wealthiest families, the gathering promised to be the most opulent celebration since before the Panic of 1819, which had temporarily stifled such extravagance.

When the night of the party arrived, Pleasant was exultant. He and Jeff donned their best clothes, Jeff's being by far the finer, and both shaved the scraggly beards they'd been allowed to grow while studying for final exams. Jeff was perhaps the most popular boy in the class and every bit the high achiever Pleasant was, but he'd recently learned that he would be unable to stay at the university and earn his degree. His father had died unexpectedly, and his older brother, believing it to be in his best interest, managed to get him an appointment to the Academy at West Point. He was leaving in August, and he considered the midsummer party to be his last hurrah in

Lexington.

Russell Cave, eight miles northeast of town, required the employment of Jeff's sleek new phaeton carriage, a purchase he considered absolutely necessary for his upcoming trip to New York, though his brother disagreed. Along the way, the young men dipped into what Jeff referred to as his "driving bourbon" and took turns at the reins. The whiskey warmed Pleasant's throat and stomach and set his head to buzzing. Night had already fallen, and the path was fairly treacherous, but the boys felt no fear. They laughed and sang as the horse pulled them down the rugged path. Pleasant's spirits, already soaring with anticipation, reached new heights as the carriage crested the last hill, and he caught a glimpse of the gathering below. His vision exploded with light. Hundreds of lanterns were strung together from tall poles that loosely corralled more than three hundred celebrants who were dancing and swirling against the backdrop of the ancient cavern. The lights reflected majestically upon the placid surface of a shallow, dawdling creek that flowed from the mouth of the cave. High above, the moon shone brightly and cast a protective blanket of silver luminescence over the jubilee.

From atop the hill, the air smelled of cooking meats and sweet confections. He hopped off the carriage, and the grass even felt airy and soft beneath his boots. More than ever he felt the desperate excitement his mother exuded when she sent him off to school. He wondered if she'd ever seen anything like it herself. The sight before him was a marvelous integration of the old and new. The cave, an ancient wonder formed in the limestone cliffs over thousands of years, had been further adorned by the imaginative artistry and energetic benevolence of a youthful people. With deliberate savoring, he absorbed the scene like a cube of sugar on his tongue.

"I feel like Oberon watching over the sprites in the forest of Athens," he confessed. It was an especially apt description considering how some had taken to calling Lexington the Athens of the West.

"I guess that makes me Robin Goodfellow." Jeff grinned roguishly as he hopped off the phaeton and took another long sip of bourbon from his hip flask.

The young men laughed merrily and sauntered down the hill to join the festivities. A valet took the reins of the carriage and led the horse downstream where fresh hay and water awaited.

As Pleasant stepped among the people he'd been sent to meet and mingle with, he was awestruck by the luxury around him. Waiters in tailed tuxedos carrying crystal glasses of sherry on silver trays circulated through the crowd. It was with some embarrassment that he realized they were better dressed than him. Off to the right were tables, chairs, and benches where the partygoers could sit and talk or take a rest from dancing. On the left was an immense serving table featuring at least a hundred dishes. He spied venison, roasted quail, breaded lamb chops, a cornucopia of fresh vegetables and melons, even oysters on the half-shell, painstakingly shipped in ice crates from Maryland. There were two barrels of brandy punch, a cask of bourbon, and dozens of bottles of French and Spanish wine. The flatware was silver, the dinnerware was fine China. Nothing but the very best.

Cleverly, the musicians were assembled on a special platform at the mouth of the cave, where an acoustically ideal forechamber allowed each perfectly executed note to wash sonorously over the dancers who had gathered on the opposite side of the creek. It was a scene that beggared all description. Pleasant couldn't help but laugh with delight.

Two pretty girls promenaded by, arm in arm, giggling at a secret joke. One of them cut an impish glance at Pleasant and Jeff. That was all Jeff needed. He immediately grabbed three glasses of sherry from a passing server's tray.

"Where are you going?" Pleasant asked.

"Every man for himself," Jeff replied gaily, "and may the devil take the hindmost!"

Suddenly alone, Pleasant was unsure what to do. He stood tall and gazed confidently at the swarm of faces in the crowd, but fought a nervous hesitation in the pit of his stomach. He settled his left hand into the inner pocket of his overcoat and held a glass of sherry with the other, anything to give them some occupation. Anxiously, he waited for an opportunity to join in somehow. From amongst the throng he heard his name being called. It took a moment to spot the source, but when he did, a wave of relief washed over him.

"Monsieur Rafinesque!" Pleasant exclaimed happily as he recognized his teacher and mentor. No one at the party could have contrasted more perfectly with Pleasant's youthful, clean, and statuesque appearance. His professor, Constantine Rafinesque, wore a long, ill-fitting coat of yellow nankeen cloth, stained all over with the juice of plants, a nankeen waistcoat with enormous pockets buttoned to the chin, and a pair of comically tight pantaloons. His beard was long and his lank black hair hung loosely over his shoulders. He was short and fat, and his receding hairline emphasized his already prominent forehead. Yet despite his singular appearance, women surrounded him.

"Ladies," the little man said with a French accent that he was helpless in trying to hide, "it pleases me greatly to introduce my top pupil, Mr. Pleasant Driscoll."

Pleasant bowed politely then gracefully took the hand of each woman in the group as his professor named her. Most were married to prominent university men, trustees and administrators.

"Happy to make your acquaintance," Pleasant said.

"I am excited to finally meet the young man of whom the professor speaks so highly," said Mary Holley, the wife of Transylvania's president, Horace Holley. She was a plain woman but not without a certain plump attractiveness. "I must say, I was quite impressed with your performance in *Catherine and Petruchio* last spring."

One of the other ladies gasped. "I knew you looked familiar! You played Petruchio, didn't you? Oh, how marvelous! Miss Holley will attest that I declared your portrayal enthralling. How did you ever recall all of those lines?"

"Through great repetition." Pleasant smiled. "I was so afraid I would forget something, I must have studied the script every night for a month."

"Well, you did splendidly," the woman said. "I certainly hope your theater company does something this fall. Perhaps another comedy. I do love to laugh."

"So, what do you think of the party, Mr. Driscoll?" Mrs. Holley asked, gesturing flippantly with her drink-free hand.

"It is quite astounding and ingeniously executed," Pleasant replied.

She nodded. "I tend to agree. You have the professor here to thank for the idea. He is the one who first proposed this location as a leisure spot."

"Is that so?" Pleasant inquired of the beaming man.

"'Tis true, I suppose. I spent several days exploring this area a little while ago. The cave itself is terrifically fascinating, but quite difficult to navigate as the creek, Dog Fennel, I believe, fills it from side to side in most places. I managed to follow it for nearly a mile before abandoning the effort when the water became too deep for me to stand. Notwithstanding the treacherous caverns within, I think you will agree, there is no place better suited for a pleasure resort."

"I can't imagine braving that dark, ominous hole," said one of the ladies, a fleshy woman feverishly wafting an ornate fan toward her face. "Do you often encounter dangers in the course of your explorations?"

Professor Rafinesque clearly relished the question. He rocked slightly from his heels to his toes, his chest somewhat protruding. "The life of a true field botanist on this continent is one full of exertions and difficulties, much like those faced by any common explorer. Foremost is the danger that attends solitude, for you may be lost, or hurt, or even waylaid by scoundrels, heaven forbid, with no friendly body to aid you. Then again, food may be scarce, the climate inhospitable, or deadly snakes may be lurking underfoot. I'd say the most obnoxious of all are the ticks, ants, wasps, and horseflies that constantly assail the tender flesh and threaten disease."

Mrs. Holley and the other ladies listened rapturously to the Professor's lively account.

"Don't misunderstand me, though," he continued. "All in all, the pleasures of botanical exploration fully compensate for these miseries and dangers, else no one would be a travelling botanist, nor spend his time and money in vain. That being said, I truly despise those who have the gall to claim for themselves the title of botanist and yet travel in carriages and steamboats. What has ever been discovered in the wild from a cushioned seat? Had I not been traveling on foot near the Red River three years ago, I daresay we'd not have the company of Mr. Driscoll with us tonight."

"Professor," the corpulent woman interjected, "you make it sound like you plucked him from under a fallen tree like a common toadstool to season your soup."

"Oh, quite the contrary, Madame. Mr. Driscoll, not much more than a pup then, came to my aid in a moment of exceptional distress. I had, quite unwisely, attempted to climb one of the many unique geological anomalies that populate that region, an enormous arch atop a great jagged cliff, and managed to find myself at a point in the climb where I was uncertain both how to proceed upward or how to get back to the ground. Being some eighty feet up, I became concerned that my life was danger. Young Mr. Driscoll, as part of a Divine scheme, I'm sure, was in my vicinity and quickly perceived my dilemma. He guided me with a most helpful tutorial about where to place my hands and feet so as to successfully reach his position at the summit of the rocky cliff.

"Owing the boy my very life, I inquired if he would accompany me on my explorations that afternoon as an assistant and guide. A proposition he accepted most enthusiastically. It was within the span of only a few hours that I began to perceive the latent alacrity of his mind and the contagious enthusiasm of his spirit for discovery. He reminded me very much of myself as a boy. I stayed with young Mr. Driscoll and his mother in their cabin for several days, teaching and testing him in the evenings and exploring with him during the days. I daresay it was one of the most joyous excursions I have ever experienced."

Pleasant had heard his teacher's recitation of the story many times, but he never grew tired of it. He too recalled the encounter with fondness, since it was the first time in his life someone had challenged his mind and led him to believe he was capable of great things. Moreover, the professor had called in several favors to get him admitted to the university.

"What a fortuitous encounter," exclaimed one of the ladies.

"It has been entirely to my own profit," Pleasant humbly replied. "Studying under Professor Rafinesque has brought me great joy and has set my life on a vastly different trajectory."

Professor Rafinesque swelled with pride at the remark and shook Pleasant's hand vigorously. "Is there a finer young man than this?"

"Mr. Driscoll, I feel we are selfishly detaining you at the expense of the young ladies here tonight who are waiting for their turn to dance with you," said Mrs. Holley.

"You are very kind, ma'am, but I daresay the ladies will find me utterly boring compared with the other fine gentlemen I see here. As a hopeless academic, I have focused all of my passions upon my scholarship. It is a lesson learned from my good teacher here."

Pleasant thought he detected a shared glance between Professor Rafinesque and Mrs. Holley that made the latter flush.

"Come, my boy," the professor broke in suddenly, "I've heard that Monsieur Mathurin Giron has baked one of his famous cakes for this event, and I insist you have some."

They graciously bid adieu to the ladies and headed toward the long serving table.

"Is everything all right, Professor?"

"*Oui*, quite, quite," he replied, mopping his forehead with a grimy handkerchief produced from one of his many pockets. A forgotten plant specimen haphazardly stored in the same pocket clung to the ragged cloth. Slices of strawberry cake, served on decorative plates, sat ready on the immense table before them. They each claimed a piece and eagerly set about sampling them. Professor Rafinesque sighed as he savored his first bite. "It certainly is a magnificent party. Such a shame they intend to ruin it with the violence they have planned."

"What do you mean?" Pleasant asked, but only reflexively. His attention was diverted to the cake. He'd eaten cake a few times before, but nothing like a decadent Giron creation. It was the finest thing he'd ever tasted. He feared everything he ate in the future would taste like sawdust by comparison.

"The duel," Professor Rafinesque said disapprovingly. "Have you not heard?"

Pleasant shook his head.

"Some dispute has come to a head, and now the parties intend to shoot it out later this evening."

"Who are the combatants, and what is their grievance?"

"I do not recall who the parties are, but the prevailing rumor is that the challenger's brother was killed by the negligence of the man challenged. Something about drunkenness and a ricocheted bullet — no doubt someone's honor has been called into question. Truly, I do not understand the ingrained obsession among Kentucky folk regarding perceived slights to honor."

"Isn't honor a virtue in a man?"

"*Oui*, one of many. What about patience, charity, empathy, and forgiveness? These are virtues as well. Are they all slaves to honor? I don't see anyone eager to put his life on the line for forgiveness."

Pleasant was about to respond, but another man interrupted.

"Professor Rafinesque, how nice of you to suspend your work for an evening to honor us with your presence. I daresay all the secrets of the natural world will have to wait until tomorrow to be discovered."

The voice belonged to Dr. Benjamin Dudley, a professor at Transylvania's medical school. Pleasant had taken an undergraduate anatomy class with Dr. Dudley and immediately recognized his mocking tone. It was the primary weapon in his teaching arsenal. No student dared attend his lectures unprepared for fear they would be mercilessly lambasted by his razor-sharp reproaches.

Dr. Dudley and Professor Rafinesque were close in age but quite disparate in appearance and temperament. Dr. Dudley was rigid and immaculately dressed. Long sideburns swept toward his chin, while a pronounced widow's peak crept inexorably toward his crown. A thin nose hooked over his delicate smirking lips. Where Professor Rafinesque's eyes seemed to dart about with excitement, Dr. Dudley's were deep-set and generally glared with solemn disinterest. An open contempt permeated the air.

"Dr. Dudley, it is always a comfort to know that your surgical skill is close by to rid us of our bad blood if the circumstances should call for it."

The doctor responded with a sneer.

"Dr. Dudley," Pleasant said, respectfully extending his hand.

The man looked contemptuously at the outstretched hand and made no attempt to meet it with his own. He looked Pleasant over with a disgusted glance before turning his attention back to Professor Rafinesque.

"Professor, I attended your lecture at the end of the term on the medicinal attributes of plants native to this region. Like always, your analysis was dizzying. I must admit, I could not comprehend it."

"Ah, a common admission from you, I am sure."

Dr. Dudley narrowed his gaze. "It was not for want of intellect that your ramblings could not be understood. It was the complete lack of actual science employed by the speaker. Your study of the natives of this region has gone to your head. You've adopted their practices and taken to considering yourself a rudimentary healer, haven't you? You French are so infatuated with the savages of this country, you are willing to delude yourselves that chanting, pipe-smoking medicine men have some real power to heal."

"It is true that some inhabitants of this commonwealth consider me a healer, a notion I do not encourage but which I am ill-inclined to fully dissuade.  For many ailments, my plants and poultices rival the crude medieval medical practices you so-called physicians have adopted from your European masters."

"Take care with your tone, Professor. You insult me."

"Heaven forbid," the professor replied with feigned concern. "None of us have forgotten how you treat those who say aught against you."

"I assume you are referring to that poltroon, Dr. Drake. Even you cannot deny that he slandered me most unjustly and that I was quite justified in challenging him to a contest of deadly instruments."

Pleasant was curious. "What was the slanderous comment, Doctor?"

Dr. Dudley rolled his eyes. "If you must know, he called me an ignoramus, a bully, and a liar."

"Absurd!" Professor Rafinesque proclaimed. "You are no liar."

"Neither am I an ignoramus nor a bully," Dr. Dudley growled. "That is why Dr. Drake had to be called to task for his outrageous comments. But being the coward that he is, a proxy served in his stead, the brave Dr.

Richardson."

"*Oui,* and I recall very well how you heroically shot the brave Dr. Richardson in the groin," Professor Rafinesque jeered. "It was a triumph of honor."

"It was a civilized airing of grievances by two gentlemen," the doctor retorted. "Something you cannot possibly understand. You will recall that after shooting Mr. Richardson, I came to his aid and stopped the bleeding that certainly would have been mortal without my intervention. Having settled our differences, we now share an abundance of mutual respect."

"What a shame you did not lay hands on his groin before the duel. Perhaps you could have cultivated a friendship without the need of pistols."

Dr. Dudley nearly choked on his drink. "Jest all you like, Professor. That is all you seem to do well. Even your so-called friends make a buffoon out of you. We've all seen your publication featuring the newly discovered fishes of John James Audubon. Any imbecile could have seen that he was only japing with you with those monstrous and fantastical drawings. But you…you just accept them wholesale with no further investigation. What kind of scientist does that?"

Pleasant could tell Dr. Dudley's words were salting a very tender wound. Professor Rafinesque inherently held his fellow frontier explorers in high esteem. John Audubon's joke had caused him a great deal of embarrassment.

"If you are accusing me of trusting a man I admire and consider a friend, I will not deny it."

"No, Professor, I'm accusing you of having your head in every cloud that crosses the horizon. One day you are adventuring for plants, the next you are decoding ancient Indian languages, the next you are trying your hand at astronomy, then medicine, then ornithology, then geology, then zoology. It makes my head spin."

"What can I say?" the professor replied defiantly. "There is no limit to my desire for discovery."

"There is no limit to your mania. If you are not careful, you will discover yourself out of your post at the university and in a room at the new lunatic asylum we keep hearing so much about."

Pleasant stood by awkwardly as the two men traded barbs. He wanted to come to his mentor's defense, but he could not summon the words or the courage to do so.

Thankfully, the squabble was interrupted when Professor Rafinesque spied Robert Wickliffe passing nearby.

"Mr. Wickliffe, how well met!" he exclaimed, clutching at the elbow of the other man's jacket and nearly causing him to spill his glass of bourbon.

"Professor," the snared man mumbled, clearly put off but not going so far as to roll his eyes.

"Have you given any more thought to our last conversation about the botanical garden? There are so many positive attributes…"

Mr. Wickliffe wearily cut him off. "Professor, I recall our conversation about the benefits of a botanical garden very well. As I've already told you, I'm interested in donating to the cause, but I'd like to talk to some of the other contributors first, as well as Mr. Holley."

The last part obviously rankled the professor, who had been sparring with the university president on a number of proposed projects. In general, Mr. Holley was not a great supporter of Professor Rafinesque's grandiose plans. He believed the professor should be spending less time out in the field and more time in the classroom, teaching students.

"Will there be any speeches tonight?" Dr. Dudley asked Mr. Wickliffe, who'd recently been reelected to the US House of Representatives.

"Mercifully, no," he replied. "After the last election, I am sick to death of politics. You try to do something to show appreciation to your constituency, and some goddamned Republican has to ruin it for everyone."

Dr. Dudley nodded and smirked at the remark, but Professor Rafinesque confessed his ignorance on the subject.

Mr. Wickliffe looked astonished. "My God, Professor, I thought everyone heard about that fiasco. After winning my seat in Congress last fall, I gave the rabble a barrel of punch as a gift. I'll be damned if someone didn't poison the whole thing with tartar emetic. The spewing began immediately, and the stench that followed will haunt me for the rest of my days. You'd think Limestone Street was one of Dante's inner circles of Hell based on the lamentations of the imbibers."

Mr. Wickliffe shook his head. "If I ever lay my hands on the hornswaggler who did it, I'll pour tartar emetic down his gullet, then I'll shove the empty bottle up his ass."

Dr. Dudley and Professor Rafinesque laughed heartily. Pleasant only smiled.

Mr. Wickliffe closely examined his face. "You look familiar, son. What's your name?"

"Pleasant Driscoll, sir."

"Perchance are you any relation to Thackery Driscoll?"

"He was my father."

Mr. Wickliffe nodded approvingly. "Thackery Driscoll was a frontiersman of the highest order. There is no end to the number of tales I've heard told about him."

"I never knew him myself, sir," Pleasant confessed. "He died shortly before I was born."

"Well, countless families in this state owe him a debt of gratitude for the protection and interdiction he provided when this place was still wild with Indians."

Pleasant nodded his appreciation.

"What of the duel tonight?" Dr. Dudley asked Mr. Wickliffe, eager to change the subject. "I've heard it's between a cuckold and his wife's paramour."

Mr. Wickliffe sipped his bourbon. "Ah yes, it should be very exciting. Though, I heard it was between the father of a runaway daughter and the girl's seducer."

Dr. Dudley cocked his head slightly to the side. "Either way, honor must be restored. Wouldn't you agree, Professor?"

Professor Rafinesque looked at Mr. Wickliffe and, not wanting to disagree with a man from whom he needed financial support, gave a sickly smile. "Of course," he uttered sheepishly.

"Come, Mr. Wickliffe," Dr. Dudley implored smugly. "I have a friend I'd like you to meet. He is breeding some of the finest horses you have ever seen."

When they had gone, Professor Rafinesque spat on the ground.

"I envy you, Pleasant," he said with a sad smile.

"Why, Professor?"

"Because you are not the odd fish that I am." He sighed. "I am foreign and bizarre. My own colleagues mock me and belittle my work. The university uses my passions against me. They know that learning and scholarship give me life, so they give me only a pittance for my time. I hardly make enough to dress and feed myself, and yet Mr. Holley shames me because of the number of university candles I use working late at night." He shook his head. "I see the sparkle in your eyes tonight. You see these beautiful people and their wealth, and you want nothing more than to be a part of them."

Pleasant could not deny it.

"I have felt that way myself. I still do, in some ways. But all of this," he gestured at their surroundings, "is something that is not meant to last. At least not how they have constructed it. They wear masks with smiling faces, but most of these so-called gentlemen would devour each other if it were to their advantage. It is not true friendship."

A shadow then seemed to cross the professor's face.

"Even more than that, the foundation of this empire is not stable."

He nodded toward a passing slave carrying a serving tray.

"It mocks God to buy and sell men and women and subjugate them like animals. They claim the black race are lesser beings — that they cannot learn like other men. But that is a farce. If they cannot learn, then it would be unnecessary to make laws forbidding their education. It is a terrible crime to prevent the education of those who desire it. Quite unforgivable." He shook his head bitterly. "Mr. Wickliffe is the biggest perpetrator. He owns more slaves than anyone in the state."

Pleasant was not unmoved by what the professor said. He could not deny the inherent injustice of the system by which the wealthy prospered.

"What would you have me do?" he asked.

The professor clutched his elbow firmly. "Seek truth, Pleasant, above all. Do not allow the Dr. Dudleys of this world, with their limited imaginations, to cripple your pursuit of knowledge. Truth is a mad scramble, a whirling blur. There are times it cannot be assembled politely into a neat book as some would have us believe, and it is not monopolized by the scholars of Europe. If at all possible, be your own patron so you have to beg no man for the opportunity to do the work that benefits mankind. Seek friendship, true friendship, and never hinder another man's pursuit of knowledge."

Professor Rafinesque forced a smile.

"I've slipped into a dour mood, I'm afraid. But seeing you here tonight is enough to lift my spirits. Please don't mistake me. I am blessed as no man has any right to be blessed. Every day I wake up and have the opportunity to do the things I love. I write, I teach, I discover, and I learn. Would that I had a thousand lifetimes — perhaps that would be enough time to satisfy my curiosities."

He patted Pleasant on the back.

"Come, it's time to have some fun. A robust dance will make everything right."

With alarming spryness, he bounded ridiculously toward the dancing area and, amazingly, secured a partner within a matter of seconds.

"He's a little warlock," Pleasant said under his breath before searching the ranks of young ladies for a partner of his own, someone he could be sure would not refuse him. As he scanned, he noticed that some of the girls were looking at him and whispering to one another. He became very self-conscious and felt his face warming with embarrassment. Most likely they were commenting on his shabby, second-hand clothes. He wished he'd saved more money and bought something nicer. One song concluded and another began, but Pleasant remained frozen in place.

Jeff, who had just finished dancing a waltz, spotted him and swaggered over with a breathless girl in tow.

"The fish aren't going to jump into your boat by themselves, my friend. You've got to cast a line."

Pleasant grinned shyly.

"Here, allow me to introduce you to Mary — Mary, Pleasant Driscoll, the second most handsome man at Transylvania University."

Jeff slapped him on the back and marched off to his next conquest.

Just as Pleasant was about to ask her to dance, the fiddle rang out boldly from the cave.

"'Durang's Hornpipe'!" Mary exclaimed. "They're starting the Virginia Reel, do you know it?"

"Of course," he said, relieved that the group dances were starting. He took her white-gloved hand and led her to where two large groups were forming up. "It's my favorite."

The dancing area had been strategically placed as close to the mouth of the cave as possible so that the chilled air from within could cool the dancers and overcome some of the summer swelter. As the song progressed, the couples intertwined, linking arms and pressing close to one another. Each face he encountered met him with a bright smile and shining eyes. He thrilled at each touch and felt enveloped by the warmth and goodwill of the group.

Later, the large groups broke up into quadrilles. Pleasant found himself coupled with a beautiful girl with long chestnut hair. She danced with the effortless grace of one well practiced, and she laughed easily and often, her joyous eyes sparkling. Once he'd seen her, Pleasant could hardly bear to look away. She was magnetic. After a number of songs, the quadrille broke apart. While the participants congratulated one another for a well-executed dance, the girl slid her arm through Pleasant's and beckoned him toward the refreshments table with the tilt of her head. Ecstatically, he accepted her invitation.

The punch had gotten a bit warm during the evening, but it was still refreshing. Pleasant wiped his face and neck with a handkerchief produced from his jacket pocket. Likewise, the girl elegantly dabbed perspiration from her brow with a delicate handkerchief of her own.

"The humidity is as unrelenting in this area as the wagering," he said. "You'd think we were at Postlethwait's Tavern for the amount of oddsmaking I've overhead tonight."

"Betting is contagious," she grinned. "Let me show you. I bet I can guess your name."

"The odds are already against you," he warned. "I have a most uncommon name."

"Is that so? Well, some say a man's name reflects his personality, or vice versa. Either way, I'll put that theory to the test."

"Very well."

She squinted as though deep in thought. "What do I know about you? Let's see, you are a pleasant-looking fellow. You speak pleasantly. You dance pleasantly. You smile pleasantly. And you seem to have a genuine overall pleasantness."

Pleasant smiled broadly. "So you've reached a conclusion, have you?"

"It's only too obvious. Your name is Imposter, or how else would you be among this lot?"

They laughed.

"I overhead some of the other girls talking about you tonight," she confessed. "You may not know it, but you've made several conquests. I predict the name Pleasant Driscoll will be scrawled dotingly in a dozen or more diaries tomorrow."

Pleasant blushed. "I saw some girls looking and whispering. I thought they were making fun of my clothes."

The girl laughed as she playfully adjusted his tie. "I like your clothes. They are very well selected, in my opinion."

"You are too kind, and a magnanimous winner. Having named me, you have won your bet. Would you be so gracious as to allow me the chance to return the favor?"

"I agree, seeing as how it only proves my point that betting is contagious."

"So, what do I know about *you*? Let's see, you have a sunny disposition, of that I am certain." He rubbed his chin solemnly. "And the sun shines most directly on the equator, or so I'm told."

"So far your facts are correct, but the likelihood of your reaching the correct destination seems very grim."

"Bear with me, my process is tried and true."

The girl nonchalantly extended her hand and encouraged Pleasant to continue.

"All right, equatorial climates are known for their exotic wildlife, like parrots and toucans."

The girl raised a suspicious eyebrow.

"But birds are a diversion, aren't they? You're trying to throw me off the scent."

"It seems you need no help in that regard."

"What, you doubt me? Where's your faith? I'm close, I just know it." He gasped. "Monkeys! Monkeys live in equatorial climates as well. And what do monkeys eat?"

The girl was totally bewildered. "Bananas?"

"Yes! And banana rhymes with…Anna, so that must be your name."

First, the girl's mouth opened in surprise, then she pursed her lips in a sly smile.

"It seems you already know the secret to successful wagering. You've managed to secure a good tip. Perhaps you're no imposter after all."

Pleasant pointed to the handkerchief that was still in her hand. Her name was embroidered in purple letters along the outer seam.

"I want you to know I meant everything I said — about your sunny disposition, the toucans, the bananas…all of it."

She rolled her eyes. "I'm sure."

"Are you a student?" he asked.

"Yes, I'm studying at Madame Victoria Charlotte LeClere Mentelle's boarding school. It is opposite Mr. Clay's estate on Rose Hill."

"This town is overrun with French educators," Pleasant said.

"Your teacher is French as well?"

Pleasant pointed toward the dancing area, where Professor Rafinesque was still enthusiastically skipping about.

"About as French as it gets."

Anna grinned. "Perhaps the French have not abandoned their quest to conquer this continent after all — their new plan is to indoctrinate us."

"Are you enjoying the party?" Pleasant asked.

"Yes, I absolutely adore dancing. I wish there were more opportunities for it. You?"

"I agree. I am new to parties like this, but I can certainly get used to them. Everything is so wonderfully happy tonight — except for the duel, of course. I tend to agree with my professor, there's no place for bloodshed at an event like this."

Anna's face suddenly darkened. Her entire demeanor changed as quick as a flash of lightning.

"I'm sorry, did I say something wrong?"

"No, of course not," she said as she hastily swept away the tears welling in her eyes. "It's just that…one of the duelists is my father. At least, he was supposed to be one of the duelists. I spoke with him earlier this evening, and he promised me he would not fight. He said he would find another way to resolve his issue with the other man."

"That's a relief," Pleasant said. "If I may ask, what was their quarrel about? I've heard a good deal of speculation tonight."

"I'm sure you have. These piranhas go into a frenzy when they smell blood in the water. It's all over an idiotic trifle. Do you know my father, some call him the Hemp Barren?"

"Yes," Pleasant replied. "Patrick Nelson, right? The biggest rope manufacturer west of the Alleghenies."

"Yes. Well, a man named Fredrick Harlan, one of his suppliers, wagered and lost an entire shipment of hemp that was due to my father during a drunken game of cards. The man who won the shipment sold it to one of Father's competitors. Without the shipment, Father was forced to temporarily halt his rope production. I think it lost him a lot of money."

"That's unfortunate."

"When Father discovered how Fredrick Harlan lost the shipment, he said he'd never do business with him again, calling him a drunkard and a lackwit."

"I take it Mr. Harlan did not take it well when he caught wind of your father's statement."

"He immediately challenged Father to a duel, and quite improperly so. There was no opportunity given to Father to publicly recant his statements, even though the whole Christian world knows he spoke true. Fredrick

Harlan is a brute, and a dangerous one at that. He fought with Andrew Jackson against the Indians in Alabama, then against the British in New Orleans. He's got many a notch on his rifle. Father, on the other hand, has never raised a hand in anger in his life. He's a peaceful man, and Mr. Harlan knows that."

"I'm very sorry."

"Me too. When I found out earlier this week that the duel would be fought tonight, it put me in a very ill state. I had a bit of an episode and spent the past few days in bed. It wasn't until I saw Father before the party tonight and he promised me he would not fight that I began to feel better. I think the dancing helped too. I feel so carefree when I hear that lively music."

Pleasant raised his cup. "Here's to peaceful endings and good music."

Anna smiled and raised her cup as well. "Hear, hear."

When she'd drained her cup, she gave it to a nearby server. "Well, I'm sure my friends are waiting. If I don't go tell them about you soon, I think they may actually burst. They are a very curious lot."

Pleasant laughed. "Please, go right ahead. I'd hate to think I was responsible for such carnage."

"Just so you know, I'm going to tell them that you are a dreadful bore," she said playfully. "I feel it is my duty to thin out your herd of admirers a bit. I'll tell them you talked of nothing but monkeys."

Pleasant bowed low. "I trust your judgment completely."

With a polite curtsy, she turned and scampered away. Pleasant sighed wistfully.

"That is a charming girl," said a friendly-faced man who had been standing nearby. He was not quite young, but probably no more than forty.

"Yes," Pleasant agreed, though somewhat taken aback. He had been so consumed by his conversation with Anna he had no idea anyone else was even remotely close to them.

"I'm sorry, I couldn't help overhearing you two," the man said. "She reminds me very much of what my wife was like at that age." He laughed. "The first time I saw her, my wife I mean, she was riding bareback on a feisty little Indian pony, all breathless and flushed. I think she was trying to jump a bevy quail. She was so preoccupied with her sport, she didn't even notice me standing there, gawking and dumbstruck."

"Have we met before?" asked Pleasant.

"I'm sorry, probably not. I'm Matthew Jouett. And if I heard correctly, you are Imposter."

Pleasant's eyes widened. "Mr. Jouett, it's an honor to meet you. Actually, I'm Pleasant Driscoll. I've seen your work, it is truly incredible — the ability to capture a moment in time so perfectly with nothing but a paintbrush, it's like magic."

Matthew modestly bowed his head. "Well, thank you. You know, for only fifty dollars you too can be immortalized. Just come down to my studio on Short Street."

Pleasant blushed. "Would that I could. I'm afraid that when Miss Nelson called me an Imposter, she wasn't far off the mark. In truth, I doubt there is a person here tonight who has less money to their name than me. I'm but a poor student."

Matthew patted him heartily on the shoulder. "There's no reason to be ashamed, my friend; it wasn't long ago that I was in your shoes myself. My father was a man of modest means. He had far more sons than he had money, so one day he gathered me and my brothers together and told us that he could only afford to send one of us to school. Having a democratic spirit, he told us to vote on it. My brothers quite graciously nominated me."

"They must think very highly of you."

"They are good brothers. They knew how much I wanted it. Anyway, I studied law at Transylvania, and when I graduated I took a clerkship with Judge Bibb in Frankfort. I was well on my way to fulfilling my father's dream of wealth and influence. There was only one problem."

"You wanted to paint."

"I couldn't imagine doing anything else. It was the hardest thing in the world to tell my father I was going to Boston to study under Gilbert Stuart. He told me he had educated me to be a gentleman, not a damned sign painter."

"Surely, he sees now how wrong he was," Pleasant said.

Matthew shrugged. "If you are doing what you are meant to do, it doesn't matter what anyone else thinks." Pleasant detected a bit of melancholy in his voice. "There is a price to following your passions, however. During the summer, business is good, but during the winters the roads get bad and folks hold a little more tightly to their money. I'm forced to travel south to ply my trade in warmer climes. Being apart from my wife and children can be…difficult to bear."

Jeff approached and tapped Pleasant on the elbow. "Sorry to interrupt."

"Jeff, I'm glad you're here. Have you met Matthew Jouett?"

Jeff politely extended his hand. "It's an honor, Mr. Jouett. Your reputation precedes you. Jefferson Davis."

"Very well met, Mr. Davis," the painter responded.

"Pleasant, the duel is about to begin. Are you going to watch?"

Pleasant was confused. "You must be mistaken. I heard it was called off."

Jeff pointed toward a gathering crowd at the fringe of the party. "Someone forgot to tell them that."

The three made their way toward the commotion and found Anna distraught and crying. Her father, a corpulent man with thick, curly hair, grossly overgrown eyebrows, and a permanently flushed face, did his best to calm her.

"Please, don't do this," Anna begged, tears streaming down her cheeks. "Please, Father. Please don't go. Just say you were wrong. It doesn't matter. It doesn't mean anything."

Her mother scoffed. "You'd have your father look like a coward in front of the whole city. You're only a child. You can't understand what's at stake."

Anna ignored her. "Fredrick Harlan is no gentleman. No one will think less of you for ignoring him."

"It's too late for that," her mother barked. "Now, dry up Anna, you're making a fool of yourself."

"No, Father, please. Don't do this!"

The man embraced his daughter tightly and kissed her forehead. "Don't worry, dear. I don't intend to die tonight. But this is something that must be done."

He gave her arms a tender squeeze as her mother looked on with an icy glare.

Mr. Nelson nodded solemnly at the steely woman and started the grand procession over the hill to the adjoining field where his opponent was already waiting. The men followed closely behind him in an excited rabble while the women stayed safely back, clustering together and speaking in hushed tones. The band took a long-awaited break.

When Patrick reached the dueling ground, the crowd around him parted to either side, creating a narrow alley where the bullets could freely fly. A dozen tuxedoed servants had brought lanterns up from the party to provide adequate light. Tension in the air became palpable as the two men confronted one another. The parameters of the contest had been decided a few days in advance. Patrick, having been given the choice of weapons, selected dueling pistols. Fredrick then selected a distance of eight paces.

Fredrick, tall and thick-chested, was truly an imposing figure. He wore his army uniform, which had grown snug since its last use in 1812, making him appear bigger still. His sandy hair was long and lay freely on his shoulders. A wild reddish beard sprouted from his massive jaw. He stood tall and fierce, unlike his portly opponent, who sighed heavily and fought to catch his breath.

"I just don't understand," Pleasant whispered to Matthew. "Isn't dueling illegal?"

"Not when it has the blessing of the kings."

"The kings?"

"The money kings, the men who rule this state — who make and enforce the laws." Matthew nodded toward a group of older gentlemen wearing expensive suits. Among them Pleasant recognized Robert Wickliffe and John Wesley Hunt.

"See the man smoking a pipe on the far right?"

"Yes."

"Do you know who that is?"

"Should I?"

"That's Governor Desha. Last year, his son killed a man in Fleming

County. The victim was traveling north to meet his fiancé in New Jersey for their wedding. Desha's son met him on the road and bashed his skull in with a horsewhip. He then took the man's horse and other belongings and left his corpse on the side of the road."

Pleasant grimaced. "How terrible!"

"Truly it was. The jury thought so too; Desha was convicted after an hour's deliberation and sentenced to death. But instead of allowing justice to run its course, Desha was given a second trial."

"What happened at the second trial?"

"He was convicted again." Matthew was incredulous. "Can you believe they are already talking about a third trial? Mark my words, Governor Desha will never allow his son to die. If they don't find a jury to acquit him before the end of his term as governor, he'll pardon the scoundrel. That's the type of power a money king wields in this state."

Pleasant shook his head disbelievingly.

"Desha is not a bad man," Matthew added. "I've spoken with him on several occasions, and I quite like him. But no father would allow his son to be put to death if he had any way to prevent it. Even if the son's sins are great, and the father's personal cost is high. Still, you only get the opportunity to rise above the law if you are a money king."

The crowd hushed. Judge Thomas Letcher, a sleepy-eyed old barrister, the agreed-upon moderator, approached the combatants.

"Gentlemen, you've come to this spot upon the challenge of Mr. Harlan for statements made by Mr. Nelson that he claims to be slanderous. Mr. Harlan, have you received satisfaction from Mr. Nelson?"

"I have not," the man hissed.

"Mr. Nelson, do you recant your statements with regard to Mr. Harlan?"

Patrick swallowed hard. "I do not."

At the sound of his opponent's voice, Fredrick's jaw clenched.

"And who have you selected as your seconds?" the judge asked.

A short man with black hair and deep-set eyes stepped forward from the crowd to stand next to Patrick. The judge shook hands with the little man.

"Mr. Pike, have you taken on the duties of Mr. Nelson's second?"

"Yes, Judge."

"Have you inspected Mr. Nelson's pistol?"

"I have, Judge, and I warrant that it is a well-maintained weapon and in good working condition."

The judge turned to Fredrick. "What about you? Where's your man?"

The burly man spat to the side. "I don't need no second."

"Yes, you do," the judge said, unimpressed and visibly annoyed. "There's a procedure for how these affairs are conducted, Mr. Harlan. Can you not find a single man to stand up with you right now?"

"I can check my own gun. There's two dozen men can attest I know how to use it well enough."

"If you can't adhere to the common traditions and practices of this ritual, then we'll not proceed further," the judge said sharply.

Fredrick scowled at the Judge, but the old man was unwavering.

"Fine," he relented, and turned toward the crowd. "Who here will stand up with me?"

No one moved.

"You don't need to do a damned thing, 'cept stand and gawk like you're already doin'."

Still, no one heeded his call. Furiously, he scanned the men assembled and waited for a response. When it was clear none would be forthcoming, he marched over to the nearest man, grabbed him by the shirt, and slung him toward the Judge.

"Here's my man," Fredrick said gruffly.

To his shock and horror, the man was Pleasant.

"You're making a mockery of this," the judge said. "This boy doesn't want to be your second."

"I truly do not," Pleasant confirmed, his heart racing.

"Just do it so we can get on with it!" a voice cried out from the crowd. It was echoed by several others.

"I'm not going to make this boy stand with Mr. Harlan if he doesn't want to," the judge said resolutely.

"Give us a moment, Judge. Let me talk to the boy," Mr. Pike said.

He and Pleasant took a few steps off to the side.

"Do you want this duel to happen?" Mr. Pike asked in a hushed tone.

"No, I don't," Pleasant emphatically responded.

"Good. Then you are just the man we need standing second to Mr. Harlan. Part of a second's job is to convince the principal to reach an accord with his opponent without coming to blows."

Pleasant was unsure. "He's not going to take counsel from me. I'm nobody."

Mr. Pike didn't seem to hear him. "We just need a level-headed person whispering mercy in his ear. You can do that as well as anyone else."

Pleasant was nearly frantic. "I know Mr. Nelson's daughter. She's my friend. What would she think if she heard I stood up against her father?"

Mr. Pike cocked his head to the side. "What would she think if she heard you had a chance to try to persuade him not to fight, and you didn't take it?"

The cries from the crowd were becoming steadier, including a few discernible jeers directed at Pleasant. With a sick feeling in his stomach, he finally agreed.

Mr. Pike looked as though he were about to hand something to Pleasant, but when he realized the boy was acquiescing, he slipped whatever it was back into the pocket of his trousers. They returned to the parley of the duelists.

"I'll do it," Pleasant muttered.

The judge gave him the same skeptical look he gave witnesses on the stand. "You're sure?"

Pleasant nodded.

"Well, let's at least have your name, son?"

"Pleasant Driscoll."

Fredrick stiffened at the name, and his eyes searched Pleasant's face with a curiosity that bordered on amusement. He opened his mouth to say something but hesitated. Instead, he turned and began preparing his pistol. The judge, Mr. Nelson, and Mr. Pike stepped away to conference with one another. Timidly, Pleasant approached the brooding man with whom he'd been conscripted to stand.

"M–Mr. Harlan," he stammered. "Mr. Nelson is a well-meaning man. Is there any way you could just agree not to do this?"

Fredrick didn't reply.

"If you two took a few moments to talk, I'm sure you can reach a more productive solution than this."

Nothing.

"Please, Mr. Harlan..."

Fredrick cocked his pistol and leveled it at Pleasant's head, immediately silencing the boy. The man looked carefully down the barrel for what seemed like an eternity before letting it drop back down to his side.

Pleasant took a deep breath. Time was running out. He knew he had to try to get a dialogue going. "Is there any message you'd like me to pass along to your family if you should be killed?"

This only elicited a caustic laugh. His breath was sour with the smell of whiskey.

"He could...I mean it's possible..." Pleasant sputtered.

Fredrick cut him off. "Tell them I'm ready."

Defeated, Pleasant did as he was told. When he approached the other men, Mr. Pike asked, "Anything?"

Pleasant shook his head. "He won't listen to me. I knew he wouldn't. It was a mistake to send me."

He felt awful, and it must have shown on his face. "Don't worry," Patrick assured him. "I don't hold anything against you, lad."

Though the man tried to put on a confident air, his hands were shaking. One last time, he looked his gun over. It was a beautifully crafted firearm, undoubtedly purchased only to adorn a wall in his study, not for actual use. To Pleasant he looked like a man heading to the gallows, not a field of honor. Solemnly, he crossed himself.

"I'm ready."

From there, things happened very quickly. The crowd went from a fevered murmur to a reverent hush. Many of the men puffed compulsively on their pipes or cigars. The two combatants faced each other then turned back-to-back. Mr. Pike found a place for himself on the front edge of the crowd, and Pleasant followed suit. Judge Letcher approached.

"When I instruct you to begin, you will each take eight paces, turn to face your opponent, and then ready yourselves. Upon my call, you will each fire one round at will. If neither man is hit after the first round, and both of you wish to continue, we will reconvene at this spot and discuss terms for a second round. Do you understand?"

Both men nodded.

"Very good. Let's begin. Gentlemen, please take your paces."

In his entire life, Pleasant had never seen a gun intentionally fired at another human being. It was surreal to think that the men who were standing just a few feet from him were preparing to do just that and that one or both of them could be killed. He hated it but could do nothing but stand by helplessly.

After taking their paces, the men turned. Patrick was breathing rapidly, his brow shimmering with sweat in the lantern light. Fredrick stood as rigid as stone, no indication of fear marring his weathered face. There was an interminable pause.

"Fire when ready!" the judge shouted.

With surprising quickness, Patrick raised his pistol above his head and fired harmlessly up into the night sky. Smoke filled the air and quickly wafted away. It took Pleasant a moment to understand that he was offering Fredrick one last chance at maintaining honor without actual bloodshed. Pleasant hoped desperately the grim-faced man would follow his opponent's lead. As the crowd waited for Fredrick's response, the tension ratcheted even tighter, holding all observers motionless, unable to even draw a breath.

Fredrick, who had raised his pistol almost as quickly as Patrick, lowered it momentarily and glowered hatefully at the other man. A new wave of resolve washed over his face, and he once again took careful aim at his opponent, who could do nothing but stand helplessly before him.

"What are you doing?" Matthew exclaimed, jumping out from the crowd.

"It's my turn," Fredrick snarled without taking his eyes off of Patrick. "I mean to make it count."

"That's bad form," Matthew implored, a few others from the crowd shouting their agreement. "Just fire into the air, and both of you will maintain your honor."

"No." Fredrick's voice lowered. "This debt must be paid in blood."

Matthew looked to the judge. "Are you going to allow this?"

The old man seemed to be at a loss for words. "Each man has one shot to spend however he wishes," he finally said.

"Are you mad?" Matthew cried. "This is an execution!"

Thinking of Anna and the desperation he'd seen on her face, Pleasant summoned all of his courage and rushed forward, placing himself directly in front of Fredrick's pistol.

Murmurs floated through the crowd.

"Out of the way, boy," Fredrick threatened.

"Just fire into the air and we can all go back to the party," Pleasant begged. "Please, Mr. Harlan. I can't let you do this."

"Step aside, or I'll send a slug through your chest."

"You'll do no such thing," the judge interjected. "You shoot an unarmed boy and you'll hang for it tonight, I swear that to God."

Sensing his opportunity slipping away, Fredrick did not wait for further discussion. With his free hand he landed a hammer-like blow to Pleasant's jaw, sending the boy sprawling. He then took careful aim and fired. The slug hit Patrick's chest with a sickening thud. The fat man staggered backward a few steps before losing his footing and falling to the ground in a massive heap. Dr. Dudley calmly stepped forward and attended to the wounded man, but there was nothing he could do. Within a matter of moments, he was dead. Around him, the grass glistened with the dark, wet blood still spilling from his wound.

Matthew and Jeff helped Pleasant to his feet. The painter dusted off his jacket. "That was very foolish, my friend. Brave, but foolish."

Jeff looked shocked. "I didn't know you had it in you, Driscoll. You're a full-fledged hero."

Pleasant glanced over to Mr. Nelson's motionless body. "Some good I did."

Matthew took him tenderly by the shoulders. "You did more than any other man here." But his words were no balm.

Fredrick, after a severe reproach from the judge, sat dourly upon his horse and watched as Mr. Nelson's body was loaded by six men into the back of an oxcart. There was no remorse on his face, but Pleasant thought he detected something else. Was it shame? He turned toward Pleasant, and the two shared a brief, sorrowful glance before he pulled sharply on the reins and spurred his horse into the darkness. He could never return to Lexington. Judge Letcher had made that perfectly clear.

As the crowd dispersed, the world seemed a blur. In the shadows, away from all the rest, he saw the money kings congregating and surreptitiously exchanging something from hand to hand. Was it money? It was with sick disbelief that Pleasant realized they had been betting on the outcome.

For the rest of the night, he was in a daze. Ladies doted on him for his courage, and men congratulated him for doing the honorable thing, but he couldn't escape the image of Patrick Nelson's frightened face as life slipped away. Incredibly, the party continued as joyously as before. The band roared, chilled Champagne was served, and gales of laughter periodically arose from some lark or anecdote. Pleasant was thankful that his jaw was throbbing from the blow he was dealt by Fredrick Harlan — the pain was the only thing tethering him to a reality he could understand.

The warmth he'd felt earlier in the night suddenly became stifling. All the wonder and excitement had been violently smothered, and his stomach was roiling. When he finally got a moment to himself, he slipped away to get a breath of fresh air. That's when he discovered Anna, sitting on the ground and leaning against a tree stump near the edge of the woods. She stared out blankly at the party still raging below. Wordlessly, he sat down beside her. Together they remained in a numb silence for several heavy minutes, his gaze fixed upon a hanging lantern that had burned out.

"I heard what you did," Anna finally uttered, strained and raspy. "Thank you."

Pleasant was reluctant to answer, not knowing exactly what to say. "Your father was very brave," he replied. "He was the better man."

Anna closed her eyes tightly as fresh tears rushed forth, her face contorted in unbearable pain. To Pleasant, she looked more beautiful than ever. Through the intensity of her pain, he could sense her true sweetness and the depth of the love she bore her father. Undoubtedly, this capacity for emotion was a double-edged sword. Bitterly, helplessly, he watched her languish, wishing he could take some of the burden from her. If it were within his power, he would heal all of her hurt and never let her feel pain like that again. For the moment, however, all he could do was sit near her and gently squeeze her hand.

She laid her head on his shoulder.

"It's all so ugly," she whispered, gazing hatefully upon the party.

After all that had happened, Pleasant could not disagree.

# Chapter 11

As the great red fog clouding his eyes finally dissipated, the world around Charles Bascom returned to focus. He found himself hovering over a grotesquely mutilated body, an old man this time, his face nothing but pulp, his skull ajar and empty. Charles was on his hands and knees, nearly paralyzed. With great effort, he managed to roll himself away from the corpse and onto his back. Getting to his feet was hopeless, but he could still move his head from side to side. The little village was quietly smoldering around him. A number of bodies littered the ground. It was oddly calm, the throbbing stillness that followed the chaos of battle. A rooster, oblivious to the carnage around it, boldly heralded the rising sun with a self-assured crow. After two weeks of starvation, Charles had finally gorged. He was both regretful and relieved.

He had no memory of leaving his tiny pit or how he'd come to the village. The last thought he could recall was gnashing fruitlessly against the reed barrier and the stone walls of his cell, calling out to his captors, who had seemingly disappeared. Since being force-fed the diviner's sage that healed him and regrew his hand, hunger was no longer a feeling he got in the pit of his stomach like an ache or grumble. Hunger was desperation — it felt like drowning, like uncontrolled rage. When hunger was present, it was his first and only priority. The feeling got stronger and stronger, until he eventually lost complete control of himself. Only after feeding did his self-awareness return. He knew he needed to try to get up, to escape, but his body would not cooperate. It was still pulsing euphorically. His tongue, like the rest of his body, was totally impervious to feeling, but it could still taste, and the taste lingering in his mouth was succulent.

For half an hour he lay there, helplessly but serenely taking in the sights around him. He looked down at his tattered uniform. It was saturated with blood and gore. The jaguar warriors were present in great numbers, maybe even thirty of them. They were busy flushing the villagers from their hiding places and herding them to the plaza in the center of the village. A mother and two young children passed by. A long gash marred the woman's worried face, and she clutched her fearful children tightly by their little hands. They stepped around him cautiously, eyeing him as though he were a viper that could strike at any moment. They wouldn't be nearly as afraid if they knew he was totally defenseless, unable even to raise his arms.

Not far away, a group of old men, perhaps village elders, cowered before two jaguar warriors. The men appeared to be pleading with the warriors, but their pleas were falling on deaf ears; the warriors just gazed on with cold, dead eyes.

Just as the euphoria began wearing off and his arms and legs once again responded to his mental impulses, one of the jaguar warriors bound his hands and feet. He also pulled loose a previously unnoticed machete that had been lodged deep into Charles's clavicle. He looked at it with indifference; he felt nothing. The warrior pulled him up to his feet and guided him over to where his fellow prisoners were shackled, including the other Americans. They looked dazed but healthy. Finney's eyes were back, and Josiah showed no sign of the sickness that had threatened his life during their initial forced march. Soñador was there too but appeared despondent.

They all knew what came next; they saw it last time. When all of the stragglers finally made their way to the gathering at the center of the village, one of the warriors held up ten fingers and shouted something in a language Charles didn't understand. No one moved. Again, the warrior shouted at the crowd. There was a low murmur as a little old woman pushed her way forward and emerged from the others. The warrior left nine fingers in the air. Two more elderly villagers came forward, but after that, no one else.

Some were nudging the elders who'd been pleading with the warriors, but they fearfully held their ground.

*They're not going to like this next part*, Charles thought.

Swiftly, seven of the warriors pushed violently into the crowd, each emerging with a villager in tow, all men. Wives, mothers, and children wailed in protest, trying desperately to pull the men away from the warriors. Their efforts earned them vicious beatings.

One of the women could not be calmed. She was middle-aged and rail-thin, less than ninety pounds if Charles had to guess, but absolutely hysterical for the return of a young man, most likely her son. The warriors savagely beat her with the blunt ends of their weapons, but she would not stop her charge. Some of the other villagers tried to hold her back, but they too could not stand up to the ferocity of the little woman's determination. She threw herself at the closest warrior and splashed him in the face with liquid from a glass bottle she produced from a hiding spot in her linen dress. Surprisingly, the warrior recoiled at the action. He grabbed the bottle from the woman and smashed it on the ground, then separated the woman's head from her body using an antique-looking sword.

Another warrior picked up the head by the hair and stuffed it into a sack he then slung over his shoulder. Utterly defeated and docile, the villagers could only cry bitter, hateful tears as the hostages were shackled together in two groups of five, just like Charles and the other blood-covered soldiers.

The walk back to the ancient city was nothing like the first march. Charles wasn't hungry or thirsty, nor was he tired or feeling any kind of pain. Even the mosquitoes, Mexico's most consistent pestilence, wouldn't bite him — not that he would be able to feel it if they did. He was still numb all over. The only things plaguing him were the terrible images that kept popping into his mind. He saw people running from him, fighting against him, striking him with weapons, and then he saw the pain on their faces as they were torn apart. Nothing was very clear, just passing flashes. After a while, like half-remembered dreams, they were all gone. He was thankful for that.

Charles counted twelve other captive soldiers, three fewer than last time. He wondered if the others were still in their cells or if the warriors had somehow gotten rid of them. They kept quiet as they marched. Unlike after they were first captured, the warriors kept a very close eye on them. *We're more dangerous now*, Charles thought. Talking was not allowed, and anyone who disobeyed would lose their tongues. It wasn't a terribly frightening prospect, since they could no longer feel pain, but it would certainly curtail communication, which could prove to be important before everything was said and done. It was a wonder the warriors didn't just cut out their tongues out of hand. As captors and conquerors, they were very clever.

After only a half-day's march, they reached the ancient city, whereupon the soldier-captives were separated from the new hostages and taken back to their pits. Once again secured in their cell, Soñador and Charles returned to the spots they had claimed across from one another. Soñador's black hair was wild in some places and matted to his scalp in others. His clothes were like shredded rags and covered with brown spatters of dried blood. Still, the man underneath the filth and grime seemed healthier than ever. A thick, dark beard framed his face. If trimmed properly, it might have even lent him an air of sophistication. Charles wondered about his own appearance after having been in captivity nearly two months, but then, what did it matter?

"I see your ear grew back," Charles said.

Soñador stroked his hand along the side of his head, momentarily forgetting that he would not be able to feel the touch, just the pressure. "I will have to take your word for it." His voice dripped with contempt, but he looked different, concerned.

Things had not been going well between the two. Since the snake incident, they had tried every conceivable way to kill one another, including a fight that ended in a biting brawl in which Charles lost his little finger and Soñador his left ear. Just as the snake's venom had no effect, neither did anything else they'd tried, leaving the two men in a constant state of paranoia and restless watchfulness.

"They are using us as weapons," Soñador muttered. He did not want to talk to Charles, but something was weighing on him, something he could not keep quiet any longer.

"I know," Charles replied grimly, "but why?"

Soñador thoughtfully ran his fingers through the dirt on the cell floor, a habit he'd been cultivating for weeks. "Some of the villages are defiant. They are refusing to pay homage to the warriors with sacrifices. I heard them talking."

Charles straightened up. "You can understand them?"

"My mother was from a village like the one today."

Soñador looked like he wanted to say something else, but he was having trouble overcoming the distaste of conversing with his enemy.

"Well, spit it out," Charles demanded.

The other man seemed to swallow back bile. "We have to help them," he finally choked.

Charles was confused. "Who? The warriors?"

"No, not the warriors," Soñador spat, exasperated. "The next village."

He closed his eyes tight and grimaced, then shook his head like he was trying to dislodge a sticky memory.

"My God," he continued, furiously pointing to his temple. "We're...eating them. Don't you know that?"

It was a repulsive thought, and it sounded even worse spoken aloud, but there was no way to deny it. Charles had not been conscious during the feeding, and there was no way to know for certain what he had done, but the evidence in the aftermath was clear enough. He'd come to his senses hovering over a dead man's body, his clothes soaked in blood and his stomach full to bursting. Not to mention the cruel images lingering in the shadows of his memory — images of unspeakable deeds. The first village had been more of a haze. Having not regained consciousness until just before they left the devastation behind, he had no way of knowing what role he'd actually played. He feared something horrible had happened, but his fears were unconfirmed until the second village.

"Well, what are we supposed to do?" he wondered aloud. "You know what happens if we try eating other things."

During the first week of starvation, they had attempted to eat the snake that had been ripped to pieces during their first brawl, but it didn't take long for the meat to come shooting into their trousers as totally undigested snake diarrhea. To date, burying the resulting filth under some dirt that collected in one of the corners of their cell had been their only collaborative effort.

"If we don't find something to eat, we will just slip into the red fog again, and that's when we're most dangerous. There's no telling where we'll wake up or who we'll hurt. On the other hand, if we do eat, it means someone else has to die." He sighed. "The only way to keep from doing harm is to kill ourselves."

It was obvious Soñador had already thought of that. "Is it even possible?" he asked sedately.

It was a fair question. The two men had choked, clawed, punched, and even stabbed each other using makeshift weapons, but nothing seemed to cause substantial harm. No matter what damage was done, everything returned to normal after a feeding. Nature had even taken a turn at trying to kill them. One night, a torrential rain fell and flooded their cell. Frantically, they fought to keep their heads above the water, but the cell filled quickly and their cries for help went unheeded. Charles pressed his face into the reeds above him and took one last gulp of air. There was nothing left to do but wait for his lungs to scream in agony, release his breath, and suck in the water that would spell his doom. Only, that moment never came. All night, he floated in the darkness, hearing the steady, resonating thrum of water in his ears but never feeling the need to take another breath. When the sun rose the next morning, the water slowly evaporated and soaked into the soil. Charles and Soñador were wet but no worse for wear.

Still, Charles wasn't convinced of their immortality.

"We haven't tried everything yet," he reminded the other man. "What if I cut your head off? Do you think you would survive that? That your body would sprout a new head or that your head would sprout a new body?"

Soñador bristled at the thought. "Why don't I cut *your* head off and find out?"

Charles didn't want to fight. That was what the warriors wanted. That was why they put him in a cell with his enemy, one they assumed he couldn't even communicate with. They wanted their captives to be distracted from what they should really be focusing on: escaping.

Then something new occurred to him. "Why do the warriors even need us? If they are invulnerable, why show caution at all? Why use us to harass these villages when they could just as easily do it themselves?"

Soñador concluded the thought. "Because they have a weakness, and the villagers know what it is."

They eyed each other warily. The unspoken reality was that whatever the weakness was, they likely had it too. They sat in silence for a time, neither wanting to destroy the tenuous peace they had established. Finally, Charles spoke up.

"So, what is it you want? You want to work together to try to get out of here?"

Soñador raised his head slowly, gave it another long thought, then nodded solemnly.

"Fine," Charles replied, "but you should know I have absolutely no intention of fighting those jaguar bastards if I can help it. You want to try to stop them, good for you. I just want to get out of this godforsaken country."

Soñador looked disappointed but not surprised. "Have you no remorse for the things you've done?"

"No," he responded bluntly. "All of that was out of my control. I wish it hadn't happened, but there's nothing I can do about it now."

The Mexican shook his head disapprovingly, then stared at his own grubby hands. He rubbed his thumbs against the tips of his other fingers, rolling away a thin film of grime. "I wasn't always a killer," he said softly. "Not even a year ago, I was a peaceful man, a farmer."

"So I've heard," Charles replied. He'd heard a lot about Soñador during the weeks his company was cutting through the jungle, hunting the bandit. Outlandish rumors about him, fueled by locals who considered him a hero, were pervasive among the Americans. One popular story was that he had amputated his own leg and fitted himself with a wooden prosthetic so that he would more closely resemble Santa Anna. Another was that he was too big to sit a horse, forcing him to ride an ill-tempered bull named Montaña instead. It was utter nonsense, but that was typical for army gossip. Still, judging from the gruesomeness of the slaughter left in his wake, Charles would have pictured Soñador to be a much harder-looking man than the melancholy figure sitting across from him. His name, which meant "dreamer" in English, seemed more appropriate.

"I had nothing," the Mexican said, his voice low and tinged with emotion, "just some pigs, a bit of dirt, and a good wife. It was nothing; it was worth nothing. But it was everything. Your people took that from me." He glared at Charles with fiery eyes. "They took everything. They twisted me into something hateful and wicked. They planted the seeds of rage and revenge in my heart and sent me down the road that has led me here, sitting in the dirt, covered in the blood of innocent people. There will be no salvation for me now. I have done too much. I will never see my wife again. We will spend eternity apart."

Wretchedly, he looked up through the reeds, his eyes searching in vain for a heaven that he could never touch. "Part of the old me, the good me, is still in here," he said, patting himself on the chest. "I was not a born killer like you."

Charles laughed. "You think I was born a killer?"

"I see it your eyes. You were a killer before this war even started, I bet." He cocked his head to the side. "How many?"

Charles was somewhat taken aback. Though the Mexican was probably just guessing, trying to better understand the character of the man he was going to be in league with, he had struck remarkably close to the target.

"Just once," Charles somberly admitted, "but it was different than the killing I've done here."

Soñador was silent.

"It was in a saloon in New Orleans," Charles continued, inexplicably feeling the need to clarify. "Two men had gotten into a fight. One of the men said that his wife had just given birth to a baby boy, and he bought a round of drinks for the whole bar. The other man was already drunk and had been brooding in a corner by himself all evening. He kept muttering about his own wife, but no one paid him any mind. When the new father patted him on the back and tried to hand him a round of whiskey, the drunk man slapped it out of his hand and put a knife to his throat. There was a madness in his eyes, and I could see he meant to do harm. Without hesitation, I pulled out my pistol and shot him in the temple."

"Did they take you to jail?"

"No," Charles said. "They bought me drinks and said I was a hero."

Soñador shook his head. "Americans glorify killing."

"I took no glory in it," Charles replied defensively. "It was something that had to be done. Turns out the man with the knife was on the run from the law. He was wanted in Kentucky for strangling his wife to death. I don't think anyone misses him."

Soñador gave a caustic snort. "So you will fight to keep innocent Americans from dying, but not innocent Mexicans?"

Charles was growing weary of the debate. "I'm done fighting for other people altogether. Nothing good has ever come of it. That doesn't change the fact that we have a common goal. Now, do you want to work together to get out of here or not?"

Soñador didn't disagree. Charles knew that was the best response he was likely to get. "Good." He reached up and shook the barrier over their heads. "Obviously, we need to get on the other side of this, but more than that, we need food and information. And I know how we can get both."

Soñador was skeptical. "How?"

"All we have to do is lure one of the jaguar warriors away from the others. We get our hands on one of those boys, and we'll have everything we need."

"Impossible," the other man said. "When have you even seen one of them come check on us? Never. We only see them when we wake up from…" He couldn't bring himself to say *eating people,* so he just waved his hand with the flick of his wrist.

Charles just tapped his finger against his chin. "We just need a good opportunity."

# Chapter 12

## 1962

Birdie whistled through the gap in his front teeth. "Got yourself a triple-header, huh?

It was a callous way of describing three funerals in a four-day span, and Violet knew she should probably be offended, but she was beginning to understand that even the business of death could get tedious, and Birdie's characterization seemed to fit the mood. Besides, it was hard to take offense to anything he said. The retired handyman turned hearse driver had an endearing rudeness that came off more affable than crass, especially when he punctuated his banter with a red-cheeked grin. She didn't even mind too much when he sometimes referred to her as his "little cactus blossom."

Normally, Birdie only worked a couple of days a week, enough to pick up a little extra cash to support his poker habit, but this week he was pulling special duty. In addition to driving the hearse, he was also transporting floral arrangements. Somehow, the address for Pendleton's Funeral Home got mixed up with the address of another Lexington funeral home on the obituary page of the *Herald Leader*. As a result, flowers had been going to the wrong places all weekend. Although Violet was proud that Henry trusted her enough to coordinate the mass floral exchange with the other funeral home, the newspaper's gaffe had certainly added to her workload.

"I don't know if I'll have time to breathe this week," Violet told Birdie as she helped him carry some of the recovered flowers from the parking lot to the parlor.

CHAPTER 12

Unlike other local funeral homes, where whole families sometimes took part in the operations, Pendleton's was a small outfit. The house itself was spacious, but with such a small staff and one sanctuary, it could only accommodate one viewing and funeral at a time, making for a tight schedule. It was Monday afternoon, and the visitation for Mrs. Sheryl Caldwell had already begun. Her funeral would be Tuesday morning. As soon as that was done, there would be a quick turnaround to prepare for the visitation of Mr. Andrew Warren on Tuesday afternoon. His funeral would be Wednesday morning. Wednesday afternoon would bring the visitation of Mr. Neil Henderson, followed by his funeral the next morning. It made Violet anxious. Henry's reputation was at stake each time someone stepped foot in the funeral home, and she didn't want to do anything that might embarrass him.

One thing she failed to take into account when she began working for Henry was how difficult it would be to live, eat, and sleep in the same place as she worked. Basically, there was no escape, no clocking out at the end of the day and putting everything aside until tomorrow. There was always work to be done. The only benefit to this obsessive preoccupation with work was that it served to temporarily divert her attention away from the secret room. Night and day it called to her, both frightening and seductive. Just knowing it was there, waiting just down the hall with all of its mysteries, was enough to sustain her. More than anything, it was a welcome distraction for her turbulent mind. Soon, the right opportunity would come along, and she could really delve into what she'd found. There couldn't be any more close calls, though. She was smarter than that, and she had resolved never again to let her impatience overcome her good sense.

As she was walking Birdie back out to his car, they passed Henry's first-floor office. The door was cracked, and she could see him sitting at his desk, leisurely scribbling in some ledger. When he saw her looking in, he managed a tight-lipped smile, which she returned. Smartly dressed and charming, he looked every bit the fastidious mortician, but recently Violet felt like she was peeking under the veil that hid his true personality, and the more she looked, the more unsettled she became.

A few days earlier, she had witnessed him execute a bold deception with such practiced ease, it startled her. It all happened the previous Friday afternoon. The land surveyor appointed by the Fayette Circuit Court as a special commissioner in Henry's lawsuit against Mr. Trimble had shown up to perform his official duties. The parties had agreed the best way to resolve their dispute was to have an unbiased survey of the property line by a disinterested party. The surveyor's report would be taken by the court as definitive evidence on the issue of ownership, barring some objection to the surveyor's methods. It was a winner-take-all situation. Henry and Mr. Trimble, both nervously confident in their claims, came out to watch as the surveyor did his work. Violet did the same. From what Henry told her, the deeds at issue were not contradictory; the neighbors simply disagreed about the location of a certain property marker. If Henry was right, then Mr. Trimble's pool house was about three feet over the line and on Henry's property. If Mr. Trimble was right, then his pool house was safely on his own land.

The anxious hostility between the two neighbors was plain enough. They refused to look at or speak to one another. Anyone with an ounce of perspective would have found the scene comical, two grown men watching a third search for an invisible line along the ground as though life hung in the balance. Mr. Trimble kept watch from his side of the line, pacing back and forth, crossing then uncrossing his arms. Henry sat in a foldout chair he'd gotten out of the first-floor supply closet. Even he appeared restive. The surveyor, by contrast, went about his work as though he were completely alone, not a care in the world. He spat and mumbled to himself and seemed to care very little about the fact that his ill-fitting pants exposed the hairiest half of an ass that Violet had ever seen. She shuddered to think about the lower half.

After toying with a variety of tripods, specially calibrated instruments, clipboards, and notepads, it was finally time for the moment of truth. The surveyor went to the spot where Mr. Trimble claimed the last marker was located, buried just beneath the surface. Alternating between a spade and a long steel pole, the surveyor prodded the area for a quarter of an hour.

When he gave up, the ground was completely aerated and the surveyor sopping wet from sweat, but no marker was found. Mr. Trimble looked concerned. Henry then led the surveyor to the area where he purported the marker was located. The surveyor only had to search for few minutes before he hit something hard with his spade. Carefully, he dug around the object as the parties gathered in close to get a look. When he had exposed the marker and wiped off the excess dirt, Violet nearly gasped. Scrawled in capital letters across the top was a single word: BERWICK.

Mr. Trimble shook his head in disbelief. He was going to lose the case. With his hands on his hips, he turned and looked at the pool house whose fate now rested in Henry's hands.

"It can't be right," he said meekly.

"Oh, it's right," the surveyor replied. "That marker's been sitting there for over a hundred years."

Violet knew that wasn't true. She'd seen it just a few weeks earlier in Henry's secret room. It had to be the same one; it was the same size and shape and everything. He must have dug up the marker from its original location, most likely where Mr. Trimble claimed it was, hid it until the time was right, then secretly reburied it so he would win his lawsuit. He was flat-out stealing from Mr. Trimble.

Violet, though shocked, seized the opportunity to ask one of the questions she'd been harboring since finding the secret room. "What is Berwick?" she asked no one in particular.

The surveyor pointed at the funeral home. "Darlin', that's what they used to call that house over yonder. Berwick House." He then produced a red bandana from his pocket and wiped hard across his forehead.

Violet was disappointed. The Berwick marker held so much promise when she first found it. In truth, she thought it was an old headstone of some sort or that it would lead to some larger mystery. A simple property marker, which had been intentionally misplaced by a greedy mortician in order to commit a blatant property theft, was infinitely less thrilling.

"All right, Pendleton," Mr. Trimble said miserably, "you were right. I'm sorry about the fuss I made. Please, can't we come to some sort of agreement about this?"

Henry was remorseless. "My attorney will be in touch with yours." He folded up his chair and marched victoriously back to the funeral home.

Violet felt sorry for Mr. Trimble. He'd been hoodwinked, and he didn't even know it. She had no idea Henry was willing to stoop so low, all for a tiny sliver of property. She wanted to say something, to reveal what she knew, but thought better of it. It was possible the marker she'd found was different, but it seemed unlikely. Mr. Trimble looked at her with the downcast shame of a rebuked schoolboy. He'd been beaten and humiliated. She forced a sympathetic smile at him and then followed Henry inside.

Before, she'd thought of Henry as a kindly loner, a good-natured soul who enjoyed his work and his solitude. But after finding the secret room and seeing how ruthlessly he swindled Mr. Trimble, now he just seemed creepy and spiteful, maybe even dangerous.

Violet tried to clear all that from her mind. A sizeable crowd had gathered for Mrs. Caldwell's visitation, and she needed to focus on the task at hand. As always, she dressed conservatively in a gray pleated dress with a black satin sash. Her hair was tied back with a thin black ribbon. Like a little mouse, she scurried quietly along the edges of the room, cracking windows for air circulation, adjusting flower arrangements, and inviting guests to visit the lounge area where soda and coffee were available. Henry had taught her how to blend in, how to be unassuming and helpful. He told her never to laugh while in the sanctuary and never to interrupt a conversation. Everything she said should be in a soothing tone slightly below normal conversational level. If someone asked her where something was, she was to personally escort the person, taking care to match the person's pace. Her misgivings about the man aside, he definitely knew his trade.

From one of the cracked windows a wasp floated into the room. At first, it went unnoticed, hovering precariously over the heads of the guests who stood unaware of the danger in their midst. But as it continued circling, erratically bobbing through the crowd, ever lower and closer, some of the mourners tensed up and awkwardly retreated. Wasps frightened Violet. Ever since getting stung as a child by one that had sadistically hidden itself under the door handle of her father's old Chevy, she gave them as wide a berth as possible. Even so, she found them terribly fascinating. The wasp was a true titan of the insect world, striking fear into creatures a million times its own size, all from the threat of a tiny little sting. Menacing, sleek, and confident despite its own frailty, the wasp restlessly patrolled the room.

Wielding a paper fan and all the bravery she could summon, Violet attempted to shepherd the wasp out a nearby window. Like a fingernail tapping on the glass, it bounced off of the window panes a dozen times before finally slipping out into the open air.

Relieved, Violet shut the window behind it. She was glad no one had been stung. Being stung at a funeral seemed like it would be a bad omen. She was about to return to her duties when something outside caught her eye. The door to Henry's greenhouse was wide open. Henry never worked in his greenhouse while there were mourners in the house and certainly would never leave the door open. Quietly, she made her way out of the sanctuary, through the south drawing room, and out the back door into a sticky afternoon heat that immediately made her scalp itch.

Cautiously, she entered the greenhouse and discovered a short man feverishly examining the plants. The greenhouse was Henry's sacred place, his refuge, and the plants inside were his cherished relics. Seeing the stranger roughly manipulate the delicate leaves and blossoms seemed like sacrilege.

"Excuse me, what are you doing?"

The man's head snapped toward Violet. "Oh, hello there. I was just examining the fine specimens you have here."

"I'm sorry, but no one is allowed in here. This is Mr. Pendleton's private greenhouse."

The man searched Violet's face. He smiled and reluctantly released the plant leaf pinched between his fingers.

"Surely, Mr. Pendleton wouldn't begrudge a fellow plant lover the opportunity to admire his garden?"

The man looked familiar to Violet, but she couldn't quite place him. He wore a navy suit and matching hat. In his front pocket was a bright orange handkerchief. His face was clean-shaven, though when he smiled he revealed tobacco-stained teeth.

"Mr. Pendleton is an obliging man, and I'm certain he'd be happy to give you a tour, but until you have his permission, I'm afraid you will need to go."

"Well, all right now, darlin', no need to get yourself worked up about it. I'll skedaddle if that's what you want."

As the man hobbled toward the exit, Violet stepped aside so he could leave. Once outside, Violet closed the greenhouse door behind her.

"Did you just wander in from the street?" Violet asked.

"Oh no," the man replied. "I'm here for the funeral."

"The funeral is not until tomorrow," Violet said suspiciously. "Today is the visitation."

"Right, that's what I meant, the visitation. Tragic loss, I knew the man well."

"Mrs. Caldwell?"

"Uh, yes, Mrs. Caldwell. That is to say, I knew her husband well. She was a sweetheart too."

The man looked over Violet's shoulder. "Looks like you've got a visitor."

Violet turned to find Mr. Trimble standing behind her. At first, she thought he was wearing nothing but his boxer shorts, a thought so shocking, her eyes went comically wide, but she quickly realized the sky-blue and red striped shorts were not his underwear but rather his swimming trunks. The beach towel hung over his shoulder helped clue her in.

"Violet, right?" Mr. Trimble asked.

Violet blinked hard and slightly shook her head to force the lingering shock out of her eyes. "Yes, uh, yes, that's right."

The little man from the greenhouse bowed politely. "Well, I should be getting back to the visitation."

Mr. Trimble watched him totter off before continuing. "This is extremely awkward, and I'm embarrassed to have to ask this, but I could use your help, if you have a moment to spare."

"Well, actually, I'm working right now, there's a visitation..."

"Of course." He nodded apologetically. "Sorry to intrude."

He had the same hangdog look on his face as when he got the bad news about the property marker.

"What's the matter?"

He laughed and scratched the back of his head. "I went for a swim this afternoon, and like an idiot, I locked myself out of the house."

"Oh, did you need to use the phone?"

"No, I couldn't possibly go in looking like this, especially not with so many people inside. Plus, after all the unpleasantness with your boss recently, I'd be too ashamed anyway."

"I can make a call for you, if you like," Violet offered.

"I really appreciate that, but, well…you see there's a little window that goes into my basement and I'm just a little too big to squeeze through, but you, tiny wisp of a thing, would probably slide right in. If you could climb in and unlock the door from the inside, you'd save me the cost of a locksmith. I swear, it wouldn't take two minutes."

Violet glanced back at the funeral home. Barring another wasp attack, the mourners would probably be all right without her help for a couple more minutes. A gracious smile crept across her face. It was the least she could do for the poor guy. "Sure, lead the way."

She followed Mr. Trimble around to the back of his enormous, dark red-brick house. It was much newer than the funeral home, a bit bigger too, though not by much. The yard was very green for early August and finely manicured. A crew came out once a week to keep everything in pristine condition. It probably cost a small fortune to maintain, but Mr. Trimble could certainly afford it. According to Henry, he owned one of the largest tobacco warehouses in the region, in addition to the lumber yard he inherited from his father. It was a little surprising he was going to so much trouble to avoid the cost of a locksmith; for him such an expense would be trivial. But then again, she didn't know his situation. It was possible that he was just as miserly as Henry, or it could just be a pride thing. All Violet knew was that his fashionable swimming trunks and tanned skin made him look like Cary Grant or some other Hollywood star. It was no wonder he was considered Lexington's most eligible bachelor.

"Normally, I have a spare key hidden in the pool house," Mr. Trimble told her, drying his salt-and-pepper hair as he walked, "but I seem to have misplaced it."

He smiled at her over his shoulder. "You probably think I'm a real slugabed, floating around in my pool on a Monday afternoon instead of going to work. It was just so damn hot out, I felt like taking a dip."

"I don't blame you. The pool looks really inviting today. I wish I could go for a swim myself."

"Really? Well, you're welcome to use my pool any time."

Violet looked at him suspiciously.

"I know." He grinned. "Henry and I don't exactly get along, but I want to try to change that. So, you don't have to ask, just come over if you ever feel like swimming. I usually keep beer in the poolhouse fridge too, help yourself."

He chuckled to himself. "At least, while the pool house is still here."

"I'm really sorry how everything has turned out," Violet offered.

Mr. Trimble carelessly flipped his right hand. "Don't worry, it's not your fault. It was mine. I was a jerk about the whole thing. I had it coming."

"I hope you and Mr. Pendleton can still work something out."

Mr. Trimble nodded. "Me too. Well, here it is." He pointed to a narrow opening about two feet wide and ten inches high. The window and the iron grating that normally covered it were propped up against the house. "Thank goodness I found a screwdriver in my shed for the grating. The window just popped right out."

Violet was unsure how to proceed. "How should I…"

"You can probably just slide in feet first," Mr. Trimble offered. "There's an old desk right under the window."

He placed his towel on the ground near the open window and offered Violet his hand. She took it and lowered herself down as gracefully as her dress would allow. She slid forward until her legs were dangling inside the basement. When she couldn't put her feet on the desk, she climbed back out and turned onto her stomach, then scooted in backward, pushing forward with her hands until her waist crossed the threshold and her feet could finally reach the desk.

"The stairs are against the far wall," Mr. Trimble instructed. "Just go straight up and take a left. You can't miss the front foyer. I'll be waiting at the door."

Carefully, Violet climbed down from the desk and squinted into the darkness. The coolness of the basement was a welcome relief from the oppressive summer heat. Rays of light cut sharply through the high, narrow windows, illuminating the dust particles in the air that seemed to hover in place like tiny underwater organisms. Once her eyes adjusted, she smoothed her dress and took a few uncertain steps toward the staircase. The basement was unfinished and smelled a bit dank, but it was pretty clean. Boxes and a few gaudy Christmas decorations were stacked neatly along one of the walls. A large, menacing furnace sat idle along another. For a bachelor, Mr. Trimble seemed to keep things pretty tidy. She was impressed.

The staircase was a simple construction of bare wooden planks. Three quarters of the way up, where they reached the basement ceiling, the stairs were enclosed by a narrow hallway that shielded the upper steps from what little sunlight could filter in. Violet reached out until she touched the walls on both sides, steadying herself as she ascended. When she reached the top, she fumbled around for the doorknob. It was locked. She ran her hands along the edges of the door. There was no way to unlock it from her side.

"Mr. Trimble," she called over her shoulder. "Are you still there?"

No reply.

Figuring he'd already gone to the front door, Violet cautiously descended back into the basement, taking care not to catch one of her heels on a step. With no banister to grasp, any stumble would result in a nasty fall. Just as she suspected, Mr. Trimble was gone when she reached the window. He'd also already reattached the window and the metal grating. Violet cupped her hands to the glass and peered out. No one was in sight.

*He'll come back in a few minutes when I don't open the front door,* she thought.

She looked at her watch. It had already been twenty minutes since she left the sanctuary. If she didn't get back soon, Henry might think she was shirking her duties. She leaned on the edge of the desk and tapped her foot impatiently. A few more minutes passed. The light in the basement dimmed and brightened as clouds passed outside. Getting irritated, Violet started knocking on the window hoping that Mr. Trimble could hear her. When that didn't work, she went back up the stairs and banged on the door to the basement.

*Where is he?*

Another five minutes passed before she finally heard something other than her own steady breathing. It was a window breaking.

*I guess he got tired of waiting for me.* She was sorry about the window, but she was also relieved that she'd be able to leave soon. For some reason, the basement made her feel even more claustrophobic than she had in Henry's secret room.

"Mr. Trimble?" she yelled. "I'm locked in!"

Hard-soled shoes plodded toward the basement door, so she backed up a couple of steps and gazed up expectantly. A shadow appeared at the lower crack of the door, but nothing happened.

"Mr. Trimble?" Violet said, more muted than before. Then she got to thinking. Outside, Mr. Trimble had been barefoot. Whoever was on the other side of the door was wearing dress shoes or boots. The shadow moved away. *Could he have found a pair of shoes before breaking the window? Why won't he open the door? Is someone else in the house?*

Suddenly she felt uneasy and quickly retreated down the stairs into the shadows. Another cloud passed, and the basement grew ominously dark. Something was very wrong. The basement was starting to feel more and more like a web. Just then, a flurry of violent crashes reverberated through the overhead floorboards, raining dust all around her.

"*Dios me salva,*" she whispered.

Frightened, she searched for anything that would either help her get out or protect her from whoever might come in. No doubt she would soon be missed at the funeral home, but Henry would never think to look for her at Mr. Trimble's house, much less in his basement. For the first time, she noticed a pillowcase sitting at the base of the stairs. It was the only thing in the entire basement that looked out of place. From its lumpy shape she could tell there was something inside. When she picked it up, it was surprisingly heavy. Quickly, she took it over to the desk near the window and dumped out the contents under the meager sunlight.

Her jaw dropped. There was money, lots of money, both cash and coins. There was also a small golden clock, some jewelry, and a mess of silverware.

"What the hell..." she whispered.

The lights came on. Stunned, she whirled back toward the staircase. The lock snapped and the door creaked open. From where she stood, Violet could not see who was coming down. She could only see dark shoes and the hem of a light-colored pair of slacks. Slowly, cautiously, the shoes marched down the steps.

"Show yourself," came an unfamiliar voice. It was a man, though the forced bravado of the command suggested youth.

Violet was petrified.

"I know you are down here. Now step out so I can see you."

"What do you want from me?" Violet squeaked.

"I want you to walk slowly toward the staircase with your hands out where I can see them."

The man took another step down the stairs, revealing a revolver clutched between his hands.

A hundred terrible things flooded Violet's mind. She was utterly defenseless. "Please don't hurt me," she sobbed helplessly.

"I'm not going to hurt you," the man replied soothingly. "I'm Lexington P.D."

Relief washed over her like cool water. She rushed toward the foot of the stairs.

Before her stood a man with a stern but kind face. She judged him to be only a few years her senior. His sandy hair was closely cropped, though slightly longer than a military cut. He wore a white button-down dress shirt with sleeves rolled up to his elbows. A badge was clipped onto his brown leather suspenders near the right waist hook. He went rigid at the sight of her. "Easy now."

"Thank God you're here. I've been locked in this basement for a while now. I heard crashes upstairs."

The man kept his revolver trained on Violet's chest.

"What are you doing in here?" he asked.

The gun flustered her.

"My neighbor was swimming…he needed me to open his door. I mean, he locked himself out and he couldn't fit…so he asked me to, and I said yes, but it was locked, the basement door I mean, and I couldn't get back out."

With his left hand, the man reached around his back and produced a pair of handcuffs.

"Ma'am, please put both your hands on the wall there to your right."

"But…I don't understand."

"Ma'am, don't make me tell you again."

Violet obeyed, and the man cautiously slid behind her. He reached up, grabbed her left wrist, and firmly pulled it behind her back, where he cuffed it. He did the same to her right wrist and then performed a quick pat-down with his left hand. Satisfied that she posed no threat, he holstered his gun and turned her around so they were facing one another.

"Why are you doing this?" she whimpered.

The question seemed to surprise him.

"What is your name?"

"Violet Romero. I live next door."

"There's a funeral home next door."

"I know. I work for Henry Pendleton."

"How did you get into this house?"

She knew the answer was going to come out wrong, but she told the truth anyway, "I came in…well, through the window."

"What did you take?"

"What did I take? I didn't take anything. Like I was trying to tell you before, I was helping my neighbor unlock his door. He locked himself out when he was swimming. If you just ask him, he'll tell you. He's around here somewhere."

"What's his name?"

"Mr. Trimble."

"You mean Paul Trimble?"

Violet nodded.

"Ma'am, he's the one who reported the break-in in the first place."

She was confused. "Mr. Trimble called you?"

"What's that over there?" the officer said, pointing toward the desk covered in the contents of the pillowcase.

That's when everything sank in, and Violet felt like she'd been punched in the stomach. A shadow crossed the threshold at the top of the stairs. It was Mr. Trimble. He had changed into a gray business suit.

"Mr. Trimble, there you are! Please, tell him what happened. You were locked out of your house. I was helping you."

Mr. Trimble plodded casually down the steps, scowling as he came. "You certainly have a lot of nerve. You know, I think she may be on drugs, Officer."

"It's Detective, actually," he corrected.

"You've got the wrong person in cuffs," Violet stammered. "This man tricked me into coming into his basement. He locked me in here. I was working a visitation at the funeral home when he asked me to come help."

"Someone at the funeral home saw him come ask you for help?" the detective asked.

"Well, not exactly. I was in the backyard when he approached me, only he was wearing a swimsuit then. Wait, th-there was one person who saw him — a short guy in a navy suit."

Mr. Trimble scoffed. "Detective, this is nonsense. It's Monday afternoon, and I've been at the office all day. My secretary can attest to that. I don't just skip work to go swimming. Like I told you when you first arrived, I came home because I have a meeting scheduled at the stable with the man who trains a couple of my horses." He nodded derisively at Violet. "When I came into the house, I caught this one robbing me blind. I tried to corner her, but she took off down into the basement. I just locked her in and called the police."

"That's not true!" Violet raged. Furious tears welled up in her eyes.

"She's been poking around here all summer," Mr. Trimble continued. "I

157

could tell she was looking for a way to rip me off. She knew exactly when I'd be gone to work and when I'd be home."

"Look at me," Violet demanded of the detective. "Do I look like I'm dressed to break into someone's house?"

Before the detective had time to respond, Mr. Trimble chimed in. "She's clever, I'll give her that. Breaking in during a funeral visitation so if anyone comes and asks, she has an alibi. Lucky I caught her in the act, or she'd have gotten out of here scot free."

The detective turned his back and began sifting through the items on the desk.

"Why are you doing this?" Violet whispered to Mr. Trimble, who had completed his descent into the basement. He leaned so close to her that his mouth almost touched her ear.

"Tell your boss nobody fucks with Paul Trimble."

As he stepped away from her, he brushed his hand across her defenseless chest. With her hands bound behind her back, she could do nothing to retaliate. Her skin crawled with sick revulsion.

The detective turned back toward her with the pillowcase in hand. "You have to admit, this looks pretty bad."

She thought she might throw up. "Are you arresting me?"

"I'm afraid I have no choice."

When they all got up to the first floor, it looked like a war zone. Dishes were broken, pictures and mirrors were thrown from the walls, chairs were toppled over, and papers from Mr. Trimble's desk were scattered all over the floor.

"What a mess." Mr. Trimble sighed as they walked past the overturned furniture and scattered documents. "You're going to pay me back for the damages. I don't care if it takes the rest of your life."

"I'll make a full report of the damages, Mr. Trimble. It would help if you compiled a list of broken or destroyed items."

"Of course, Detective."

The detective turned back to Violet. "You ever been in trouble with the law before?"

"No," she responded sullenly. "Never."

"I don't believe that one bit. I bet she's not even in this country legally. Will you boys look into that too?"

"Sir, you've got quite a chore ahead of you, cleaning up this mess. You should get to it and let me handle the police work. I'll be back in a few minutes to ask you a few more questions for my report."

Outside, a light blue Ford Galaxie with a single flashing light on the driver's side roof was parked in the driveway behind Mr. Trimble's red Corvette convertible. As they descended the front porch steps, a squad car came squealing in from the highway, sirens howling.

"Looks like your ride is here."

He motioned for the officer driving the car to go next door.

"What are you doing?" she asked.

"You told me that someone may have seen Mr. Trimble come ask you for help. We're going to see if your story checks out."

He then took Violet by the elbow and led her across the property line toward the funeral home. Naturally, the commotion had drawn all of the visitation attendees outside, where they bore witness to Violet's utter humiliation.

"Detective," she whispered. "Can you please take these handcuffs off me?"

He shook his head. "I'm sorry, this is standard procedure. It's for your safety and mine."

Henry, as composed as ever, ran his hand through his dark hair and straightened his tie as he approached Violet and the detective.

"What's this about?" he demanded.

"Are you Henry Pendleton?"

"Yes."

"Do you know this girl?"

"Yes. She works for me."

"Mr. Pendleton, I just found her in your neighbor's basement with a pillow case full of valuables. It looks like she was stealing."

"It's not true…" Violet began.

"Don't talk," Henry sternly commanded.

He glanced at the policeman's badge.

"Detective..."

"Arnold Webster," the detective finished.

"Detective Webster, you are mistaken. This girl is incapable of doing something like that."

"So you say, but she was caught red-handed."

"There he is!" Violet exclaimed. "That man, over there in the navy suit. Oh, thank God he's still here. He can vouch for my story."

Detective Webster squinted at the gathered crowd until he spotted the man to whom Violet was referring and beckoned him over with two quick curls of his pointer finger. The man seemed surprised. He pointed at himself. "Me?"

"Yes, you," the detective said impatiently.

The little man wobbled over.

"Sir, did you speak with this young lady earlier this afternoon?"

The man nodded. "I surely did. We spoke out back in the greenhouse."

Henry cut a curious glance at the man.

"What is it you talked about?"

"I was admiring the plants in the greenhouse, and she came to tell me I was out of bounds, so to speak."

"What happened then?"

"I went back inside to pay my respects to Mrs. Caldwell."

"Did you see a man approach this young lady before you went back inside?"

"A man?"

"Yes," Violet barked. "You remember, he was wearing swimming trunks."

The little man looked confused. "No, can't say that I did."

"You're certain?" the detective asked.

"I think I would recall something like that."

Violet was flabbergasted, "Why are you lying?"

"That'll be all," the detective said. "Thanks for your cooperation."

The little man flashed a yellow grin. That was when it finally occurred to Violet where she had seen him before. He was in the cemetery a few weeks earlier, the day she tried to kill herself. A clean shave and new clothes had nearly transformed him into a new man; he'd even ditched his cane, but there was no way to disguise those yellow teeth. Rhodes was his name. He'd told her that he had a sick aunt, and he'd come up from Atlanta to make preparations for her. Why was he lying for Mr. Trimble?

She turned to Henry. "It's not true. Don't believe them."

"Be quiet," he responded tersely.

"Please, I swear, it's not how they say it is. He's lying…"

Anger flashed across Henry's face, contorting his smooth features.

"Violet, shut up. Don't say another word."

He stood with his hands on his hips, thinking, seething.

"I'll call Brian."

# Chapter 13

**1845**

It was an hour until dawn, and the posse was getting restless. They had been coaxed from their beds by the promise of imminent violence, and if Sheriff Carr did not send them on their way soon, they would fulfill that promise one way or another. Many of the men were just as likely to kill each other in a barroom scrap as they were the man they'd been called to find. The sheriff motioned for them to gather around, but many were too undisciplined or too groggy to heed his call, so he let loose a high, cutting whistle so piercing, it caused a few of the raucous men to flinch.

"Listen up, boys, this is how it is," the sheriff bellowed. "Pleasant Driscoll is a fugitive of the law."

Out of the corner of his eye he saw a woman standing on the fringe of the crowd, her face awash in the orange light of a lantern. It was the last face he wanted to see. She was severe, beautiful but severe.

"I hereby deputize each and every one of you men for the limited purpose of bringing Mr. Driscoll back to Lexington. By my reckoning, he's heading north to Cincinnati. He's got people up there, business associates and such. If he beats the news, they will have no reason not to help him."

It was hard to keep his train of thought. Sheriff Carr tried to imagine what was going through the woman's mind as she watched him speak. Her face would never betray her true feelings. The sheriff glanced at his watch.

"You've got an hour before dawn, and he's got a good head start. He hasn't yet slept, so look for him to bed down somewhere north of Georgetown."

"What's the bounty on this feller?" one man cried out above the rest.

"Twenty-five dollars," Sheriff Carr replied. "That's from the city of Lexington." He checked his own pockets. "I'll put in another four bucks myself."

"That's dead or alive, mind ya," added Jacob Bell, the night watchman who had first gotten the sheriff earlier that night.

"Ain't you coming with us?" another man called to the sheriff.

"Chasing fugitives is a young man's game," Sheriff Carr replied. "I'd fall to pieces in the saddle."

"Sheriff, I figured you'd want to be the one to put a bullet in this bastard."

The sheriff clutched his gun belt with both hands. "You boys are the bullet, I'm pulling the trigger right now."

Laughs and a few cheers erupted.

"Get outta here, you sons of bitches, and don't come back without Pleasant Driscoll."

Unable to contain their enthusiasm any longer, the posse tore out into the darkness, their torches blazing, a chorus of wild shouts following the stampeding herd.

"You reckon they'll find him, sheriff?" Mrs. Cullen asked. She had been sent from Anna's room upon the arrival of the coroner. She looked more miserable by the minute.

Jacob laughed. "Those idiots couldn't find their own peckers if they were wrapped in hunnert-dollar bills and set on fire."

Sourly, Sheriff Carr lumbered down from the porch toward his mount. Obstructing his path was the woman, the one he didn't want to see, probably the only woman in Lexington who didn't want the posse to catch up to Pleasant: his mother. Outwardly, a person would be hard-pressed to guess that she was suffering. Her face was placid, almost serene. But Sheriff Carr knew better. Her whole life had been dedicated to Pleasant. Both his most ferocious advocate and his harshest critic, she'd hitched her wagon to his star, indelibly linking herself to his fate, and now she would be consumed in his descent through the atmosphere. Sheriff Carr thought about passing her by. There was a time when he could have been so cruel, but not anymore.

He no longer had the whiskey to drown the memory of his cold deeds. Besides, the sheer gravitational force of her indomitable will brought him to a dead stop when he reached her side. Unable to face her directly, the two stood next to one another, stock still, staring out into opposite directions.

She had known him back in the old days, and she probably thought he was the same man. Maybe he was, but he didn't feel like it. He didn't know what she wanted from him, and he'd never been good with words. At times that was a humiliating curse, but at the moment it seemed right.

The woman's right hand crept up from underneath her woolen shawl. Unsteady and shaking, she clasped Sheriff Carr by his arm. Finally, they looked into each other's faces as they had not done in many years. There was still strength in her grip and defiance in her eyes, even though her world was wrought with destruction. Her request was clear. She wanted mercy for her child. Gradually, her grip loosened until her hand fell away completely. Sheriff Carr gave her a solemn nod. He didn't know what else to do. She read his face intently, and then her gravitational pull dissolved and he was able to walk away.

Weary down to his bones, Sheriff Carr mounted his horse and began the ride home. His army days were long gone, but the forced marches that he had endured in the endless summer swamps and bayous were still alive in his memory. This felt strangely similar, except that he no longer had the resiliency of youth. On his left, dawn was breaking imperceptibly slow. It was like waiting for water to boil. If he kept his eyes on it, it would never happen. Dark purple gave way to crimson and then to bright orange.

Harvest was nearly complete, and the tobacco patches were vacant except for the dotted rows of stumps where the burley once stood.

*God, I could use a drink,* he thought.

The pain in his shoulder was starting to creep across his chest. Like a dog retreating to its favorite spot under the porch when hurt, he longed for his cushioned armchair. The road forked ahead of him. The path on the right would lead him home, to breakfast, to coffee, to rest. The left path would lead him to that other place. For reasons he couldn't explain, he froze.

There was no sense in dallying. He'd never ignored his intuition before, and he wasn't about to start. He tugged left on the reins and spurred his horse forward. At first the gelding took an easy pace, trotting briskly along the dirt trail, but as curtains of sunlight began descending among the trees, the sheriff felt like pushing. The trot turned into a hurried canter, then to an all-out gallop. Riding hard, the morning mist and fog swirled in his horse's wake, and the wind pushed against the sheriff's leathery face, making him feel like the wrinkles were being pushed smooth, like he was going back in time, becoming younger. It felt like hell was chasing him, grasping out. And so he tore down the path. But there was no real escape. When he slowed back down to a trot, his joints screamed in pain. Out of breath, he touched his face. The wrinkles were still there. He was still an old man.

The gaping entrance to Russell Cave stood before him, rising seamlessly from the earth like a fold in a crumpled blanket. Sheriff Carr dismounted and led his horse down to the edge of the creek that lazily flowed from within the cavern. He took off his hat and rubbed his sleeve along his forehead to sop up his perspiration. It was a cool morning, but the ride had worked him up. He looped his horse's reins around a low-hanging branch and hobbled along the creek toward the mouth of the cave.

Time slowed. He saw things with a clarity he thought had abandoned him long ago. The sky was turning to a cruel, eternal blue. The dew on the high grass soaked through his trousers just above the top of his boots and trickled down his calf.

A rustling from the overgrown woods across the creek disrupted his wondering thoughts like the crack of a whip. Instinctively, he drew his pistol and took a knee, rapidly surveying the scene before him. Through the foliage, he caught a glimpse of a large, dark figure. He craned his neck forward until he realized he was looking at a saddled but riderless horse. His heart fell. He'd seen the horse too many times to mistake it as anything other than Pleasant's. The fool hadn't gotten out of Lexington after all.

With a grunt, he pushed himself back up to his feet and splashed across the creek. He took the nervous horse by the bridle and led it over to where his own mount was resting. After securing it to the low branch, he scanned for any sign of the missing rider. Nothing. A buzzard circling overhead in the distance gave him a moment's pause, but he decided that was nothing. If Pleasant had killed himself, the buzzards wouldn't have found him this quickly. No, Pleasant had come to this place for a reason. It was sacred to him.

At the cave's opening, the cool autumn air turned frigid. The sheriff had no desire to get wet, but he no longer had the balance or the leg strength to bound from stone to stone. Instead, he slogged through the knee-deep water as best he could, trying not to raise any more noise than was absolutely necessary. Desperate men are unpredictable. He needed to find Pleasant before Pleasant found him. The ceiling was high enough that the morning sunlight could reach a fair distance into the cave, but the sheriff knew he wouldn't be able to go on much longer without a lantern or torch.

As he approached the threshold of sheer darkness, he spied a flicker of light emanating from the narrow opening to a small side chamber. Bracing himself for what he might find, the sheriff lowered his head and ducked silently inside. Sitting next to a lantern on the muddy cavern floor, soaking wet and shivering, his knees tucked up against his chest, was the shell of the man Sheriff Carr once knew.

"On your feet," he commanded.

Pleasant weakly lifted his head, his eyes swollen.

"I said get up," he barked.

Pleasant awkwardly pushed himself to his knees, ripped off his waistcoat, and scooted toward to the sheriff. With full resignation of his fate, he reached out and grabbed Sheriff Carr's gun, pressing the barrel to his chest.

"End this misery," he pleaded. "I cannot bear it another minute."

In that instant, Sheriff Carr felt a strong sense of déjà vu. He jerked his pistol away from Pleasant, nearly losing his balance. When he found his footing again, he put his pistol safely back into its holster and then furiously attempted to jerk Pleasant to his feet, but the other man went limp, and Sheriff Carr only succeeded in stumbling to the ground himself.

He grappled with Pleasant for a few more moments, but his strength quickly gave out, and the two men ended up sitting next to one another on the muddy ground, both struggling for breath.

"Tell me it wasn't you," Sheriff Carr demanded when he'd recovered enough to speak.

When Pleasant refused to answer, the sheriff grabbed him by the scruff of the neck. Pleasant tried to wriggle free, but Sheriff Carr would not relinquish his grasp.

"Tell me you didn't do that to Anna," he repeated, his voice shaking. "It doesn't look good, but if you say it wasn't you, I'll believe it."

"It was me. I did it."

Sheriff Carr let go. "No, you're lying. Why are you lying?"

Pleasant's face contorted with pain, and he pounded his forehead with his fists.

"Pleasant, why?"

He shook his head. "I put it all on her. I couldn't admit to my own failings, and I blamed her."

"What did you blame her for?"

"For the rose bushes," Pleasant said, with a caustic laugh. "She trusted him as a friend, and the jealous bastard tricked her with the damned rose bushes."

"Who?"

"Who?" Pleasant echoed, dazed.

"Pleasant who gave Anna rose bushes?"

Pleasant sobered. "The devil."

"I don't understand."

"Do you think God is just?" Pleasant blurted.

The sheriff realized Pleasant wasn't in his right mind. He took off his hat and looked up at the ceiling of the cave. "Men like us better hope he ain't."

Pleasant's eyes looked like black reflecting pools in the lantern light. He panted deeply through his mouth. "Why even take me in?" he asked. "Save everyone the trouble and just put me down right now. I want to be here. I want to be bone and dust and stone."

Sheriff Carr spat. "I ain't taking you in."

Pleasant turned toward the sheriff, but the other man did not meet his gaze.

"The posse has gone north. They think you are heading to Cincinnati and then northwest. You need to go east into the mountains, then south."

"I don't understand."

"I made a promise to your momma a long time ago. Gonna keep it or die trying."

Pleasant shook his head. "I'm not running from this."

"You don't have a say in the matter. You stay here and you'll be strung up before sundown."

"So be it."

"No, not so be it, you selfish bastard. Your momma sees that and you've as good as killed her too."

Pleasant grabbed the sheriff's arm with a frenzied grip. "The pain I carry is unbearable."

The sheriff shook him off. "And yet it shall be borne. I ain't your judge, and I ain't gonna be your executioner. You have to live with what you done. Your torment is your punishment. You want to see true justice? Well, this is it."

He could see Pleasant hardening against the advice. His thoughts were transparent.

"You kill yourself and you'll be damned forever."

The words landed like fiery coals on Pleasant's head. He pulled so hard at his dark hair that tufts came out in his hands.

"This is a big country, Pleasant. A man can get lost out in the fringes and change himself in the process. All he needs is time."

The soothing sound of flowing water permeated the chamber.

"Where would I go?" he asked bitterly.

"Texas. Kansas. Hell, go to New Orleans, that's where I went when I was figuring things out."

The sheriff struggled to his feet and helped Pleasant do the same.

"You've got a second chance, son. Been a lot better men than you or me who deserved one but didn't get it. You squander it, you'll have hell to pay. I guarantee that."

Sheriff Carr had an urge to embrace the man, but he didn't.

"You know how to stay out of sight during the day?"

Warily, Pleasant nodded.

"Then go on. I can't risk being seen with you. Your horse is hitched next to mine by the creek."

Pleasant sobered himself and looked at the sheriff with suspicion. "This is more than a promise to my momma, isn't it? This feels like atonement."

The sheriff chewed on his lip. "I failed you, boy. I should have been there for you, but I was too broken myself. You know I loved Anna too. She lived with a broke heart more than half her life, and I'm the one who done it."

The old sheriff felt twenty years worth of shame thumping in his aching chest. "I tried to come back and make amends. God knows I did. But I didn't do it right. I wish I'd done it right."

"What do you mean?" Pleasant asked.

The sheriff drew a heavy breath. "I've kept this secret for too long." He wiped his mouth nervously on his sleeve. "Look at me, Pleasant. Don't you know this face? I had longer hair then, and a beard. Imagine me younger, with hate in every word I uttered."

Pleasant searched the older man's face in the flickering lantern light.

"It was me, Pleasant. You were there when I done it. You tried to stop it, but damned fool that I am, I done it all the same. I was the one that killed Anna's daddy."

Pleasant shook his head in disbelief. It appeared he wanted to refute the sheriff, but he was simply unable to formulate any speech. The truth of what the old man said shook him to the bone and jarred him back to lucidity.

"Did you hear me?" the sheriff screamed. "It was me that done it!"

Pleasant let out a guttural cry and struck the sheriff in the jaw, sending a jolt of pain through his head that made his vision go black and red. Still, it somehow eased the sheriff's internal torment. He gathered himself and grabbed Pleasant by the shirt with both hands.

"It was me!" he cried again. "I wounded that poor girl in a way she just couldn't mend. I done it, and I wish to God I could change it. I'd give anything to change it. I've been crushed under it."

Pleasant tried to break free of the sheriff's grasp, but his hands were like iron.

"You ain't the first man that done something unforgivable," the sheriff barked. "Eat the pain, Pleasant. You eat every goddamned bite. That is your punishment, boy. Now get the hell out of here."

Pleasant was temporarily paralyzed by the sheriff's revelation. He ambled backward slowly in disbelief for several steps before turning toward the chamber's narrow entrance and stepping through, pausing only long enough to take one last look at the old man.

After he had gone, the sheriff plopped back down in the mud and rested for another half hour. He knew he needed to get going, but he was too weary to stand, and he suspected he'd never be able to do so again. It was a strange feeling to have finally admitted his secret to Pleasant. At least one of them. It put him strangely at peace.

He searched his coat for his tobacco pouch but then remembered that he'd left it at home. Instead, he found the literary journal Mr. Clinton had made such a fuss about. He didn't even remember picking it up. Absentmindedly, he flipped through the pages. Twenty minutes later, he was dead.

# Chapter 14

**February 11, 1846**

*Lexington Observer and Reporter p. 3, col. 3*

*Missing Fayette County Sheriff Found Dead – Murder Suspected!*

*More than five months after the horse of Fayette County Sheriff Joseph Carr was found wandering alone on the streets of Lexington, the remains of Carr himself have finally been discovered. The mystery surrounding the disappearance of Carr has been the fodder of much talk and speculation in Lexington since last fall, and now county officials say they have reason to believe he was heinously murdered.*

*On Tuesday morning, about day-light, Mr. Thomas Hardin, the new owner of the sprawling estate surrounding Russell Cave, was exploring his property with his brother when he discovered a tattered jacket bearing Carr's badge caught in the weeds near the mouth of the aforementioned cave. Upon inspecting the small chambers within, the two gentlemen happened upon a most grisly scene. The corrupted remains of the late sheriff lay torn apart by scavenging animals upon the floor of the chamber. The sheriff was identified by the coroner based upon the clothes and pistol remaining on his person.*

*Scrawled upon the chamber wall at the point of a knife was the number 29. Investigators believe this number was a reference to the bounty placed on the fugitive Pleasant Driscoll's head by Carr just hours before the latter went missing. The number was likely a message from Sheriff Carr meant to reach from beyond the grave to identify his murderer. The now infamous Driscoll, former pride of the community, fled Lexington last September after a servant witnessed him viciously murder his wife, Anna Driscoll, by strangulation. Also found within the cave was Driscoll's waistcoat, indicating his presence with the sheriff before his demise. The timing of Carr's disappearance in light of his heated pursuit of Driscoll led many to believe the latter had a hand in the death of the good sheriff, even before he was found. The incriminating inscription on the cave wall and waistcoat removed all doubt.*

*Despite this gruesome and terrible discovery, Lexington citizens have no reason to fear for their safety. As was recently reported by this newspaper, officials in the state of Louisiana have confirmed that Driscoll was killed in a New Orleans saloon three weeks ago. Lexington citizens agree that Driscoll's ignominious demise was far too easy a punishment for the inhuman wretch.*

*A special election will be held in one month's time to officially fill the office vacated by Carr. Deputy Sheriff David Hickman, who has been the acting sheriff since Carr's disappearance, is the only man who has yet announced his candidacy.*

*Funeral services for Carr will be held Friday morning at 10:00 at the First Presbyterian Church. Following the services, he will be laid to rest in Lexington Cemetery.*

# Chapter 15

**1962**

Not even the refreshing brace of a late summer breeze could curb Violet's fury upon being released from the Fayette County Detention Center. She sizzled in the passenger seat of Brian's car. The whole ordeal had been an unmitigated hell, right down to the last minute of her incarceration, when the smug and vilely obese secretary in charge of processing releases was more preoccupied with pushing back her cuticles than doing her job. When Violet turned to Brian and referred to the woman as a "bitch heifer," she meant for it to be a whisper. It wasn't. She hoped the woman didn't hear her. She did. Her paperwork was misplaced for a full two hours. Violet was almost delirious with rage.

Brian was unusually quiet as he drove. He seemed troubled. Violet had come to see him in a new light since he took on her representation. His surliness had somewhat diminished, at least with regard to her, and he seemed to project genuine concern for what had happened. When he first visited Violet at the Detention Center, she had been despondent. Never having been in trouble in her life, she found it unsettling to be treated like a criminal.

"I didn't do it," she told him, her lip quivering.

He took her hand and squeezed it with genuine consolation. "I know, and I'm going to help you."

She believed him. He visited her every day, inquiring about her treatment and explaining what steps he was taking to try to secure her release. Waiting for him in the visitor's room was the most hopeful part of her day. Trudging back to her cell afterward was the most disheartening.

The days passed with a sluggishness that bordered on complete stasis. Imagining two more years in lockup, which was what the police interrogator told she was looking at if she didn't cooperate, frightened her very much. But just when she started coming to terms with her likely conviction, the charges against her were suddenly dropped and she got word that her release was imminent. She received the news with both relief and apprehension. Until she got out, she worried that something could happen or that the powers that be would change their minds. So when Brian asked her if she'd like a change of clothes for her release, she got angry at him for jinxing things, but the thought of putting on something of her own, something other than her oversized prison smock, was just too appealing. It was either that or do the unthinkable and wear the dress she had on when she got arrested. She was far too superstitious even to consider it. In all of the anxious excitement, Violet had been too distracted to give Brian any further instruction on the matter and, of course, he brought her the ugliest dress from her closet, the one in which she hid the duplicate key to Henry's secret room. But he also brought a matching pair of shoes, a ribbon for her hair, and a necklace he thought she might want. The outfit he'd put together was not ideal, but there was a certain thoughtfulness to it that was kind of sweet.

"Is it true that the charges against me were dropped because Mr. Pendleton agreed to dismiss his lawsuit against Mr. Trimble?" Violet asked when they stopped at a traffic light.

"I'm afraid so." Brian sighed. "I wish I could take credit for you getting you out of there, but there was just nothing I could do. Trimble had you dead to rights."

"So that was Trimble's plan all along, bait me into his house, accuse me of theft, and ruin my reputation, all just to get leverage over Henry? All because of a few feet of property?"

Brian offered a consoling smile. "That seems to be the long and short of it."

He switched on the radio to fill the heavy silence that followed, but Violet switched it back off.

"Someone needs to arrest that asshole. He kidnapped me. Maybe I want to press charges against *him*."

"False imprisoned."

"What?"

"Technically, it would have been false imprisonment. What he did to you."

"Whatever."

Violet sulked, but as the miles passed she could feel her spirits begin to lift, at least a little. She looked forward to having a private shower and a decent meal. The prison slop, almost all of it from a can, had played havoc on her digestion and kept her in a constant state of abdominal discomfort. In order to start the cleansing process, she fasted for the twenty-four hours prior to her release. Her hunger only added to her overall crankiness. For some reason, she also dreamed about curling up in bed with a hot cup of tea. She'd never had tea in bed in her life, but that was the safest, most desirable thing she could imagine during the long, lonely nights on her hard bunk.

There was no doubt that she was not cut out for prison life. The other women she saw at the detention center had been a much harder breed. Their eyes were dim as they peered out of their cells, staring dismally at the miserable years spread out before them. Violet just did her best to disappear. She wasn't supposed to be there, after all. It was like she had accidentally fallen into an exhibit at the zoo. It was all a horrible mistake, and she knew she'd eventually be discovered and rescued, but it was important not to get eaten by the lions before help could come.

Brian nervously tapped his hands on the steering wheel as he pulled into the funeral home's parking lot.

"I think I should go in with you," he said, putting the car in park.

"Why?"

"I'm concerned about Henry. He's not acting right."

"How so?"

"This is going to sound stupid, and it's not like I care or anything, I'm just saying it was really, you know, weird."

"What?"

"Well…he yelled at me yesterday."

"He yelled at you? For what?"

"Does it matter? This is Henry we're talking about."

The two sat in silence as Violet considered this.

"Okay. Yeah, you'd better come in."

She was glad he did. The house was wrecked. Chairs were overturned, papers were strewn all over the floor, and several of the floral prints had been pulled from the walls.

"Oh my God!" Violet gasped.

"Shh," Brian whispered, "listen."

Faintly, there was a scraping coming from upstairs. Brian stared uncertainly up at the ceiling. Violet stared uncertainly at Brian. He carefully removed his suit jacket and draped it across the bannister at the foot of the staircase. "Better go check it out."

"Wait," Violet whispered anxiously. "What are you going to do if it's an intruder?"

He paused and grinned. "I don't know. Probably trip you and book it."

Violet rolled her eyes.

They cautiously tiptoed up each carpeted step. When they reached the second floor landing, it became apparent the sounds were coming from Henry's bedroom. As they stealthily approached the door, Violet realized that she had inadvertently placed her hand on the crook of Brian's elbow. She pulled it back, embarrassed, but immediately reached for him again when the scraping began anew.

Brian eased the door open a crack and peeked in. He squinted, then relaxed and pushed the door fully ajar. In the center of the room, between the foot of his bed and a large dresser, Henry was dragging a crowbar roughly across the narrow floorboards. When it finally caught a board, he yanked it up with surprising force, splintering it. With the board out of the way, he slid down to his belly and reached his arm into the floor opening, grunting as he reached. He pulled out an empty mason jar, cursed savagely, then tossed it back into the hole he had created. Defeated, he collapsed back down to his stomach.

"Henry, what the hell are you doing?" Brian asked.

Henry looked up and noticed Brian and Violet for the first time. He casually pushed himself up to his knees, ran his hand through his wild hair, and slunk backward to sit on his ankles. His clothes were filthy, and dirt was smeared across his face and arms.

Exasperated, he snarled at Violet. "You just had to go over there, didn't you?"

Violet was startled by his tone. "Go where?"

Henry laughed scornfully. *"Where? she asks.* Oh, I don't know. Can you think of any place you've been recently that has caused some controversy? Anything come to mind at all?"

Violet didn't respond.

Henry tossed his crowbar aside, and it landed with a clanking thud. "I mean, do you have anything rattling around that goddamn head of yours? Are you really so naïve?"

"It's like I told Brian…" she began, but Henry cut her off.

"Oh, I know all about the brilliant ruse. A more clever trap was never devised. Tell the little neighbor girl you're locked out of your mansion and get her to crawl into the basement. I mean, gosh, who wouldn't fall for it?"

Violet was indignant. "How could I have possibly known what he was going to do?"

Henry lowered his gaze and shook his head. "You have no idea what you've done, what you've cost me."

She wanted to argue, but Henry's disheveled appearance and hateful grimace gave her pause. She wanted to mention the property marker she'd found in his secret closet, to confront him with his own treachery, to let him know that none of this would have happened if he hadn't tried to cheat his neighbor in the first place. Wisely, she kept quiet. Something was going on with Henry, and she didn't want to push him.

"Do you realize I haven't had a funeral here in two weeks? The phone has absolutely stopped ringing. Do you know why? Because no one trusts dead mommy or dead daddy to a funeral home where a thieving Mexican might steal their wedding bands or their gold teeth."

"Henry!" Brian exclaimed. "Jesus Christ, man, you are way out of line. You know she wasn't stealing anything from Trimble."

"Yes, Mr. Todd, I understand that," Henry snarled back. "But do me a favor, will you? Go door to door in this godforsaken city and explain that to everyone else. Explain that Miss Romero wasn't breaking into the neighbor's house; she'd just been duped by an elaborate scheme perpetrated by one of the most prominent men in the community to extort the local mortician. My reputation will be restored in no time."

He laughed caustically. "And guess who's leading the chorus of gossip? My own goddamn organ player."

"Henry, I know you're angry, but Violet is not the enemy here."

Henry looked at Brian in feigned amazement. "Says the other person making a laughingstock out of me."

"Excuse me?"

"Brian, do you know how many members of the local bar have warned me about you? That is a serious question. I want you to guess. Not going to? Seven. Seven fucking lawyers have taken me aside and warned me about your alcohol-drenched embarrassments. Each one had a story about you, and no two stories were the same. Seven. Here's a little free advice for you, Counselor. You're going to get disbarred. It's only a matter of time."

It was Brian's turn to be indignant. "I've done a good job for you, Henry, and you know it. With all due respect, what I do outside of work is my business."

"With all due respect, Mr. Todd, making an ass out of yourself is not going to bring her back."

Brian's face deadened. "Henry, I know you're not referring to who I think you're referring."

Henry rolled his eyes. "Your wife is dead, Brian. You hear me? She's dead. Deeeeeeaaad. Jesus, you've got to let it go."

The hate in Brian's eyes scared Violet. "Fuck you, Henry. You heartless bastard."

Henry seemed to find that funny. He smiled with cruel amusement and rose to his feet. "It's true. I'm a heartless bastard. But it's well past time somebody stopped sugarcoating things for you. Your grandfather would shit a holy brick if he knew how you turned out. Squandering your family's goodwill with your whiskey-soaked benders and publishing those half-baked novels. Oh, that's right. I've read some of your little space stories. I imagine some pretty serious favors had to be called in to get that garbage in print."

Brian's jaw clenched tight, but he still couldn't help blushing. He glanced at Violet, then quickly down to the floor. "Why are you doing this?" he asked, swallowing his anger. "Violet and I have only been trying to help you."

Henry approached Brian, stopping just inches from his face.

"Violet," Henry smirked, "would you please let Mr. Todd know that his wife is dead and she will continue being dead until the end of time."

She didn't have time to respond. Brian landed a left hook squarely on Henry's left temple, sending him flailing across the room, but not to the floor. Once Henry managed to get his feet back underneath him, he calmly tucked in his shirt, which had come halfway out, and ran his hand through his hair again.

"Good," he said calmly. "Good."

Brian was still in a fighting stance, his fists clenched.

Henry pointed toward the door. "Get the fuck out. You're fired."

Brian straightened himself and breathed heavily.

"What? Something else to say?" Henry asked.

Brian didn't respond.

Henry nodded at Violet. "I guess you want to get paid for representing this one."

He reached into his back pocket and produced a leather wallet. From it, he pulled a large handful of creased bills, then tossed the bills in Brian's direction, scattering them across the scratched and battered floor.

Henry turned his attention to Violet. "You're fired too. I expect you to be out when I come back."

"That's not fair," she said weakly.

Henry just shrugged.

"Mr. Pendleton, something is clearly going on with you. Just talk to us."

Henry sighed deeply with frustration. "No, I've got to go. If you're not gone when I come back, I'm calling the police."

With that, he passed between them and left the room.

"Where could you possibly be going right now?" she blurted after him.

"That's no longer your concern," he called over his shoulder. "Just lock the door when you leave."

When he reached the bottom of the steps, he must have glanced at the mess around him. "Or don't. What's the point," he yelled, then slammed the front door.

Brian and Violet were shell-shocked. The jarring ugliness of the scene upset Violet's stomach, so she sat down on the corner of Henry's bed to regroup. Brian's face was drawn with worry and repugnance.

"What just happened?" Violet asked weakly.

Brian shook his head and tried to speak, but his voice caught in his throat. He coughed into his fist and tried again. "I don't know. Did I just punch Henry?"

Violet nodded.

"I thought so," he said, then rubbed his hands down the sides of his face. "What the hell was he looking for under the floorboards, anyway?"

"Money?" Violet guessed.

"I don't think so," Brian said as he kicked at some of the bills Henry had tossed on the floor.

"I guess I'm out on the street," Violet mumbled.

Brian drew a deep breath and let it out slowly. He leaned against the wall, not trusting his legs to support his weight unaided. "No, don't worry about that. I've got a client who owns a motel at the edge of town. The rooms aren't fancy or anything, but they're clean. I'll take you there. He'll give you a good rate until you figure out what to do next."

"Thank you," she replied.

"I can help you gather your things too if you'd like," he offered.

Violet jammed her hands down into the pockets on her dress. When she did, a strange look suddenly crossed her face. She had nearly forgotten. From her pocket, she produced an oddly shaped key.

"What is that?" Brian asked.

Violet pointed toward the hallway. "Before we go, there's something you should see."

# Chapter 16

Clack tried to muster the will to stand as a group of young girls blithely approached his cart, but knowing the effort would be wasted, he kept his seat. The girls wore clean linen dresses and giggled into their hands. As they passed, the scent of cotton candy hung in the air, surrounding them like an aura and filling Clack's dank cart.

"Bitches," he muttered.

He'd known a hundred girls like them — vapid, insufferable ninnies. He could probably sell them some candy, maybe even one of his love potions, but those were nickel and dime items. He needed to sell some of his top-shelf merchandise if he ever planned on getting anywhere. His top shelf was actually a hidden compartment in the floor of his cart where he kept the white dog moonshine. It was a tough setup because his stock was doubly illicit. He could usually spot an undercover dry agent, but it was harder to tell the difference between one of Lamont's goons, who were looking for unsanctioned sales in Lamont's territory, and regular unaffiliated goons who just wanted a drink. Selling to the wrong man could get his legs broken, not that it would make a huge difference.

Pierre plodded through the sucking mud to Clack's cart. He leaned his slight frame on the hinged wooden counter that held a jar of pickled eggs and a small chalkboard featuring a price list that Clack changed several times a day, depending on where he set up and who was around.

"You getting your keep?" he asked in a thick French accent. Pierre was actually from Mississippi, and his name was really Timothy. For whatever reason, he thought people were more willing to overpay when dealing with a Frenchman. To Clack, it seemed exhausting.

"This town's for shit," Clack replied.

Pierre shook his head. "We shall see. Things always pick up when the sun goes down."

Clack spat tobacco juice in the direction of his spittoon. It missed.

"Pretty soon you are only going to have one clean thing in this heap, and it will be the spittoon." Pierre laughed.

His own cart was immaculate, partly because of what he sold — perfumes, tonics, and pharmaceuticals — and partly because he hated disarray. Pierre bought both of the carts from the same woodworker, so they were identical in every way, but Clack's mistreatment made his look like a cautionary tale for the other.

Clack owed Pierre a lot, which he hated for reasons he couldn't quite understand. Pierre showed Clack mercy when no one else would, and it wasn't out of pity either, at least as far as Clack could tell. Pierre was a genuine soul. Somehow he was graceful, a thought that made Clack uncomfortable. As bald, middle-aged men went, Pierre was nothing special — he certainly couldn't be described as successful — but he lived happily. He had no family, no property, and he was forever being accused of being a dandy. From time to time, Pierre would get run out of town; it was the nature of his work, but even that couldn't dampen his spirit.

Pierre took a deep breath and held it with satisfaction as he looked up at the darkening sky. "I think the rain is all done. It's going to be a lovely night." He smiled brightly. He said it with such conviction, Clack almost believed him.

"I'm going for a stroll. Will you watch my cart?"

Clack nodded.

"*Ah! Merci.*"

Pierre gently placed a peppermint candy on Clack's counter and winked. When he was out of sight, Clack rolled his eyes and flicked the candy into the mud. He rested his head in his hands and watched the discarded candy collect flies. The flies annoyed him. The candy annoyed him. Everything annoyed him.

With a grunt, Clack slid off of his stool and onto his feet. They ached tremendously, but nature was calling. He unrolled a canvas curtain to cover his display and then stumbled down the wooden steps of his cart toward the darkness of the nearby woods. The air was swampy, and his shirt was damp with sweat. It was a wonder he ever needed to piss at all, considering how much he perspired. When he reached the edge of the woods, he unbuttoned his trousers and let out a slow breath until he managed to coax out a steady stream that splattered noisily on the leafy undergrowth.

He relaxed his head and stared straight up, resting his hands on his hips. The moon swam under the brightly fringed clouds that lumbered monstrously across the night sky. Had he waited for his eyes to adjust to the darkness, or had he any awareness of his surroundings whatsoever, Clack would have realized that he wasn't alone. A few yards away, a hulking man leaned motionlessly against a tall pine.

"Will anyone miss you when you're gone?" the man asked in a low, flat tone.

Clack nearly levitated from the jolt of fright and adrenaline at the sound of the voice. In his haste to turn around, he tripped over his own feet and rolled awkwardly to the ground. Piss sprayed up from his tiny penis like a fountain, hitting him in the face and chest.

"Jesus Christ!" he squealed as he fumbled at his fly, trying to control the renegade stream. Unable to stop the flow, he rolled onto his side and waited for his bladder to drain. The stranger watched unflinchingly.

"What the hell is wrong with you?" Clack asked as the stream slowed to a dribble and he was able to button up and get back to his feet.

"Will anyone miss you when you're gone?" the man repeated. He wore a dark gray suit that was worn and dirty.

"That's a helluva question to ask a guy trying to use the privy," Clack shot back, though still not totally in command of the timbre of his own voice.

As the man approached, Clack started to make out his sallow, bearded face. His eyes were ferocious and seemed to be nearly glowing.

"Some men have families — people relying on them. Some men are drunkards and the sort. What type of man are you?"

Sensing danger, Clack lied. "Not that it's any of your business, but I've got more children than most men my age."

"How many is that?"

"Three, er, that is, five."

The stranger smirked. "Well, which is it? Three or five? One of those figures is mistaken by two."

"Definitely five." Clack laughed nervously. "I nearly forgot about the twins. Born just a few days ago."

"Five children? You're a virile young man. How old are you? Seventeen?"

"Nineteen and half. Closer to twenty really."

The stranger lowered his large frame down onto a felled tree. He motioned for Clack to sit down next to him, something Clack was not interested in doing.

"Well, c'mon then, rest those bum legs of yours."

Clack did as he was told. There was no sense in trying to run. He wouldn't make it three steps before the huge man had him, if he were inclined to pursue.

The man stretched his legs out in front of him, crossing one over the other at the ankle. He straightened his arms out behind him and braced them on the log.

"You smart?" he asked.

Clack shrugged.

"You afraid of me?"

Clack nodded.

The man nodded back. "Good."

"I've become a bit of a sporting man recently. There's a certain pleasure in it — relieves some of the drudgery of this life. Such as it is."

"What type of sport?"

"Patience, friend." The man smirked. "That's yet to be determined. Where are you from?"

"Here. Coffee County, born and bred. Live a few miles that-a-way." Clack tilted his head leftward.

The man looked in the direction Clack indicated. He looked back at Clack and clicked his tongue against the roof of his mouth.

"I thought you was smart," the man said.

Clack looked back at him innocently.

"That's twice you've lied to me already. I know a North Georgia accent when I hear it. I'd say you're from Rabun County or Towns County, roundabout Hiawasee."

"Rabun," Clack acquiesced.

The man grinned. "No, sir, you can't hide an accent like that. I'm from Tennessee myself."

There was a moment of silence. Clack didn't know how to respond.

"And I know you ain't got five younguns neither. Hell, I'd wager you've yet to even get that tiny pecker wet."

Clack was indignant, but he kept quiet.

"I know it's hard to tell," the stranger continued, "because of my calm disposition, but you are in a goodly amount of peril at this precise moment. Can you understand that?"

Clack remained motionless.

"Do you know I aim to kill you?"

"You...don't..." Clack stirred.

"Speak up," the man demanded.

"You don't have to," Clack croaked.

"That's true, I don't. But I'm gonna, and there's not a goddamn thing you can do about it neither. Bet that makes you feel pretty bad about the world, don't it?"

"Please..." Clack started to be beg, but the stranger cut him off.

"Let me finish. I'm gonna kill ya, *unless* you do two things. Number one, tell me the truth and nothin' but. Number two, win a little game of my choosing. What do you say?"

Clack's mouth was cotton. He nodded.

"Good. There's a third thing, but it's just a trifle. We'll see if you get past the first two things before we cross that bridge. Now, before we get started,

186

to emphasize just exactly how important rule number one is, I've got a little demonstration for you."

The big man produced a large, serrated Bowie knife from a leather sheath on his belt. Clack went cold at the sight of it. The man handled the blade with an alacrity that suggested great skill. He pointed at Clack with his left hand, his finger just inches from the young man's face. To Clack's astonishment, he slid the knife around the extended finger like he was peeling an apple, until the finger fell to the ground.

"Pick it up," the man ordered as he wrapped up the fresh wound with a strip of cloth from his pocket.

Clack's stomach turned as he plucked the severed finger from the dark mud. It was cold and rigid in his hand. He held it out to the man, who looked thoughtfully at his own mutilated hand.

"Naw, you hold on to it. I don't want you forgettin' what type of man you are dealing with. Now, let's get to business. Start with your name."

"I've had a few."

"No matter. So have I. More than once I've been mistaken for the devil." The man grinned.

"I got my first name at the orphanage, I reckon. The sisters called me Silas Bucket."

"Don't believe I've ever heard that surname before. You pulling my leg?"

Clack shook his head solemnly as he glanced down at the knife still in the man's hand.

"It was supposed to be a joke about how fussy I was. You know, I cried so much, they needed a bucket."

"Did you know your folks at all?"

"I'm told my mother was a teenager from Savannah whose dentist liked to dabble in gynecology when his patients were under ether. She was from a nice family, so I had to be gotten rid of. She had me in a cabin deep in the Chattahoochee. As for the dentist, I was told he was found dangling with the Spanish moss from the oak in his backyard. Don't know if he done it himself or if someone done it for him — either way, it was justice, I reckon."

"What name do you go by now?"

"Clack," the little man responded as he tapped the metal braces on his legs together. "When I was three, I got the polio. It wrecked my legs and any chance of someone adopting me, but it didn't finish me off. The sisters at the orphanage were disappointed about that, I'm sure. I ain't complaining or anything; those old cooters raised me up, so they deserve my respect, but I'll be damned if they didn't treat me like Quasimodo."

"What do you do?"

"I own that cart over yonder. Got something for everyone — tonics, sweets, maybe something a little harder, depending on who's asking."

"I'm asking."

"Look, if you work for Lamont, I don't sell any of that other stuff anymore."

"I don't work for Lamont."

Clack tilted his head. "In that case, maybe we could reach an agreement. I've got enough moonshine in the bottom of my cart to make you a good bit of coin. Take it, it's yours."

"You're trying to bargain with me, but there's nothing you have that I want. I don't drink, and I don't need money. I've got more than I need."

"Then maybe I could unburden you some of that extra cash. Lighten your load a bit, and you can be on your way."

The man shook his head and chuckled. "Salesmen. Tell you what, that gives me a good idea. I think I know the game now. You're a flim-flam man, aintcha?"

"Well..."

The man displayed his knife again, gently turning it so that it glistened in the moonlight.

"Yessir, I reckon I am."

"All right, then tell me about your best scam."

"What do you mean?"

"Don't play dumb. Salesmen are the same the world over. They think they're the cleverest beasts to walk the earth. Bitter and hateful, most of 'em, but industrious. I'll give y'all that much."

Clack racked his brain. Most of his cons were petty and only marginally effective. He spent most of his time convincing teenagers that he had potions that would clear their complexion or improve their memory to help with exams. In reality, he was selling sugar water mixed with some coloring and moonshine. Once, he convinced a man to buy a squirrel that he claimed would gather walnuts from the man's backyard into a bucket while the man slept. He set a squirrel loose in the man's backyard and sat an empty bucket next to his back door. During the night, Clack came creeping back and put a few dozen nuts in the bucket. The next day he came back with another squirrel, claiming that he'd gotten the first one to come back to him. The man gave him thirty dollars to turn the squirrel loose for good, which Clack gladly did. Neither was seen by the man again.

Clack thought the story was amusing, but he didn't think it was good enough to satisfy the dark stranger. He couldn't even think of a good lie. Even if he could, he had a bad feeling the stranger would sniff it out and carve him up like the finger he clutched in his hand.

"Well. Whatcha got?" the stranger demanded as he wiped the blade gently against his pant leg.

"There's so many good ones, I'm just trying to think of the most impressive."

"Horseshit. You're stalling. Get on with it, I'm running out of patience."

Clack was drawing a blank, and it must have showed on his face, because the man flipped the knife in his hand and straightened himself into a striking position.

"No, no…all right, I'm ready. I've got it now."

The stranger relaxed and nodded at Clack to continue. "Don't be nervous, salesman, but your life depends on this."

Clack took a deep breath. "I guess I'll tell you about the Hickory Grove revival."

"All right. Let's hear it."

"I reckon I'd better start at the startin' place."

"That sounds like as good a place as any," the stranger replied as he put the dagger back in a sheath on his belt.

"I was at the orphanage in Rabun County until I was eleven years old. Nobody thought I'd ever get adopted because of my legs, least of all me, but one day an old biddy from Marietta named Betsy Mackey strolled in and picked me out like she was gettin' a side of beef from the butcher. She told the sisters that God had spoken to her and revealed that even the most wretched soul deserved a family and that she was called by the Lord to give the gift of her love to a young person with no other prospect for happiness. In truth, she was more worried about her impending incapacity due to chronic gout and the expense of her care than she was in saving poor souls in a Christian sort of way. I was an investment, and she trained me to be an obedient little nurse who could tend to her hypochondria. If I misbehaved, she would lock me in the little closet under the stairs with nothing but a candle and her old Bible. You see, Betsy was a regular pew-jumping Pentecostal who followed the revival circuit from county to county with the never-ending hope that one of the traveling preachers would cast the sickness from her body for good."

"Did any of that religion take with you?" the stranger asked bemusedly.

The question came as a relief to Clack. It meant the stranger was interested. "Hard not to pick up something when you're in church every damn day," he replied, forcing a grin. "But most of the time I was just plotting my escape."

The stranger rolled his eyes. "It wouldn't be too hard to give a gouty old lady the slip, even on them dinky legs."

"You're right about that; physically getting away wasn't the problem. But I was smart enough to know that I needed a little bit of jingle in my pocket if I was gonna get very far, and old Betsy's money was in the bank, outta my reach. That's when I came up with my best scam."

"If you're gonna tell me that you robbed an old lady, I think we can skip to the end. I ain't impressed."

"Just hold your fuckin' horses, that ain't what I'm saying. It was much better than that. You see, I got this idea one day, and I spent hours and hours thinking about it and waiting for the right time. It wasn't until the revival at the Christ Covenant Church in Hickory Grove that I finally got my chance.

"A preacher named Watkins had come up from his church in Dahlonega to rekindle the spirit of God at old Christ Covenant. He had a reputation for laying hands on the sick in moments of spiritual fervor, so I knew Betsy would make sure we were sitting on the front pew.

"Brother Watkins was in rare form the last night of the revival — screamin' and hoppin' around. Things were as perfect as they were ever gonna get, so I sprung my plan. In the midst of the pandemonium, I grabbed old lady Mackey's Bible and waddled my way up to the altar. Generally speaking, it's hard to know when something out of the ordinary is happening in a Pentecostal church. Earlier that night, a fifty-year-old cotton farmer ran up and down the aisles, whoopin', and hollerin', and speaking in tongues, and no one batted an eye. But when I stood in front of everyone on my weak legs with my little fists clenched and my eyes all fiery, everything got real quiet. That's when I knew I had 'em."

Clack paused.

The stranger, who had been listening closely, stirred. "Well? What'd you do?"

Clack got up and stood in front of the stranger. He closed his eyes and concentrated, remembering exactly what he'd said on that hot Georgia night.

"*Isaiah,* I began, almost whispering so everyone would have to strain to hear me, *told King Hezekiah that God would answer his prayer and help him defeat the approaching Assyrian army if Judah would simply stand up and resist them. Hezekiah obeyed, and the Assyrians were defeated.* Nobody moved. So I went on.

"*Today I tell you that God has made the same promise to this church that he made to Judah. If we can find the courage to confront the evil in this community, we will prevail against it.*

"The congregation's curiosity was through the roof. I could see it on their faces as I gripped that old Bible so tight, you could hear my palms rub against the leather cover.

"*God spoke to me and told me that there is wickedness among us. There are wicked people sitting under this roof tonight. As I lay sleeping in my bed last night, God whispered in my ear and told me the sins of my neighbors. Many of the things he told me I didn't understand. I asked the Lord why he was telling me such horrible things. I told him that I was just a boy, and he said, 'They must know my power and repent!'*

"Old Betsy looked like she popped a hemorrhoid. I don't think I'd ever seen her more uncomfortable. Still, she didn't try to stop me.

"*Adultery. Greed. Covetousness. Theft. These are the things I heard from the Lord. These are the things I heard about the people sitting in this very room. Repent now, and I will not share your secrets. There will be no need.* No one budged.

"*Now ain't the time for the meek and timid. I can see you don't believe a twelve-year-old boy could be chosen by God to relay His holy message, but you are dead wrong and your souls are in danger. Now repent!*

"Brother Watkins, started getting antsy and tried to cut in. *Yes, my dear boy, we are all sinners and would all be destined for the pits of Hell if not for the grace of the Lord, zippity do, blah, blah, blah.*

"I couldn't let him steal my thunder, so I held my ground. *No, the Lord demands repentance tonight!*

"*I think you'd better find your seat,* Watkins growled in my ear, but I just shook my head. *I cannot. It is not my message, and it is not my decision whether to deliver it.*

"I raised my face up to the ceiling, held my arms out wide, and rolled my eyes back in my head and then began convulsing. After doing that for a spell, I stopped and pointed at the town grocer.

"*T.W. Tyree!* I yelled. *God has told me about you!*

"Keep in mind this fella was the chairman of the deacons and one of the church's main financial backers. Ha ha! When I called his name he went ramrod stiff.

"*Repent, T.W.!* I screamed.

"*Of what?* he hollered back at me.

"That's when I laid it on him. *Your infidelity!*

"Boy, that got things a buzzin'. He hemmed and hawed, saying, *Now wait just a minute, boy.* But I just kept at him.

"*Repent T.W. Repent for sinning against your family. Repent for sinning with another member of this congregation.*

"There was another big gasp from the congregation.

*"God whispered it in my ear. He told me that T.W. has gone to bed with one of his sisters in Christ, and if he does not repent, they will both be stricken with suffering and disease and strife for their sin. So you must repent, T.W., or God will show his might.*

"I could see T.W. was not having any of it, but just when I thought my plan had failed and I was about to have the whippin' of a lifetime, a sobbing voice from across the room rang out, *I repent. Oh, God Almighty I confess my sin. Please forgive me.*

"It was Jane Marcum! Her eyes were shut tight, and she clutched a handkerchief to her chest as she said it. I'll never forget the look on her husband's face. He was as dumbstruck as everyone else. That's when the place erupted. I wanted to take advantage of my momentum, so I held up my hands for silence. Quickly, I picked out another fella and kept going.

*"Thomas Henderson! Repent now or the Lord will show his might!*

"Now, this old boy must've seen the writing on the wall, because he immediately made for the door.

*"Stop right there! I told him. You cannot escape the Lord's judgment. He is the creator of the universe, and his will cannot be undone. God told me about the intoxicating liquors you have been distilling in the darkness of your cellar while your neighbors were sleeping. He told me that you engage in drunkenness, debauchery, and sexual perversion.*

"Thomas cracked straight away. He dropped to his knees and started sobbing.

*"Do not cry like a sissy, Thomas! The Lord is disgusted by such effeminate sniveling. Stand up like a man and repent for the evil that you have allowed to possess you!*

"He did as he was told and begged for forgiveness at the altar while I called out a half dozen more people just to the stir the pot a little. You'd have thought the joint was a madhouse the way everyone was crawlin' around and wailin' and callin' out to the Lord. In the meantime, I made sure to get the offering plates started again. Folks dumped everything they had into them! The place was in such an uproar, no one saw me swipe the money and slip out the back!"

Clack was nearly out of breath. "And that's the story of the Hickory Grove revival."

When he'd finished, there was nothing but the sound of a distant barn owl to fill the stagnant air.

The stranger shifted on the fallen tree. "All right, so how'd you do it?" he finally asked.

Clack smiled coyly. "I'll gladly tell you, but you've got to promise I'm free to go — unharmed."

The stranger considered the offer. "If it's as clever as that shit-eating grin on your face says it is, then I'll leave you be. Now, how'd you know all that stuff about them folks?"

Clack winked. "I got it from the Bible."

The stranger was not impressed with that answer. He grabbed Clack by the arm with an iron grip and forced him to sit next to him again on the fallen tree.

"I think you're lying."

"Swear to God, I'm not," Clack squealed.

"Ain't no way you got all them stories from the Bible."

"Let me finish, please," Clack choked out, holding back fearful sobs. "It was old Lady Mackey's prayer list. She kept it tucked in her Bible on an old bulletin between Proverbs and Psalms."

The stranger loosened his grip a little.

"The bitch was a gossip whore, and she wrote everything down on her 'prayer list.' I found it one day when I was locked under them steps for actin' up. That's when I hatched my plan, you see."

The stranger let go of Clack, and the two men stared intently at one another. Finally, the stranger burst out laughing.

"The goddamn prayer list! I gotta give it to you, kid, that's good. That's real good."

Clack allowed himself to laugh nervously along with the bigger man, but he couldn't keep the tears from streaming down his cheeks at the same time.

The stranger slapped Clack's leg hard enough to make him grimace.

"Relax, Clack. I like the story."

"Good God. You scared me. I thought you were gonna cut me up like you did this finger," Clack said, handing the forgotten digit back to its owner. "Geez, why did you cut that thing off anyway? You coulda scared me good enough without doin' that. Don't you think you'll be wanting that again at some point?"

The stranger nonchalantly tossed the finger off into the woods, then unwrapped the cloth from his hand.

"Don't worry about it. I'll just grow another."

Clack smirked. "That's a trick I'd like to see."

The stranger raised an eyebrow. "All right. I normally wouldn't do this, but you've earned it."

He produced a small deerskin medicine pouch from under his shirt. It was hanging on a long, leather strap around his neck. He reached his mutilated hand into the pouch and pulled it out, empty. He laughed as he recognized his mistake. Whatever was inside, he couldn't grasp it without his index finger, so instead he tilted the top of the bag into his good hand and watched as three bean-like items poured out.

"What's that?"

The stranger held his hand out to Clack, who leaned forward to get a better look.

"Are they beans?"

The stranger chuckled. "Yessir. Magic beans."

He popped the little gray objects into his mouth and threw his head back to help him swallow. The hairs on Clack's neck stood on end as the stranger's eyes glowed like the dying embers of a fire. He looked on in disbelief as a new finger unfurled from the nub on the stranger's hand.

Clack couldn't help himself; he reached out and touched the new finger.

"Blessed are those who have not seen and still believe," the stranger said blasphemously.

"You are the fuckin' devil," Clack uttered.

The stranger lunged at Clack and grabbed him by the face, baring his teeth and chomping just inches from his nose. Clack pulled back and fell to the ground in terror, much to the stranger's delight.

"Naw, I ain't the devil," he said, laughing. "Like I said, these are magic beans. They'll cure anything. Take 'em for any ailment, and they'll make you better than new."

Clack's heart was still racing as he made his way to his feet for the second time.

"What about heart failure?" he asked, clutching his chest.

"I'd say so," the stranger replied. "I bet they'd even fix them busted legs."

That got Clack's attention. "Can I have one?"

"Hell, no. Why should you get one?"

"C'mon now, don't hold out on me. I'll give you everything I've got."

The stranger shook his head. "I already told you, you ain't got nothin' I want."

Clack sulked. "Please?"

The stranger stroked his black beard as he reconsidered. With a slight nod of his head, he motioned for Clack to come closer. He turned the deerskin pouch upside down in Clack's hand, and a single gray bean came tumbling out. Clack examined it as closely as the moonlight would allow.

"So, what is this anyway?"

The stranger smirked, "Panacea."

Fearing the stranger would change his mind, Clack popped it into his mouth. He'd never been good about taking pills, so he bit the little bean in half — it was chewy and salty. He swallowed it and waited.

"How long does it take?" he asked. His heart was beating out of his chest.

"For me, it starts working almost immediately."

The two men waited. Clack's heavy breathing filled the air.

"I think I feel something," he said with a start.

"Well, get out there and try out them new legs!" the stranger encouraged.

Gingerly at first, Clack began walking, then trotting, then running. He ran as far as adrenaline could take him before the familiar tinge of searing pain shot through his body, and he collapsed in the mud. The stranger roared with laughter.

Clack was humiliated. The stranger had done to him what he had done to hundreds of his customers.

"The more a person wants something, the more willing they are to believe any ridiculous thing," the stranger said, shaking his head. "You should know that better than anyone."

"But I saw your finger grow back," Clack said as he climbed up from the ground for a third time.

The stranger looked down at Clack without pity.

"Will you at least tell me what I just swallowed?"

The tall man thought for a moment. "I think that's fair," he smiled. "I met a man about a month back, up in the mountains of North Carolina — has a little cabin on a ridge near a path I often travel. This fella had a mushroom farm, of all things, and he grew some of the best mushrooms in the South, or so he claimed. I spent a little time with him, and he showed me his little operation. It was very impressive."

"So it was a mushroom?"

"Huh? Oh, God no," the stranger laughed. "Naw, I put my knife far enough through one of the old man's ears that it came out the other side of his head. Then I used an iron skillet to crack his skull just enough for me to get at that sweet gray meat on the inside."

Horror washed over Clack as he realized what he'd just done.

"I had a good helping right then and there," the stranger continued, "because it's always best when its fresh, but I dried out the rest and made some jerky pellets. I've considered making some with a hickory smoke, but who am I kidding? They taste great the way they are."

Clack dropped down to his knees and retched.

"You are a leaky little bastard," the stranger said as he took a step back. "The only thing you haven't done since we met is shit your pants."

"Please just leave me be," Clack begged. "I did what you asked."

"Almost," the stranger reminded him. "There's still one little trifle remaining."

"What?" Clack asked fearfully.

"You've got to nominate a substitute. This stuff don't grow on trees," the stranger said, nodding to the empty pouch in his hand.

"You want me to pick out someone to die?"

The stranger shrugged. "You can look at it that way if you want. If you want to be all noble about it, I can still take you."

In the distance, Clack saw Pierre returning from his walk, a fresh rosebud pinned to his lapel and a broad smile on his face as he tipped his cap to some passing ladies.

"I've got just the man," Clack replied flatly.

# Chapter 17

Brian was uncomfortable milling around Henry's house, especially after punching him in the face and getting fired, but there was nothing he could do. Violet was on a mission, and he saw in her face that nothing was going to stop her. She led him to a broom closet, then through a tiny hidden door that was almost too small for him. A nail caught his suit jacket and ripped it.

"Oh, sorry," Violet said. "I meant to warn you about that."

There wasn't much space inside the little room, so the two kept bumping into each other in the dark.

"Where's the light?" Brian asked.

"I don't think there is one. I had a flashlight last time I was in here."

Brian pulled a book of matches from his pocket and struck one. Light washed upward and filled the space between him and Violet. Her face glowed in the orange light, and her eyes reflected the flame. The image made Brian pause just long enough for the cheap match to burn down to his fingertips. He cursed and quickly lit another.

"I've only got a few more of these."

"Here," Violet said as she grabbed a candle from a nearby shelf.

Brian lit it, then found another and lit it too. He looked around the little room.

"So what is this, exactly?"

Violet took a long breath and exhaled. "I'm not sure. I only had a few minutes to look around when I found it."

"Whoa," Brian exclaimed.

"What!?"

"Look at this." He pointed to a framed wreath. "Do you know what this is?"

"Just a wreath, I thought."

"No, look closer. See what it's made of."

Violet picked up the frame and squinted as she drew her face close to it. "Looks like…thread?"

"Hair," Brian replied. "They used to do that in the old days when someone died. Saw one of these in a museum once."

Violet's mouth opened at the revelation.

"Gross," she whispered, making Brian laugh.

"What?" she asked, narrowing her eyes.

"Nothing."

Her face fell a little. "I know you think I'm an idiot."

Brian was surprised. "Why would you say that?"

"Because you always look like you're angry at me. And you're always around when I do stupid things. Like the night at Cuppy's. And this whole thing with Trimble."

Brian furrowed his brow. "That's not what I think at all, Violet. All these things that have happened, you have to know that they were out of your control. And you were only trying to help that prick Trimble. I wish more people were like that."

"You wish more people helped pricks?"

"No. I wish more people were kind when they didn't have to be."

Violet shrugged. "Some good it did. Anyway, I never thanked you for everything you did when I was in jail. It meant a lot to me. And thank you for standing up to Henry when he said those things earlier. I know I don't deserve the help you've given me."

Brian reached out and touched Violet's elbow. He wanted to make her feel better, but he didn't know how.

"I know we got off to rocky start, but I can tell that you're a good girl."

He blushed. "You've just had some rotten luck. More than most."

"You going soft on me?" Violet smirked.

"Ah, nuts." Brian grinned. "We both know I'm an asshole. But sometimes it's good to have an asshole on your team."

Violet pointed to some small clumps of dirt on the floor. "I didn't tell anyone this before, but you know the property marker that surveyor was looking for a few weeks ago?"

"Of course, the one in the backyard."

"Yeah. I found that exact same marker right there on the floor before the surveyor came. I didn't know what it was at the time. It wasn't until I saw what the surveyor dug up that I knew it was the same. It had BERWICK written on it."

Brian sighed heavily. "So that's why Henry was so confident about his case. He had an ace up his sleeve."

"He's not who he says he is," Violet said solemnly.

"I'd say not," Brian agreed, then added, "but nobody really is."

Violet looked up into Brian's eyes, then down to the floor.

Brian wished he knew her thoughts. She held everything so close. He brushed his hand across his back pocket. He could feel the outline of a folded piece of paper against the fabric. He needed to talk to Violet. There were some very difficult things that he had to say, things he had tried to say over and over, but couldn't. It still wasn't the right time, but it needed to happen soon. For the past few weeks, he thought about her often, always evoking very confusing emotions.

"Look at these books," Violet suggested, pointing past Brian's shoulder.

She squeezed past him and picked up the book on the far end of a row of ten or more on a makeshift shelf. As they shifted awkwardly toward another shelf, one that appeared to be made for viewing, Brian accidentally stepped on Violet's foot. She grunted in pain.

"Sorry."

"I bet you're an amazing dancer." She grimaced.

"Hey," Brian said indignantly. "I do all right for myself."

"My toes disagree."

"Well, usually when I dance I don't have to do it in a tiny little dungeon room. When I've got space, forget about it, sister, I'm poetry in motion."

Violet turned toward him and put a hand on her hip. "Name one dance you know how to do."

Brian pretended he didn't hear her. "Let's have a look at that book you've got there."

"That's what I thought."

Violet set the book down on the viewing shelf and pulled the candles closer. It was bound in leather and had a thin leather strap wrapped several times around its width. The edges were worn thin, and uneven pages protruded from all sides. Gently, Violet began unwinding the leather strap.

"Did you hear that?" Brian asked.

Violet tilted her head and listened carefully. "I don't hear anything," she said after a few silent moments.

"I thought I heard footsteps," Brian whispered.

"You're just jumpy."

She once again started to unwrap the book.

"C'mon, Violet, we've got to get going."

"Just give me a minute. Aren't you curious what this stuff is?"

"Yeah, but it's really not smart for us to be here right now. Need I remind you that you just got out of jail an hour ago?"

Violet's nostrils flared.

"My advice to you, as your attorney, is that we cease trespassing on this property."

Violet was unconvinced.

"Maybe you'd like to have supper at the detention center? How was the food there? Pretty good?"

"All right, stringbean, let's scram," Violet said as she crouched down and opened the secret door. "Blow out the candles before you come out," she instructed as she shimmied through the opening. "I don't want to add arson to my rap sheet."

"Good idea," Brian replied. "You've got to work your way up to that. First, you should master burglary. You know, get away with it one time, then we can talk about maybe doing some arson. *Maybe.*"

When Violet giggled, Brian realized that it was the second time he had made her laugh that evening. It made him feel good. He also recalled how she'd touched his arm as they approached Henry's room together. With some annoyance, he shook off the feeling.

"What's that on your shoulder?" he asked as they exited the broom closet.

Violet froze midstride. "Please get it off," she commanded through clenched teeth.

Brian picked a dust bunny off of her dress and held it up for her to see. "Just some dirt. Geez, now who's jumpy? What did you think it was?"

"Loxosceles reclusa," she replied.

"Huh?"

She shook her head. "Nothing. Hey, I need to grab a few things before we go, do you mind?"

"No, but let's do it quickly,"

He followed her to her room and watched as she darted around, tossing things into a canvas bag that she pulled out from under the bed.

"Can I help?"

Violet paused, the backs of her hands resting on her hips and her mouth pursed to one side as she thought. She swept a tuft of hair that had fluttered across her forehead behind her ear.

"Yes, actually. I'd like to take my bicycle with me. Do think you can go get it while I get some stuff?"

"I didn't know you had a bike. I thought the hearse was your only set of wheels."

Violet ignored the comment. "It's in the basement. Just roll it out the storm doors, and I'll meet you out front."

"All right, but hurry. I don't want to be here when Henry gets back."

When Violet nodded, Brian rushed down the main staircase into the foyer and then back into the kitchen area, where the narrow entrance to the basement was located. Brian pulled open the door and fumbled his hand along the wall inside to flip an unresponsive light switch. He sighed and squinted into the dark stairwell. He thought about turning and reporting back to Violet, but he didn't want to waste any more time.

The wooden steps creaked noisily as he navigated into the darkness, where a cold, metallic odor hung in the air. When he reached the bottom, he stumbled, thinking there were more steps. His feet slapped awkwardly against the tile floor as he fought to regain his balance. Something crunched underneath his shoes. Once again, he struck a match. There were only two left. Glass and filament from a broken light bulb littered the floor.

Brian held up the match just long enough to orient himself to the room before it burned out. The only other time he had been in the basement was the day Henry first retained him as counsel. Brian was quite hungover at the time, or maybe even still a little drunk, and he didn't remember much about it other than the fact it also served as the embalming room. The memory made him instinctively reach for his flask, which he kept forgetting he no longer carried. He lit the next match.

A long metal gurney stood like an island in the middle of the room. Shadows flickered across it as the flame from the match burned precariously down the thin matchstick. Brian stepped closer. There were dark pools collecting in the corners of the gurney-top. With his eyes, Brian followed the stream of dark liquid to its source. At the far end of the gurney he saw two lumps of fur. Confused, he moved even closer, leaning toward the two mounds. It wasn't until his match had burned out and the darkness once again swallowed him that his brain registered what his eyes had just seen.

They were cats. Two headless cats.

"What the fuck?" Brian whispered. He stepped backward until he bumped into a countertop, knocking a tray of embalming tools to the ground with an ear-jarring clatter. The stillness that followed was just as deafening. Brian felt like he wasn't alone. Someone else was either in the basement or had been very recently — someone perverse enough to mangle stray cats. He wanted to leave as quietly as possible, but he'd gotten turned around in the dark, and glass crunched under every step.

As his eyes adjusted, he noticed the nearly imperceptible glow of the pilot light to the furnace on the far wall. If he remembered correctly, the furnace was near the stairwell. Using it as his North Star, Brian shuffled toward it. Upstairs, the front door opened and closed with a thud. *Violet leaving,* Brian thought. He wanted to call out to her and warn her that someone else might be watching them, but he held his tongue.

Brian drew closer to the pilot light. It had a strange design. There were two small flames burning so low, they were barely on at all. They were high on the furnace. Too high. Having closed the gap to just a few inches, Brian grew uneasy with the little flames. They weren't burning at all, just glowing, and they seemed to emit a putrid smell. With sick dread, Brian struck his last match.

There was no furnace. Standing before him was Henry, his mouth dripping with blood and his glowing eyes staring hatefully into Brian's. With stinking breath, he blew out the match.

# Chapter 18

**1962**

**(A note in Brian Todd's pocket)**

*Henry,*

*I'm sorry for doing this to you. Everything I own is boxed up and sorted. Please know that the last thing I wanted to do was inconvenience you, especially after all the kindness you've shown me. That's why I feel I owe you an explanation.*

*When I first showed up on your doorstep, I wasn't looking for a job. I know that's what I told you, but I couldn't think of anything else to say. The embarrassing fact is that I had been following you. Not you, exactly, but the person you happened to be talking with that day: Brian Todd. You see, Brian and I have a terrible connection, even though he doesn't know it. I am responsible for the death of his wife.*

*My father is a drinker. He always was, but it got worse when my mother died. I put all of my plans on hold and looked after him for a time, but he was more than I could handle. He wouldn't work. He wouldn't take care of himself. All he ever did was get blackout drunk and beg me to take him to my mother's grave. He obviously couldn't drive himself — he could barely stand most of the time. One night, in my selfishness and hatred, I said some unforgivable things to him, and I gave him his keys. I told him if he wanted to be with my mother so badly, he could just go, that I wouldn't stop him. I was just so tired. It was disgusting and selfish, but I didn't want him to come back.*

*He ran a stop sign and collided with another car that night, a couple visiting California on their honeymoon. The woman was killed, the man lived, and my*

206

*father went to jail. I felt so sorry for what I'd done to that poor man. Years passed. I lived in agony for as long as I could, but I needed to know if he had moved on. If he had, then maybe I could too. I tracked him down to Kentucky to check. I followed him for days. When he came to your funeral home, I didn't know he was your lawyer. I thought maybe he'd lost someone else. I had to find out more. That's where you found me.*

*Although I made my decision earlier today to do this thing I've done, seeing Brian at Cuppy's further convinced me that I've done the right thing — the only honorable thing. He is not over his wife's death, and he seems fairly determined to destroy himself.*

*Tell Brian I'm sorry. Tell him that if I could trade places with his wife, I gladly would. I know what I'm doing tonight won't bring her back, but it will take me out this world and hopefully bring Brian some measure of comfort.*

*This is my confession and my apology, such as it is.*

*Goodbye,*

*V*

# Chapter 19

**1931**

For the first time she could remember, Genevieve considered doing something unthinkable: disobeying. It was an odd feeling. She loved obeying. She loved following the rules and getting good marks. But as she lugged the box of old journals and books down the back steps to the alley behind the office, she felt the overpowering urge to defy her boss's order to trash them as historically irrelevant garbage. He had flipped through a few of the box's contents when the man from the auction house brought them to the Lexington Historical Society's office, but not enough to really appreciate what he was seeing.

The box wasn't just the unsold portion of an estate sale; it contained the remnants of someone's life, someone's thoughts and meditations and confessions. Even without reading a word, Genevieve could not fathom just throwing the manuscripts out. The journals alone represented countless hours of toil and struggle, of innumerable heartfelt reflections. To her, pushing the box into the trash felt like snuffing out the dying embers of someone's once blazing existence.

The thought crossed her mind once again. *What if I didn't throw this box away? What if I just kept it for myself and gave it the attention it deserved? Who would that hurt?* Of course, the rule-following part of her knew the obvious answer. *You already have more than enough work to do cataloguing the old collections. That's what you are actually getting paid to do and, even now, you aren't sure you have enough time in the day to get it done before Mr. Marshall's deadline. He is the expert. Just trust what he says and do your work.*

Genevieve's internal battle raged for her entire break. The trashcans in the alley behind the office were all full. It was Tuesday. She knew that the garbage truck came every Wednesday morning. Sometimes, when the trashcans were full and additional trash was set out beside them, the garbage crew would take the extra rubbish. Then again, sometimes they didn't, much to the ire of Mr. Marshall. It really just depended on the mood of the crew that particular day.

After equivocating for a good while, Genevieve decided on a compromise. *I'll leave the box out here like Mr. Marshall said, and if the garbage men don't take it tomorrow, I'll take that as a sign that I should keep it myself. If it's gone, then there was nothing in this box that the universe wasn't okay with discarding.* Satisfied with her own mental bargain, Genevieve gingerly placed the box on the ground. She tried to turn and go back inside to work, but hesitated. With her foot, she pushed the box a few inches away from the trashcans, then rushed away to avoid an obsessive episode.

Genevieve was passionate about her work. At least, she was passionate about what she imagined her work would someday be. History was not dead to her. It was violent and beautiful, heartbreaking and sensual. She loved original source material much more than she loved derivative works. She liked to make up her own mind about what people meant when they took the time to write something down. That was why it was so difficult for her to respect a man who would toss out crucial clues about the way people lived a hundred years ago. Maybe he was right. Maybe it was inconsequential drivel from yet another failed southern estate. Maybe his time was too valuable to fiddle with that sort of thing, but hers wasn't.

Genevieve was only eight months out of college, but already she was becoming disillusioned with the real world. In school, everyone revered the pursuit of truth and scholarship. She took a job with the Lexington Historical Society because she thought that same reverence would continue. To her disappointment, even the historical society was beholden to the almighty dollar. Curators needed salaries, bills had to be paid, and space was limited. On top of all that, there was a depression on, and everyone was terrified of ending up in the soup line. Sometimes things just had to be jettisoned to make room for the exhibits that would bring in donation dollars.

Genevieve was proud of her academic record and even more proud of her stint as president of the Transylvania University History Club. Under her tenure, the group raised funds to buy a proper memorial plaque for Samuel Constantine Rafinesque, a nineteenth Century professor at Transylvania who died a pauper and was buried in an unmarked grave in Philadelphia. Rafinesque had been a quirky and controversial figure during his tenure at Transylvania, but Genevieve loved his work because it dripped with his authentic wonder at the natural world. She spent many long nights in the university library poring over Rafinesque's writings, getting to know him, to understand him. She loved touching his books, feeling the same paper under her fingertips that he felt so many years ago.

In 1924, even the university that had unceremoniously fired Rafinesque a century before finally came to understand his unappreciated genius. A contingent from Lexington successfully lobbied to have his remains disinterred and reburied in a crypt under Old Morrison, the oldest building on campus. The History Club donated a memorial plaque for his tomb that gave a beautiful recounting of his incredible life and his many contributions to science. Genevieve wrote it.

The late nights of studying piled up, however, and kept Genevieve from interacting with her peers like a typical college student. She was cordial and engaging in class, but she never accepted any invitations to extracurricular activities. Instead, she was content making picnics for herself and reading some odd book or journal at the arboretum. Nothing brought her more satisfaction than lying on her blanket and dreamily thinking about the past as the sun warmed her skin.

But those lovely summer days seemed long gone. It was winter, and the box issue was only adding to her gloom. By the time Genevieve took her usual seat on the bus that took her home, her thoughts were completely consumed by the box and whether it would still be waiting for her when she got to work the following morning. She already regretted leaving its fate to chance. Who was she kidding? She desperately wanted to see what treasures it held.

The entire ride, she kicked herself for her folly. Genevieve lived in a little bungalow with two other girls, a graduate student and a nurse. If it had not been her turn to cook supper that night, she would have gone straight back downtown to the office to rescue the little box. True to her typical form, though, responsibility trumped personal caprice, and Genevieve went home and threw together some cream chipped beef on toast.

That night, her sleep was restless. When she finally managed to doze, she had the same nightmare she always had when she was stressed. She dreamed that she was back in college and she was taking a test in a class that she had forgotten to attend all semester. The dream always conjured the same anxiety. *How could I have forgotten to go to this class? I vaguely remember the first day and the professor discussing the syllabus. Oh god, my grades will be ruined!* As always, it was not until her despair reached a fever pitch that her brain could mercifully rattle her awake.

Genevieve beat her alarm clock by twenty minutes. She decided just to abandon the struggle for rest and hurry back to the office to see if her mistake was going to be a temporary or permanent one. In an effort to catch an earlier bus, Genevieve skipped breakfast. Her annoyance rose to a brewing anger as she arrived at the bus stop just in time to see the taillights of the six fifteen bus to downtown speeding away down Rose Street. Genevieve stood, hungry, cold, and fuming until she stepped onto her normal bus over a half hour later.

At the office, Mr. Marshall had arrived early. He caught Genevieve as she came through the door and held a painfully one-sided conversation about how he hated when the paperboy placed his newspaper in a different spot on his front porch every morning. Genevieve squirmed as she looked for an opportunity to escape the clutches of his interminable musings. Twice she turned to leave. Both times, she started with, "Well, I should probably..." but Mr. Marshall powered through.

Genevieve tried to control her irritation through measured breathing, but her anxiety persisted. *There's no way I'll get to the back alley before the garbage truck gets here.*

As Mr. Marshall droned on, he interrupted his own reflections about the correct way to fold a letter before mailing it. "Oh, I nearly forgot. I'm afraid I'll be adding something else to your plate, work-wise, and I wanted to discuss it with you."

Genevieve leapt at the opening. "Of course, sir. Just let me go get my notepad," she said as she rushed out of his office and down the hall. She pretended not to hear as he offered one of his own notepads. Genevieve clomped down the hallway across the hardwood floors, something she generally tried not to do because it was so unbecoming, but niceties were suspended due to emergency. She burst through the back door and scrambled down the steps only to discover the trashcans were empty and the box was gone. Her heart sank but quickly revived when she saw the garbage truck lingering at the end of the alley. Genevieve took off in an all-out run. A dozen painful strides later, she stopped briefly to take off her encumbering Oxfords then proceeded with a sprinter's gait in her stocking feet.

"Stop!" she called. "Please hold up!"

The two garbage collectors regarded the shoeless girl, first with bewilderment, then amusement. The older of the two, a slick-haired goon, put up both his hands as Genevieve approached.

"Hold up there, doll face. Where's the fire?"

Genevieve fought to catch her breath. She became aware of the ice-cold pavement under her feet as the effects of her initial adrenaline wore off.

"I'm very sorry," she panted, "but you just picked up a box of books back there, and it's not trash."

The goon smugly placed a toothpick in his mouth and looked at his partner, a chuckling teenager. "Did you pick up a box of books?"

The nervous boy shook his head and chuckled again.

"Sorry, miss, I think you're mistaken." The goon shrugged.

Genevieve did not hide her irritation. "Sir, I assure you. There was a box of books by the trashcans behind our building. I put it there last night. Now it's gone."

The goon, seemingly enjoying her agitation, smiled. "I don't know what to tell you, girly. There ain't no box."

Genevieve huffed. "If it wouldn't inconvenience you too much, could you look in the back of your truck there? I'm sure it will be on top of the heap."

The goon folded his arms. "No can do, union rules. I put the trash in the back. Another fella unloads it from the back. If I start unloading from the back, my foreman will be on my ass. I'm not about to put another man outta work by doing his job."

Genevieve was speechless with frustration.

"That being said," the goon continued, "if you wanted to take a look for yourself, I ain't gonna stop ya."

Genevieve hated the glee beaming from the goon's face, but she wasn't about to let it keep her from getting what she wanted. "Fine," she said defiantly. She then walked over to the side of the converted flatbed dump truck and climbed up on one of the oversized tires. Standing on her tiptoes, she peered over the side of the huge steel container affixed to the back of the truck and scanned the huge pile of trash. The odor was very strong, and it made her want to gag, but she wasn't about to give the garbage collectors that kind of satisfaction. After a long initial review of the pile, she didn't see the box.

"What's going on back there?" a voice called out from the cab of the truck. "We movin' or what?"

"C'mon, girly, we got stops to make. You see what you're looking for yet?" the goon asked.

Genevieve felt rushed. *It's got to be here. Where is it?* There was just so much garbage and everything blended in together.

"There!" she exclaimed. "I see a book!"

She leaned as far as she could over the side of the steel container and managed to pick up an old-looking hardcover with the tips of her fingers. As she did so, out of the corner of her eye she caught the goon craning his neck to look up her dress. Her left hand still holding on to the side of the truck, Genevieve used her book hand to pull her dress tightly against the back of her legs. She quickly hopped down off the tire, her cold feet landing on the pavement with a jarring impact.

Resisting the urge to slap at the goon's face, Genevieve gathered herself as best she could. "You are well suited for your profession, sir. You truly are a garbage man."

The goon looked at the teenager and pretended to stifle a laugh. "Thank you." He beamed, tipping an imaginary cap toward Genevieve.

She was cold and embarrassed. Her feet hurt, and there was a mystery slime smeared across her backside from when she used the book to keep the goon from peeping up her dress. Still, Genevieve felt satisfied that she'd managed to save a piece of history. Eagerly, she flipped through the pages of her salvage to see what treasure she'd rescued. Her satisfaction melted into dismay. It was just a worn copy of a Nancy Drew novel, *The Secret of the Old Clock*. She just let the book fall from her hands. At first, she wanted to cry, but her discouragement quickly changed to anger. She was angry with herself for playing stupid mental games. She wanted the books from the very beginning. *Why didn't I just take them, everyone else be damned? Never again. From here on out, I'm not going to let the things I want slip through my grasp.*

Back inside the office, she cleaned up as best she could. She was so disgusted with herself, it was hard to see her own reflection in the bathroom mirror. But the more she thought about it, the angrier she got at Mr. Marshall for deciding to throw the books out in the first place. He was supposed to be a good steward of history, faithfully preserving it and passing it on to the next generation. How could he call himself a true historian?

Unable to control her resentment at losing the box, Genevieve went back down the hallway to confront Mr. Marshall.

"There you are!" he exclaimed as she marched in and sat down, scowling. "I was about to send out a search party."

He looked at her empty hands. "All that time, and you couldn't find your notepad? Here, just take mine."

Genevieve knew what she wanted to say, but she was having a difficult time finding the right way to start. Confronting authority went against her very core.

"Now, like I was saying before, I have something new for you," Mr. Marshall continued. "I know that you are already busy, and you are doing a very good job indeed. I think that's why I feel so confident that you will be fine, even if I add something else to your duties. What do you think? Are you up for a challenge?"

"Sir, you shouldn't have thrown out that box yesterday," Genevieve blurted.

"What's that?" Mr. Marshall asked, adjusting his glasses.

"That box of old books and journals that were brought here yesterday. I think it was a mistake to throw them out."

"Oh really? Why is that?"

"Because that was history that we can't get back now. I know they didn't look like much, but I'm sure we could have gotten something useful from them. And what are we doing here if we aren't learning from the past?"

Mr. Marshall leaned forward in his chair and pointed toward Genevieve. "I'm glad to hear you say that."

He reached under his desk and produced the box that Genevieve had been obsessing over.

"Before I left yesterday, I had the exact same thought. Now, I'm not sure there is much we can really learn from the contents of this box, but I think that would be a wonderful assignment for someone like you, a bright, energetic young person who is trying to make a name for herself."

Genevieve was shocked. Tears welled up as she let out a relieved laugh. "Yes! Of course."

"Wonderful. I know that it will take some time to get through the material, but I expect a well-crafted analysis of these documents from…ummm," he paused and tilted his head back slightly to look at the outside of the box through his bifocals, "uhh…the estate of Berwick. Does six months sound reasonable?"

Genevieve picked up the box. "That sounds perfectly reasonable, sir. Thank you."

Her boss tilted his head forward and tapped his pencil on the edge of his desk. "This is a great opportunity for you to show me your mettle, Genevieve. Do a good job with this assignment and I'll consider recommending you for the graduate program in the History Department at the University of Kentucky. I'm still on the alumni association board, you know," he said with a self-satisfied grin.

# Chapter 20

**1962**

Even though Violet was flustered and rushed, she still felt sad at having to leave the funeral home. She only took the job as the means to an end, but it had been surprisingly good for her. She'd grown to feel proud of her work. Up until an hour ago, Henry had even been a friend and a mentor. The terrible things he said changed all of that. It hurt her deeply that he despised her so much. She caught a glimpse of her troubled face in the mirror, and it made her angry. "Fuck him."

Downstairs, there was a clattering. Brian must have knocked something over in the basement with her bike. A few moments later, she heard the front door open and close.

"Jesus, he's really hustling," Violet thought as she scurried out into the hallway with her overflowing bag in tow. She couldn't blame him for wanting to be gone before Henry got back. Henry would have been justified in having Brian arrested for punching him in the face like he did. Hell, it was Kentucky — Henry would've been justified in shooting him.

Violet tried to catch up to him before he got upset with her for dawdling. When she reached the first floor landing, another crash sounded from the basement, giving her pause. She looked back in the direction of the sanctuary.

Everything became very still.

Violet was not sure what was happening. She'd definitely heard someone at the front door a few moments before. Could Brian have somehow made a noise in the basement, come up to the front door, and then gone back down into the basement so quickly? Was the crash in the basement a delayed reaction to Brian's jostling around in the dark — maybe something that he'd nudged that hung precariously unbalanced until it finally toppled over? Had Henry come back?

Gently, she sat down her belongings and tiptoed her way to the basement door, which was open. Standing at the top of the steps, Violet squinted fearfully into the darkness. She heard muffled grunts and heavy breathing float up from below.

"Brian?" she called timidly.

There was a half moment of silence before a desperate shriek pierced out from the darkness: "Run!"

The terror in Brian's voice sent an electric jolt through her spine. Plodding footsteps suddenly slapped against the tile of the embalming room floor. By the time the stairs starting creaking, Violet knew she'd waited too long. Henry flew out of the shadows, his face dripping with blood and his eyes aflame. She held up her hands to stop him, but he was too big and moving too fast. His lunge was high and powerful, launching him nearly horizontally into her chest and slamming her shoulders to the hardwood floor with a resonant thud. All the air in her body seemed to pop, leaving her writhing in suffocating pain.

Her hands, through instinct, pushed desperately against Henry's neck, keeping his gnashing teeth, which were clamping with feral power, just out of reach of her face. She tried without success to inhale, but the writhing weight of Henry's body wouldn't allow it. Her vision began to tunnel from the lack of oxygen. Henry snapped closer and closer, blood spattering on Violet's cheek and into her gaping mouth. A new wave of panic gave her just enough adrenaline to push his neck back again. His skin felt like clay in her hands.

With all her remaining strength, Violet slid her hands up Henry's neck to his cheeks and then his forehead. Darkness was moving beyond the periphery of her vision as she pressed her thumbs into his eyes as deep as they would go, which, it turned out, was a long way. His eyeballs gave way as Violet pressed all of the jelly out of them. Leveraging her thumbs against his eye sockets, she finally managed to twist his head in a way that rotated him off of her body.

With the pressure on Violet's chest gone, she gasped for air in moaning heaves. It felt like breathing through a straw. Henry, now on all fours, moved his head in a jerky, searching way. He could no longer see. Violet scrambled backward away from him, scooting across the smooth floor. Twice she tried to regain her feet and failed, both times falling hard. Henry seemed to track the racket she was making and began crawling toward her in the same reckless way he'd pounced up the basement stairs.

Violet continued crawling backward until she slid into an upright lamp against the wall. The lamp toppled over and the glass globe shattered against the floor. Henry lunged at the noise and smashed his face against the wall as a result.

While the lamp distracted him, Violet finally managed to regain her feet and run from the room. To her dismay, Henry followed her, skillfully tracking her by the tapping of her hard soles on the wood floor. Violet hopped on one foot midstride and slid one shoe off, and then the other. She skidded to a stop and tossed one of the shoes into the sanctuary, where it hit a pew and bounced to the floor. Henry was after it in a flash. Meanwhile, Violet went the opposite way and ducked into the casket showroom on the other side of the house. Without hesitation, she climbed into the first casket she saw and lowered the upper panel; the latch clicked as it closed.

At first, all she could hear was her own panting breath, which she tried to modulate by inhaling through her nose and exhaling slowly out of her mouth. When she got that under control, she strained to listen for any sign of Henry. Faintly, she could hear the sound of his clambering hands and knees. For a moment it seemed like he was going away from her, but just as quickly, he was back. He moved with terrible swiftness. Violet could hear him sniffing like a dog around the lid of the casket.

She was in an extremely vulnerable position should Henry open up her hiding place like a can of sardines. Once again, she would be forced to fight him using her already weakened arms. Henry jostled the casket, causing Violet to catch a yelp in her hands. He jostled it again, harder. Then he started shaking it with all his might. Violet braced her hands against the cushioned walls inside and grimaced in anticipation. Suddenly the shaking stopped. Violet waited. Before she knew what was happening, the casket was knocked off of its pedestal and onto the ground. Henry flipped the casket onto its side, then upside down, then onto the other side. The absolute darkness within the box added to Violet's disorientation.

From above, Henry started scratching. At first it sounded like nails against the fine grain wood, but it soon changed to squeaking, like windshield wipers. Then there was silence. A minute passed, then two. Violet didn't hear Henry scramble away. For all she knew, he was still there, waiting for her to pop her head out like a whack-a-mole. After a few more minutes, she decided to test the water.

"Henry, are you there?" she said softly.

Nothing.

"Henry?" she called louder.

Still nothing.

Violet wasn't sure which way to roll the casket to get it upright. She felt around until she found the side that had some curvature, the top. She shifted hard to the left, tipping the casket back to an upright position with a thunderous boom against the hardwood floor.

*Geez, if that doesn't draw him back, I don't know what will.*

No longer able to stand another moment of confinement, Violet decided to risk everything and make a run for it. She pushed hard against the lid. It didn't budge. She pushed again, forcing her knees up against it as well, but it was locked in place. Dread washed over her. Violet had never been a fan of tight spaces. She once almost had a panic attack when she got stuck in an elevator for fifteen minutes between floors. The casket was much tighter than the elevator, and darker. Her breathing picked up again. It felt like she was inside a hot sleeping bag.

"Brian!" she screamed, her voice giving out. "Brian, Help!"

Yet another wave of panic struck her. If Brian was battling Henry, he didn't stand a chance. Brian was bigger and stronger than Violet, but Henry was an unstoppable force. The fact that Brian did not come help her while she was fighting off Henry's savage attack at the top of the basement stairs made Violet think that he was probably hurt very badly. Or maybe he had simply run off to save himself. And if either thing was true, then nobody was coming to save her.

The air was so hot and thick, Violet labored to breathe. Her body jerked instinctively at the prospect of suffocating, so she began punching and kicking with all of her might. Even with the cushioned lining, her fists ached from the repeated strikes.

It was hard to think clearly with her own panicked gasps echoing in her ears, so she made an effort to calm herself and focus. She took a deep, deliberate breath and slowly released the air with a long, steady exhale. She did it again and again until she finally managed to slow her racing heart.

*Okay, now think. What do I need to open a locked casket?*

The answer was obvious: *A key.*

*Now, where are the keys? On Henry's key ring. Shit. Are there any others?* She answered her own question. *Just the copy I made for the secret door.*

The thought hit Violet like a jolt. She was wearing the dress in which the key was hidden!

*Thank God Brian has no sense of fashion!*

She reached into her pocket. It was empty.

"No!" she wailed and desperately patted herself down, checking every pocket on her dress. *The key must have fallen out while I was fighting off Henry. But then again, it could have fallen out when he flipped the casket over too.*

Violet felt underneath herself as much as she could, but her mobility was very limited. Nothing was there. She used her feet to search the bottom of the casket as well. Her toenail clinked against something hard. *The key!*

Methodically, Violet worked the key up the side of the casket, first with her foot, then with her other foot, which she tucked under her calf, then her knee, and ultimately with the very tip of her middle finger. When she actually secured it in her hand, she let out a relieved sob.

*Okay, you're not done yet.*

The casket was completely dark, and she still needed to find the keyhole.

She pushed at the cushioned lining until she could feel hinges on the left side. *All right, other side.* Desperately, she pushed against the lining, but it was too thick. With animal aggression, she began ripping at the lining until she'd torn it off the entire right side and it was resting in pieces on her belly. Again she ran her fingers up and down the right panel, as though she were reading braille.

But then a horribly defeating thought dawned on her. *You idiot! There's no way this key will work from inside. That's not how keys work.*

She let the worthless key slip out of her palm and onto the cushioned lining beneath her. Hopeless, hot, and breathless, she lay perfectly still. She tried to accept the fact that she was going to die a horrible death. Tears streamed down her cheeks, but she made no sound. Her discomfort was unrelenting. For the second time in her life, Violet wished that she could just die painlessly in her sleep.

# Chapter 21

**1848**

For two more killing cycles, Charles worked on his plan. It was not going well. For the hundredth time, he took a mental inventory of what he and Soñador had been able to learn about their situation and their physical condition.

Without a doubt, the jaguar warriors were using the "affected" prisoners as a tool to terrorize the local population into providing them with human sacrifices. From what Charles could gather, the jaguar warriors had the same affliction as the prisoners; they could only eat one thing: people. More specifically, Soñador was convinced that they were only able to digest human brain matter. Charles was not yet completely certain of that.

The scheme implemented by the warriors was fairly simple. For weeks, the prisoners were starved. At a certain point during their deprivation, the red fog would set in. Charles and Soñador could never remember anything after that happened but would invariably regain consciousness post-feeding, while covered in human gore and unable to move. Although mobility eventually returned in full, they felt very sluggish for several days after gorging and were easily controlled by their captors.

The jaguar warriors never gorged like the prisoners. Instead, they periodically ate bean-like morsels from the pouches around their necks. Charles hypothesized that eating smaller amounts more regularly probably helped prevent the red fog from setting in with the warriors.

The ranks of the prisoners were dwindling. After the last killing cycle,

Charles counted only eight remaining prisoners, including himself. Thad and Josiah were gone. Charles suspected they'd been killed. What he didn't know was whether the jaguar warriors were killing the prisoners or if the villagers were somehow doing it. Charles and Soñador had not yet figured out what, if anything, could truly hurt them.

Charles considered the things that he and Soñador needed. First, they needed to get out of the cell. That was obvious. Also obvious was the fact that they needed to do so without all of the warriors knowing. Between himself and Soñador, Charles figured they could probably overpower one or two of the warriors, but it would be impossible to take on their entire force. Even more importantly, they needed to do so while in the correct state of mind. If they got to the point of the red fog, they lost their ability to control themselves in any way. Charles and Soñador also needed to know how to kill or permanently injure the warriors, and they needed the weapons to do it. Having none of those things, all they could do was wait until something changed or they learned something new. So they waited.

To pass the time, they tried talking, but conversation between Charles and Soñador was tricky to say the least. When the topics of politics, imperialism, morality, or religion came up, the conversation usually ended with some form of body-mutilating fight between them. Growing tired of such a tedious outcome, the two began seeking common ground on more polite topics. The best one they eventually found was agriculture.

At first, the two talked of the different crops that they'd grown in their former lives. They discussed methods of irrigation, the challenges presented by their respective climates, and the hundreds of other minutiae of farming that farmers have discussed since man first graduated from the hunter-gatherer lifestyle. Several times, they even found themselves laughing at common problems. Before long, they were trading jokes and talking about girls they'd known.

Soñador even told Charles about the first girl he ever kissed. He was twelve years old, and he'd gone to his cousin's *quinceañera.* Soñador explained that the quinceañera celebration was a momentous occasion for young women in Mexico. It was a big party thrown by the family of a girl turning fifteen years old that marked the girl's passage into womanhood. Soñador had never been to a formal party, so he was quite nervous. To make matters worse, his older sister told him that he'd be expected to dance with girls, or everyone would think he was a dullard. On top of that, he explained that he was an extremely bashful boy, so the anticipation of the event was a source of overwhelming anxiety for him.

On the way to the party, he told his father about how nervous he was. His father had chuckled and handed him a beat-up old flask.

*"Take this,"* he'd told Soñador. *"Any time you feel nervous tonight, find a private place and take a sip."*

Although Soñador had seen his father drink from the flask on several occasions, he did not actually know what his father was drinking. It happened to be tequila. When Soñador got to the party, he immediately found a secluded spot and took a sip. The taste was powerful, and it nearly choked him. After taking the drink, he waited for a few minutes, but he didn't feel any less nervous. Convinced that he hadn't drunk enough, Soñador held his nose and drained the entire flask.

From what he could remember, the party had been the time of his life. He had laughed and danced and felt quite wonderful. But the next morning, he woke up vomiting in his uncle's chicken coop, where his grandmother had made him sleep. His sister taunted him relentlessly, telling him that he was real Casanova.

*"Why do you keep saying that?"* Soñador had asked.

*"You don't remember? Oh, Soñador, you fell in love last night."* Soñador recalled his sister batting her eyes and lifting her chin with her interlaced fingers while saying, *"Mi amorcito! Mi amorcito!"*

Soñador had no idea who she was talking about until later that day when the whole family went to the town plaza and the open-air market. With glee, Soñador's sister pointed to a thick-legged, pimple-riddled girl drawing water from the town's central well. The girl saw Soñador and waved at him enthusiastically. Soñador's face lost all color, and once again his sister laughed mightily.

*"I wouldn't laugh too much, hija,"* Soñador's father had chimed in. *"I'm going*

to have buckets of tequila at your quinceañera so that the boys will pay some attention to you too."

"*Papa!*"his sister cried.

His father laughed and winked at Soñador, who managed a weak smile back.

Charles found the story very amusing. "What exactly is tequila?" he asked. "I assume it's like whiskey, but I truly know nothing about the stuff."

Soñador grinned. He looked around the filthy cell and at his own grimy apparel. "Tequila is what makes all of this...all of life...not so goddamn terrible. It makes your friends feel more like your brothers. It blunts the sting of tragedy. It makes wisdom look like foolishness and foolishness look like brilliance. And it compels you to expose your deepest feelings to the people who matter most to you." He laughed. "Or whoever is around, really."

"Sounds exactly like whiskey." Charles smiled.

Soñador rested his head against the hard rock of the cell wall and sighed deeply. "Actually, I'd give anything to have a bottle right now. Though I doubt it would have the same effect on me anymore. It would just make me shit my pants like everything else I put down my throat."

Charles shrugged. "Well, not *everything* makes us shit."

Soñador tilted his head in confusion.

Charles ran his fingers across his own stomach to imitate a little running man. He then picked up the little man with his other hand, the little legs still kicking furiously in the air, and dangled him over his open mouth. After tormenting the little man, whose muffled screams Charles imitated in the back of his throat, Charles finally dropped him into his chomping teeth.

Soñador looked truly horrified, like someone had just lifted up his grand-mother's dress and spanked her naked bottom in front of his grandfather. He couldn't believe Charles could make light of the unspeakable repulsiveness of what they had done.

"You know...people," Charles needlessly explained. "I was trying to say that we can eat people."

"Yes. I know what you meant," Soñador replied with disgust.

Charles licked the tips of each of his fingers like he was sucking chicken grease off of them, all the while locking a penetrating gaze on Soñador.

Despite himself, Soñador began to chuckle. It started as a snort but then came from deep within his belly. Charles eagerly joined him. Soon the two were doubled over with hysterical laughter.

"You are demented!" Soñador finally managed to utter.

Charles felt an unbelievable relief in discovering that he could still laugh. It felt very good, and for a moment he didn't feel like the monster he had become. He would have liked for the moment to last longer, but to the amazement of the prisoners a new voice addressed them from above.

"What are you laughing at?" a little boy asked.

Soñador and Charles shielded their eyes from the midday sun as they looked up through the woven reed thatching. For the first time since their capture, they had a visitor.

# Chapter 22

**1962**

Violet pretended that the casket was sinking into the ocean near a beautiful reef. She imagined there was a glass portal through which she could watch enormous schools of fluorescent fish swarm in artful spirals over the brightly colored corals and seaweeds that waved faintly with the tide. A curious octopus even emerged from his hidden home and suctioned one of his arms on the glass as if to say hello. From the ocean floor, the casket no longer seemed like a tortuous, inescapable prison, but more like a safe little haven.

Violet knew that even in this construct of her mind, she would never get out again. She would never float back to shore, open her little vessel, and feel misting breeze or the soft, wet sand under her feet. Still, it was infinitely more bearable than merely suffocating in the dark. Here, she could just lie peacefully and enjoy the beauty of the hidden underwater world until she fell asleep and drifted off into a painless death. There was a certain relief in not having to actually face the real world any longer. All of those problems were done. They didn't involve her any more.

Just as she felt herself blacking out, something struck her vessel, and sharp jets of water began spraying inside. Violet jolted with the atmospheric change. There was another strike, and then another. Water began pouring in — except it wasn't water. It was light. Violet struggled to come back to her senses.

Brian peered into the little hole he'd created. "Violet?" he whispered.

"Yes, I'm here," she croaked.

"Henry's still here. He's gone absolutely wild. He's trying to kill us."

"I know. Please help me out, I'm trapped."

"Shush," Brian demanded. "I think he's coming back down the stairs. I have to hide."

"Brian, don't leave me!" Violet cried out, but he was already gone.

Even though she was still terrified, the rush of fresh air revived her, and knowing that Brian was still alive also gave her hope. Through the hole, she could barely hear what was happening around her. The stillness in the room was thick, like just before a lightning strike. It was in that crushing silence that a new voice softly filtered through the density.

"Stay where you are. When he comes back, I'll lure him away and you can get her out," someone whispered to Brian. Violet strained but did not hear Brian respond.

Within moments, the erratic slapping of bare hands and feet on the hardwood announced Henry's return to the casket room. Violet held her breath and listened to his approach. Henry slung himself from wall to wall with complete abandon. His forehead thudded sharply against the top of the casket, and his face slid across the surface until he buried his nose as deeply into the newly created hole as he could penetrate. Rediscovering his prey sent him into a renewed paroxysm of fury. His arms and legs flailed recklessly and ineffectively at the casket's hard mahogany.

Yet again, Violet felt utterly defenseless. Henry gnashed his mouth into the hole, chomping at her with teeth that were starting to break into shards. When that proved unsuccessful, he tried jamming his hand through the small hole, peeling back the skin of his forearm on the jagged edges. With unbelievable strength, he gripped Violet's thigh and tugged it upward, making her shriek in pain. Reflexively, she shimmied free of his grasp and shifted herself as far away from the hole as she could. Because Henry could not get his elbow through, he had no angle to regain his hold on Violet. Even still, he showed no signs of relenting.

"Here now! Over here!" a man yelled from somewhere else in the house. Henry paused momentarily and listened. When the man repeated his call,

Henry bolted away. Violet did not wait to call out to Brian.

"Hey, are you still there?" she said in a low voice.

A few seconds later, he leaned his face over the hole. "I'm here."

"You have got to get me out of this fucking thing."

"It's locked. I'll have to keep busting it open with the ax."

"No, don't. That will just draw him back here. Oh my god," Violet remembered. "The key! I have it."

She fumbled underneath herself until she found it and then pushed it through the hole with shaking fingers. No sooner had Brian popped the lid open than she sprang into his arms. Violet tried to thank him, but she was too overcome by emotion to speak. Brian returned her embrace with genuine relief that she was okay.

"Brian, your face!" she exclaimed. Blood was trickling from his forehead, down his cheek, and onto his neck. His face was red and swollen, and his shirt was ripped to shreds.

"He almost killed me," Brian explained, picking up the ax lying near the casket that Violet just escaped. "He's changed. He's like a cannibal. I really think he was trying to eat me. I put this ax into his chest, right into his heart, but it didn't stop him."

Violet frowned. "I know. I think I squeezed his eyes out of his head. It didn't faze him."

"We've got to go right now."

Violet nodded, and the two made their way out of the casket showroom. Just as she cleared the threshold, she crashed squarely into a man who was hurrying down the hallway. Fearing it was Henry, Violet thrust her hand out defensively, her palm firmly striking the man's nose with a muted pop. He grunted in pain and covered his face with a small, grungy hand.

"Fuck! Why did you do that?" he whined, blood flowing freely over his mouth and chin and dripping onto his white suit. The man was very short and had a bulbous head.

"You!" Violet gasped.

"You know him?" Brian asked.

"Rhodes. He was the one that lied for Trimble. I saw him in the cemetery

230

and then in the greenhouse the day I got framed for burglary. He's the one that lied to Detective Webster, denying that Trimble told me that he'd locked himself out of his house."

"I can explain," Rhodes grunted. His eyes were still watering from the palm strike to his nose.

"What are you even doing here right now?" Violet asked.

Brian looked over Rhodes's shoulder down the hallway. "Guys, let's talk about this another time. Henry is still lurking around here somewhere."

"I've incapacitated him," Rhodes said in his thick Georgia accent. "At least temporarily."

Brian was baffled. "How did you do that? He was unstoppable. And, no offense, he's about three times your size."

"Every monster has a weakness," Rhodes replied, pinching the bridge of his nose with a handkerchief from his pocket.

"Brian, I don't know what's going on, but I know that we can't trust this little cretin," Violet snarled.

"This little cretin just saved your lives," Rhodes retorted. The bleeding seemed to be stopping, so he wadded up his handkerchief and stuffed it back into his pocket. "I don't care if you trust me or not. I'm not asking you to do anything except get out of here and away from danger. I can explain myself if you give me a chance, but now is not the time. I've been searching for Henry for many years, and now that I've found him there's a lot I need to do."

"Violet, I agree that there's a lot of explaining to be done, but I also agree with this guy that we need to get out of here." Brian looked to Rhodes. "Should we call the police?"

"No. At least not yet. I need some time to get him in proper restraints so he doesn't hurt anyone else."

"Well, should we stay and help you then?" Brian offered.

"No. Please. Just give me some time to do what I need to do. Can we agree to meet here tomorrow? I'll explain everything then, I promise."

"Like that means anything," Violet sneered. "He's probably robbing the place."

"Young lady, you have no idea what it is your dealing with. That man downstairs is possibly the most dangerous being on the face of the Earth. There will be a time of reckoning between the two of us. I know that I owe you a sincere apology, but I think in the end you will appreciate why I've done all of these things."

Violet was skeptical.

"Like I said. We will meet here tomorrow and everything will be explained. Now go. Get cleaned up. Get some rest."

Brian gently pulled Violet by the elbow. "Come on, Violet. I think he's right. Do you really think we're going to be able to explain what happened to the police?"

"Okay." Violet relented. "But I've got a terrible feeling about all of this."

"As you should," Rhodes warned.

# Chapter 23

Charles judged the little boy to be about seven years old, but he was so malnourished and small, he may have been older. The boy squatted near the edge of the pit and looked down curiously at the two men below. He wore a dingy white linen shirt with matching pants. On his shoulder was a black howler monkey that mimicked the boy's inquisitive posture.

"Hello there, *hijo*," Soñador cooed, careful not to scare the boy away.

"I'm not your hijo," the boy replied without fear.

"Of course not. Please take no offense. What are you doing all the way out here? Are you alone?"

"No," the boy said. "I'm here with Chalo."

"Where is Chalo?" Charles chimed in. "Is he nearby?"

The boy laughed and nodded to his monkey. "Yes, he's right here. We are out on an adventure today."

Charles and Soñador glanced at each other. Neither was quite sure how to proceed, but both sensed an opportunity was presenting itself.

"What luck!" Charles told the boy, rising to his knees. "My friend and I are also adventurers."

"You are?"

"Yes! And explorers to boot."

"What are you exploring down there?"

"Well, we have hit a small bump in the road. You see, my partner and I were searching for a cavern in this forest where a great chest of treasure

233

has been..."

Soñador grabbed Charles by the arm, startling him and nearly triggering him to violently retaliate.

"My friend," Soñador said to Charles, imploring him with his eyes to play along. "You cannot just reveal the secret location so carelessly."

Charles caught on immediately. "Ah. Yes, of course. There I go again — always saying too much! I'm just so eager to get out of this pit, I'd gladly share our bounty with someone who could help us escape."

"What bounty?" the boy asked.

"Don't you think we should tell him? Maybe he could help us," Charles suggested.

"This little kitten?" Soñador asked, pointing up at the boy. "How could he possibly help?"

"I'm no kitten!" the boy said indignantly. "I'm a jaguar."

"What's your name, boy?" Charles asked.

"Gonzalo," the boy replied proudly.

Charles rubbed his chin and pretended to examine the boy closely. "Are you strong?"

Gonzalo flexed his scrawny bicep. Although there was no perceptible muscle at all, he strained mightily, causing his little fist to tremble. Charles and Soñador leaned closer to the reed thatching to get a better look. The boy, momentarily losing confidence in his claim under such close scrutiny, stole a glance at his arm. Completely reassured by what he saw, he smirked with self-assuredness.

Charles and Soñador nodded at each other in silent agreement.

"Who put you down there?" Gonzalo asked.

Soñador slumped back against the cell wall in feigned exasperation. "We were traveling with a party of twelve other men. One of those men was my dastardly brother, Hernando. We were getting very close to the location of the treasure, when he incited a mutiny among the men and they stuck us in this pit. They were greedy and wanted our share of the riches."

"What kind of treasure is it?" Gonzalo asked.

"Why, Spanish gold, of course!"

"Think they've already found it by now?" the boy wondered aloud.

Soñador smiled deviously. "No. Only I know the secret location. They put a knife to my throat and made me tell them where it was, but I lied. I suspect they have already discovered my lie and will come back here soon to beat the truth out of me. If I can escape before they get here, then we can go claim the treasure for ourselves!"

Gonzalo looked skeptical. "Who is this gringo?" he asked, pointing at Charles.

"This is my best friend in the world and a brave man," Soñador replied without hesitation. "When the other men took me prisoner, this man tried to convince them to let me go. In the end, they just left him here too."

Gonzalo rocked back and forth on his haunches as he thought. He pointed upward to a spot over his shoulder that Charles and Soñador could not see and patted his stomach three times. Chalo shrieked a staccato burst of monkey calls then hopped away.

"So what do you think, young man? Will you help us get out of here?" Charles asked.

"Maybe," Gonzalo replied. "What do you want?"

Soñador pushed his hand through the reed thatching and pointed his finger in several directions. "Can you see what the men have used to secure this barrier in place?"

Gonzalo got up and walked around. "There is a big iron lock attached to this thing," he said as he kicked the barrier and then squatted back down where he was before.

Soñador looked at Charles. "Maybe he could smash the lock with a large stone?"

"I honestly doubt that. If it really is made of iron, it would take more than a rock to smash it."

Chalo came waddling back up to Gonzalo, holding a piece of fruit that Charles did not recognize.

"Your monkey is very clever," Soñador said.

Gonzalo took the fruit from Chalo and kissed him on the head. "He's my best friend in the world and a brave man," he said, echoing Soñador's words.

Gonzalo produced a small knife from his pocket and cut the fruit in half. He then cut a small piece from the center and handed it to Chalo, who greedily jammed it into his mouth making Gonzalo giggle.

"Will you help us?" Charles asked again.

The boy took a wild, sloppy bite of fruit so that the juice ran down his chin and dripped onto the ground. "Maybe," he managed to mumble with his full mouth.

Soñador was growing impatient, but he was careful to disguise it. "What else do you need to know before you decide?"

Gonzalo considered this. "I need to ask you something first."

Soñador shifted restlessly. "What? I'll tell you anything you need to know."

Gonzalo sat the remains of his fruit on the ground and cautiously checked over both of his shoulders. He then leaned close to the reed thatching and motioned for Soñador to do the same.

"What is it?" Soñador whispered as he pushed his ear close to the thatching.

"Are you the Cuco?" the boy whispered, then retreated back to his squatting position at the edge of the pit to watch Soñador's reply.

Soñador laughed.

"What is that?" Charles asked. "I don't know this word, *Cuco*."

Soñador held eye contact with Gonzalo. "It's the made-up monster that parents use to scare children into doing their chores and going to bed. No, hijo, I'm not the Cuco."

"I'm not your hijo," Gonzalo repeated coldly.

"I know I look filthy, sitting in this muddy pit, but I'm no monster. I'm just a man who needs the help of a brave boy."

Gonzalo scooted backward on his haunches. "You're lying."

By this point, Soñador's patience was ebbing. "If you don't help get us out, then we will die. Those men will come back and cut our throats. Can you live with that, letting two innocent men die when you have the power to help?"

Gonzalo patted his shoulder. "Chalo, come."

The monkey scrambled nimbly up the boy's back and onto its perch. Gonzalo then stood up and began to back away.

"Where are you going?" Charles cried in sudden desperation.

"If they cut your throats, it won't matter," Gonzalo replied.

"How can you say such an awful thing?" Soñador demanded.

The boy pointed at Soñador's neck. "Because I've already done it, and it didn't seem to bother you."

Soñador slapped at his neck until the little knife that Gonzalo had used to cut fruit pulled free from his flesh and fell to the ground. The boy had deftly plunged the blade just below Soñador's jaw while whispering into his ear. Soñador growled in frustration, picked up the knife, and lunged at the reed thatching. Unleashing all of his pent-up aggression, he stabbed violently at the reeds with all of his might. Within a half dozen jabs, the fragile blade broke from its rudimentary wooden handle.

Charles grabbed Soñador by the shoulders and slammed him back against the wall of the pit. "Goddamnit, Soñador, calm yourself. We could have used that knife."

Soñador pushed Charles back to his side of the pit but did not escalate the fight. The realization set in that they had completely misplayed their one opportunity to get out. To their amazement, however, when they looked back up, Gonzalo had his face pressed against the reeds with his hands cupped against his face to help his eyes focus into the darkness of the pit. When he saw the prisoners turn their attention back to him, he pushed himself away once again.

"Soñador?" the boy asked.

"You've heard of him?" Charles asked.

"You lie," Gonzalo whimpered. "That's not him. Soñador is a great warrior. He's fighting the gringos, and soon he will come help us fight too."

"He's not that great of a warrior," Charles said, rolling his eyes.

Gonzalo, who had been remarkably wily and under control during the whole interaction, was clearly becoming distraught. He squatted on his haunches and thought deeply.

"If you are Soñador, then what is the secret sign of his men?"

"I don't care who you think I am, you little flea. If you aren't going to help us then leave us in peace," Soñador snarled.

"What are you doing? This little boy clearly admires Soñador. Why won't you just prove that you are him, for Christ's sake?" Charles implored.

"You don't know the sign because you aren't him. You are just trying to be cruel because I won't free you."

"How would *you* know the sign of Soñador anyway?" Soñador said with a snarl. "Are you a gringo spy?"

Gonzalo spat at Soñador through the reed thatching, his monkey howling angrily on his shoulder. "Die in there, monster. I'll never help you. I'll find the real Soñador, and he will come back and skin you alive for being an imposter. Then I will tell him how to deliver the true death to you. I have seen it done. Then you will be nothing, and even the vultures will vomit you out when they try to eat your stinking rotten flesh."

Charles perked up. "You know how to kill this man? His kind?"

"Of course I do! That's why they sent me and Chalo on our adventure."

"Who sent you?" Charles asked.

Gonzalo straightened up and shut his mouth tightly.

"It's a secret, huh? That's okay. Maybe I can guess, and then you won't have to tell me."

Gonzalo shifted uncomfortably but did not say *no*.

"Okay, you said, *that's why they sent me*. And we were talking about the true death. Whoever it was wanted you to spread the message about how to kill...us, our kind. So you've seen others like us? Men who can be stabbed in the neck and not die?"

Gonzalo said nothing but watched Charles very carefully.

"Hmm...so who would've sent you? The jaguar warriors?"

"They are my enemy," Gonzalo blurted, unable to control his anger.

"Of course, of course. They are threatening villages, aren't they? Taking sacrifices."

"They are devils. They are from the pits of hell," the little boy said.

"It's okay, little one," Charles reassured him. "They are enemies of mine as well. They have captured me and changed me into…this. So maybe your parents sent you?"

Gonzalo shifted his gaze to the ground.

"Oh, my boy, I'm sorry. Were they taken?"

"My father was taken. My mother was eaten."

"Terrible, terrible. So it was your village then? They sent you out looking for soldiers, those who could help you fight off the jaguar warriors, didn't they?"

Gonzalo nodded.

"But you're in a rush, aren't you?"

"The jaguar warriors are coming back in a few days," Gonzalo said forlornly. "They have demanded ten more people. We need fierce soldiers to fight them and kill them. I need to find Soñador. I told everyone that me and Chalo would find him and bring him back to help us."

"I am sorry for the troubles you have seen, young one, but the wonderful news is that you have succeeded! You found Soñador."

"That is not Soñador," the boy said with disgust. "The real Soñador would have killed a gringo like you."

Soñador had been silent while Charles and Gonzalo spoke, but his expression softened as he heard the boy's plight.

"You are a clever boy," Soñador finally said. "I have seen many grown men with less wisdom and bravery."

Gonzalo scoffed.

"It's true. When we lied to you about why we were trapped down here, you saw right through it. And I know that when you use that cleverness, and really think about things, you will help us get out of here."

The boy was intrigued. "Why would I do that? Because you claim to be Soñador?"

"No, not because of that. I don't care who you think I am. I could be Santa Anna himself. It doesn't matter. Here's what matters. Your enemies are my enemies. You know that they are my enemies because you see me now being held against my will in this stinking cage with an ugly gringo."

Charles bit his tongue.

"You have seen how the jaguar warriors use us, have you not?"

The boy nodded. "They starve you and set you loose like ravenous dogs on our village."

"That's right. Neither of us wants that. Look, one of three things will happen if you get us out of here. One, we will go and kill our enemies, the jaguar warriors, which helps you. Two, we will go and escape into the forest, never to be seen again, which helps you because there will be two fewer monsters attacking your village. Three, we immediately get out of here and try to kill you. That's the scariest option, right? But we could never catch you, could we? You know all the secret paths and hideaways. "

The boy tapped his finger against his lip as he thought about what Soñador was saying. "Why don't you just overtake the jaguar warriors when they come to get you out of your pit?"

"Trust me, we would try if we were in our right minds. When we don't eat, however, something takes over us and we can't control ourselves any more. We can't think or talk or plan. All we can do is eat."

"Yes, that's true," the boy admitted. "I have seen it myself. After you eat, you become very slow. That's when we've killed a few of you."

Charles wanted to ask how they did it, but he sensed that Soñador was getting through to the boy and didn't want to interrupt.

"What if I brought you food so that you weren't hungry? Then you could kill the jaguar warriors when they come to get you."

Soñador frowned. "I wish it were that easy, hijo, but we can only eat one thing that keeps us from getting hungry."

Gonzalo timidly tapped his own forehead.

"Yes," Soñador replied.

"Do you know where to find something…like that?" Charles asked.

The boy thought deeply. "I could hunt and bring you a bird head or something."

"We've tried eating the animals that fall into our pit. It doesn't work. We think it has to be human. Do you know if there are any dead bodies?"

Gonzalo scrunched his face in disgust. "No."

"Maybe your little friend there?" Charles suggested, pointing at Chalo.

"Monkeys are kind of like little hairy humans. They are clever like humans."

"No!" Gonzalo yelled. "I'd rather die than…" The boy abruptly looked over his shoulder and paused. "I think something is out there. I have to go. I'll come back later."

He disappeared quickly from the prisoners' sight. They listened intently for a long while, but they heard nothing.

Charles slumped back into his spot. "Now what are we going to do?"

"We're going to have to eat the boy," Soñador said flatly.

# Chapter 24

"What Henry said — was it true?" Violet asked.

Brian was too preoccupied with preparing the hotel room's foldout bed to look up. "Which part?"

"That you were a writer."

Brian glanced at her but then quickly went back to work with the fitted sheet he'd found in the closet. "Come on, let's try and get some rest. It's been a helluva day."

"So it *was* true?" Violet said as she gave some much-needed assistance on the sheet's far corner.

Brian sighed. "Yeah, so what?"

She waited for him to say more.

"What?" Brian demanded.

"Nothing. I don't want to make you mad."

"Okay, then let's go to bed. The big bed is yours. This contraption is mine. Tomorrow we…"

"I mean, surely you wouldn't be mad if I asked just one more question, though."

Brian growled. "Let me guess. You want to know what type of stories I wrote?"

"No, I already know that." Violet grinned. "Space stories, right?"

"Yes, space stories. La-di-da. Happy now?"

"Can you tell me one of your stories?"

"Definitely not. You wouldn't appreciate it."

Violet was mildly offended. "Don't be a jerk. You think my tiny little brain can't comprehend the depth of your genius?"

"Ha. That's not what I meant. It's just that my stories were kind of an acquired taste."

"But they were published, right? So somebody must've liked them."

"Yeah. Someone did," Brian said softly. "How about this? I'll trade you. You tell me something I don't know about Violet Romero, and I'll tell you one of my stories."

Violet squinted cautiously.

"And I don't want any *my favorite color is blue, I love pizza, I hate mean people* bullshit either."

Violet extended her hand. "Deal."

Brian took it and gave it a firm shake. "Okay, before I tell you one of my stories, I have one other condition."

"Oh my God," Violet said in feigned exasperation. "I hate lawyers. What now?"

"Even if you don't like the story, you can't just shit all over it."

"Eww, gross."

"I mean that figuratively. Geez, grow up."

Violet nodded enthusiastically, then plopped down on her bed and sat cross-legged, leaning against the headboard.

"You ready?"

"One second." She grabbed one of the pillows and squeezed it tightly in her lap. "Ready!"

Brian sat on the corner of her bed. "I can't believe I'm doing this. Umm, let's see, which story? Probably my favorite was a little book called *Remembering Death*."

"What a depressing title!" Violet blurted.

"Hey! What did I just say?"

"Sorry, sorry," Violet said, zipping her lips and locking them with an invisible key.

"Now I know what comes to mind when you think about science fiction stories, but this wasn't your run-of-the-mill tractor beam, alien invasion story."

"So it was boring," Violet teased.

Brian glared at her. Again, she locked her mouth with an invisible key. Brian held out his hand. "Here, give me that." Violet rolled her eyes and grudgingly handed him the invisible key. He pretended to put it in his shirt pocket.

"The story started with a middle-aged television repairman living with his family in a little suburb outside of Cincinnati. The man was pretty normal. He had a wife and kids and a decent little house with an unattached garage, where he liked to tinker with lawnmowers and things, nothing fancy. The only extraordinary thing about the man was that he periodically got these wild, vision-like memories. None of the memories made any sense, but other than being uncomfortable and somewhat frightening, they didn't really cause him any harm. Sometimes years would pass in between these episodes, so he didn't think too much about it. Still, he never told anyone because he worried that he might be a little koo-koo.

"Then one day, while the man was fooling around in his workshop, the memories came on stronger than ever. He felt compelled, for inexplicable reasons, to gather up some of the spare television components he had lying around and start building a strange contraption. He had no idea what he was doing, but at the same time, he seemed to know exactly what step came next. The man worked for hours without stopping until whatever he was building was done. Exhausted and confused, he flipped a switch on the side of the gizmo. A single red light appeared through a glass bulb on top. He stood there for a long time, gawking at his creation. Just when he started feeling foolish, a flood of lights surrounded the man with terrible swiftness, and he lost consciousness."

"I thought you said there weren't any tractor beams," Violet interrupted.

"Who said it was a tractor beam? It could have been some type of alien diversionary device. Like an intergalactic smoke grenade."

Violet rolled her eyes. "God, you're a dork."

Brian ignored her. He was getting caught up in the story, which Violet

244

couldn't help finding adorable.

"The man woke up, unsure where he was. He looked out a viewing port of the space ship and saw that he was in some unknown galaxy. Earth was nowhere to be seen. Needless to say, he started losing his shit. Then to make matters worse, an alien being came sliding into the room. It looked like a huge slimy snail except without the shell. The filthy smell of the spaceship was suffocating. The snail started communicating with the man telepathically."

"I think it would help if I knew the man's name," Violet interrupted again.

"Why would that help?"

"I dunno, I just don't feel a connection to a man with no name."

"I can't remember. The name doesn't matter that much for purposes of the story, though."

"Hmmm." Violet scrunched her nose disapprovingly.

"Fine, his name was…Vincent."

Violet laughed. "Vincent!?"

"Yeah. What's wrong with Vincent?"

"On second thought, yeah, he seems like a Vincent. You may continue."

"Anyway, as I was saying, the snail started communicating with the man, er, Vincent, telepathically. He tells Vincent that his name is Glorp and that he is a Rayron, a race of carbon-based beings from across the universe."

"The alien's name was Glorp?"

"Actually, in the book, he didn't have a name. I just added that because I thought it would help you 'connect' with him."

"Oh. Well, I don't really need to connect with the alien. You don't have to call him anything."

Brian was getting impatient. "I'm calling him Glorp, goddamn it!"

"Glorp told Vincent that the thing Vincent built in his garage was a Rayron beacon. Once Vincent activated the beacon, the Rayrons came and got him. *How did I know how to build that thing?* Vincent asked. Glorp said it was because Vincent was actually a Rayron too, and he had innate Rayron knowledge. *How could that be?* Vincent wanted to know. *I've lived my entire life as a human.* Glorp explained that the Rayrons were an ancient race of beings. They were very wise and technologically advanced. But life as a Rayron wasn't exactly a bowl of cherries. The Rayrons had no physiological ability to feel pleasure. As a matter of fact, the only physical sensation they could feel was pain, and the only thing that even remotely resembled pleasure to a Rayron was defecating."

"Pooping?" Violet asked, sticking out her tongue in disgust.

"Yeah...that's what defecate means. That's why their home planet and everything on it smelled so terrible. Anyway, because life was so miserable for the Rayrons, they began looking for ways to improve their existence. The first major thing they discovered was how to computerize their consciousness. Essentially, they figured out how to put all of their individual thoughts into machines, which could then potentially live on forever. Certainly, that was a better option than their snail form, but it was a cold existence, without feeling or emotion.

"The next thing the Rayrons discovered was how to transfer their consciousness to other organic life forms. After that, they began scouring the universe for suitable life forms to transfer into. Of the hundreds they found, one was far and away better than all of the others: humans. Humanity was the pinnacle of sensation. Humans felt physical and emotional pleasure much more intensely than all other species. To the Rayrons, living in human form was euphoric to the point of being considered paradise. The main drawback, of course, was that humans were mortal and the Rayrons only knew how to transfer consciousness out of their own snail bodies, not how to transfer consciousness out of anything else. So once a Rayron transferred into a human, the Rayron was stuck there for good.

*"Why don't I remember being a Rayron then?* Vincent asked Glorp. Glorp went on to explain that once a Rayron was transferred into a human, his memory was wiped. The Rayron existence was so miserable that even the memory of it could diminish the human experience to the point of ruining it. That's why Vincent couldn't remember his former life. Unfortunately for Vincent, however, the process failed to completely wipe his former memories. That's why he would get the periodic episodes of flashbacks. It was a rare, but not unheard of, snafu in the memory wipe process. To make

matters worse, the flashback episodes were almost certainly going to get more frequent and more intense as life went on.

"Glorp presented Vincent with a choice. He could get his memory rewiped, which would help him achieve the pure human experience once again, or he could do nothing and live with the knowledge of his misery as a Rayron. The only problem with rewiping was that there was no way to differentiate between a Rayron memory and a human memory. Everything had to go. Basically, Vincent would lose the birth of his children, the love he shared with his wife, and the thousands of sweet memories he'd created over the course of his life as a human."

"What did he choose?" Violet asked, clutching the pillow tightly in her lap.

Brian paused dramatically. "He chose to live with the memories, even though it meant holding on to a lifetime of horrific flashbacks from his former life as a Rayron."

"Wow," Violet whispered. "What made him so sure he was making the right choice?"

Brian deliberately tapped the tip of his nose with his finger three times and grinned.

"What is that? What are you doing right now?" Violet asked.

"That's the thing that made Vincent certain about his choice. You see, when Vincent's kids were young, they had a little, scruffy mutt named Rascal. Rascal was the ultimate playmate, and the kids absolutely adored him. But one day, Vincent's youngest daughter…" Brian stopped, snapped his fingers, and extended a beckoning hand out to Violet.

Violet quickly caught on to what he wanted. "Oh, uh…uhh…Candace!" she yipped with delight.

Brian laughed and nodded approvingly. "But one day, Vincent's youngest daughter, Candace, went looking to play with Rascal, only to find him dead inside his doghouse. Vincent remembered holding Candace for an hour as innocent tears streamed down her four-year-old cheeks and onto his shirt. His soul ached for his little girl and the bitterness of her first taste of loss. Finally, when she'd calmed down, he turned her face toward his. He took his finger and tapped the tip of her nose three times, making her giggle despite herself. *I love you, sweetheart,* Vincent told her. *I love you too, Daddy,* she replied. Vincent decided he'd rather die than live without memories like that."

Violet let the story sink in. "That's very…"

"Stupid?" Brian interjected.

"No, not stupid, sweet."

"Well, there was a lot more that went into the story obviously — character development, plot twists, etcetera. I'm just telling you the condensed version. The full story was kind of funny — or at least it was to me."

Brian seemed to get lost in thought.

"What?" Violet prodded.

He chuckled. "Nothing."

"Come on, what are you thinking about?"

"My wife. She used to read my stories when we were dating. She couldn't wait until a whole book was done, so she made me give her each chapter as I finished them. I used to tell her to be patient because I was still in law school at the time, and I didn't really have time to write. Oh man, that didn't fly, though. She pestered me until I gave her new material. She was the perfect reader for an aspiring author, though. She boosted my ego because she loved everything. Really, she just loved me. All I ever wanted to do was make her laugh."

"Did it work?"

Brian again looked thoughtful. "Yeah, I think so. Once, we were driving somewhere and I caught her giggling. I asked her what she was laughing at, and she said that she was just thinking about the Rayrons. But she was such a tenderhearted person. I also once caught her wiping a tear away, and I asked her what was wrong. She said the same thing — she was just thinking about the Rayrons."

Violet felt a pang in her chest. "You're a lot like Vincent, I guess."

"Yeah, I guess so," he agreed.

The two sat in a heavy silence.

"So, now it's your turn. Tell me something I don't know about you."

A cloud suddenly came over Violet's face. She twisted the amethyst ring on her finger. She knew what she had to tell Brian, and it made her sick to her stomach. After two false starts, she cleared her throat instead and slid awkwardly off of the bed. "Will you just give me one minute?"

She barely got the bathroom door closed before she melted to the floor and wept tight, silent sobs into her hands. She was unable to wrangle the raw force of her guilt, so she leaned her back against the tub and pulled her knees into her chest while her shoulders convulsed.

She couldn't wait any longer. It was time to confess to Brian what she'd done — that she was the one responsible for the death of his biggest fan, his tenderhearted reader. With all the strength she could muster, she stood up, turned on the faucet, and splashed her cheeks with cool water. She took a moment to stare hatefully at her own reflection. *Whatever he says to you, you deserve it*, she thought.

Her courage mustered, she opened the bathroom door and stepped back into the room. Brian had fallen asleep on the foldout bed.

# Chapter 25

**1848**

"You're going to have to do it," Soñador said.

"The hell I do," Charles was quick to reply.

"You are already a killer. What is one more life?"

Charles shook his head in disbelief. "Who do you think I am? Genghis Khan? You've taken more lives than me, you asshole!"

"There is a big difference. The men I killed were soldiers, in battle."

Charles raised an eyebrow.

"Or at least they were going to be in battle at some point. Maybe I got to them a little early. Still, I never killed women or children."

"I never killed women or children either."

"Liar! My wife was killed…"

"You can stop right there. I was not part of that. I would never be a part of that."

The two fell into silence.

"The red fog is going to set in soon," Soñador said. "Your eyes are already starting to burn red. We have to be ready for the boy if he decides to come back here. Otherwise, we are just going to kill more innocent people."

"This has to be left to chance, then," Charles said as he ripped the last brass button off his tattered jacket. He showed both sides of the button to Soñador. An eagle was embossed on one side. The other side was smooth, except for the button loop.

"If it lands with the eagle facing up, you do it. If it lands with the button hole facing up, then I do it."

Soñador grudgingly agreed. Just as Charles prepared to make the flip, though, Soñador stopped him. "Only if I can make the toss."

Charles shrugged and handed him the button. "Suit yourself."

Soñador drew an uneasy breath and tossed it in the air. It bounced off of the reed thatching above and clinked along the stone floor of the cell. Both men leaned in to inspect the result.

Soñador angrily slapped the wall of the cell. Charles handed Soñador the knife blade that Soñador had previously broken in frustration after Gonzalo refused to help them get out of the cell.

"I will be just as guilty in this as you," Charles said. "And I will help if you need it."

Soñador hung his head. "Just when I start to think I can't become any more corrupted, I find myself doing some new, unimaginable thing."

"What we are about to do is horrendous, but like you said, how many other innocent people are we going to kill if we stay enslaved here?"

"This feels far worse, though," Soñador replied. "When the jaguar warriors unleash us on the villages, we don't know what we are doing. We aren't in our right minds. But this," he said, looking at the knife blade in his hand, "is something far worse. We are choosing to do this."

Charles leaned forward, demanding eye contact with Soñador. "I don't want to make this any worse than it already is, but we have to bolster our resolve if we are going to accomplish this." He paused. "You know we are going to have to get him into the cell to hide his body."

They both looked at the reed thatching. The largest grid opening was about the size of an apple.

"We will have to pull him through, piece by piece, so that the jaguar warriors don't notice that we have fed and that we aren't in the red fog."

Soñador clearly had not considered that particular detail. He rested his head against the stone wall. "Has God abandoned us completely? Maybe there is something else we could do."

"Like what?" Charles asked.

"We could find out from the boy what it takes to kill us, and then do it.

Then we don't have to kill the boy, and we won't be used to kill anyone else."

Charles shook his head. "You know that he won't tell us that. He *thinks* that if he gets us out of here, we are going help his people fight against the jaguar warriors."

Soñador narrowed his eyes at Charles. "If he could get us out of here, that *is* what we would do."

Charles hesitated. "Right."

Before Soñador could respond, they heard footsteps rustling nearby. The noise stopped before anything came into view.

"Little jaguar, is that you?" Soñador called.

There was no answer.

"Gonzalo? Are you there? We can't see you."

A meek voice replied, "Yes, it's me."

Charles grabbed Soñador by the arm, then nodded encouragement.

"Come closer, hijo. Talk to us. Did you have any luck finding what we asked you to find? Our special food?"

"No," the boy whimpered. "I couldn't find what you wanted."

"Come here, hijo, we want to see you."

Gonzalo stepped into view. Charles could see that the boy had bloodstains on his white shirt.

"Are you okay? What happened?"

"I'm fine," the boy lied as he suppressed his tears. His shoulders lifted each time he sniffled.

"Something has happened, I can tell," Soñador pressed.

Gonzalo shook his head as he wiped his nose with his arm. Without explanation, he lay down on top of the reed thatching and thrust his arms through the holes. Charles and Soñador were so shocked by the act, they weren't sure what to do.

"What are you doing, hijo?" Soñador whispered to the boy through the thatching.

"Take it," Gonzalo said, unable to control his sobbing.

For the first time, Charles and Soñador realized that Gonzalo had something in each of his balled-up hands.

"What is this?" Charles asked.

"Just take it," Gonzalo replied with exasperation.

The captives examined what they had been given very closely.

"Is this the special food we asked for?" Soñador asked.

Gonzalo pulled his arms back through the thatching and sat back on his haunches.

"Sort of."

A sickening realization overtook Charles. "Where is your little friend, Chalo?"

Gonzalo buried his face in his arms. "He's in Heaven now. The Virgin Mary took him."

Charles sighed with deep regret. Before, when he suggested eating Chalo, he only did so in jest. Both he and Soñador had come to the conclusion long ago that only human brain would suffice to nourish them and keep them out of the red fog. Killing that monkey and scraping out its brain was probably the hardest, most heart-wrenching thing the little boy had ever done. Charles couldn't imagine telling the boy that he had done so in vain. It was evident that he loved that damned monkey. Charles figured he must have reached a truly suffocating level of despair in order to kill him, just for a chance at fending off the jaguar warriors.

Soñador's guilt was perfectly transparent. He looked at the little piece of meat in his hand then shook his head at Charles. Despite knowing that Chalo's brain was worthless and that killing Gonzalo was the only way out, Charles also knew that there was no way Soñador could kill the boy now. Charles suspected Soñador would also stop him from trying. In unspoken acceptance of the situation, they just ate Gonzalo's sacrifice.

Although it tasted rancid, it did not immediately come back up or out the other side. The three sat in dejected silence for a good while.

Thunder sounded in the distance. It rained often there in the jungle, but most storms were quick to start and quick to end. The clouds rolling in overhead suggested much more significant weather on the horizon.

That's when Charles noticed something that restored his spirits.

"Soñador! Your neck wound — it's healing!"

Soñador, once again forgetting that he couldn't feel anything, reached up to his neck where Gonzalo had stabbed him. "Are you certain?"

Charles leaned in close. "Yes, it's gone! Gonzalo, come see. It worked!"

Gonzalo stood up and looked down at the prisoners. There was no relief or happiness in his eyes, only determination. "The warriors will be back soon. They will attack tonight."

"How do you know?" Charles asked.

"Because that's how long they gave my village to give up sacrifices."

"How many will come for us?"

"Probably one, maybe two. They will unlock the lock and hold meat over you like this," Gonzalo said as he imitated holding something above his head, like he was holding a turkey leg out to a begging dog. "While you are reaching for the meat, they put iron collars around your necks and attach the collars to a horse with chains. That's how they lead you to the village."

"You have seen this before?" Soñador asked.

"Yes, many times," Gonzalo confirmed.

"How many?" Soñador pressed.

Gonzalo broke eye contact and held up one finger.

"They will expect us to act as though we are in the red fog," Charles mused aloud. "What does that look like? If they think we are in our right minds, then they won't open the cell."

"Like this," Gonzalo said. He growled in an exaggerated low tone and clawed overhead. He then snapped his teeth over and over like a rabid wolf.

Gonzalo stopped his imitation abruptly. He turned his head and cocked his ear to the side.

"They are coming," he said and scurried away.

"Gonzalo, wait!" Charles whisper-yelled after him. "You didn't tell us how to kill them! Come back!"

The last of the sunlight was beginning to fade from the sky. Although they were still in their right minds, the monkey brain was like eating rotting meat. It didn't have the same satiating effect as human brain. In fact, Charles felt quite nauseous. Both of their eyes still burned brightly. They were on the cusp of the red fog. Nevertheless, a sense of calm settled over them.

"You were a mighty warrior before all of this," Charles said quietly.

"As were you," Soñador replied. "Fierce and merciless."

"Do you remember that feeling? That feeling of strength?" Charles asked. Soñador nodded resolutely.

"Good, it's time to be warriors again. We must trust each other if we are going to prevail in this."

Soñador looked down in deep consideration of the thought. "We have been enemies in every way imaginable. We have tried to kill each other, over and over again."

"Yes," Charles acknowledged. "But we have a common enemy now."

"We also have a common obligation to the boy," Soñador said. "Swear to me that if we escape, you will help me come to the aid of Gonzalo and the villagers."

Charles hesitated.

"Will you help them?" Soñador asked.

They could both hear approaching footsteps.

"First things first," Charles replied.

He started growling and snapping his teeth as Gonzalo had shown him. Soñador followed suit.

A jaguar warrior knelt down on top of the thatching and peered inside at the prisoners. His face was devoid of any emotion, and his eyes were dark and vacant. Apparently satisfied with what he saw, the warrior took a key from a pouch tied to his loincloth and unlocked the giant iron lock keeping the cell's ceiling in place. Once opened, another warrior appeared and dangled a piece of succulent gray matter at the end of a rope above the pit to divert the attention of the prisoners while the first warrior secured them in iron neck harnesses. Although Charles was merely playing the part of a mindless cannibal, the meat did actually look and smell especially appetizing. He found it difficult to ignore his hunger. For a moment he wanted to forget all about the plan and make a realistic play for the meat.

But as the first warrior leaned in close to Soñador to apply the neck harness, the prisoners snapped into a combat posture. The warrior was visibly startled when Soñador grabbed him by his outstretched arms and flung him to the bottom of the pit. Charles swiftly robbed him of his dagger and savagely sawed through his neck until his head was completely severed.

The second warrior was too slow to react. He only managed to a run a few steps in complete retreat before both of the prisoners bounded with impossible strength from the pit and overtook him. Months of rage and frustration came spilling out as they brutally separated the warrior into pieces.

Victorious, but once again on the verge of the red fog, the men quickly moved to devour the meat the second warrior had been dangling. Only then did the fire in their eyes subside and their full senses return. Sitting next to each other amid the gore and carnage, they embraced and laughed in relief. It was something they never thought they would feel again: freedom.

From the shadows of the forest, a small form emerged. It was Gonzalo.

"Thank you, my brave little friend," Soñador said. "Don't be afraid. We won't hurt you, I promise."

"I'm not afraid," he said flatly, then disappeared down into the pit where the first jaguar warrior lay decapitated. A moment later, the severed head popped out of the hole, and the boy climbed out after it. He kicked it toward the place where Charles and Soñador were sitting.

"See how it still moves?" he asked.

Sure enough, the warrior's eyes were still blinking, and he was mouthing inaudible words with his distorted face.

"He is not dead yet," the boy said. He looked around until he found a large stone. With cold determination, he smashed the stone against the head until he'd broken through the skull. Then he reached his small hand inside the hole and fished something out.

"What is it?" Charles asked, leaning forward.

"Here, take it," Gonzalo said as he put it in Charles's hand. Soñador and Charles leaned in close to the object to see what it was in the last of the fading light. It looked and felt like a perfectly round stone about the size of an avocado pit.

"Is that it?" Charles asked. "Is he truly dead now?"

"No," Gonzalo replied. "If you put this in the ground where the dirt has been drenched thoroughly with blood, it will grow like a seed. After some time, the man will be whole again, and he will remember all of his old grudges."

"Absolutely amazing," said Charles with a true sense of wonder. "You've seen this happen before?"

"Not me," he replied, "but others. That's when they made a great discovery. Because it grows like a plant, we can destroy it like a plant."

Gonzalo removed a small canteen strapped to his back and uncorked the top.

"Smell it," he said.

Soñador took the canteen and put it under his nose. "Vinegar."

Gonzalo then poured out the liquid onto the object in Charles's hand. Immediately, it hissed, and a thick white vapor rose from it. The object turned black and shriveled down to the size of a prune.

"Now, he's dead," Gonzalo said, taking the object from Charles and tossing it over his shoulder. "It's like an old bone."

"I'll be damned," Charles said, shaking his head. "Plant and animal as one. Simply amazing."

"Yes," Soñador said as he used Gonzalo's stone to crack open the skull of the second warrior and then remove the round object inside with a wet, sucking noise. "It's a real magical wonder."

Once again, Gonzalo poured vinegar on the object, causing it to shrivel and die. He also found the small leather pouches the warriors carried around their necks and gave them to Charles and Soñador.

"It's food for them, I think," he explained.

Inside, Charles found small gray pieces of dehydrated meat. He put one of the pieces in his mouth and swallowed it whole. It was one of the finest things he ever tasted. Charles nodded to Soñador that it was all right. Soñador also ate a piece.

"It will help keep you from becoming monsters," Gonzalo said. "There's something else." He motioned for the two men to follow him. Just inside the forest, they saw a horse tied to a tree with a man secured by the neck in tow. When the man saw Gonzalo, he began raging and thrashing wildly but he was held safely in place by his neck restraint and a long wooden rod attached to the horse's harness.

"Let's kill it," Soñador said, knife in hand.

"Wait a moment," Charles replied, grabbing Soñador by the arm. "He's not a jaguar warrior. He's a prisoner like we were. Let's give him some meat and get him out of the red fog."

Soñador reluctantly agreed but cursed Charles viciously when the man bit off one of Soñador's fingers as he shoved some of the dehydrated meat into his mouth.

It took a while, but the man calmed down and began talking.

"What's he saying?" Soñador asked as he lit a torch to see better.

Charles almost failed to realize that the man was speaking in English.

"Charles, is that you?"

"Who are you?" Charles responded. "I don't recognize you."

"It's me, Virgil! Charles, thank God! Please let me loose."

"Who is it?" Soñador asked.

"He's one of the men from my company," Charles exclaimed. He started to pull the lynchpin from the clasp in the iron neck harness.

Soñador held out his hand, imploring restraint. "Wait."

Charles paused.

Soñador continued in Spanish. "I don't know this man. What is he going to do when you free him?"

Charles laughed. "Thank us, I'd imagine."

"Are you vouching for him?"

"Yes, I'm vouching for him," Charles scoffed as he opened up the neck restraint and cut the ropes binding Virgil's hands. "He's a good man."

Once freed, Virgil snatched the pouch of dehydrated meat Charles had taken from the dead jaguar warrior and then bull-rushed him. Charles toppled over and watched helplessly as Virgil bolted into the forest like a wild animal.

Stunned, Charles climbed to his feet and looked back at Soñador. "Well, fuck."

"You could do the same," Soñador said flatly. "I won't stop you."

Charles looked at Gonzalo and then slapped Soñador on the back. "First of all, you couldn't stop me. Second of all, why would I leave now? We've got the element of surprise, and I'm in the mood for a bit of sport."

# Chapter 26

**1908**

"*Abuelo*, tell us a story!" The little girl tugged on her grandfather's trousers just as sleep was overtaking him. He straightened up in his rocking chair and instinctively put his hand on top of his granddaughter's head. The nearby fireplace crackled, and the smell of tamales wafted in from the kitchen.

"Ah, *mi conejito*. But we are about to eat. You want to hear a story now?"

"Yes, yes, please!" she exclaimed.

The other grandchildren also began to chime in. "Yes, please, abuelo. Tell us a story!"

"Very well. Which story would you like to hear? Do you want to hear about the night your *abuela* fell in with love me? There's a lot of kissing in that one!"

"Ewww, no!" the children cried.

"How about I tell you the complete history of Mexico, sparing no details?"

"No, abuelo, that's too boring. Please tell us an exciting story. Tell us something scary!"

"Something scary, huh?"

"Not too scary, Papa," said the man's daughter, who happened to be passing through the room as she calmed a crying baby.

"Okay," he replied, winking at the children. "Nothing too scary. Come sit on the floor, *niños*. Abuelo will tell you about the little boy with the monkey."

The old man leaned forward in his chair and cleared his throat.

"Once upon a time, there was a little boy who lived with his parents in a small village at the foot of a great mountain. The boy was scrawny and shy. He had no friends because he was poor and dirty. His mother, seeing that he was lonely, paid a month's wages to buy the boy a pet monkey from a traveling merchant. The boy loved the monkey more than anything, and they played together in the forest every day. The monkey was very clever and could climb trees to bring the boy fruit."

The old man imitated a monkey howling, then puffed out his cheeks and pulled out his ears, making all the children giggle.

"The village was a quiet, peaceful place. One night though, a band of monsters came to the village and demanded children to eat. The villagers, who loved their children, told the monsters *no* and tried to send the monsters away. They stabbed the monsters with pitchforks and burned them with torches, but nothing worked. The monsters were invincible. As punishment for not giving up the children, the monsters came back to the village time and again and simply stole the children from their beds.

"The little boy with the monkey wanted to stop the monsters, but he knew that he was too small and too weak to slay them himself. Under a full moon, he prayed to the Virgin Maria de Guadeloupe for help. He prayed with all of his heart, which was innocent and pure. To his great astonishment, she appeared and asked him what he wanted.

"*I want to protect my village and stop these monsters that are stealing all of the children,* he said.

"*I will answer your prayer,* she replied, *but you must give me your monkey in return.*

"The boy was torn. The monkey was his best friend in the world and a brave companion. On the other hand, the village children were being gobbled up. Tearfully, he gave the Virgin de Guadeloupe his monkey. In return, she gave the boy two monsters of his own. The boy was frightened when he saw the two fearsome monsters.

"*Won't they try to eat me?* he asked.

"*No,* the Virgin de Guadeloupe replied. *Because you have given me your most treasured possession, I will bless you and they will not bring you any harm.*

*They will obey your every command.*

"She gave the boy some holy water as well. *Instruct your new pets to go to the monsters where they live, and then pour this holy water into their ears.*

"The boy took the holy water and the two monsters and hid them in a secret cave near the village. Every night, he sneaked out of bed and collected his two monsters and the holy water and traveled up the mountain to where he knew the other monsters lived. He instructed his two monsters to go into their camp while they rested and pour the holy water into their ears. The boy's monsters were very quiet and sneaky. Each night they did as they were told, and each night several more monsters were killed. The boy even came to enjoy the company of his monsters. Over time, they became his good friends.

"After nearly a month, the other monsters became very fearful because they did not understand how so many of their fellow monsters were dying off. They were supposed to be invincible, after all. They all became so scared, they decided to leave the mountain entirely and search for a new place to the live. It didn't take long after that for the villagers to notice that none of their children were being stolen any longer.

"*What has happened?* they asked amongst themselves. *Why have the monsters suddenly left us alone?*

"The little boy brought his two monsters out of hiding and said, *The Virgin de Guadeloupe answered my prayer and gave me these two monsters to control. They have rid our mountain of the ones who were terrorizing us.*

"The boy thought the villagers would be happy and would welcome his new friends, but they were very afraid.

"*Please,* they begged, *You must kill these monsters too. They frighten us. Someday they may steal our children like the others had done.*

"Once again, the boy was sad because he had to make a choice.

"*You don't have to kill us,* the monsters said. *We will do anything you tell us to do. If you want us to leave and never return, then we will do so.*

"*Very well,* the boy said, *but you may never harm another person for the rest of your days.*

"The monsters began to cry. *We will do as you say. But how will we eat? We*

262

*will starve to death.*

"*Fine,* the boy replied. *You may still eat children. But only wicked children who disobey their parents and shirk their chores.*

"With that, the boy sent the two monsters away, one going north and the other going west."

The old man lowered his voice to little more than a whisper.

"To this day, the two monsters still seek to snatch disobedient children from their beds at night. That's why it is so important to mind your parents and work hard. Otherwise...rawwwr!!"

The children screamed in glee at the final flourish, then ran from the room in feigned distress.

The old man sat in his rocking chair, laughing.

An old woman stood in the doorway, drying her hands on a dishtowel and shaking her head. "I think you love that story as much as they do, Gonzalo."

The old man gingerly got up from his chair and walked across the jaguar pelt stretched out on the floor in front of the fireplace. He placed his hand gently on the back of her neck and kissed her on the cheek. "Yes, I suppose you're right. Let's eat. It smells wonderful!"

# Chapter 27

## 1962

A laser-like beam of sunlight sliced through the tiny space where the hotel room curtains failed to fully overlap, slowly baking Violet's eyelids until she awoke from a deep, dreamless sleep. When her initial disorientation wore off, she looked over to the cot where Brian had fallen asleep. He was gone. His blanket was neatly folded and the pillow stacked on top. There also was a note written on the hotel stationary. Violet's body ached all over from the previous night's ordeal, but she managed to roll out of bed and retrieve the note.

*Violet – I'm sorry I wiped out last night. Getting your ass kicked really takes a lot out of a guy, I guess. I have some court appearances today that I can't miss, but I didn't want to wake you before I left. I should be back this afternoon. Please do me a favor and stay in the room today and get some rest. You should be safe here, and we can make a plan for what to do about Henry when I get back. Was last night even real? These bruises tell me yes — but my mind still can't believe it! Anyway, I told the front desk that you'd be calling for breakfast. Don't worry, I'll take care of the expenses. Feel free to do the same for lunch. Okay, I'm out of here. Hopefully, Henry is not waiting for me at my apartment! If I'm not back by this evening and you think something has happened, then do the smart thing...and come risk your life to safe my ass! —Brian*

Violet smiled as she finished reading. Brian was right; she was very hungry. She hadn't eaten since she left the jail the day before. At first, she thought some eggs and toast would do the trick, but as she looked at the room service menu, her order got a little out of control. By the time the bellhop left her room with his tip, she sat down to a portable dining cart containing a plate of bacon, eggs, and hash browns, half of a grapefruit, a large glass of orange juice, a carafe of coffee, and an unrealistically tall stack of pancakes. Violet was amused with the mountain of food before her. She ate greedily and then sighed in blissful discomfort when she finished. Next, she took a long, hot shower to wash away the last of the prison grime that she felt covering her skin. The water was nearly soothing enough to make her forget that she was almost killed the night before.

As she went through her bag to get fresh clothes, she came across the leather-bound book she'd taken from Henry's secret room. Violet set the book down on the bed and inspected it curiously while she finished drying her hair. The cover of the book was worn shiny-smooth. Violet dressed and plopped down on the bed next to it. She took a deep breath and untied the leather-binding strap like she was unwrapping a Christmas gift. The ink was severely faded, but with the aid of a nearby lamp and a good deal of squinting, she could make out the words, written in a flourishing old-style cursive.

*June 30, 1849,*

*It scarcely seems possible that, after such a fantastical ordeal, I now find myself safe and free on American soil. Even now, my shaking fingers struggle to guide this pen. I am still testing my faculties for anything other than savagery. Nevertheless, I feel I must document my progress as I attempt to understand this malady that now afflicts me. I plan to write in detail about my capture by the jaguar warriors and the application of the transformative sage. Now that I am free, I have the time and opportunity to implement the many experiments I devised during my capture.*

*The purpose of my research is to answer one seminal question: do I still possess the fundamental elements of humanity? Do I still live? Is this life? Can a man live if there is no threat of death? I do not yet know, but I shall learn as much as I can. First, it is imperative that I memorialize the circumstances that led to my current condition, as I do not know how this disease will affect my memory as time progresses.*

*Today, I read a newspaper here in New Orleans that stated General Taylor is now President Taylor. Having been in the wilderness for more than two years, I suppose I should have expected to resurface to radical changes such as these. Still, I find this lapse of time unsettling.*

Violet was captivated. She continued reading, but from the outset, it was very confusing. The book read like a diary or journal, yet the things written inside could not possibly be real. The writer detailed a disease that he had contracted in the wilderness of Mexico that gave him a hunger that was only satiated by eating, what he called "gray meat." At first, Violet did not understand the term, but after a number of references, from context she came to the chilling realization that the writer meant human brain.

He spoke of the "red fog," which would occur when he could not find enough gray meat. The way it was described, it sounded very similar to what happened with Henry: visceral anger, followed by superhuman strength and murderous rage. The writer also wrote of being completely impervious to physical pain, aside from hunger, and having the ability to regenerate lost or mutilated body parts.

Violet dived deeper into the journal, carefully turning the delicate old pages. The writer never named himself, other than describing himself as a fiend or a monster. But the more Violet read, the less he sounded like a monster. He often wrote quite poetically, inserting Spanish and French phrases throughout. It was also clear that he carried a terrible guilt and self-loathing with him and a strange compassion for the people he encountered. He seemed determined to make amends for past "atrocities."

There were several entries in which the writer expressed severe fatalism about his condition and contemplated administering the "second death" upon himself to end the anguish in his mind. Still, there were other entries in which he also delighted in what he called the "redeeming splendor of life" and the many wonderful things that managed to calm his tormented soul. One entry was three pages long, all about how incredible it felt to go exploring in the wild without having an explorer's traditional concerns. He did not have to fear man, beast, weather, or physical hazard. He could experience the natural world in the most incredible way: as a truly unaffected spectator. The only caveat was that he needed to stay fed in order to function at his full ability.

Violet found one entry about the specifics of the man's diet both fascinating and horrifying.

*January 28, 1854,*

*Gray meat is best and most satisfying when eaten directly from a live or very recently deceased contributor. If it is not harvested within a few days of the contributor's expiration, it starts to lose its luscious flavor and becomes less palatable. After a week or so, the meat has a rancid flavor and leaves a foul aftertaste in my mouth. Though, pragmatically, the effect of the gray meat is the same, regardless of when it is consumed. Small wounds and fingers can reform within minutes of consumption. Limbs and gaping wounds mend within the half hour. No seasoning or herbs have any effect on the taste of the gray meat; only freshness matters in that regard. It can be cured and turned into something called "charqui." Doing so helps it maintain some of its freshness and allows me the freedom to roam about the countryside without fear of having the "red fog" set in. While eating the cured gray meat is sustaining, it feels very much like slow starvation. I feel perpetually famished and irritated.*

*I have measured carefully the minimum amount of meat I need to sustain myself, and it comes to approximately one harvested adult every five days, more if I am recovering from significant wounds. This reveals a truly grisly reality. More than seventy souls must perish in order to sustain me for a single year. I am horrified and sickened at the thought of it. But there is no substitute for it. I have tried eating all varieties of plant, animal, and mineral, to no avail. Only gray meat from monkeys come close. It is such a fleeting and sickening form of satiation, though, it cannot realistically be counted on except in an emergency. Anything other than human gray meat my body rejects, forcefully.*

*The only way I can justify my continued existence is that I have chosen only to eat from those in whose death I played no part or for whom justice demands their demise. For that reason, I have become a very capable bounty hunter, with the one peculiarity being that I do not collect the bounties. There is a great deal of satisfaction in tracking down murderous outlaws and dispatching them. Especially the ones who fancy themselves quick draws. I derive great entertainment from watching the dismay on the face of a man who has put six quick rounds in my chest, only to watch me take a very deliberate draw of my own pistol and carefully take aim at his heart.*

*Certainly, if I wanted more meat, or fresher meat, I could easily have it. But preying on the innocent would repudiate my right to live. Fortunately for me, there is enough death in this frontier country that I rarely feel utterly deprived. Although I often feel seduced by the call to devour the meat of the accidental stranger, thus far I have resisted those appalling urges.*

Morning turned into afternoon, but Violet could not quit reading the journal. The more she read, the more she was convinced that it was not a work of fiction, but rather the tortured musings of a man simply trying to find his place in the world.

*September 2, 1858,*

*Freed once again from the clutches of a would-be grave! Somehow, calamity has transformed itself into triumph as I have now settled a debt that was long overdue.*

*I have not written in some months. I attribute this lack of documentation to a general malaise that has persisted in me for some time, diminishing my interest in my work and other endeavors. But a macabre humor has taken hold of me of late to a reinvigorating degree.*

*As big as this country is, especially here in the west, it can feel quite small at times. By some cosmic luck, I once again encountered the scoundrel, Ezra Green.*

Violet recalled that name from an earlier entry in the journal. She flipped back through the pages until she found it again. The writer had been traveling through a little gold mining settlement in California when he heard from locals that there were a rash of grave robberies. The town employed a one-legged man to keep watch over the cemetery at night, but he had been murdered in cold blood when he confronted the robbers. Determined to help, partly out of necessity from his ever-present appetite and partly due to boredom, the writer let it be known to everyone he encountered that he had acquired two golden teeth. He flashed his teeth at the local watering hole, at the post office, and at the makeshift church. Once he was convinced of the fame of his smile, he faked a heart attack in the middle of the town's main thoroughfare and was pronounced dead on the spot.

The writer expected that he would be hastily buried and then quickly visited by the would-be grave robbers, at which time the writer could administer some frontier justice. His plan was foiled, however, when the town undertaker, Ezra Green, extracted his gold teeth right there, on the spot, in the middle of the road with some pliers. Unable to spring back to life without raising some very serious questions, the writer was forced to continue playing dead. Before he knew it, he was buried and waiting for grave robbers that would never come.

The writer said it was the only time since his emancipation in Mexico that he was once again inflicted with the "red fog." After two weeks of starving in the cheap wooden coffin, he finally lost consciousness. He awoke an indeterminate amount of time later, bloated and gorged, amongst a dozen bodies littering a recently vacated Indian camp. At first, the writer was worried that he had broken the only meaningful covenant he had placed on himself (his vow not to kill innocents). But he noticed that there were frontiersmen among the dead. As fate would have it, he had stumbled upon the aftermath of a regional skirmish between natives and settlers and was merely a scavenger of the fallen.

It took three days for him to reorient himself and travel back to the mining town where he had publicly "died." He had to go back to collect his personal belongings, including his most valued possession, his journal, which he had set aside in a secret place before his death scene in the middle of town. When he went back to the cemetery where he had been buried, he saw the splintered wreckage of his coffin. With amazement, he determined that he must have dug his way out of the grave by hand. The writer wanted to confront Ezra Green but decided it was best not to return to town.

Violet flipped ahead in the journal and continued reading the entry from 1858.

*Last Saturday, fate took me to Oregon City, where I hoped to find a room for a few days. I needed repose to think about some longer term plans for myself. Within fifteen minutes of my arrival, I was accused of stealing the horse upon* which I sat, a crime that truly I did not commit. I had purchased the horse from a trader in San Francisco a year prior.

Damnation to the justice system of this territory. Before sundown I was convicted of the crime and hanged. It marked the second time in my travels that I have been executed as an innocent man. Innocent of the charges levied against me, at least. Still, it is quite irksome, not to mention inconvenient, to be strung up so impulsively.

Although I could easily have escaped, I played my part faithfully. The people of the west are obsessed with convicts and bounties. It does me no good to accumulate infamy as a wanted man. So I accepted my death sentence willingly, in order to close the matter. I have resurrected myself from the dead many times now and have some alacrity for the business. From the gallows, I was taken to the shop of a local cabinetmaker who also held the role of town undertaker. To my delighted astonishment, it was Mr. Ezra Green. I do not know what circumstances brought the villain to Oregon from California, but I dared not look a gift horse in the mouth.

Quickly, I devised my scheme. As soon as Green left me alone in his workshop, I got out of my coffin, the noose still hanging from my neck, and collected a number of arbitrary items from a nearby rolltop desk. I jammed the items in my various pockets and got back into the coffin. Shortly thereafter, Green returned and, true to form, got to work pilfering my corpse. He turned out one of the pockets on my breeches and found his own pocketknife. When he saw it, his eye twitched. He examined it carefully and then looked over his shoulder at the desk. Warily, he walked over to the desk and shuffled some of his papers around. Muttering to himself, he put the knife down amongst the clutter and returned to me.

While he was distracted, I discreetly took out another item, a pocket watch inscribed with E.G., and held the chain so that when I crossed my hands together, it lay on top of them. Old Green came back to me and immediately noticed the watch. He spun in place and called out that whoever was there should reveal himself. He looked under the table and behind the door but found nothing. When he picked up the watch from off of my hands, I squeezed the chain ever so slightly, giving just a small bit of resistance. The old man's breathing began to pick up. He leaned in toward the coffin with his ear nearly touching my nose to listen for breathing. *Of course, he heard none other than his own. He slapped my face and then my crotch. I could hardly keep myself from laughing, but I continued to lie perfectly still. Up to that point, my eyes had been lifeless and glossy, but open. Gingerly, he used his thumb and forefinger to close them.*

*I heard Green back away and then pull up a seat at a table across the room. When I heard the uncorking of a whiskey bottle, once again, I made an advantage for myself from his distraction and opened my eyes. When he had consumed enough courage from his bottle, Green returned to me and audibly gasped when he saw my eyes open. Without delay, he went to his desk and began searching frantically. He came back with a needle and thread. With shaking hands he proceeded to sew my eyelids closed. Again, it took all of my fortitude to keep from laughing. He finished and left the room. I heard him walk down a short hallway and then up some stairs.*

*Blindly, I climbed out of the coffin yet again and searched somewhat clumsily for the pocketknife on the desk. Once found, I cut the threads binding my eyes and got back into the coffin. A few minutes later, Green returned.*

*It had gotten dark outside, which was all for the better for my sport. Green was carrying a candle when he came back to the side of my coffin. Feeling that the time was finally ripe, I waited for him to turn his back to me, then I opened my eyes, sat upright, and whispered his name. I shall never forget that moment. A jolt went through Green like someone split his skull with a railroad spike. When he turned toward me and saw my reanimated body sitting in the coffin, he let out a shriek that could scarcely be identified as human. Then his legs went to jelly and gave out on him completely. He fell to the ground, dropping and extinguishing his candle. Three separate efforts to get back to his feet failed. In the end, he tried to crawl away but only managed to go head-first into his wood-burning stove, knocking himself out.*

*I could not bring myself to dine upon Mr. Green. While he was a rascal and a thief, he was not a killer and did not deserve death. I left a simple message for him on a piece of paper that I pinned to his shirt before leaving. "Respect the dead."*

Violet managed to read over half of the journal by the time Brian knocked on the hotel door just after four in the afternoon. She drew back the window curtain to peek outside before unlatching the bar lock and letting him in.

"Hey, how are you feeling?" he asked as he stepped inside. His battered face contrasted starkly with his business suit and briefcase.

"I'm...better," she replied. "How was court?"

Brian laughed. "Well, as it turns out the very subtle bruising on my face is somewhat noticeable. I had a judge say to me, and I quote, 'Damn, son, I've seen rotten bananas less bruised.'"

Violet suppressed a smile. "Let's look on the bright side. At least *my* face doesn't look like that."

Brian laughed. "I'm very happy for you. Did anyone try to contact you today?"

"No, it's been quiet. But there's something you should know."

Brian loosened his tie and sat down on the cot.

"When we were in that secret room in Henry's house, I took a book from the shelf."

Brian held up a hand. "Wait, didn't I just get you out of jail for burglary?"

"Yes, yes, very funny. But seriously, you have to hear this. It's a journal from a long time ago, more than a hundred years ago, and it was written by someone who has whatever Henry has."

"And what does Henry have?"

"I'm not sure, but I think it's some type of disease. And I think Henry somehow got a hold of this book because he wanted to learn more about what's afflicting him."

"I sincerely doubt that, Violet. Does that journal talk about invincible, rage-filled, monster people who have an insatiable bloodlust?"

Violet put her hand on her hip and tossed the journal to Brian. "As a matter of fact, it does."

Brian caught the book somewhat awkwardly and then opened it to a page that Violet had bookmarked. When he finished reading, he snapped the book closed with one hand.

"I think it's time we go back to the funeral home and talk to Rhodes."

# Chapter 28

**1938**

Genevieve was so consumed by her own thoughts, she didn't see the young man approach until he was standing right in front of the long table where she was working. It was getting late, and the university library browsing room was nearly empty.

"Hello," he said. He couldn't have been more than twenty-five years old.

Genevieve, who had been resting her chin in the palm of her hand, sat upright. "Hi," she replied, refocusing.

"The thing is," he started, but hesitated. He was handsome, with an earnest face and shockingly blue eyes. "I'm sorry, I'm not very good at this, so I'll just say everything as plain as I can."

She squinted a bit to signal that she was trying to understand what he wanted.

He pointed to a table at the far side of the room where a stack of books sat in disarray under the illumination of a small lamp. "I was studying, and I saw you sitting here, doing your reading. And the thing is, you had this look on your face that was very nice. I don't know how else to say it. You looked like you were thinking about something wonderful, and it made me want to think about whatever it is you were thinking about. I can't concentrate on anything else. I keep reading the same paragraph over and over." His face turned red. "It sounds ridiculous when I say all this out loud."

Genevieve was at a loss for words, which made the boy even more uncomfortable. His hands were jammed so deeply in his pockets, the outline of his knuckles protruded through the chalk-dusted fabric of his trousers.

"You don't have to tell me if you don't like. It's just, I know I'd beat myself up later if I didn't ask."

Genevieve bit the eraser on her pencil. She was used to getting attention from men. Most times she found it to be an annoying distraction from her work. But as she watched the current distractor withering helplessly under her gaze, she couldn't help but feel compassion for him. He was unlike the cocky, goldfish-swallowing fraternity boys who normally approached her, full of over-the-top bravado. It was clear to her that he was being compelled, against his will, by some implacable force. Even just standing in her presence, he looked like someone trying to see how long they could hold their hand over a candle flame. He stood, half-turned away, ready to retreat across the two-tone tile floor back to the safety of his own table.

Finally, Genevieve smiled, an act that appeared to reactivate the boy's breathing.

"I'm just reading some old correspondence," she told him. "I'm working on my doctoral dissertation."

The boy eyed the papers lying in front of her. "What's your discipline?"

"History," she said proudly.

The boy nodded. "And there was something in those letters that made you look so..." he searched for the right word, "contented?"

Genevieve chuckled and gently touched one of the letters with her fingertips. "I suppose so." She looked over her shoulder to ensure that no one was within earshot. "They're love letters."

The boy's eyes widened. "Really?"

"Yep, nearly a hundred years old too."

"Who wrote them?"

Genevieve sighed a little. "A pair of tragic lovers, desperate for one another. They lived here in Lexington, but that was way back in the early days of the city. Their gift, and the thing that always makes me swoon, is how good they were at expressing their hope and longing."

"But you say they were destined for tragedy?"

"Sadly, yes. I've spent years researching their rise and fall in Lexington society, as well as their deaths. My advisor complains that my scope is too myopic, but I've also discovered, and written, a great deal about the geopolitical landscape of that era to placate him."

A troubled look crossed the boy's face.

"What is it?" Genevieve asked.

"So even knowing the outcome of their story, you still..." He turned his hands over in the air as he attempted to conjure the word she had used.

"Swoon?" she volunteered.

The boy nodded, grateful that she didn't make him actually say it. "I guess it seems sad to think of two people wanting happiness together but never getting it."

Genevieve touched her hand to her neck as she considered this. "It's funny, I've spent a lot of time thinking about this recently — what it is to be happy. You know, I'm not sure happiness is achieved like arriving at a destination."

"No?"

Genevieve thought about how to explain her thought. "I assume that you are a student here."

"Graduate assistant," he replied. "In the Mathematics department."

"Smart guy, huh?"

The boy laughed and looked away. "No, I wouldn't say that. I just have a knack for numbers."

"In your undergraduate studies, did you happen to read *Pride and Prejudice*?"

He nodded. "Not as part of any class, but yes, I've read it. I like to read."

"I adore that book, but it took some self-reflection for me to really understand why."

"I take it it wasn't just the happy ending?"

"No, that's nice and everything, but that wasn't what made me feel a pang in the pit of stomach. It was when Mr. Darcy and Miss Elizabeth started to understand how foolish they'd been, when they started to hope that maybe the feelings of the other person had changed. When they finally began to expose their own true feelings and experience the naked vulnerability that goes along with that."

"And you get the same feeling when you read these letters?"

"Yes, but more so. Because it was real. And because it didn't last forever. When a matter is doubt, and all may be won or lost at any moment, the excitement can be rapturous. Much more so than happiness as an endpoint, which seems passive to me. If I had to try to summarize the thought, I would say the mere possibility of happiness is, in fact, where real happiness lives."

The boy stewed on this.

"Has anything ever made you feel that way?" she asked him.

He tilted his head to the side. "When I draw, I suppose."

"You're an artist too?"

"It's just a hobby, but it makes me feel connected to people because it's sort of intimate, I guess." He pointed to the letters. "I really wish I could do that."

"What?"

"Say something, beautiful."

"Why can't you?"

The boy ran his hand bashfully through his hair. "I'm good with numbers, not with words."

"It's possible to be good at both, I think."

"Well, then maybe you can tell me the secret. How do you say something that gives someone a pang in the pit of their stomach?"

"Hmm, let's see." Genevieve put her elbows on the table and then rested her head in her hands. "Above all, you have to be genuine. Then you have to think of something kind and from the heart that leaves you a bit vulnerable."

The boy looked overwhelmed by the advice. "Oh geez, is that all?" he joked.

"Why don't you give it a try right now?"

He shook his head and retreated a couple of steps to escape the radius of the suggestion. "Right now? No, I'm sorry. I can't think of something that fast."

"Don't even think about it. Just say something to me that is genuine and vulnerable."

"Genuine and vulnerable," he repeated.

"Yes. We've been chatting for a few minutes. We've learned a few things about each other. So, tell me something nice."

The boy took a deep breath and stared down at the floor. "Okay. My only thought right now, in this particular moment, is that I would like to listen to you talk more. I like how you see things, how you describe things, and the sound of your voice. It makes me wish I'd spent more time coming up with clever ideas of my own. Then maybe you'd want to listen to me talk too. And you'd look forward to seeing me again."

Genevieve was not prepared for such a heartfelt message. She blushed. "Well done."

The boy's face burned bright red in turn.

"What's your name?" she asked.

"Clark."

"I'm Genevieve," she said as she wrote out her telephone number on a scrap of paper torn from her notebook. "I'm not doing anything tomorrow, so if you'd like to take me somewhere, you can reach me here."

Clark took the piece of paper with a look of surprise and disbelief. He smiled and nodded at her. Then, almost in a daze, he walked back across the room to his table and collected his things. Before leaving, he approached Genevieve again.

"May I borrow your pencil?" he asked.

Curious, she handed it over to him.

"You've inspired me to give a title to one of my sketches," he said as he wrote something in his sketchpad and then tore out the page. He slid it to her, face down, across the table.

He smiled. "See you tomorrow."

After he was gone, Genevieve turned the paper over. It was a skillful rendering of her, sitting at her table, wistfully looking into the distance at nothing. Underneath was the title: "The Possibility of Happiness."

And just like that, as suddenly and quietly as the first firefly appearing on a summer night, the heart that Genevieve had carefully protected for so long was in danger of being stolen by a boy named Clark.

# Chapter 29

**1962**

The front door of the funeral home was unlocked, so Brian and Violet cautiously entered. Violet was shocked. The place was systematically wrecked. All of the framed art was ripped apart and strewn on the floor. Chairs were overturned, gaping holes spotted the walls, and all of the plants were uprooted from their pots.

"Jesus," Brian said as he looked at Violet. "This is probably pretty satisfying for you."

"Why's that?" she asked.

"You've only been fired for one day, and the place has really gone to shit."

Violet smirked. "This is…too much."

Brian kicked at a pile of documents and debris on the floor. "Who do you think did this, Henry or the little man?"

Before she could answer, Rhodes limped into the foyer. "It was the little man," he said wryly.

Brian grimaced when he heard Rhodes's voice. "Sorry, we were just a little shocked. You've certainly been busy."

Rhodes sighed. "It's probably hard to believe one crippled old man could do so much damage."

Violet ran her fingers across one of the holes in the wall and looked inside. "You're looking for something, aren't you?"

Rhodes nodded.

"But you haven't found it yet?" Violet continued.

"No, I haven't."

"How's your nose?" she asked.

"Fucking broken," he said, touching it gently with the tips of his fingers.

"I'm sorry about that. I really didn't mean to hit you—it was just a reflex."

"It's fine," he grumbled.

Brian leaned into a nearby room, peered warily into the dark, and then flipped on the light. "I assume that since you are not torn into pieces, Henry has been sufficiently contained somehow?"

"Yes, it took some doing, but I managed to confine him in a safe place."

"Can we see him?" Violet asked.

"Of course, but first let's sit down for a moment and talk. I'm sure you have lots of questions." He nodded toward Henry's office so that Violet and Brian followed him inside.

It felt strange to sit in Henry's office with everything in disarray. Henry was such a fastidious man, she'd never seen anything he owned out of place. Staring at the empty desk drawers strewn across the floor, along with their contents, made Violet feel uneasy, like she was disturbing an ancient pharaoh's tomb.

If the surroundings had the same effect on Brian, he didn't show it. He wasn't even seated before shifting into attorney mode.

"Okay, let's start with the basics. Who are you?"

Rhodes took a flask from inside the breast pocket of his suit jacket. "Silas," he said as he took a long pull from the flask. "I truly don't know my surname, one of the many downsides of being an orphan, but I've used Rhodes for more than thirty years now, so that will do."

"Why are you here?"

Rhodes pointed out the open door and toward the sanctuary. "I've come to bring an unholy fiend to justice."

Brian laughed and looked at Violet. "So many new questions now. Okay, why are you bringing unholy fiends to justice? How did you know Henry was an unholy fiend? And also, what the fuck is happening to Henry?"

Rhodes held out both of his hands and lowered them slowly to get Brian to take a breath. "Look, the bottom line is this. That thing in there looks like a man, talks like a man, and holds himself out to be a man, but he's not. He's not even alive anymore, at least not in the traditional sense."

"What other sense is there?" Brian asked.

"For all intents and purposes, the man you knew, Henry, is dead, but he has a condition that lets his body and mind keep going. It's a condition that lets him keep the appearance of a human being but causes him to change when he doesn't get enough to eat. That's when he reveals his true form, and he becomes the thing you saw last night."

"Last night, I think Henry would have started gnawing on me if I didn't fight him off."

Rhodes smirked. "Henry's appetite is different than ours. There's no way for me to say this that will make it sound any less crazy, but the only thing he can eat is brain matter. Human brain matter, to be specific."

The room fell silent while Rhodes's words soaked in. Brian shook his head. "Maybe I'm still fucked-up from last night. I feel like I just heard you say Henry only eats brains?" He looked at Violet. "Nothing from you? You are okay with this revelation?"

Violet just shook her head with feigned dismay. She wasn't exactly shocked by what Rhodes was saying, because she had just spent the day reading from a stolen journal about a person who had the same condition. She thought about telling Brian and Rhodes what she had discovered, but she thought better of it. It seemed more like a time to listen than a time to talk.

"It just can't be true," Brian stammered. "I went to lunch with Henry lots of times, I saw him eat other things, I'm sure of it."

"I should rephrase," Rhodes acquiesced. "It's true that Henry *can* eat anything he wants, but brain matter is the only thing from which he can garner nutrients and ultimately digest. He really had the perfect setup here. As a mortician he had access to a never-ending supply of brain matter. It was really genius."

Violet leaned forward in her chair and rested her head on her hands. "So what made him that way?"

"An excellent question, but to answer that I need to give you a little more background on my own story. You see, Henry is not the only one of his kind. I met another one like him about forty years ago when I worked in a traveling apothecary down in Georgia. That was when I witnessed one of these monsters brutally murder my employer and friend, Pierre."

"How did you know the murderer was like Henry?" Brian asked.

Rhodes snorted. "Because I watched him cut off his own finger and then grow it back right in front of my eyes. He simply fed, and then his body repaired itself." Rhodes once again pointed toward the sanctuary. "In a few minutes, you will see how Henry has regenerated himself too. Last night, I watched him grow brand-new eyeballs. It was quite remarkable."

Violet shivered as she thought about her thumbs squishing deep into Henry's eye sockets in her desperate attempt to escape from his vicious attack. She shook away the thought and continued to press Rhodes for more information.

"Did you see that man eat your boss's…brain matter?"

"Yes, I was hiding under my cart when he attacked Pierre. I ran out to try to fight him, but as you can see, I have significant physical disadvantages because of the polio. I did everything I could. I even offered myself in his place, but he just slapped me away like an insect. Then the man did something peculiar. He abducted me and kept me as an involuntary travel companion for months. It was the most horrendously distressing time because I was in constant fear for my life. I knew that at any moment he could kill and eat me."

Rhodes held out his hands. "Obviously, he never did. But the whole time I was with him, I just kept wondering why? Why won't he kill me? I'm nothing special. I kept coming to the same conclusion: loneliness. He could essentially live forever, but it was a meaningless, tiresome existence. I think he liked having me around to talk to. And boy did he talk. He told me everything. His name was Virgil, and he hailed from Tennessee. He said that he came from a well-to-do family and that politics was in his future before he disobeyed his father and volunteered to go to the war in Mexico.

"He admitted that his company committed some heinous acts in the name of winning the war, but eventually they overextended into the jungle and their carnage caught up to them. A group of warriors who wore jaguar pelts over their heads ambushed them. These warriors were impervious to rifles and swords. When they got wounded, they simply regenerated. The warriors marched the men in Virgil's company to an ancient Aztec pyramid, where they were forced to eat a hallucinogenic sage plant that apparently changed their physiology and made them like the jaguar warriors.

"Now, you two are probably wondering why the warriors would do that. Why heal their enemies and essentially make them immortal? It all revolved around a dirty little secret that the warriors did not want anyone else to know. They weren't, in fact, immortal. They were just very, very hard to kill. The problem was their work was very dangerous. They harvested brain matter by force from little tribes and villages across the Yucatan. Even though they were superior warriors and killers, at some point the secret of their weakness became known. Every now and then, villagers were able to take one of them out during their raids. As part of an apparent cost/benefit analysis, the jaguar warriors press-ganged soldiers from the American and Mexican armies to do their work for them. When starved, these men changed into creatures like the one you encountered last night: wild, ferocious, and lusting for blood. Once fed, however, they become paralyzed as their bodies heal, making them easy to recapture. The jaguar warriors unleashed these wild men on the villages when they failed to provide sacrifices as tribute.

"Virgil said that he was enslaved by the jaguar warriors and used for this purpose many times. Virgil was only released from his bondage when another man from his company freed him. His name was Charles Bascom. What happened after that, I don't know. Once he was freed, Virgil immediately fled and ultimately came back to America. He had no idea what happened to Bascom.

"I learned a great deal about the condition from which Henry now suffers during my time with Virgil. But he kept one critical piece of information from me."

"How to kill the afflicted?" Brian surmised.

"Precisely. When I learned all I felt like I could learn from Virgil, I used my wits and escaped. That's when I decided to go to the source of the story. I went to Mexico in search for more information about the afflicted. Against all odds, I tracked down a man who belonged to the Holy Order of Judgment and Redemption, a group who hunted these types of monsters. He was quite surprised to learn that one of the 'cursed men,' as he called them, was still living. He rallied members of the Holy Order to come to America. Using techniques their fathers had used half a century ago, they worked with incredible speed in locating Virgil. He was found in a secluded cabin in the Appalachian Mountains. There, they held a trial, found him guilty, and administered a final execution that destroyed Virgil for good. At long last, I had justice for Pierre."

"But what brought you here, Mr. Rhodes?" Violet asked. "How did you know Henry was one of these cursed men? And why did you lie about me to the police that day?"

"Seeing how easy it had been for Virgil to survive here in the U.S. for so long, I had a gut feeling that Charles Bascom, the man who helped Virgil escape from Mexico, could still be alive too. My purpose for finding Mr. Bascom was twofold. First, I wanted to bring him to justice for his many atrocities as well. Second, I wanted to see if he had any knowledge of the location of the diviner's sage plant that changed him. Its mere existence is a threat to all humanity. Just like the cursed men, it needs to be destroyed.

"Now, all I knew about Bascom from Virgil was that he was from Lebanon, Tennessee, and that he had killed a man in a barroom brawl in New Orleans just before leaving for Mexico. I tracked down the heirs of Bascom's family, but they said that the family lore was that Charles never returned from the war. I almost abandoned my search at that point, but something inside me told me there was still more to discover. I went back to New Orleans and scoured newspapers in libraries until I found what I was looking for: there was a short article about the justified homicide committed by Bascom. The man he killed was a fugitive from Kentucky named Pleasant Driscoll.

"So, following that lead, I came to Kentucky and learned more about Driscoll. In his day, Driscoll was well-to-do in Lexington." Rhodes pointed to the floor. "And this was his house: Berwick. Everything crumbled beneath Driscoll's feet when blight knocked out his vineyard, which was heavily financed. His creditors called in the debt, and Driscoll lost his mind. He blamed everything on his wife and strangled her to death before fleeing town in the middle of the night. The local sheriff found and confronted him during his flight and, it is believed, Driscoll murdered him as well.

"Several months ago, I visited this house and met with Henry. I told him I was interested in the history of Berwick and asked if I could look around. He was very gracious and allowed me to wander freely on the grounds. This is before your arrival here, I believe, Miss Romero. Anyway, I didn't get much out of the visit. Once again, I was feeling discouraged, so I went where I always go when I'm stuck: back to the library. To my astonishment, that is where I solved the riddle.

"You know that stupid old saying, *It was in the last place I looked*? Well, I'll be damned if it wasn't in the last place I looked: an illustrated book containing all of the portraits of Matthew Jouett. Look, I have it right here for proof."

He handed the book to Violet.

"Look on page 49, the portrait titled *Hero*."

Brian stood behind Violet as she flipped through the pages. When she got to page 49, she gasped. There was no doubt. The hair, the mouth, the intense gaze. It was Henry.

"Are you saying that Henry is really someone named Pleasant Driscoll?" Brian asked. "This portrait was painted over a hundred years ago."

Rhodes nodded vehemently. "Trust me, I had doubts as well. It defied all logic that Pleasant Driscoll could still be alive. That's when I developed my theory and then put my plan into action. A plan in which you were collateral damage I'm afraid.

"Pleasant Driscoll wasn't the one who got shot in that New Orleans saloon. Driscoll was the killer, and he somehow just assumed the identity of the man he killed, Charles Bascom from Lebanon, Tennessee. It makes perfect sense that after all of these years, when everyone who had ever known him or seen his face was long dead, that he would come back home. Turning Berwick into a funeral home was simply a stroke of brilliance.

"Now, I needed a way to make absolutely certain that I was right. That's where your part of the story begins. I knew that if there were some sort of scandal involving the funeral home, Driscoll's food supply would dry up. Then I could observe him and see for myself if his behavior matched what I learned watching Virgil. Would his character shift? Would he become erratic and easily provoked? Would his eyes start to burn? My plan actually worked better than expected. Driscoll must have become lazy in squirreling away food for the lean times, because he started to starve. It probably helped that I broke into the house while he was at the cemetery filling in for Miss Romero, who was in jail, and stole all the brain matter I could find. You know, the frozen stuff and the jerkies and what have you. Honestly, I didn't expect him to go into the full rage. But it actually helps me illustrate to you just how dangerous a man he really is.

"Just today, I received word that a member of the Holy Order will arrive tomorrow to convene and preside over Driscoll's trial."

"How does this trial work?" Brian asked.

"I will present evidence of Driscoll's guilt, and then he will be given the opportunity to rebut it."

"What crime is he being charged with?" Brian asked.

"There is only one crime for which the Holy Order will administer the final death. The murder of a truly innocent person."

"You're going to have to unpack that a little. If he's been eating people for over a hundred years, isn't that kind of a..."

Brian paused, and Violet could tell that he was searching for some phrase other than *no-brainer*.

"A sure thing?" Rhodes volunteered.

Brian nodded.

"Yes, I have no doubt that Mr. Driscoll has collected a substantial body count over the span of his unnatural life. But there is a huge problem."

"No witnesses," Violet interjected.

Rhodes pointed at her and winked. "Bingo. As you can imagine, this can be a very difficult obstacle to overcome. The only reason the Holy Order was able to condemn Virgil was through my eyewitness testimony about him killing Pierre. As of now, we have no eyewitnesses to any of Pleasant's murders."

Violet thought about the journal she had been reading from Henry's secret closet. There were a number of entries that alluded to some of the writer's victims. Quickly recalling the stories, though, she didn't remember any that involved an innocent person. In fact, the writer talked extensively about an ethical code of conduct by which he found his food.

"What makes someone truly innocent?" she asked.

"The Holy Order gets pretty strict when it comes to that point," Rhodes replied. "Essentially, the victim cannot be a murderer themselves or be committing a vile crime against the accused at the time they were killed."

"If Henry has committed a crime, though, he should be tried according to the laws we have here, not some shady monster council from Mexico," Brian said.

Rhodes shrugged. "I don't disagree with you in principle, but the Holy Order is dedicated to ridding the planet of this scourge. If the U.S. government, or any government for that matter, found out that someone like this exists, I fear they will only try to harness these powers and ultimately proliferate what we are trying to stop."

Brian looked as though he grudgingly saw the wisdom in what Rhodes was saying, but Violet could tell it rubbed him the wrong way.

"Okay, so there are no witnesses. What evidence are you going to present against Henry then?" Brian asked.

Rhodes patted a stack of old books, newspapers, and ledgers. "The murder of his wife, Anna Driscoll. The evidence was very well documented against him just after her death, when he was still a fugitive of the law."

"Interesting," Brian said, thumbing through Rhodes's stack of evidence.

"Can we see him now?" Violet asked.

"Yes, I think it's time. Follow me." Rhodes got up gingerly from his chair in a way that revealed his age. Brian and Violet followed him out of the office toward the accordion doors that led into the sanctuary. He slid the doors open but paused.

"You'll recognize the man in here better than the man you saw last night, and you'll want to let your guard down. Don't. For lack of a more polite word, he's a monster."

Violet nodded and then peered over Rhodes's outstretched arms. The sanctuary matched the rest of the house. It looked like a riot had broken out. Rhodes led them through the threshold and down the center aisle toward the catafalque where a casket serenely lay.

"I handcuffed him and tied him up in rope to completely immobilize him. If he has any leverage at all, he will just break off appendages until he can wiggle free."

When they got close enough, Violet noticed that the casket had a hole hacked into the top of it. It was the same casket in which she'd been trapped and almost killed. She swallowed back the panic and kept moving forward.

"I had to gag him. As you well know, he is a master deceiver. He'll get his opportunity to talk during the trial, but until then, he'll have to just talk to himself."

From the inside pocket of his tattered suit, Rhodes produced a comically large kitchen knife. He crept up next to the casket and stood on his tiptoes to peer into the hole on top. He then started to open the top panel of the casket but halted, his eyes darting back and forth across the room. Eventually, they landed on the ax that Brian wielded the previous night propped up against a wall.

"Better go grab that," Rhodes said as he pointed at the ax with his knife. "If he somehow gets out, we can't stop him, but we might be able to slow him down long enough to get away." He appeared to think about that comment. "Well, at least you kids with your strong legs can get away."

Rhodes took a determined breath, then lifted the head panel up with a swift upward push of his hand. Unfortunately, he had too much adrenaline behind the motion, and the panel immediately bounced closed again. For a brief, chilling moment, Violet saw Henry's face, bound and gagged, his piercing eyes locked intently on her own.

"Let me," Brian offered as he approached the casket and carefully opened it up and then locked the panel in place.

Once again, Pleasant's gaze was fixed on Violet. He tried to speak, but his mouth was duct-taped closed.

"See his eyes, his skin? All perfect again," Rhodes said in awe. "I'm feeding him every few hours to keep him in his right mind. We don't want a repeat of last night."

"Do you think he's suffocating with his mouth taped up like that? What if his nose gets stopped up?" Violet asked.

Rhodes smirked. "He's fine. He actually doesn't need to breathe at all. I think he absorbs oxygen through his skin. I held his head underwater for twenty minutes last night, and he didn't even struggle."

Violet didn't like the thought of Henry suffering. "You've been torturing him?"

Rhodes scoffed. "Torture? How? This man doesn't feel pain."

"What is it exactly that you're trying to get him to tell you?" Brian asked.

"You know, when I was a young man, and I was traveling around with the apothecary, I met all kinds of people — people from every walk of life and from all over the world. Do you know what everyone had in common?"

Violet shook her head.

"No one could lie to me. Well, I take that back. Someone *could* lie to me, but not successfully. I always sniffed it out."

"And you think Henry is lying to you about something?"

"Yes. Mr. Driscoll here is a remarkable man. He has an unparalleled intellect and an obsession with obtaining still more knowledge. My gut tells me that he has not been content to just sit idle all these years doing nothing but working funerals and eating. I think he has put his considerable scientific talent to use, specifically his botanical talent, and he has recreated the diviner's sage that changed him into this being before you. When I asked him last night if this was true, I could tell that he lied to me when he said *no*."

"Why would he want to recreate it?"

"Think about it. It's the key to immortality. There would be untold wealth and power for whoever could unlock that secret and keep control of it. Think of the geopolitical implications as well. You thought the atomic arms race and the space race have threatened the balance of the power in the world? Imagine if a nation owned the knowledge to create nearly indestructible super soldiers? Or the cult of personality that could accompany a leader that never aged and never died."

"Henry's greenhouse is chock full of plants. I take it you didn't find any sage there?" Violet asked.

"No, nothing. I've also torn this place a part looking for evidence of even a sample of the sage. No luck. You know, the Holy Order has a theory about the sage's origin, and I think they are probably on to something. Basically, they believe that the sage grew on top of one of the ancient Aztec head burial pits. You know how the Aztecs performed human sacrifice and beheadings and whatnot? Well, apparently, they tossed all of the heads into one big hole in the ground — thousands of heads. The theory is that the ground was so saturated with brain matter that over time, a new and strange connection developed between the soil and the vegetation. Some diviner's sage, which Aztec shamans would sometimes eat to have religious visions, spontaneously grew there, except it had new and incredible qualities. Ostensibly, someone eventually ate it and its powers were revealed.

"The rest is as predictable as human nature. As with all things of great power, it ultimately came under the control of the ruling class. When the Spanish came, the Aztecs were defeated, but that ruling class went deep into the jungle and continued to thrive. Some Spanish defectors that saw the potential in controlling the sage likely joined them, and together they formed a pseudo-Christian sect that terrorized Mexico.

"It occurred to me that if Mr. Driscoll wanted to recreate the conditions for the sage, he would need two things: seeds from the original plant and soil with the correct nutrients. When his greenhouse turned up empty, I thought about other places where he could be tending to the plants. The most natural choice was the cemetery. He's constantly there taking walks, and the place is littered with bodies, which are slowly absorbing into the soil. That was a dead end, though. Then I thought, maybe he's making his own soil — a sort of brain compost, if you will. But again, I've found no evidence of that here, neither the human compost nor the sage seeds."

"Isn't it possible that he didn't recreate these plants?" Violet asked.

"No," Rhodes snapped. "No one can lie to me."

Violet couldn't help but feel pity for Henry as he lay in the casket, completely immobilized. She sensed he was trying to say something to her with his eyes, but whatever that message was, she couldn't understand it.

"I think he's had enough interaction for now," Rhodes said as he unlocked the casket panel and lowered it closed.

From inside, Violet could hear Henry trying to speak through his gag.

"Ooooooodeeee Oooo!" he yelled. "Oooooooodeeee Oooo!"

Rhodes just shook his head. "His days of killing and deception are over. It's time he accepted his fate and realized that he isn't the god he thinks he is."

Rhodes walked Violet and Brian back to the front foyer of the funeral home.

"So when does the trial begin tomorrow?" Brian asked.

"I'm expecting the member of the Holy Order to arrive at Bluegrass Airport in the morning. I'll fill him in on the details of the situation, he'll inspect the premises to see if there's anything I've missed relating to the sage plants, and then we will begin the trial after that."

Brian stroked his chin, preoccupied with something. "Sounds good. We will try and get here midafternoon then."

Rhodes smiled. "I'm sorry, but the hearing is closed to all spectators. Only those presenting evidence will be allowed entry."

Violet could tell that this rankled Brian.

"Mr. Rhodes, we have been directly affected by the actions of this man. I think we have a right to be in the room when the charges against him are levied. We may be able to testify to some point or other."

Rhodes gently guided Brian by the arm toward the door. "I understand your frustration, but this proceeding is secret for a reason. Once a verdict is rendered and the sentence is enforced, I promise I'll let you know."

As an afterthought, he turned to Violet. "Miss Romero, this may come as a surprise, but your wealth will likely be greatly enlarged tomorrow. I found Mr. Driscoll's will yesterday. It appears that once he is executed, you stand to inherit his entire estate, minus my fees for the investigation of this matter, of course. Still, considering what I've found in currency alone, that is quite a lot of money, not to mention property. Mr. Driscoll has been quite an aggressive investor these past hundred years."

Violet was shocked by the announcement, and it showed on her face as she and Brian walked out the door and onto the front porch.

Rhodes, clearly impatient for them to leave, started closing the door. "It was very good talking with you both. Again, Miss Romero, I hope you can forgive me for how I treated you before. Everything I did was for the greater good. In the end, this will all work out very well for everyone, especially you."

"Please contact me at my office when everything is settled," Brian said, handing Rhodes one of his business cards.

Rhodes took the card and quickly put it in his pocket without looking at it. "Of course. Goodbye now."

"Are you okay?" Violet asked Brian when they got back into his car.

"Yeah, why?"

"I've never seen you back down so easily."

Brian lifted an eyebrow. "Oh, I'm definitely going to that trial tomorrow, and so are you."

"We are?"

"There was no point in arguing with Rhodes, because he's clearly got his convictions, but nothing could keep me away from it. It's all so strange, and it doesn't feel right. I mean, what the fuck is going on here? This is all madness!"

Violet was relieved that Brian was not about to drop the matter. "I know what you mean."

"I have a lot to do between now and tomorrow," he said, his eyes glazing over with an imaginary to-do list. "Where would you like me to take you?"

"What do you have to do?" Violet asked.

"I want to do a little research, you know, bone up on my history. We don't have the full story here, and there's just so much to try to uncover. There really isn't enough time."

Violet nodded. "In that case, let's split up now. I'll take the hearse. I know where the spare keys are hidden."

"You've got something you want to go check out too?"

"Yeah, it might be nothing, but I think Henry was trying to tell me something just now."

"Call me in the morning?" Brian asked.

"I don't know your number."

Brian reached into one pocket, then another, until he found a pen. He pulled the top off of it with his mouth and motioned for Violet's hand. It tickled her palm as he wrote, but the numbers were clear. When he finished, he held her hand a little longer.

"Be careful," he said.

She laughed.

"I'm serious."

"All right. I will be."

Brian let go and once again reached into his pocket. "Here's some money to get a room for the night."

"Don't worry," she said, waving him off. "I've got it."

"Oh, that's right, you're the heiress to a fortune."

Violet rolled her eyes. "Shut up, stupid. Now get out of here."

# Chapter 30

**1962**
**(Revelations)**

Violet rummaged through the mess on the countertop until she found the coffee tin. Mercifully, there were enough grounds inside for a decent pot. She shook the tin at Brian. "We're in luck!"

The trial was about to begin, but the Inquisitor, a very serious-looking man, saw Brian's ragged appearance and gave him ten minutes to gather himself. Outside, the sun was setting. Brian looked like he hadn't slept at all.

"I'm sorry I couldn't talk when you called," he said, rubbing his bleary eyes. "I was just feeling overwhelmed."

"Don't worry about it," Violet said as the coffee maker began percolating. "I take it you found something, though?"

Brian's eyes flashed. "You could say that."

"Does it have anything to do with the lady who came here with you?"

"My star witness." He grinned.

Violet was wearing her black dress, the one she usually wore when she worked funerals. The trial had a similar feel to it. "So, what's going to happen?" she asked. "Is he guilty?"

"It's complicated," Brian replied. "I don't understand the procedure with this whole thing, or how it will be decided, or who even makes that call. And I really don't like it. We have a judicial system that for some reason we are just going to ignore. I didn't think about it until now, but I probably have some ethical obligation to report this to bar association."

Violet didn't know how to feel. Henry had been good to her. There were times when he felt like her only friend in the world. He knew terrible things about her, things that no one else did, but he didn't judge her, and he never betrayed her trust. On the other hand, his rampage two nights prior was the most frightening thing she'd ever experienced. He was completely out of control, and his raw, hateful rage turned her blood cold. There was no doubt that he would have killed her and Brian if Rhodes hadn't shown up and helped them escape.

Brian, exhausted, leaned against the kitchen wall. "What about you? Any luck with your mystery endeavor?"

"As a matter of fact, yes," Violet said coyly.

Brian waited, but Violet didn't volunteer anything more. "Do you want to tell me what it is?"

"I do, but I think I'd like to keep it to myself for the time being. It has to do with something Henry tried to yell through his gag yesterday. I think I have discovered something that could be important."

Brian looked like he wanted to keep prodding, but he resisted the urge. "Okay, well, if you ever want to fill in your old pal Brian, just let me know. Oh, and remember, it's Pleasant."

Violet was confused. "What do you mean? What's pleasant?"

Brian nodded in the general direction of the sanctuary. "Henry Pendleton isn't his real name. He's Pleasant Driscoll."

"That's right! Man, this is going to be hard to get used to."

Rhodes poked his head into the kitchen area. He didn't try to hide his contempt. "Are you sufficiently revived yet?"

When Brian and Violet arrived at the funeral home for the trial, Rhodes initially refused to let them in. He reminded them that the proceedings were not open to the public and that they needed to leave immediately. Things were getting heated until the Inquisitor himself stepped in and heard their appeal to stay. Brian explained that they had information that would be directly germane to the accusations against Pleasant. The Inquisitor decided to hear their evidence.

"We'll be right in," Brian assured him. He waited until the little man limped out of earshot before winking at Violet. "I've got a couple of surprises for old Foghorn Leghorn there."

"Oh my God," Violet said.

"What?"

She smiled as she poured coffee into a Styrofoam cup and extended it to him. "You're actually loving this, aren't you?"

Brian looked offended. "Violet, a life is on the line here."

She pulled the cup back as he reached for it and raised an eyebrow.

"I mean, I suppose I feel a sort of…nervous excitement. But that's not weird."

Violet gave him the cup. "I didn't say it was."

"I just feel underprepared. I think I'm close to truth. With more time, I could work out some of the blank spaces."

Violet touched Brian's elbow. "Before we go in there, I want to tell you something, but I don't want it to be weird. So just know ahead of time — this isn't weird, okay?"

Brian looked down at her hand. "What the hell is happening right now?"

"You're making it weird," she said sternly.

"Sorry."

She took a breath and steadied her gaze. "Brian. You are a good lawyer. And despite being unbelievably cocky and an insufferable jerk, I think you may just be a good man too. What I'm trying to say is, I believe in you."

Brian's mouth opened, but he was unsure how to respond.

"Okay, that *was* weird," Violet admitted.

Brian laughed. "So weird."

"Hey, I was being nice."

"You kind of sounded like my father just now."

"Forget it — you're going to stink in there. You're going to blow it."

Brian laughed. "Now you sound like my boss."

"See if I ever say anything nice ever again…"

"All right, I'm sorry. I take it back. Thank you for believing in me." He nudged her chin softly with his fist. "And for the record, I think you'll make an excellent father someday."

Coffee in hand, Violet and Brian entered the sanctuary, where they were slightly taken aback. It appeared that Rhodes had been busy as well. The place was still wrecked, but it had been straightened up considerably. The pews were turned upright and put back in their proper places, the broken vases and pictures had been removed entirely, and the small wooden lectern was back in the front of the room near the catafalque where Henry's casket lay. The Inquisitor sat in one of two identical, velvet-lined seats offset to the left of the catafalque.

Brian and Violet took a seat next to one another in the second pew from the front on the right side. Behind them, in the third pew, was Brian's so-called star witness, an older, fastidiously dressed woman Violet had never met. Next to her on the pew was a banker's box full of books and papers. She looked very uneasy. Rhodes was on the left side of the room in the front pew, his chin tucked down as he struggled to look through his smudged bifocals at a legal pad full of notes.

Outside, the wind was picking up, and thunder rolled in the distance. Inside, the room was filled by a nervous energy that was becoming more palpable by the second. The Inquisitor examined his pocket watch and then stood up. He was not a tall man, but his bespoke suit and effortless confidence gave him gravitas.

"I think we are ready to begin," he said. "Please allow me to introduce myself. I am the Inquisitor. My name is Miguel Quinteiro. I am here on behalf of the Holy Order of Judgment and Redemption at the request of Mr. Silas Rhodes."

The Inquisitor spoke softly and with the faint hint of an accent, but his words were deliberate and clear. He took a thin silver tin from his inside breast pocket and removed a cigarette.

"For over one hundred years, the Holy Order of Judgment and Redemption has had one directive: to assess and pass judgment on the actions of those who can no longer be held accountable by the laws of man."

He put the cigarette to his lips, where it dangled precariously.

"Our work is very simple. If one is judged by the Holy Order to be guilty of an unjustified crime against humanity," he paused to light the cigarette and take a long draw, "then we administer justice by executing the offender."

Brian stood up. "May it please the court?"

The Inquisitor held up a hand. "Please, this is not a court of law, and your formalities are not necessary. Be respectful, but speak freely."

Brian nodded in acknowledgement. "Thank you. Sir, I'm just having a hard time understanding exactly what all of this is. By what authority do you act?"

"A fair question. The Holy Order received its commission and authority by the request and consent of those who were once terrorized by a race of beings in Mexico known as the 'cursed men.' Mr. Todd, thousands upon thousands of innocent people were savagely murdered by beings just like Mr. Driscoll before the secret to their vulnerability was discovered and the people's yoke of bondage was finally broken. Most of the cursed men were killed during the initial insurrection. The Holy Order hunted the remainder in the years that followed, driving them to the edge of extinction. My father was a member of the Holy Order, and his father before him. I have sworn an oath to continue in this calling. In truth, there are very few members of the Holy Order left, just as there are very few cursed men. Those who remain still adhere to the principals of the founding members and protect their vital knowledge."

Violet cleared her throat and stood up. "The cursed men that you find, are they all given a trial like this?"

The Inquisitor shook his head. "In the beginning, no. The original members of the Holy Order worked for total eradication. And they were very successful in their work. According to my grandfather, it was easy to find the cursed men back then. The true monsters among them left great swaths of suffering in their wake. They were dispatched rather quickly. Much later, it was discovered that some of the cursed men were different. They were leading productive lives, lives that aided humanity and did no harm. That was a very trying time for the Holy Order. Many of the members adamantly held to the original tenets of eradication. Others felt torn. Some of the cursed men had become cursed against their will and were in fact good men. A rift developed between the members until a compromise was reached to hold the cursed men accountable through trial. The righteous were allowed to live. The rest were killed."

Brian was still not pacified. "Why not just have him stand trial in a normal court of law? This isn't the jungle. He has protections under the Constitution."

The Inquisitor shook his head. "You must understand. That simply could never happen. How could the public ever comprehend this man's existence? He is over one hundred years old, and he looks like he is thirty and in perfect health. How do you prosecute him for the crime of murder, a notorious historical murder nonetheless, when no one could possibly believe that he was even alive when the crime occurred and nearly all of the physical evidence has been lost to time?"

"But isn't that what we are about to do? Take scraps of evidence to piece together a ramshackle trial?"

The Inquisitor seemed irritated. "Yes, that is what we are about to do, and the world will be better for it. Have you been watching the news? Humanity is on the brink of annihilation. The last thing the world needs is for the world's superpowers to discover and covet a new weapon." He pointed at the casket. "And that is exactly what they will find in that box, a new weapon, a new advantage for them to exploit at the expense of innocent human life. I simply won't allow it."

The Inquisitor punctuated his last statement with an intense stare, which was accompanied by the timely crash of nearby thunder. Violet felt uneasy by the veiled threat. Until then, the Inquisitor had seemed mostly benign, if not amiable.

"That being said," he continued. "Mr. Driscoll has managed to keep his secret for many years. If he is acquitted, then I will let him continue about his business. If he is guilty, then I will administer the final death to him tonight. That may not fit your elevated sense of justice, but it will have to do. You have no other choice in the matter."

The Inquisitor narrowed his steely gaze on each person in turn to see if there was any further resistance. When he was satisfied that none remained, he flicked his cigarette filter onto the floor, walked over to the casket, unlocked the head panel, and lifted it up.

"Let's get the defendant out. Mr. Todd, some assistance please."

Brian walked over to the casket like he was approaching a coiled rattlesnake.

"Don't worry, he is immobilized. He can't hurt you," the Inquisitor said. "He is heavy, though."

Brian opened the lower panel of the casket and tentatively took hold of Pleasant's legs. The Inquisitor took hold of his torso. After a three-count, they lifted him out with a grunt and then stood him upright. He was still bound tightly with rope from below his knees to the middle of his chest. The Inquisitor pulled the duct tape from his mouth, allowing him to spit out a table napkin that had been jammed inside.

"How are you feeling, Mr. Driscoll?"

"Well rested," Pleasant replied dryly.

The Inquisitor smirked. "Are you hungry? We need you to be in your right mind if we are to continue."

Pleasant shook his head.

"Very well. Now, we can continue one of two ways. We can leave you tied up like this, or I can untie you and we can continue this proceeding like civilized people."

"I don't think that's a good idea," Rhodes started but was quickly waved off.

"I'll have to incapacitate you another way, of course," the Inquisitor said.

Pleasant nodded his agreement.

"Very well. Mr. Rhodes, are Mr. Driscoll's hands shackled?"

"Handcuffed, yes."

The Inquisitor untied the rope's knots, causing it to unravel from Pleasant's body and fall limply to the floor. Pleasant was wearing the same shredded suit he'd been wearing since the night he attacked Brian and Violet. His hair was matted, and dirt was smeared across his face. Still, despite looking like he'd crawled out of his own grave, he was the vision of health.

"Please hold out your arms," the Inquisitor directed him.

Pleasant obeyed. The Inquisitor retrieved a case from under his velvet chair. He opened it and withdrew a polished machete. With a single, violent downward slice, he cut off Pleasant's hands, which thudded to the floor, along with the handcuffs.

The older woman, Brian's witness, gasped and reflexively lurched forward, grabbing Violet by the shoulders in terror.

Startled, Violet screamed. "Jesus Christ!"

Brian turned around and calmed the woman. "Genevieve, remember what we discussed. You're going to see things tonight that may be disturbing, but it's okay. You'll be just fine."

The woman, panting in fright, slowly released Violet from her grasp. Her hand instinctively clutched at a wedding band that hung from a delicate chain necklace. "Yes, of course," she said. "I just wasn't prepared for that."

With his hands removed, the nubs of Pleasant's wrists looked like raw steak. Violet was surprised that they did not bleed.

The Inquisitor used a handkerchief to wipe down the machete and then carefully placed it in the open coffin. "This will be nearby if you misbehave." He pointed toward the hands on the floor. "You can always regrow those later if you are acquitted."

He positioned the second velvet-lined chair behind Pleasant and bade him to take a seat. After lighting another cigarette, he returned to his own seat.

"All right, I don't want to draw this out any longer. Let's get down to business. Mr. Rhodes, what allegation do you assert against this man?"

Rhodes leaned on his cane and grunted his way to his feet. "The charge is simple. On the night of September 12, 1846, Pleasant Driscoll murdered his wife, Anna Driscoll, in cold blood."

The Inquisitor carefully removed a piece of lint from the sleeve of his suit jacket. "Would you like to present evidence or question the accused?"

"Both, sir."

The Inquisitor nodded. "Very well, go ahead."

The room fell silent except for the rain that had started pelting the windows. Rhodes made a show of positioning the lectern to face Pleasant and then piling a stack of documents on it. He then took on the mannerisms of a television lawyer. With one hand supporting his weight on his cane and the other stroking his chin, he looked up to the ceiling and appeared to think deeply about how he wanted to begin. Finally, his Georgia accent rang out dramatically.

"Pleasant Driscoll, did you kill your wife?"

All eyes turned to Pleasant.

"Yes," he replied flatly.

The answer hung in the hollow air. Rhodes was caught off-guard. Stunned, he looked at the others in the sanctuary. It was clear he expected more resistance.

"You killed her?" he asked again.

"Yes," Pleasant repeated.

Rhodes turned to Brian, his free hand on his hip. "Well, that was easy."

"Did you act in self-defense?" Rhodes continued.

"No."

"Was her death justified in any way?"

"No."

"And were you ever prosecuted for this crime?"

"No."

Rhodes looked to the Inquisitor and shrugged. "What else is there to prove? He admits it. Without any qualification, he has admitted that he committed an unjustified crime against an innocent person. He killed his wife, and he escaped justice." He pointed at Brian with his cane. "Nothing he says can possibly overcome this confession."

"Does that conclude your presentation of allegations against Mr. Driscoll?" the Inquisitor asked with apparent indifference.

Rhodes seemed distressed by the Inquisitor's lack of reaction to the confession. "There's nothing left to prove, right?"

"I agree," Pleasant said. "What is the point of continuing? I admit guilt."

The Inquisitor leaned forward and pointed at Pleasant. "You are not in control of this proceeding, Mr. Driscoll. I am. We will continue with the questioning until I am satisfied. Now, Mr. Rhodes, do you wish to continue, or are you through?"

It appeared to Violet that Rhodes did not want to yield the floor but was unsure what to ask next. He shuffled through some of his papers until he could think of a new line of questioning.

"After you killed your wife, what did you do?"

"I fled."

"Where did you go?"

"Russell Cave."

"According to the newspapers, the County Sheriff was found dead at Russell Cave. Did you kill him too?"

Pleasant shook his head. "No."

"But you saw him there?"

"When he found me there, I was ready to die. I asked him to kill me, but he wouldn't do it. I even scuffled with him to give him a reason to do it. Still, he stayed his hand. He told me that my punishment was to live with my guilt. Then he told me to go south."

Rhodes was incredulous. "You expect us to believe that he just let you go? The reports surrounding his disappearance detailed how he was leading a posse to find you. He even put a bounty on your head — twenty-nine dollars, dead or alive. He scrawled the number on the cave wall before he died, for Christ's sake."

Pleasant remained adamant. "I didn't kill him; he was a close friend."

"Yes, and Anna Driscoll was your wife," Rhodes spat back.

The words appeared to sting Pleasant. "I'm ready to accept my punishment for that, at long last."

The Inquisitor grew impatient with the questioning. "He denies killing the sheriff. Unless you have some convincing evidence he did it, or a witness that saw him do it, you'll need to move on."

"Fine," Rhodes acquiesced. "Where did you go when you went south?"

"New Orleans."

"Why there?"

"I don't know."

"Well, how did you come to assume the identity of Charles Bascom? Did you kill him too?"

"No, I simply seized on an opportunity. I was in a saloon with the real Charles Bascom when he got into a drunken fight. He pulled a knife on a Creole man, who produced a pistol and shot him. All night, he'd done nothing but talk about meeting up with a company of volunteers from Tennessee heading down to fight in Mexico. I paid the coroner ten dollars for all of his belongings and an extra five to say the dead man was Pleasant Driscoll. When I went through Bascom's pockets, I found his commission papers. Impulsively, I made the decision to simply follow Bascom's path to war. It was an easy way out of the country, and truthfully, I thought it would lead to my destruction. Something I wanted desperately at the time."

Rhodes shuffled more papers, and there was a long pause before he repeated his original question. "So, you didn't kill Charles Bascom?"

The Inquisitor had enough. "Just take a seat Mr. Rhodes, I'll take over."

Rhodes tried to look indignant, but Violet could see he was relieved.

"After New Orleans, you went to Mexico, correct? Did you take lives there?"

"Most likely," Pleasant admitted. "It is almost certain that I killed men in battle, but I really can't know that for sure."

"Soldiers killing other soldiers in war does not necessitate action from the Holy Order. However, your company was renowned for its brutality toward civilians, no?"

"The company suffered from the reputation earned by a few individual soldiers. I participated in action only against military combatants."

The Inquisitor looked disgusted. "Alas, there is no one to contradict your own self-serving testimony. How fortunate for you."

For the first time, Pleasant appeared irritated. "It was not fortune, it is truth. I have already confessed to a capital offense. Why would I hesitate to confess to all? You can only kill me once. Once is enough."

Brian stood up and signaled to the Inquisitor. "Mr. Quinteiro, may I speak?"

The Inquisitor reluctantly nodded.

"From what I can gather, the only way you can reach a determination of guilt against Mr. Driscoll is through his own admission, or through evidence from eyewitnesses or other reliable sources."

"Yes, that's generally how prosecutions work."

"May I ask him a question that may help us focus this proceeding?"

"By all means?"

"Mr. Driscoll, other than your confession of guilt about the death of Anna Driscoll, are you prepared to admit that you have unjustly killed any other person in a way that could be deemed a crime as defined by the Holy Order?"

Pleasant spent a moment in thought. "After being taken prisoner by the cursed men in Mexico, I was driven into the red fog through starvation and then set upon innocent villagers."

Brian looked to the Inquisitor.

"Mr. Driscoll's time as a prisoner and slave to the cursed men is well known to the Holy Order. After his escape, he rained down terror on the cursed men. His amnesty for that time is irrevocable."

Brian looked back at Pleasant. "Since gaining your freedom from the cursed men, have you taken an innocent life?"

Once again, Pleasant took several moments to consider before answering. "No," he replied.

"Mr. Quinteiro, you are always free to come back here at any time to present new charges against Mr. Driscoll, correct? There's no statute of limitations or double jeopardy or anything, right?"

"That is correct," the Inquisitor agreed.

"Then why don't we keep our focus on the real issue, the death of Anna Driscoll. Otherwise, this is just going to be an endless fishing expedition."

The Inquisitor folded his hands on his lap. "You make a good point, Mr. Todd. Let us continue with the allegations at hand." He looked to Rhodes. "Would you like to add anything else about the death of Mrs. Driscoll?"

"Not at the moment," Rhodes replied. "But I would like the opportunity to rebut any evidence presented by Mr. Todd."

"You shall have it," the Inquisitor agreed. "Mr. Todd, go ahead with your presentation of evidence."

"I'd like to call a witness," Brian said, motioning toward the woman sitting behind him. "Where would you like her to sit?"

Just as he asked the question, lightning struck with a startling crack, and all of the lights went out. The wind howled and beat savagely against the windows.

"Someone stop him!" Rhodes shouted. "Don't let him escape!"

The Inquisitor struck his lighter to reveal that Pleasant hadn't moved from where he was sitting.

"Are you all right, Mr. Rhodes? You seem skittish," the Inquisitor said.

"I'm perfectly fine," Rhodes said sheepishly.

"We have lots of candles," Violet volunteered. "Sometimes we do candlelight wakes here."

"Thank you," the Inquisitor replied. "Would you be so kind?"

Violet felt her way out of the sanctuary and to the first-floor supply closet, where she found a box of fresh candles, which she collected, along with as many candlestick holders as she could carry. At the Inquisitor's request, she lit the candles and placed them in a circle around Pleasant's chair. Everyone else was given one to hold. The glowing lights cast long shadows on the wall, giving the sanctuary a more antiquated and somehow sinister quality.

"Madam," the Inquisitor said to Genevieve. "Come take a seat so that everyone may face you."

Nervously, she did as she was told. The Inquisitor sat on the front pew next to Rhodes. Out of habit, Brian stood to conduct his direct examination. Before getting started, he walked over to Genevieve and whispered something in her ear that made her smile and relax her rigid posture a bit. Violet estimated that Genevieve was either in her late forties or early fifties. The candle she was holding illuminated her round face, which possessed soft but handsome features.

"Professor, please tell us your name and what you do."

She took a deep breath. "My name is Genevieve McLean. I'm the director of the Lexington Historical Society."

"How long have you worked there?"

"In my current position? Nearly eight years. But I've been with the LHS for thirty-one."

"Do you have any other occupation?"

"Yes, I'm also a tenured professor of history at the University of Kentucky. I've been teaching there for seventeen years."

"And that's where we met yesterday, correct?"

"Yes, although I'm still very disoriented about this whole thing. I'm not altogether sure I am in my right mind or that I'm even awake. I still can't believe that we all just watched a man get his hands chopped off, and everyone was perfectly fine with that."

"Trust me, I know exactly how you feel. I'm only a couple of days ahead of you on this journey, ma'am. Now, Professor, do you know Pleasant Driscoll?"

"In a manner of speaking, I suppose. I've never met Mr. Driscoll, but I daresay I know about his time in Lexington better than anyone."

"What do you mean?"

"As a historian, I am the foremost authority on Pleasant Driscoll and Berwick House. My doctoral dissertation focused on the Reform Era in Central Kentucky, and a significant component of my academic research centered on Mr. Driscoll's estate as a case study. I am familiar with nearly every recorded facet of his life until his death in New Orleans in 1846." She looked somewhat troubled. "Well, purported death."

"It must come as a shock to see him alive and well today?"

Genevieve's mouth tightened into a sardonic smile. "That is an understatement, to say the least. I still can't..." She trailed off. "This just seems so impossible. There are so many questions I want to ask him." She glanced at Pleasant but quickly looked away.

"What caused you to focus on Mr. Driscoll?"

"Many years ago, the historical society received all of the surviving journals, ledgers, books, and papers from Berwick House by donation after an estate sale. I started my research there, but it took me to many other sources. It was a significant part of my life's work."

"Would you call yourself an expert?"

"On the subject of Pleasant Driscoll? Yes, I would."

Rhodes could hold his silence no longer. "Isn't it convenient that Mr. Todd miraculously discovered the world's foremost scholar on a man who supposedly died over a hundred years ago on the eve of his trial?"

"What are you saying, Mr. Rhodes?" the Inquisitor replied.

"I'm saying this is bullshit. All of this could be made up."

Brian interjected. "Yesterday, I contacted a close friend at the university and asked if anyone in the history department had knowledge of Pleasant Driscoll. I was immediately referred to Professor McLean. After speaking with her for fifteen minutes, I was convinced of her unsurpassed knowledge. I admit that it was extremely fortunate that I was able to find her on such short notice, but I assure everyone here, she is the real McCoy. If you don't believe me, I suggest we do a test."

The Inquisitor seemed inclined to agree. "What do you propose?"

"Let's ask her some questions about Mr. Driscoll. Professor McLean will write down her answer, then we'll hear from Mr. Driscoll to see if the answers line up."

"They could have planned this," Rhodes exclaimed. "What if the questions are rehearsed?"

The Inquisitor looked at Genevieve. "Professor, have you ever spoken to Pleasant Driscoll before?"

"No," she replied.

"How about a man named Henry Pendleton?"

"Who is that?" she asked.

"That's Mr. Driscoll's current alias."

"Oh, well, then no."

"Has Mr. Todd coached you in any way?"

Genevieve squared up her shoulders proudly. "He just told me to tell the truth."

The Inquisitor turned back to Rhodes. "I'm going to allow this. You can ask questions of Professor McLean too if you like."

Rhodes huffed but nodded in agreement.

Brian handed Genevieve a pad of paper and a pen. "Let me start with a couple of straightforward questions. How old is Mr. Driscoll, and where did he grow up?"

Genevieve did some arithmetic in her head, pointing at invisible numbers in the air. She then wrote down her answers, tore the piece of paper out of the pad, and handed it to Brian, who showed the Inquisitor. After the Inquisitor reviewed what she wrote, Brian showed Rhodes as well.

"Okay, Mr. Driscoll, could you please answer the question?"

Pleasant also had to take a second to think. "I suppose I currently am 153 years old. I turn 154 in a few months."

Brian smiled and pointed to the paper. "Professor Mclean was correct. Now, where did you grow up?"

"With my mother in the mountains near Red River Gorge. Today that is Powell County. Back then, it was part of Montgomery County, I suppose."

Brian excitedly pointed to the paper again. "Look! *Red River Gorge in Montgomery County 1808–1821.* Two for two!"

Pleasant glanced curiously at Genevieve. She smiled bashfully in return.

Rhodes was not impressed. "That's nice, but it isn't even relevant to anything that's going on right now. How about something more to the point? Where did Pleasant and Anna Driscoll go the night he murdered her?"

"Objection!" Brian cried.

"Don't do that," the Inquisitor said, annoyed. "Objections don't exist here, Mr. Todd. I don't need your help sorting through the testimony, and there's no possibility of preserving an objection for appeal. There is no appeal. Professor, please just write down your response."

Genevieve complied and once again passed the paper to Brian.

The Inquisitor looked to Pleasant. "Mr. Driscoll, your response?"

"If memory serves, we went to a party at the home of a friend, Philip Carter."

"Three for three," Brian said.

Rhodes was still not satisfied. "Okay, and what did you eat at the party?"

Pleasant shook his head. "There's no way I can remember that."

Brian jumped in as well. "Mr. Quinteiro, he's not being realistic. I can't even remember what I ate three days ago."

Before the Inquisitor could respond, Genevieve spoke up. "I know."

"Professor," the Inquisitor said, "is there something you'd like to say?"

"Just that I know what they ate that night. Well, at least I know what was served. It was fricasseed veal with rice croquettes and baked apples."

Rhodes tried to dismiss her. "How could she possibly know that?"

"It was printed on the social page of the newspaper the week of Mrs. Driscoll's death," Genevieve said matter-of-factly.

The three men were speechless.

Genevieve continued, "I don't think you understand me when I say that knowing what happened in this house all those years ago has been part of my life's work, if not my obsession. Preserving knowledge of the past and piecing together its mysteries has given me purpose. None of you know me, so I understand your skepticism, but you can rest assured, everything that I know is supported by the surviving sources. I don't have them all here tonight, but I have quite a few. I can certainly make them all available for your review."

Brian beamed. "May I continue with the questioning?"

"Looking forward to it," the Inquisitor said.

"Professor, please tell us about your research."

"It started in 1931 when we got the box of manuscripts from Berwick — this estate, actually," she said as she motioned to the house around her. "As a new graduate and freshly minted historian, I had a great deal of energy for the project. I just never expected that what I would find in that box would consume me like it did."

"And what was that?"

"Well, I had heard of Pleasant Driscoll and Berwick House before. Back then this place was run down, on the verge of condemnation," she said as she motioned to the room around her. "It was commonly thought to be haunted. If it hadn't been named a historic landmark by the state, we probably wouldn't be sitting here right now."

"Go on," Brian urged.

"I knew Pleasant Driscoll was enigmatic in his time, that he was a scholar, a scientist, an entrepreneur, a farmer, and a poet. But what I learned from the surviving journals and letters was that, above all, he was a husband. My god, the letters I found."

She looked at Pleasant. *"Should misfortune ever find me out of your favor, I pray to be unmade and reduced to my elements, so that the offending attributes can be easily removed, and I, with Divine hands, can be reformed more perfectly to satisfy your temper. And if I still please thee not, I pray to be remade as a frog and banished into the forest where I may find a companion to whom I would be better suited."*

Genevieve smiled.

"Your correspondence was unlike anything else I had seen from that time. It was sweet and quirky and full of life. That's what I found in the box from Berwick that inspired my obsession for finding the truth, your correspondence with Anna. I couldn't comprehend someone who wrote those wonderful, beautiful things doing something like…what you are accused of doing."

"Can you tell us more about the relationship between Mr. Driscoll and his wife?" Brian asked.

"Of course," Genevieve said. "They had a tragically unlikely romance, which began with death and ended with death."

"What do you mean began with death?"

"Pleasant and Anna began courting just after Pleasant's father killed Anna's father in a duel."

Pleasant interrupted. "I'm sorry, but I have to stop you. I admit that you have an impressive knowledge of my life, but you are mistaken regarding a key point. A man named Fredrick Harlan killed Anna's father over a business dispute. My father was long dead by then."

Genevieve seemed confused and then gasped and covered her mouth. "This is incredible! You didn't know? Oh my god, how heartbreaking."

"I don't understand. What do you mean?"

Genevieve had to pull herself out of her own racing mind. "Are you telling me that you didn't know that Fredrick Harlan was your father?"

"No, Thackery Driscoll was my father."

Genevieve shook her head resolutely. "Thackery Driscoll couldn't have been your father. The timing doesn't work out. From December 1807 to October 1808, it is well documented that he was in Pennsylvania recruiting families for his guide services to settlements in Kentucky. There is no documentation that your mother went with him. You were born in November 1808, just one month after his return. Not only that, but he returned in very poor health, and he died before you were even born. The only information I could find was that it was from 'illness.'"

"I was told consumption," Pleasant said.

"Ah, I always wondered that!" Genevieve exclaimed and then became embarrassed at her own excitement.

"So, you are saying my mother was unfaithful while he was away, and I'm a bastard?"

"Please forgive me. No, that's not exactly what I'm saying. According to my research, Thackery Driscoll was never married, not to your mother or anyone else. He was an adventurer and a lifelong bachelor. I don't think he ever had a relationship of any kind with your mother."

"That simply can't be. Why would she lie to me?"

"I believe she was a young, unwed mother, in a very precarious position, who was just trying to give you the benefit of the Driscoll name, which was well-respected in Kentucky at the time. She knew that since Thackery Driscoll was dead, he wouldn't dispute the claim."

"But how do you make the leap to Fredrick Harlan?"

Genevieve's eyes lit up. "The short answer is because of your grandmother, Mernia Harlan."

"And the slightly longer answer?" Brian asked, careful not to test the patience of the Inquisitor.

"The duel between Patrick Nelson, Anna's father, and Fredrick Harlan was quite notorious. As a matter of fact, anti-dueling laws in Kentucky became more strictly enforced because of it. Try as I might, though, I couldn't find much in my research about Fredrick Harlan. I tracked down a notation regarding his birth in some public records in Virginia, but there was little else. Since that gave me the names of his parents, I decided to see if I could find anything about them. That turned out to be quite helpful.

I found their gravesites in a little cemetery behind Antioch Presbyterian Church in Richmond, one of the oldest churches still standing in Kentucky. On a whim, I went inside to speak with the pastor. Wouldn't you know it, he knew the Harlans' names. They were church founders, and Mernia had bequeathed the family Bible to the church's library. He showed me, and just like most Bibles from those days, there was a family record in the front. It had numerous entries, including one for her only child, Fredrick. That's where I made an unbelievable discovery. Below Fredrick's name she'd written *Pleasant Dris*."

Genevieve couldn't help but smile. "She was a true grandmother. Even though illegitimate, she couldn't bear to leave her only grandson out of the family tree."

Pleasant appeared distressed by the revelation.

"The fact that you stood as his second in the duel," Genevieve continued, "I always thought that was proof that you knew."

"I did not," Pleasant confessed. "He pulled me randomly from the gathering crowd. I tried in every way to stop it."

"After the duel, Fredrick Harlan was never heard from again," Genevieve said somberly. "Not to brag, but I'm good at tracking down this sort of thing. It was like he ceased to exist from that day forward."

Pleasant looked like he was about to add something but thought better of it.

Rhodes cut in. "Coming from a fellow bastard, no one loves a good *who's my real father?* story more than me, but none of this matters a hill of beans."

The Inquisitor agreed. "He's right, Mr. Todd. You need to get to the point, and get there quickly."

"Of course," Brian said, then turned back to Genevieve. "Professor, did you find anything important in your research that would shed light on Mrs. Driscoll's death?"

"Yes. The thing is, Mr. Driscoll..." she hesitated, "well, he's not telling the truth. At least not the whole truth."

"How so?" Brian asked.

"To put it plainly, he didn't kill Anna Driscoll."

"Then who did?"

"No one," she replied firmly. "She killed herself."

Rhodes held out his cane in front of Brian, as though it could stop him from pursuing his line of questioning. "Oh no no no no no. Don't even start down that path. There has always been speculation about that, but there was absolutely no proof of suicide."

Genevieve's eyes went wide. "There was, it just wasn't discovered. When Sheriff Carr's body was found inside Russell Cave, all of his personal items found at the scene were given to his widow. According to the police ledger, there wasn't much: a pocket watch, a knife, his pistol, a few coins, a literary magazine called *The Pioneer*, and the sheriff's investigative notebook. This piqued my interest because nowhere in the police records could I find anything about the contents of this notebook, and I thought it would certainly have some clues about what happened to Mrs. Driscoll. It took months of genealogical research, but I managed to track down the only living relative of the sheriff. All of my work paid off one afternoon in Baltimore, Maryland, in the sweltering attic of Sheriff Carr's stepdaughter's, great-grandson. In an old rolltop desk filled with decades worth of random junk, I found this..."

Genevieve handed her candle to Brian and then opened her leather satchel, withdrawing a weather worn copy of the first edition of *The Pioneer*.

"At the time, I was so focused on finding the sheriff's notebook, I just set this aside. I almost didn't even open it. For hours I rummaged through that hot attic. But when the notebook was nowhere to be found, I came back to this and flipped through the pages. And that's where I found it, on page 29, a handwritten note."

She reached into her satchel once again, this time removing a small piece of paper in a plastic sleeve.

"Could you please read it?" Brian asked.

Genevieve produced a pair of glasses from her satchel and beckoned for Brian to return her candle. Holding the paper at arm's-length, she began reading aloud.

*Pleasant, my darling,*

*I fear that I must put an end to my anguish tonight. I have loved you and will always love you. I am sorry that I am broken and that I have brought ruin down upon you. If I could just go back and think wisely, I would not have accepted the roses. It was an innocent folly that has proven devastating. Thank you for lifting me up from my dark places all of this time. I no longer can stomach for you to bear that burden. Do not blame yourself, my darling. I pray that God has mercy upon my soul and allows me to enter Heaven. I hope it is a cheerful place. With all my love forever, Anna.*

"Everything started to make sense after I found this," Genevieve continued. "The number 29 scrawled on the cave wall was not a clue about Sheriff Carr's killer. It wasn't referring to the bounty on Mr. Driscoll's head. It was a page number. He was dying, and he wanted to make sure someone found this note."

"May I see it?" Pleasant asked.

Genevieve nodded. Brian took the note and held it in front of Pleasant's face, since he was unable to hold it himself. Pleasant read it over once more, fighting to mask the anguish that was overtaking him. Violet was shocked. She found that she had unknowingly clutched her hands to her chest. She also felt ashamed that she too had, at one time, intended to take her own life in the same house.

"Mr. Driscoll, why did you say you killed your wife when you didn't?" Brian asked. Pleasant didn't respond.

"How do we know that was really written by Anna Driscoll?" Rhodes asked.

Genevieve pointed at the box of documents she'd brought with her to the funeral home. "I have her diary and an assortment of her letters for handwriting comparison if you like. I further challenge you to find paper manufactured this century made of the same material."

The low rumble of thunder filled the ensuing silence. It sounded to Violet like the storm was moving away.

"I need to hear the truth, Mr. Driscoll," the Inquisitor said as he leaned forward from his pew. "Did you kill your wife?"

Pleasant visibly shook as he fought to maintain his composure. "Yes," he replied, his teeth clenched.

"Then you are saying this note is not genuine?"

Genevieve bristled at the question but remained silent.

"It's real," Pleasant admitted. "But when she wrote it, she was already dead in…" Unable to finish, he thumped his chest with his wrist.

"Just tell us what happened."

Pleasant looked to the ceiling and bit his bottom lip, choking back his emotions. "I can't," he croaked.

"You will," said the Inquisitor sternly.

Pleasant struggled to gain control of himself. "Back then, I was succeeding in every way imaginable. After years of work and planning, I finally managed to build this estate and get my vines in the ground. Anna and I had spent several years before that, draining away her inheritance in France and Spain as I sought the perfect grapes for my hybrid. I promised her that I'd earn it all back ten-fold once my plans came to fruition."

Pleasant spoke in such a low tone, his voice melded neatly with the back end of some rolling thunder. He paused and looked at the room around him like he was seeing it again for the first time. "God, I was so self-assured."

"Go on," Brian urged.

"Just as my vines were beginning to come into maturity, they were stricken with a fungal blight, which I traced to rose bushes that Anna had planted at the ends of every row. She'd received the bushes as a gift from a neighbor, coincidentally one of my creditors. She thought they would add a marvelous touch of beauty to the otherwise mundane hillside. She had such an acute sense of beauty."

"Do you believe the gift was designed to destroy your vineyard?" Brian asked.

"I cannot say for certain. I always sensed a covetousness in the man."

"Toward what?"

"Toward Anna. That's why I supposed the roses were just a harmless gesture of his genuine affection for her. It is possible his intent was more sinister. If so, his outward tediousness belied his shrewd cunning. Whatever the motive, he exposed a fatal flaw in my planning. Through sheer overconfidence, I'd failed to diversify my position. I'd left myself vulnerable to calamity, and indeed, calamity found me. Without my wine, I could not produce enough income to pay my creditors. I was on the edge of ruin.

"During that time, I became…unlike myself. I was short-tempered and spent my days raging against my misfortune. I said unkind things to Anna. I blamed her." Pleasant struck his thigh with the nub of his wrist. "I neglected and mistreated the most precious thing in my life. The night…it happened, she tried to reach out to me. Desperate to feel loved once again, she reached out to me, but I was cold."

Pleasant bowed his head in shame. No longer able to hold back his emotion, his shoulders shook as he noiselessly wept. Once again he fought to regain his composure. Angrily, he forced himself to continue.

"I dallied in the stables once we arrived home that night. As I lingered there seething, it began to dawn on me how I'd mistreated my wife, how unfairly I'd put all of my own shortcomings on her shoulders. Finally coming to my senses and determined to make things right, I went to her, but the door to our room was locked. I knocked, but there was no reply. Sensing catastrophe, I kicked in the door, only to discover the most terrible vision. She was hanging from the bed frame, her beautiful face gray and vacant. Her eyes were open, but the life in them was drained away. I was too late. I lowered her body and then laid her down on the bed. I knew in that instant that everything was shattered. All happiness was gone forever, and I only had myself to blame."

Brian put his hand on Pleasant's shoulder. "It was tragic, and you were angry at yourself, but you didn't take Anna's life."

Pleasant tried to pull himself together. "She always carried a sadness with her. We shared so many happy days, but no matter what, the sadness was there. And the worst part is that I actually remember times when I felt sorry for myself because I was tired of trying to be the happiness for us both. It was in that self-pity that I let her slip into the ultimate despair. I should have been more steadfast. I should have shown her more love. I should have helped take that pain away from her or at least helped shoulder more of it myself. She was the only thing that mattered. Every day I try to remember the details of her face, but it has faded so completely from my mind, I'm not sure I would recognize her if I saw her. The image of her limp body hanging from that rope, and her eyes, devoid of life — that's what never fades." He paused. "And neither does the guilt. I am indelibly linked to it."

Genevieve blew out her candle and abruptly stood and walked over to Pleasant's seat, careful to avoid the candles surrounding it, and gracefully knelt beside him.

"I have read her journals and her letters," she said softly. "I'm not a medical doctor, but by any modern standard, Anna suffered from depression. You are a man of science, so I know you understand that what was happening with her was a sickness. It was beyond her control, and it was beyond your control. Psychiatric health was simply not advanced enough at that time to give her the help she needed."

Pleasant shook his head in disbelief.

"You know that it's true," Genevieve continued. "And throwing your own life away now may assuage the guilt you feel, but there is a better way to do that. Take her journals. Read them. You were the greatest happiness of her life. If you would just read her words, then can see how wonderful you made her feel for all those years. If you do that, I think you can finally process this loss the way you need to."

"I've heard enough," the Inquisitor said. "Mr. Rhodes, do you have anything further to add?"

Sensing that any further effort on his own part would be futile, Rhodes just shook his head.

"I'd like to look at your source material, Professor," the Inquisitor said. "But barring any irregularities there, Mr. Driscoll's life will be spared for now. Keep in mind, Mr. Driscoll, there is no such thing as double jeopardy with the Holy Order. If new evidence is presented against you, we will do this again. Who knows what barn, or basement, or CIA filing cabinet Professor McLean will get into next. And God only knows what she'll find there."

Brian looked at Violet with a subdued smile. He helped Genevieve back to her feet and squeezed her hands in his own before guiding her back to her pew.

"That brings me to Mr. Rhodes's next allegation," the Inquisitor said, looking at Pleasant. "According to him, you are in possession of the transformative sage that turned you into a cursed man."

"I've searched everywhere on this property and questioned him at length," Rhodes interjected. "He denies having some, but I know he does. I can tell he's lying."

"Is that true?" the Inquisitor asked.

Brian was suddenly alarmed. "Before he answers, what are the consequences of possessing such a plant?"

"Relax, Mr. Todd," the Inquisitor replied. "The penalty for possessing the sage is not nearly as draconian as a crime against humanity. It would just need to be destroyed."

"Examination of such a plant, if it existed, could prove scientifically beneficial," Pleasant said, still trying to gather himself. "In time, maybe a countermeasure to the malady that afflicts me could be developed."

The Inquisitor was resolute. "The Holy Order's edicts with regard to the sage are absolute. To my knowledge, it has been completely eradicated. If you have some, it must likewise be destroyed."

Pleasant paused and locked eyes with the Inquisitor.

"Before I left Mexico, I harvested some of the sage used by jaguar warriors, or what you call the cursed men. Since then, I've carefully maintained the purity of the seeds as closely as possible."

"I fucking knew it!" Rhodes cried out.

"Where is it now?" the Inquisitor demanded.

"I took it to a secret place and put it in the trust of someone who could keep it hidden for me."

"Mr. Driscoll, the edicts are absolute."

Pleasant bowed his head slightly in defeat and then looked at Violet. "Did you find it?"

Everyone turned toward her. She nodded.

Pleasant smiled, despite himself. "I knew you would. Go ahead, you can give it to Mr. Quinteiro."

"It's out in the hearse," Violet said, standing up. "Give me just a minute."

"While she does that, maybe I could take this opportunity to go relieve myself," Rhodes said, also struggling to get to his feet.

"No, Mr. Rhodes, I'd prefer if you stayed. We will handle this business quickly, then you can go do as you please."

A flash of anger crossed Rhodes's face, but he quickly hid it. "Well if I spring a leak, you'll have a mess on your hands," he joked, pointing to Pleasant's severed hands on the floor in front of him.

The Inquisitor did not laugh. "He who would pun would pick a pocket," he said grimly.

Violet rushed out of the sanctuary and came back a few moments later holding a green plastic flowerpot with a humble-looking sage plant growing inside. She walked over to where Pleasant was still sitting.

Pleasant rose and examined the plant carefully in the candlelight. "This specimen is at least a hundred generations removed from my original sample, but I believe I have kept its integrity pure."

"Does it still have its transformative effects?" the Inquisitor asked.

Pleasant shook his head. "I don't know. It would have been unethical to subject any other person to this curse, so I have limited my research to what I can surmise from its biological makeup."

The Inquisitor approached Violet and caressed one of the leaves of the plant with his fingers. "Is this all of it?"

"There used to be more, but at the moment, this is all that's left."

Rhodes also began to approach. "May I inspect it?"

"That's not necessary," the Inquisitor replied. "Out of caution, we will destroy it even if it does not have the transformative properties."

Rhodes took another step closer to Violet. "It's just I've been hunting cursed men for so long, and I've heard about this sage. I didn't know if I'd ever get a chance to see it. If I could just get a quick look, I'll know what to look for in my future investigations. I'll be better equipped to rid the Earth of this scourge."

Pleasant stepped between Rhodes and Violet. "The abnormal qualities of the plant are microscopic. From its outward appearance, it just looks like a sage plant."

"I understand," Rhodes said with rising contempt, "but what harm would it cause for me to just take a look?"

Having heard enough, the Inquisitor picked up the handcuffs from the floor and grabbed Rhodes by the arm.

"Get your hands off of me," Rhodes snarled.

The Inquisitor handcuffed him to one of the side handles of the heavy casket.

"What are you doing?" he cried as he pulled fruitlessly on his tethering.

The Inquisitor lit another cigarette. "Rhodes, you have your usefulness, but don't delude yourself. I know you think of yourself as some great con artist, but your motivations have always been transparent to me." He took the plant from Violet. "You think this will heal you — make you young and immortal."

Rhodes just glowered at the Inquisitor.

"Well, you can't have it. It doesn't bring life. It brings death."

"Who are you to deny me?" Rhodes seethed. "I spent my life looking for that fucking plant. I've earned it." He pointed to Pleasant with his free arm. "Why should he get it, and not me? He had everything. It wasn't enough. He was an entitled prick. But me, I had nothing! I have been crippled and destitute my whole life. Why can I not improve myself?"

Violet gasped. "So that's why you lied to the police about me. You were trying to use the charges against me as a bargaining chip to blackmail Pleasant into giving you the sage."

Rhodes just snarled at her.

The Inquisitor took the sage from Violet. "I'm going to help you, Mr. Rhodes. I'm going to give you the greatest gift of your life, freedom from this fool's errand that has enslaved you. If Mr. Driscoll speaks truthfully about this being his only surviving plant, then once this is gone, it will be extinct from the face of the Earth. And you will finally be free to move on."

Rhodes lunged for the plant, but the casket, which was locked into place on the catafalque, kept him from reaching it. "Don't do that! Please! I'll do anything!"

"We should destroy this at once," the Inquisitor said and then looked to Violet. "You seem to know where everything is in this house. Can you find us some lighter fluid?"

Violet thought for second. "Umm, yes, I think so."

"Good, please go. Everyone else, let's reconvene out back."

"Don't do this," Rhodes growled ominously as they left the sanctuary.

Violet shielded the flickering candle with her hand as she made her way down the creaking stairs into the basement. Like the rest of the house, there was clutter everywhere, a result of Rhodes's manic search for the transformative sage. Rhodes was responsible for a lot of needless suffering. But even after all of that bad behavior, Violet still felt sorry for him. Life had dealt him an unfair hand. He was sad and lonely, a feeling she knew all too well. She truly hoped that he would be able to salvage the rest of his life and find some happiness once the sage was gone for good.

The lighter fluid wasn't in its usual place, since the shelf had been completely cleared, but she quickly found it amongst the debris on the floor nearby. It felt about half full, plenty left for the task at hand. Going back up the stairs, Violet once again shielded the flame but startled herself when she realized that she was doing it with the lighter fluid tin.

*Wouldn't that be my luck,* she thought, *surviving this nightmare only to blow myself up.*

There was enough ambient light filtering into the stairwell from the main floor that she just blew out the candle and proceeded cautiously up the steps. Outside, the storm had subsided. Violet no longer heard rain spraying against the windows. An uneasy silence took its place. She came back to the sanctuary to rejoin the group, but they were already gone. Quickly, she moved up the left side aisle, causing the candles on the floor to flutter as she passed by them. Just as she reached the rear door leading to the back yard, she paused. Something wasn't right.

*Where did Rhodes go?*

Slowly, she approached the casket where he'd been handcuffed. Rhodes was gone, but the handcuffs were still there, hanging from the side handle.

322

The scene didn't make any sense to her. She looked over her shoulder at the empty pews.

"Rhodes," she said, almost whispering. There was no reply.

As she turned back to the casket, she nearly tripped over something on the floor. Near her foot was one of Pleasant's hands. Violet instinctively recoiled, as though she'd just seen a rat. As her heart settled, she came to the frightening realization that there were now three hands on the floor, not two. She looked inside the casket where the Inquisitor had placed his machete. It was gone. Everything started to become clear.

While Violet had never been a particularly fearful person, neither had she ever been particularly brave. It wasn't until she battled with Pleasant during his fit of rage that her will to fight and survive had been tested. Like that night, a sense of impending violence started to wash over her, and a feeling began to rise from the pit of her stomach. It wasn't panic or helplessness, like she expected; it was something more obstinate and fierce. It was a feeling of determination.

Keeping her head up and focused on the room around her, Violet slipped off her heels. She instantly felt more agile and ready. Quietly, she crept toward the back door. With one decisive movement, she opened it and slipped through the crack.

Moonlight sliced through the breaking clouds to illuminate the brutal scene unfolding outside. Violet struggled to process it all at once. Rhodes was halfway between the back of the funeral home and the greenhouse. Kneeling next to him was Brian. Rhodes cradled his left wrist between his torso and the back of his right arm. The blood soaking into his white seersucker looked black as ink in the pale light. He held the machete in his right hand with the blade hovering just inches above the back of Brian's neck. Genevieve, a few steps away, was shaking violently in shock and fear. She held the potted sage plant in her hands. The Inquisitor's body lay on the grass just a few yards away from the back exit, his head a few feet beyond that. Pleasant, whose legs were hacked to pieces, was trying to belly-crawl in the direction of Rhodes.

"Give it to me!" Rhodes barked desperately at Genevieve. He lifted the machete into a striking position over Brian. "I swear I'll cut his fucking head off!"

Time slowed to a crawl in the density of the moment. Without hesitation, Violet took off in a dead sprint toward Rhodes, her bare feet falling soft and quick on the wet grass. Even as it was unfolding, Violet recognized that she was in the defining moment of her life, one she likely wouldn't survive. But unlike the night she tried to kill herself, she wasn't filled with pain or darkness. Now, once again at death's door, all she felt was love. Love for her friends. Love for all the happiness she'd experienced in life. And love for knowing that she could be counted on when she was needed most.

In her last few steps toward the unsuspecting Rhodes, time began to slingshot back to its true speed. With all the force she could muster, she buried her shoulder into Rhodes's spine, sending them both sprawling upon the ground. Rhodes was dazed, but his mania helped him recover quickly. From his knees, he swung the machete at Violet, who was on her back beside him. She blocked the strike with the lighter fluid tin that, she was surprised to find, was still in her hands. The liquid inside sprayed over them both.

Brian tried to take advantage of Rhodes's preoccupation with Violet. He reached for Rhodes's arm but only managed to grab the machete by the blade. Rhodes yanked it free, slicing deeply into Brian's hand. Brian screamed as he pulled his hand back. Just as Rhodes prepared to hack downward on Brian, who was vulnerable, Violet rushed between the two of them. She took Brian into a protective embrace as the blows fell across her back. Violet didn't know how many times she'd been struck, but it felt like enough to do the trick.

Rhodes, remembering his true mission, rushed toward the terrified Genevieve and grabbed a handful of sage leaves from the plant. He shoved them triumphantly into his mouth and then hobbled off into the darkness like a wounded animal.

Brian held Violet upright, unsure how to aid her. "Pleasant," he cried out. "She's hurt. We've got to help her." There was panic in his voice.

Violet felt her vision begin to blur. "I'm so sorry, Brian," she said, coughing blood onto his shirt. She tried to speak again, but the words wouldn't come. Just before everything went black, she heard Pleasant's voice.

"Quickly, feed her the sage."

# Chapter 31

**February 14, 1839**
**(A Valentine Note From Pleasant Driscoll to Anna Driscoll)**

*Just one day for loving, that's all they've set aside.*
*Just one day for loathing I could easier abide.*
*We shall take the latter and loving is all we'll do.*
*As for the day of loathing, we'll sleep that one through.*

# Chapter 32

**1962**

When she woke up, Violet did not know where she was and could not remember how she got there. As she stirred, Pleasant, who had been sitting in a chair by her bedside, put down the book he was reading and leaned toward her.

"Water," Violet managed to rasp.

Pleasant put a cup gently to her lips and helped lift her head slightly from the pillow to take a drink. "I can't tell you how glad I am to see you awake," he said.

Violet vaguely recognized the room. Out the window, the sun was setting in a brilliant orange and pink sky.

"Where am I?" she asked.

"You're in your old room here at the funeral home."

"I can't feel my arm," she said as she lifted it up and touched her thumb to each individual finger.

"Just give it a little time," Pleasant suggested. "You've been through a lot, and you're still groggy."

Slowly, Violet began to remember the pandemonium that followed Pleasant's trial. She recalled how Rhodes had gone mad and savagely attacked her with a machete before stealing the transformative diviner's sage. Violet turned her head to examine Pleasant.

"Your hands are back," she exclaimed.

Pleasant looked down and turned his hands over. "Yes, I've eaten. I'm back to full strength."

Violet's face was full of worry. "Rhodes ate the sage, didn't he?"

"Yes, he did."

"And did I?"

Pleasant nodded solemnly. "Violet, I thought you were going to die."

To her surprise, the Inquisitor came into the room. He smiled broadly at Violet and stood at her bedside.

"I thought I heard you talking in here. I'm glad you've come back to us, Miss Romero. How are you feeling?" he asked.

Violet was dumbfounded. "How are you alive? Did you eat the sage too?"

He chuckled as he took a long draw from his cigarette. "Yes, many years ago."

Pleasant took Violet's hand, which started tingling like a thousand pinpricks as circulation once again began to flow.

"There's a lot we need to tell you," he said. "But if you want to rest for a while longer, it can wait."

"No, please tell me. What happened?" Tears began to well up. "Am I like you now? Am I cursed?"

Pleasant smiled. "I think you're a lot like me. But not like that."

"But I ate the sage."

"The sage had no effect, Violet. Apparently it has mutated into an inert state. Of course, I'm happy that you did not have to go through the transformation, but I would be lying if I said I wasn't disappointed that my work in maintaining it all of these years has been for nothing."

Violet grappled with the news in her mind. "What happened to Rhodes then?"

"He's dead," the Inquisitor said flatly. "He took a dangerous gamble cutting his hand off like that, and the house won. At least we were able to finally put that devious little mind of his to good use, huh, Pleasant?"

Pleasant suppressed an embarrassed smile and changed the subject. "The Inquisitor here is a man of many talents, it seems. Somewhere along the way he has become a very skilled field surgeon. When I knew him, long ago, all he knew how to do was inflict wounds, not heal them."

"An education I received in a little conflict in Europe," he said as he helped Violet sit up in her bed. She winced in pain as he lifted up the back of her t-shirt and examined the dressings over her fresh stitches. "You were sliced up pretty good, but Mr. Todd managed to stop the blood loss long enough for Pleasant and I to...recuperate from our own wounds. Just so you know, I gave you a pretty aggressive dose of anesthetics to dull the pain."

Pleasant looked her in the eyes. "What you did was extraordinary, Violet, simply extraordinary. I have rarely witnessed that type of selfless bravery."

Unable to control her relief, Violet started to cry. Pleasant sat down on the bed and gently embraced her. "Soñador, can you go wake Brian? He's in the sanctuary. He told me to let him know the moment she came to."

"Of course," the Inquisitor said.

"Henry, er, Pleasant," Violet corrected herself. "Was that man not really from the Holy Order? Was the trial fake?"

"He is indeed from the Holy Order," Pleasant replied. "And the trial was very real. You know, I helped him establish the Holy Order in the time after our escape from the cursed men. He is probably the most honorable man I've ever known, which is why he was entrusted with maintaining the Holy Order. If I'd been found guilty, he would have done his duty."

Pleasant chuckled to himself. "You know, I wasn't totally sure it was him when I first got out of that casket. He has a bit of an accent when he speaks in English. Then again, I'm sure he'd say the same thing about my Spanish."

"I just don't understand," Violet said. "Why did you go through with the trial to begin with? The whole time you knew that you didn't kill your wife. Did you just want to die?"

Pleasant looked ashamed. "No, even after all this time, I still want to live."

"But you thought you deserved to die?"

"I suppose so."

"What about now?"

Pleasant fiddled with one of the buttons on his suit jacket. For the first time, Violet noticed that he had cleaned up and put on fresh clothes. "It is a strange thing," he said somewhat reluctantly. "Professor McLean's testimony has affected me greatly. While you were resting, I spent several

329

hours talking with her. Fascinating woman. Unbelievably kind."

Pleasant sighed deeply. "It has been my own hubris, Violet, that stunted me all these years. It was a product of keeping only my own counsel, believing that no one else could ever understand. But it was foolishness."

He looked at the book he'd just sat aside. "I can't pretend that reading from Anna's journals and seeing her in my mind like I did during the good times hasn't resurrected an ancient pain. But it's quite different now. I needed help that I couldn't give myself. Genevieve has broken and reset a bone that never healed properly. For the first time since I can remember, I feel…unstuck."

Just then Brian came racing into the room, still disoriented from sleep. "You're okay!" he exclaimed.

Violet could see that he was genuinely elated, and it made her happy. "I heard you tried to make me into a brain-eating monster," she said with feigned scorn, then cut her eyes toward Pleasant. "No offense, Pleasant."

Brian laughed. "Wait, so you didn't want that? Oh boy, do I ever feel like a goof. Good thing Pleasant isn't the science stud he keeps telling everyone he is. No offense, Pleasant."

Pleasant grinned as he got up, allowing Brian to replace him on the edge of the bed. "I suppose I deserve that. I'm going to go find Soñador. The last thing I need is for him to snoop around and find more evidence against me."

"How are you feeling?" Brian asked. His hand was wrapped tightly with gauze and an ace bandage from where he'd grabbed the Inquisitor's machete by the blade during Rhodes's rampage.

Violet gingerly leaned back against the bed frame. "Like skewered lamb."

Brian's eyes went wide with excitement. "You would not believe the crazy shit I saw while you were dying. We held the Inquisitor's severed head next to his neck and force-fed him some of these brain beans that Rhodes had. The thing just magically reattached, and he hopped up like it was nothing! I tell ya, there may be some serious merit to being one of those monsters."

Violet shook her head. "Nope. Not for me."

Brian's voice got softer. "How can I ever thank you, Violet? I literally owe you my life."

Her face darkened. "Brian, there's something I need to tell you. I've needed to tell you for a long time, but I couldn't find the courage to do it."

"Before you say anything, let me show you this," Brian said as he reached into his back pocket and pulled out a note. Hesitantly, he opened it and handed it to her. She immediately recognized her own writing.

"How did you get this?" she asked.

"When I came here to get you some clothes a few days ago, I found this on your dresser. I know it was a horrific violation of privacy for me to read it, much less take it. I have no justification. I can only apologize."

Violet was once again overcome with emotion, both anger at the invasion of her privacy and fear about what Brian might say next.

"I have been looking for a way to talk to you about this," he continued, "but the moment was never right."

"It isn't fair that you saw that," she said.

"I know. But can we please talk about what's in it?"

Violet nodded.

Brian got up from the bed and sat in the chair where Pleasant had been reading. "Did you know Samantha and I only went to California on our honeymoon because of me? She wanted to go Niagara Falls, but I told her that was super corny, and I convinced her that Hollywood would be better because we might see someone like Audrey Hepburn or Dean Martin. The night she died, we were on our way back to the hotel. We'd spent the afternoon out in Westridge at one of the shooting locations for *Space Lagoon*. I wanted to get some pictures of us on the iconic boulder where they kill the alien commander at the end of the movie. Do you know the scene?"

Violet shook her head.

Brian blushed. "Nor should you. It was a very obscure movie. Samantha was unenthusiastic about going. We actually made a deal that if she went, then she could drive the rental car. Seeing the boulder was a predictably underwhelming experience, but she was a good sport. On our way back, she wanted to stop at a diner to get a cheeseburger, but I convinced her it would be better to wait and eat when we got back into the city. Looking

331

back, I made so many choices, any one of which could have led us away from that intersection or put me in the driver's seat instead of her. If I'd just listened to her about any one of those things, she'd still be alive. I would be with my wife, and you'd be in college out in California. But the stars aligned, and she's gone."

Violet clenched her jaw to fight for composure. "If I hadn't given him those keys..."

"Violet, we can't play that game. That was one factor in a thousand. I'm far more responsible than you by that logic."

She shook her head. "No, my actions came from a place of anger. Yours didn't. And when I saw how poorly you were doing that night in Cuppy's, I felt so responsible."

Brian sighed. "That was rock bottom for me, Violet. But I am very thankful for that night, and I'm thankful that you came to Kentucky. When I found myself in the back of that hearse — talk about the ultimate wake-up call. I realized that I'd let my grief get out of control. I was no longer taking responsibility for my life."

He retrieved a small item from his front pocket and handed it to her. It was a thirty-day sobriety chip.

"This is really silly, I know. But it does actually mean something to me, and you had a huge part in helping me get here."

Violet was surprised at how proud she felt as she looked at the chip. When she gave it back, she held his hand. "Brian, I'm so sorry about your wife. I am unbelievably sorry. I would do anything to..."

Brian reached out with his other hand and cupped her cheek. "Violet, it's okay."

She leaned slightly into his palm. "I need your forgiveness."

Brian's face filled with compassion. "You have it. Of course you have it. But that's not what you really need. You need to forgive yourself. Let go of the burden that you've been carrying."

"I want that so much," she sobbed as she leapt out of bed and hugged him, squeezing him as tight as she could, letting years of hurt and shame and anger melt away. Her back stung, but for the first time in a long time, Violet felt good.

"Brian, do me a favor," she said. "Can you close your eyes?"

"Yeah, sure," he said, kissing the top of her head. "Why's that?"

She laughed. "Because I just realized that I'm not wearing any pants."

A few minutes later, Brian and Violet entered the kitchen, where Pleasant, the Inquisitor, and Genevieve were all sitting at the little table. At the sight of Violet, both Pleasant and Genevieve stood and offered their seats.

"You must be absolutely starving," Genevieve said. "These cupboards are bare bones, but I think I saw a packet or two of instant soup. Would you like some of that?"

"Yes, I think I would," Violet replied. "Let me help you."

"Don't even think of it. Sit down and rest."

Brian took a seat at the table. "So, Pleasant, what's next for you? Will you try to reopen the funeral home?"

Pleasant tilted his head slightly to one side and shrugged. "Perhaps. The funeral home model works quite well in terms of keeping my cupboards stocked, so to speak."

"Well, I know how resistant you are to change," Brian replied, smiling. "I saw that old Jouett portrait of you. You've had the same haircut for literally 140 years."

Genevieve laughed heartily at the comment. "I thought the same thing!"

"If you are open to proposals, I may have an intriguing opportunity for you," the Inquisitor said to Pleasant.

Pleasant ignored Brian's comment. "What's that?"

The Inquisitor interlaced his fingers and put his hands behind his head. "You may be interested to learn that the white whale resurfaced a few months ago."

Pleasant raised an eyebrow. "Where?"

"Argentina."

Brian looked at the Inquisitor and then at Pleasant. "Okay, I'll bite — what white whale?"

"A person the Holy Order has been trying to find since the beginning," the Inquisitor said. "Public enemy number one, as you Americans would say."

Pleasant crossed his arms and leaned back against the counter. "It is believed that he was a conquistador, the man who discovered the Aztec priests who maintained and protected the transformative sage. When he came to understand the power of the sage, he exploited it and a deadly cult grew around him. He was the reason Soñador and I were transformed and used to terrorize innocent villages in the mountains of Mexico. After we escaped, we killed off all of his acolytes, but he managed to slip through our fingers."

"How does a hunting trip sound?" the Inquisitor asked. "It could be like old times. When we're done, you can come back, change your name, and start a new funeral business."

Genevieve was tending a pot of nearly boiling water on the stovetop. "As a historian, I have to say, it gets very difficult to keep track of people who change their names so frequently."

The Inquisitor laughed. "That brings me to my next proposition. Genevieve, I've never encountered a more impressive investigator. How would you feel about taking a sabbatical from the university and the historical society? I think we could use your expertise in tracking our prey."

"No, I don't think so," she replied, pouring the instant soup into the water and stirring it. "My greatest thrills come from finding long-lost documents, not going on monster assassination quests."

"What if we strike a bargain? I have a feeling we could answer a great number of historical questions for you. I have been an eyewitness to many important events in my long life."

Genevieve paused and considered this. "I've always had to work hard to make my discoveries. Seems almost like cheating to have someone just tell me the secrets of the past. But then again, why make things harder than they need to be?"

"It would be a most advantageous partnership," he assured her.

"Hey, Violet, I've got a question for you," Brian said.

"Hit me, stringbean," she replied merrily, then winced in pain as she accidentally rubbed up against the chair back.

"How did you know where Pleasant's sage was hidden? Rhodes was a son of bitch, but he was a crafty guy, and even he couldn't find it."

"Thank you for that backhanded compliment," Violet said. "It was actually something Pleasant tried to call out when he was bound up in the casket. He was trying to say *Bootie boo*."

Brian widened his eyes sarcastically. "Oh, gotcha. Well thanks for clearing that up. Makes sense now."

Violet laughed. "Bootie boo is what Randall T. Lick always called me. He's this little old pervert who lives at Eastern State Psychiatric Hospital. All this time I had no idea why he kept coming to the funeral home to check out the caskets. Little did I know Pleasant had a deal going with him. Randall kept an eye on Pleasant's secret garden project hidden in the woods on the Eastern State property in exchange for a deluxe ride to the other side. Why him, Pleasant? Just to torture me?"

Genevieve ladled soup from the pot to a bowl and then placed it in front of Violet on the table. She looked at Brian and pointed at the pot on the stove. He held up his thumb and forefinger to indicate he'd take a little bit himself.

"There was a scientific component to his selection, albeit a macabre one. During the Spanish flu outbreak in Lexington in 1918, many patients were moved to Eastern State for treatment. The hospital was so overwhelmed by the number of dead, it put hundreds of bodies into a mass grave on the property. I planted my sage on the purported mass grave site to try to emulate the growing conditions of the Aztec burial pits, thinking that the transformative effect came from soil containing high densities of human remains. It appears it did not work."

"I see why you chose the spot, but why Randall?"

"Randall was actually the head groundskeeper at the Lexington Botanical Gardens before he was committed to Eastern State. His expertise in the field of horticulture is unmatched. I was really fortunate to find him."

Violet smirked. "Yeah, lucky us." As she blew the steam away from her soup, she perked up. "Something else has been bothering me — Pleasant, why did you rebury the Berwick property marker to cheat on your property dispute with Paul Trimble?"

"How do you know I cheated on it?"

Violet had nearly forgotten how she'd broken into Pleasant's secret room. "Don't worry about that. Just answer the question."

"I'm actually glad you reminded me of that. All of this excitement with Rhodes, I nearly forgot about our dear neighbor. Brian, please tell me you haven't dismissed my lawsuit yet."

Brian raised his eyebrows. "I haven't."

Pleasant seemed relieved. "Good. I think you'll forgive me for stretching the boundaries of fair play when it comes to Mr. Trimble. You see, I caught him doing something very naughty a little while back."

# Chapter 33

August 22, 1963
*The Lexington Herald p. 1, col. 2*

*Lexington Man Accused of Double Homicide Pleads Guilty*
    *Lexington businessman Paul Trimble pleaded guilty to two counts of 1st Degree Murder on Wednesday morning in Fayette Circuit Court.  In exchange for Trimble's guilty plea, prosecutors with the Commonwealth Attorney's Office agreed not to seek the death penalty at sentencing, which is scheduled for next month.  Trimble has been charged with killing his former girlfriend, Barbara Carlisle, and her companion, Buddy Trigg.*
    *Although Carlisle and Trigg were reported missing in 1961, foul play was not initially suspected, as the couple was believed to be on an extended trip to Brazil in South America, where Trigg owns a residence. The case gained statewide and national attention in May of this year, however, when the skeletal remains of Carlisle and Trigg were discovered buried under the foundation of a pool house built behind the home of Trimble, located on Leestown Road.  The pool house was the subject of a property dispute between Trimble and Henry Pendleton, the proprietor of Pendleton Funeral Home on the neighboring estate.  Civil pleadings for trespass filed against Trimble alleged that the pool house on Trimble's property encroached three feet upon Pendleton's tract of land.  On May 10th of this year, a Fayette Circuit Judge entered an order for the demolition of the encroaching structure after granting Summary Judgment in favor of Pendleton.  Workers noticed the remains during the destruction of the pool house and notified the Lexington Police Department.*

*Trimble, who confessed to police that he killed Carlisle and Trigg in a jealous rage, now faces a potential for two life sentences in prison. Pendleton could not be reached for comment.*

The End

# Afterword

Writing *Pleasant Surprises* required that I take a little foray into Kentucky's unique history. For all you nerds out there clamoring for even more juicy details about the Bluegrass State, keep your pants on and check out the following books, all of which I consulted during my research:

Lexington: Queen of the Bluegrass
  By Randolph Hollingsworth

The Response of Kentucky to the Mexican American War, 1846-1848
  By Damon Eubank

Constantine Samuel Rafinesque
  By Leonard Warren

New Flora of North America
  By Prof. Rafinesque

A Life of Travels and Researches in North America and South Europe: Or Outlines of the Life, Travels and Researches
  By C.S. Rafinesque

Lexington Heart of the Bluegrass
  By John D. Wright, Jr.

Jouett-Bush-Frazer: Early Kentucky Artists
  By William Barrow Floyd

History of Fayette County, Kentucky
  By Robert Peter, M.D.

Wicked Lexington, Kentucky
  By Fiona Young-Brown

Kentucky's Governors
  By Lowell H. Harrison

# About the Author

Wesley Moor is the guy pictured above. Born and raised in Kentucky, Wesley revels in Bluegrass culture. Wesley's interests include (in no particular order): cigars, world flags, karaoke nights, banana ice cream, and front porch sitting.

**You can connect with me on:**

⌘ https://www.instagram.com/wesley_moor_novels

Printed in the USA
CPSIA information can be obtained
at www.ICGtesting.com
LVHW050357261023
762117LV00001B/34